Robert Herbert Story

Life and Remains of Robert Lee

Robert Herbert Story

Life and Remains of Robert Lee

ISBN/EAN: 9783744661294

Printed in Europe, USA, Canada, Australia, Japan

Cover: Foto ©Raphael Reischuk / pixelio.de

More available books at **www.hansebooks.com**

LIFE AND REMAINS

OF

ROBERT LEE, D.D.,

F.R.S.E.,

MINISTER OF THE CHURCH AND PARISH OF OLD GREYFRIARS;
PROFESSOR OF BIBLICAL CRITICISM AND ANTIQUITIES
IN THE UNIVERSITY OF EDINBURGH;
DEAN OF THE CHAPEL ROYAL OF HOLYROOD;
AND CHAPLAIN IN ORDINARY TO THE QUEEN.

BY

ROBERT HERBERT STORY,

MINISTER OF ROSNEATH;
AUTHOR OF "ROBERT STORY, OF ROSNEATH: A MEMOIR;" "CHRIST THE CONSOLER," &c.

WITH AN INTRODUCTORY CHAPTER BY

MRS. OLIPHANT,

AUTHOR OF "THE LIFE OF THE REV. EDWARD IRVING,' &c.

IN TWO VOLUMES.

VOL. I.

LONDON:

HURST AND BLACKETT, PUBLISHERS,

13, GREAT MARLBOROUGH STREET.

1870.

LONDON:
BRADBURY, EVANS, AND CO., PRINTERS, WHITEFRIARS.

CONTENTS

OF

THE FIRST VOLUME.

CHAPTER I.

EARLY LIFE.

Object of this Work—Birth of Dr. Lee—Independence and Perseverance—Course at College—Plan of Life at St. Andrews—College Records—Study of Principal Campbell's Works—Licensed to Preach—Ministry at Arbroath—Letter of Dr. Stevenson—Inverbrothock Sermons—Qualities as a Preacher—Sermons on Special Subjects—Deficiencies of the Scottish Service—Reading the Scriptures—The Church at Inverbrothock—Removal to Campsie—Recommendations—Rev. Dr. Muir's Letter to Dr. McLeod—Rev. Thomas Guthrie 1

CHAPTER II.

"NON-INTRUSION" AGITATION.

Settlement at Campsie—State of the Religious World—Evangelical Movement in Scotland—Spiritual Independence—The Church Courts—Ten Years' Conflict—Duke of Argyll's Bill—Mr. Lee and the Non-Intrusion Party—Act of Queen Anne—Imprudent Step taken by the Established Church—The Veto Law—Dangerous Character of the "Non-Intrusion" Contest—Democratic Constitution of the Scottish Church—Speech in the Presbytery of Glasgow—Close of the Struggle—Letter on Church Affairs—Letter of the Rev. W. G. Smith . . . 19

CHAPTER III.

LIFE AT CAMPSIE.

Mr. Lee's Marriage—His Mental Energy and Personal Activity—A Friend's Recollections—Devotion to the Work of his Parish—Episcopal Pretensions—Programme for Prayer Meetings—Letter on Mormonism—Trip to Tweedmouth—Extracts from Diary—Letter to a Younger Brother—Preaching at Campsie—Extracts from his Sermons—Early Publications—Candidate for the Chair of Theology in Glasgow—A Trap for catching Stray Thoughts—Freedom of Will—Arnold's Lectures on Modern History—Theological Systems—Orthodoxy—Forms of Church Government—Catholic and Protestant Unity—Personal Reflections—Plan of a Protestant Brotherhood—Church Orders—The Secession—Appointed to the Church and Parish of Old Greyfriars—Last Sermon at Campsie   42

CHAPTER IV.

EDINBURGH.

Church of Old Greyfriars—Historical Reminiscences—Parish and Congregation—Character and Opinions of Mr. Lee at this time—His Theological and General Reading—Public Worship—Restoration of the Order of Deacons—First Views of Edinburgh—Translation of the "Theses of Erastus touching Excommunication"—Erastianism—Handbook of Devotion—Degree of D.D.—Visit to Tweedmouth—Death of his Father—Burning of Old Greyfriars—Record in Dr. Lee's Diary—Presbytery of Edinburgh—Debate on the Abolition of Tests — Ministerial Communion — Correspondence—Study of German—M'Phail's Ecclesiastical Journal—Evangelical Alliance—Sermon on George Heriot's Day—The Hospital System—Home Life—Highland Tour—Amusing Encounter with Dr. Candlish   76

CHAPTER V.

CHAIR OF BIBLICAL CRITICISM.

Institution of a New Professorship in Edinburgh University—Dr. Lee's Appointment—Royal Chaplains in Scotland—Pluralities—Installation—Remarks in Diary—Inaugural Lecture—Verbal Inspiration—Interpretation of the Scriptures—United Presbyterians—Election of Mr. C. Cowan as M.P. for Edinburgh—Jewish Disabilities Bill—The Lord's Day in Scotland—Sunday Trains—Denominational Grants — Speech at a Public Dinner—Uneventful Years—Duties of the Professorial Chair—Book-buying—Miss Napier—Reading in 1848 and '49—Books commented on—Westminster Assembly — Suspected of Heresy —Clerical "Detectives"—Extracts from Diary 114

CHAPTER VI.

PUBLIC LIFE.

Ecclesiastical Titles Assumption Act—Dr. Lee's Opposition to the Bill — Fictitious Titles — Discourse on Papal Infallibility—Letter from Sir William Hamilton—Thoughts on Popery and Protestantism—Member of the General Assembly—Private Communion—Ancient Revenues of the Church—Stipends of the Country Clergy—Disastrous Effect of the Repeal of the Corn Laws—Extracts from Diary—University Tests—Dr. Muir's Proposal—Religious Instruction in Schools—Ragged Schools—Dissension—Lord Murray's Speech—Solution of the Problem—The United Industrial School—Speech on Education . . . 145

CHAPTER VII.

REPUTE WITH THE RELIGIOUS WORLD.

Dr. Lee's Relation to the Clergy—Schemes of the Church—Evils of Sectarianism—Repute with the Religious World—Charged with "Rationalism" and "Unitarianism"—Sectarianism in Edinburgh—Intimate Friends — Lord Murray's Advice — "Dull Wasps Sting"—Correspondence—Lord Palmerston on Fast Days—Sermons on the Laws of Nature—Discourses on Toleration—Sermon on the Lawfulness of War—Letter of Mr. Combe—Dr. Lee's Preaching—His Congregation—The Reference Bible—A "Free" Church Reviewer—Visit to Campsie—Extracts from Diary, 1855—The Teaching of the Spirit . . . 199

CHAPTER VIII.

TOUR ON THE CONTINENT.

Address on National Education—Physiological Teaching—Mr. George
Combe—Letter of Dr. Hodgson—Educational Questions—The
Lord Advocate's Bill—Ecclesiastical Opponents—Inconsistency
of the General Assembly—Encounter with Dr. Pirie—Tour on
the Continent—Claims Prophetic Gifts—Paris—Sincere Faith of
Catholics — Swiss Scenes — Geneva — The Rhone Valley — The
Righi—Zurich—Embarrassed Licentiate—Prophecy—Extracts
from Note-book—Diary, 1856—Banks of the Clyde—Single
Blessedness—Family Discipline—Home Life . . . 232

CHAPTER IX.

DR. SLOWMAN.

Dr. Slowman's Parish—Opposition to his Induction—Theft of Hours
—Dignity of the Pulpit — Reproving Cruelty—Visit to Dr.
Slowman—Mr. Alpha and Mr. Omicron—The Priest and the
Schoolmaster—Christian Mysteries—Advantage of a Liturgy—
Was Dr. Chalmers a Great Man?—An Uncharitable Young
Divine Reproved—Sin against the Holy Ghost—Falsehoods in
the Pulpit—Prayer for the Dead—The Happiness of Heaven—
Mania for Sermons — Justice in Small Matters — Unfulfilled
Projects 264

CHAPTER X.

SOMBRE RECORDS.

Restoration of Old Greyfriars Church — Opening Services — The
Annuity Tax—Local Demagogues—Speech in the Presbytery—
Mr. Moncrieff's Bill—Letter to Lord Campbell—Letter to Mr.
Combe—Mr. Combe's Work on the Relation between Science
and Religion — Correspondence with Mr. Combe — Sermon
preached on a Fast-day appointed by Government—Evangelization of India—Preaches at Crathie—Publication of the Sermon
—Letter to Sir James Clark—University Reform—Conversation
regarding Mr. Buckle and his Work—Principal Barclay's Ap-

pointment—Extracts from Diary, 1857-8—Sombre Records—Death of Mr. George Combe—Death of his Daughter Jane—Bereavement—Lord Murray's Death   285

CHAPTER XI.

INNOVATIONS.

Public Worship in Scotland—Exodus from the Church—Reform of Church Service—Dr. Lee's Tastes and Views—First Innovations—Printed and Read Prayers—Knox's Liturgy—The Westminster Directory—Difference of Usage and Law—Act of Assembly of 1707—Opposition—Overtures on Innovations—Proceedings in the Presbytery, 1859—First Speech on Innovations—Resolution of the Presbytery—Report of the Committee—Case before the Assembly—Rev. Dr. Bisset's Motion—Decision of the Assembly—Satisfactory End of the First Fytte of the Controversy .   327

ERRATA.

Page 29, line 15 from foot, *pro* "is it sinful?" *lege* "it is sinful."
Page 33, line 16 from foot, *pro* "our difficulty," *lege* "one difficulty.'
Page 129, line 6 from foot, *pro* "he," *lege* "Dr. Lee.'
Page 363, first foot note, *pro* "1869," *lege* "1859."

NOTE.—I beg to record here my obligations to those gentlemen who have kindly helped me by contributing to these volumes, either letters of Dr. Lee's, or memoranda of their own, or who have in other ways assisted me. I ought especially to name the Rev. Professor Stevenson, the Rev. Robert Paisley, Mr. A. K. Rice, Mr. J. R. Findlay, Mr. Robert Cox, W. S., the Rev. Dr. Rorison, the Rev. Dr. Cunningham, the Duke of Argyll, Mr. Grant Duff, M.P., the Rev. Dr. Wallace, and the Very Rev. Principal Tulloch.

R. H. S.

INTRODUCTION.

I cannot but feel that I am undertaking what some
may think a work of supererogation, and others an
impertinence, in thus interposing, as if with the intention
of introducing the following memoir, or the subject of it,
to the reader. Such, however, is not my intention; but
simply to furnish to the English public, necessarily unacquainted with many of the details, what little preliminary explanation it may be within my power to give.

Dr. Lee's life belongs to a singular crisis in Scottish
Church history, a crisis which we cannot yet fairly judge,
since it still exists, but which has already moved a per-
sistent and obstinate nation to reconsider some matters
upon which it appeared to have come to very firm resolutions, and to take, or at least show an inclination to
take, the first step into new ways. Church politics are
so much out of the ordinary course of life in any other
country, but still retain so large a share of public interest in Scotland, that it is difficult to convey any very
clear idea of the position of affairs to a larger world than
that in which the controversies and events here recorded
originated. But let the reader suppose to himself a

yearly parliament, not like Convocation divested of all power, but still retaining, and not unwont to exercise, supreme authority within its own *milieu*, endowed with historical precedents and records stretching back across several centuries, records of positive laws which have been obeyed by a nation, and of resistances which have been the beginning of many a momentous movement; let him imagine this parliament to meet in an ancient capital, not so full in the current of the world as to have its ears deafened by the continual din; among a people full of intelligence, shrewdness, and a moderate but universal education; let him suppose it open to the discussion of subjects which interest every man, by men representing, if not the highest genius, yet a very good average of the ability and cultivation of the country, its discussions taking place openly where all the world may hear,—and he will readily be able to understand how it is that these ecclesiastical parliaments interest and occupy the mind of Scotland. It is true that the picture becomes at once less picturesque and less important, when we reflect that for more than a quarter of a century there have been two of these assemblies, each carrying with it the warm support of a section of the people, and each claiming an equal right to the historical antecedents of the Church of Scotland. Unfortunately such is the case; but that it should be so is but an evidence the more of the warmth with which the Scottish nation has always thrown itself into ecclesiastical affairs.

This is not the place to discuss the origin of the Free Church. The history of the movement which brought it about is sketched, to some extent, in the following pages. My own feelings are those of regret, but of respect for the leaders of that remarkable movement; but it is not, perhaps, to be expected that those who feel the daily sting of the division, and know how the *prestige* and influence of the universal Church in Scotland has been impaired by a rent so grievous, should look upon it with feelings as placid. The great controversy which thus ended in 1843, is not, however, the chief point, or even one of special interest, in the life of Dr. Lee. His individual action upon the Scotch mind belongs to a different period. The most real and important effects of a great religious convulsion are not always those which are most immediately apparent at the time, just as in a separation of human interests it is not the wounds of natural affection, the mutual grievances and sense of injury, that are of most real consequence to the world, or to the parties themselves; but rather the strange inevitable impulse of ever - increasing severance, the push and thrill of energy with which each bursts from the side of the other. The one who possesses the most fiery disposition may be carried on by that indignant impulse to every exaggeration of self-will. The other, if he has the grace, may pause ere the new currents sweep him to one hand or the other, and ponder his changed circumstances. Such examples occur daily and hourly in the world. And such was the effect upon Scotland of the great disruption of her Church. The Free Church carried away much of the fiery fervour, the absolutism, the stern sway of dogma, which have always more or less marked the national mind. The revolutionary and democratic principles which are latent in Presbyterianism came to the surface. What many wise men fear from the disendowment of the Irish Church took place at once in this section of the Scotch Church, so suddenly, and by its own will, disendowed. It came under the sway of the always prejudiced, always hasty, slow-learning, unsympathetic crowd, and has since drifted further and further, year by year, back to the ancient intolerances, the old bigotries, the stern bondage of tradition. Traditionalism in Scotland is not the thing it is in Rome, or even in England. It has no grace of nature, no associations with the beautiful to lend it any charm; yet it has claims which move as deeply in their way. Independence, which means corporate self-will; and equality, which means the sway of the loudest voice and strongest *physique*, are to the Scotch peasant religionist, traditions, as attractive as is the worship of the Blessed Mother to the Italian. The Free Church has been carried by the impulse of severance into this sea full of shoals and secret dangers. It was the peril involved in the very act which was to make her free.

The Established Church, on the other hand, left behind in this unexampled way, had a most singular part to play. The very sight of the vanishing brother, tearing away all bonds of the lawful and practicable, and rushing wildly into a world of absolutism, where all the conditions of nature were to be set aside for his convenience, was of itself a startling spectacle, and to many of those who remained behind it must have been very evident that this convulsion was indeed but the natural issue of some of the principles which had always been most cherished by the Scotch religious mind. It may be said even that until the great event of 1843, the Church of Scotland had never fully faced and accepted its position as an Established Church. It had accepted as its right the humble provision made for it by the state, but it had never once consented to submit itself to the state in return for that provision. The conditions of existence which Rome herself has been compelled to accept, where her ministers are supported by the state, Presbyterian Scotland has never submitted to. There have been moments of compliance, times of decadence or weakness, when she has imposed unpopular ministers upon the resisting people, and otherwise bowed herself unwillingly to political restraint; but such proceedings have always been against the principles of the Church. Her endowments, it is true, are small, perhaps not worth the sacrifice, in any respect, of a dearly prized liberty. But she has never allowed, even to herself, that the privileges of her position, such as they are, the homely provisions guaranteed by the state, were attended by penalties which must be accepted with them. There can be no union without a resignation on the part of one party or the other of some of its rights, but this fact she had never fully comprehended or acknowledged; utter independence was at once her tradition and her hope. In ancient days this principle had been carried so far, that a meeting of Assembly forbidden by the state was instantly reopened and reconstituted by the President or Moderator, in prompt, instantaneous defiance of the state; an event which, even in these reasonable days, might almost, we believe, be repeated still, were Queen Victoria's Lord High Commissioner, mildest and most inoperative of viceroys, to take the same obnoxious step, so strong is the tradition of absolute independence in the Church. That restraint which every ecclesiastical body inevitably submits to, which the Catholic Church accepts with an ill grace, which the Church of England hugs to her bosom, the Scotch Church has done her best to ignore: and it was only after the disruption of 1843, when the absolutist portion—the religionists who would obey no secular laws, and claimed unlimited freedom — had gone forth from her bosom to find it, that the Church of Scotland fully awoke to the fact that the bonds between Church and State were mutual bonds, and that she had a certain allegiance to give, as well as benefits to receive. The sensation, perhaps, rather bewildered some of the older clergy, but it at once impressed the reasonable, active, and orderly mind of such a man as the subject of this memoir. It struck a new note altogether in the ecclesiastical harmonics. It turned the ship's helm almost imperceptibly in a new direction. It suggested many questions to the old corporation, which, by dint of new circumstances, was thus compelled to make a new start. If this were so, if its activities had an actual lawful bond upon them in one direction, if it had accepted, without fully perceiving it, this new discovered obligation of political allegiance, this restraint which every Church in the world has to bear, and which in Scotland lies more lightly than in any other country, what was then to be the issue :—submission in consideration of the advantages secured? or prompt repudiation of the bond altogether? The latter part had been chosen by the seceders. The former was now taken, for the first time with its eyes open, by the Established Church. And thereupon arose new questions :—What to do with the energies thus shut out from the traditional field of fight, the long-waged battle against patronage, the despotic power of excommunication, all the fierce delights of a continual struggle? What, if one looked within instead, and mended one's self, was the suggestion made by Dr. Lee—a suggestion never accepted kindly by any body, lay or cleric, and by the cleric, people say, still less kindly than by the lay.

Had the natural temper of the subject of this memoir led him to plunge with apostolic fervour into the much-

needed work of evangelizing the country, there is no
doubt that he would have carried popular sympathy
far more warmly with him. Had it been the intolerable reproach under which Scotland lies of being at once
one of the most religious, most educated, and least moral
of peoples, which had stung him to labours illimitable, it
would have been an easier matter to explain his position
and elucidate his works. But such was not the impulse
of his character. He did his own work with care and
conscience, working in his special pastorate as few men
work. But he was not a missionary born. His talents
were of an economic order, if we may use the word,
administrative and constructive. The details of practical existence moved him more than the arguments of
abstract theology; and, in one special point, a certain
enthusiasm possessed him. That admiration for the
beautiful institution of Common Prayer which seizes by
moments the Ultramontanist as warmly as the Presbyterian had laid hold upon his mind at some time or
other of his career, and worked in him as every suggestion of good works in the true patriot. When he turned
his quick eye within the Church to mark what most
wanted doing inside instead of without, his gaze lighted
upon the weakest point of Scotch religion, its worship.
Nowhere is there more true piety, nowhere more Scriptural knowledge, but Scotland still says her prayers as
she was compelled to do when she said them on the hill-
sides, with the Covenanter sentinel ready to warn her of

the approach of the red-coats. The hasty worship of that stormy period still known in every country side as the time of the persecution, has been preserved with curious superstition through two tranquil centuries. John Knox's severe and solemn Order had been cast aside in the hurry of flight and extremity of danger. It was too new to be carried in the bosom of the hunted minister, whose Bible was enough for him to carry; and with an incredible fond human faithfulness the whole country has clung to the sketch of extempore, hurried, irregular worship of which Claverhouse's troopers were the grand promoters. The Church of Scotland in its days of perpetual conflict had other things to think of; and now, when peace had come, and when the first suggestion of healing its own wounds within was made, it is not wonderful if the eyes of the younger section of the Church fixed upon this point of weakness. It can scarcely fail to be with a smile that the larger audience outside the local boundaries will contemplate a controversy as to whether or not an organ should support the voices of singers in public worship. This is the ludicrous side of the question; but the real question in such matters of order is the same as that which so often arises in the more subtle points of doctrine, whether a people with all its unborn energies is to be hampered and bound for ever by the custom adopted in a special time of difficulty and trial? It would be not much less rational to say that because our noblest forefathers have been from time to time imprisoned and tortured in the cause of freedom, we their peaceable descendants should wear prison dresses, and mark ourselves with traces of an imaginary rack. Nature rejects such overstrained and artificial signs of remembrance, and why the Church should labour to keep them up is one of the mysteries which it is so difficult to solve.

The other cognate subject in which Dr. Lee's deepest interest was engaged, and which is of more fundamental importance still, was the relaxation of those severe and voluminous formulas of faith to which the Church of Scotland claims the adherence of her clergy. It will be easily perceived what natural connection exists between the two. Dr. Lee, however, did not stand so entirely at the head of this movement, or impress it so strongly with his own individuality as was the case with the more immediately practical question in which he stood first and for some time alone.

These, then, are the special movements in which the life of the Scotch Church has developed itself in its latest stage; and their guidance, direction, and stimulation especially in respect to the reformation of worship, was the chief work in the latter part of the life of Robert Lee. His aim was not to bolster up any fictitious union between the Church of England and his own. Naturally, a minister of the Scotch Church, believing in the validity of his own orders, and feeling himself a duly authorized administrator of the mysteries of God, can scarcely, except in the exercise of Christian charity, feel strongly drawn towards a Church which ignores his position altogether, and treats his pretensions with contempt. His desire was one which, as we have said, an Ultramontanist may feel just as truly as a Presbyterian, a desire to secure that blessing of Common Prayer which, as Providence has arranged, finds its chief home in England, to his own people. He considered it a great, perhaps the greatest, means of securing the interest of the masses in religious services, giving it perhaps thereby an influence beyond that which experience would allow. But there is something in the sentiment of common worship, in the sound of the response, in the personal share taken by a multitude in the actual services of religion, which rarely fails to make a deep impression upon those who are unused to it. Whether it be the Catholic, accustomed to services of which he is merely a devout and sympathetic spectator, or the Presbyterian, habituated to those of which he is a spectator, anything but devout:—the fact remains of course on both sides that the solemnities of Rome, and the bald and homely Church services of Scotland, do actually secure the attendance of the common people as the Church of England very generally fails to do. But other causes are no doubt involved in this comparison of results. And it was the institution of Common Prayer on which Robert Lee had set his heart.

The question is far from being decided now. It will in

all likelihood go on fluctuating until the elder party of Conservatives have died out of the Scotch Church, and the younger men reign in their stead, when no doubt Common Prayer will by one means or other be attained, together with some certain smoothing down of the sharp angles which were pointed by persecution. The effort, indeed, is one to withdraw from the Church the rusty old armour in which her limbs have stiffened for long tranquil centuries, after the use and need of it was past. In this pious endeavour are mingled other motives which may or may not work successfully, but which are undeniably animated by the purest patriotism. The state of religious affairs has been changing in Scotland for many years. The country is no longer a " unanimous hero nation." That fact which has just been made certain in respect to Ireland, with startling effect, that the land-owners are almost all of one creed and the rent-payers and occupiers of land almost all of another, is gradually coming true of Scotland also; and the perilous character of such a fact to all classes, but especially to the higher class thus isolated, can scarcely be over-estimated. It has already done much to lose for the Scotch nobility the hereditary weight and influence they once possessed; and which it would be salutary for the country, as well as important to themselves, that they should possess. That something might be done to neutralize the attractions held out from the other side of the border by the ancient and noble ritual of the Church of England, and that the more refined and cultivated classes might be in some innocent instances conciliated in their tastes and religious sentiments, and drawn back to the form of faith which has found most acceptance with Scotland in general, was no doubt also in Dr. Lee's mind. Even if it reclaimed no wanderers, it would at least have the effect of penetrating the peasant's intelligence with some glimmering insight into the wants of his landlord's presumably more highly cultivated mind, and touch the landlord at the same time with some sympathy for the peasant. It may be too late to hope for any further result, but even that would be something gained.

Such is the story of the " Innovations," so called with that somewhat grandiose nomenclature peculiar to the country. It is unnecessary to make any summary of the arguments which will be found at length in the following volumes. But the changed aspect of affairs is sufficiently remarkable, and may interest any observer of men and their ways. In the first part of the present century, the Church of Scotland suffered herself to be drawn into a fierce crusade against everybody who presumed to diverge from the formulas of orthodoxy, or to throw too personal and vivid a light even upon undeniable truths. In this, its third quarter, the same Church, having received many serious and some alarming lessons, is found in the attitude so strange to churches and corporations, of examining her own deficiencies with the view of amending them. In the one case, she showed herself to be bent upon smothering all gleams of independent vision, and securing conformity at any price. In the other she has assumed the more candid position proper to humanity, and begins to think of inaugurating reforms by the correction of herself. It is unnecessary to point out which of these attitudes is the most Christian, which the most promising for after-efficiency. Let us hope that in this attempt to adapt herself in all truth and faithfulness to the age in which she has to work, she may not lose sight of that greatest of all innovations, the crusade against vice, misery, and every evil, which in every country, in whatsoever method may be most practicable, and not in one stereotyped fashion, is the great and chief occupation of every branch of the Christian Church.

ROBERT LEE, D.D.

CHAPTER I.

EARLY LIFE.—ST. ANDREWS.—ARBROATH.

" Our life is compassed round with necessity; yet is the meaning of life
itself no other than freedom, than voluntary force; thus have we a warfare;
in the beginning, especially, a hard fought battle. For the God-given mandate,
Work thou in well-doing, lies mysteriously written in Promethean, prophetic
characters in our hearts; and leaves us no rest, night or day, till it be
deciphered and obeyed—till it burn forth in our conduct, a visible, acted gospel
of freedom."—CARLYLE, *Sartor Resartus*, ii. 9.

IN these days of profuse biography it may be thought
that an apology is needed for a work like this. Why
add another to the store of books which strive to preserve from the common oblivion the memories of so
many of the great company that has passed away?
The only valid plea is found when the life, whose
records are given to the world, has not only been one
round which many interests and affections have clustered,
but one also which has been full of useful activities—
fruitful in enduring influence and work. The history of
such a life cannot but profit men, if it be fairly told to
them. And such a life makes its silent claim to our
grateful memory, all the more irresistibly and pathetically,

when it has, during its mortal course, been often mis-judged and evil spoken of.

Though this age can hardly incur the reproach which Tacitus levelled at his own—" incuriosa suorum ætas "—yet it has sometimes happened that its annals have not been fullest of those names to which it has owed the most. The debt possibly has not always been clearly understood ; and so has not been frankly acknowledged. To set the life's claim, therefore, of any good and useful man plainly forth is—while to those that knew and loved him a pious and tender duty—to the world in which he lived and moved, an act of justice which helps it to be just. And this task having been proposed to me by those to whom the memory of Robert Lee was dearest, I thought that I ought to try to perform it. I felt that he and his work had been much misunderstood and misrepresented ; that the work he wrought had been a great and good work ; and the man himself a man so bright, courageous, indomitable, warm in heart, high in purpose, just in judgment, faithful and unselfish in duty, that we, at least in Scotland, could not let him pass without some memorial of his career, and of our gratitude and sorrow.

This seemed due to him of whom one who knew him well, realising the dull blank which his removal has left, writes regretfully ;—" I wish he were here ! Presbytery had no more enlightened defender, and the Church of Scotland no more loyal son."

Though destined to leave his mark so broadly on the Scottish Church, Dr. Lee was not a Scot by birth. His native place was across the Border, at Tweedmouth, in the County of Durham. Like many another man who has won a notable place in Scottish annals, he was of humble birth. He was born in November, 1804, and by-and-by was sent to school at Berwick-on-Tweed. When he had absorbed all that the Berwick Grammar School could impart, he turned his eyes northward to the generous portals of the Universities of Scotland. But the want of money kept him back. He had not enough to live on and to pay his fees. His was not, however, a nature to yield to wants and difficulties. He had learned the craft of boat-building. He built a boat and sold it, and with the price in his pocket started for St. Andrews. He entered College in the Session of 1824—5; and went regularly through the usual eight years' curriculum required of candidates for Holy Orders.

His course was brilliant and successful. In the classics he appears to have eclipsed all rivals. He took the first prize in the Senior Greek class; and in the Latin, or "Humanity," was, as his professor's certificate bears, "uniformly the first scholar; discovered an ardour of mind and a vigour of talent altogether uncommon; and obtained the highest honours."

Dr. Chalmers was in those days Professor of Moral Philosophy and Political Economy—two branches generally united in the Scottish Universities—and he testifies that Mr. Lee "soon reached a station of high and honourable eminence in the class and maintained it to the end, having distinguished himself greatly by his appearances at the oral examinations, and still more by the style and talent of his written compositions." He won the first prize for general eminence in Moral Philosophy; the first prize for an Essay on "The Origin, the Rights, and the

Advantages of Property;" and the first prize for an Essay on "the Use and Necessity of Endowments for the Support of Education."

Altogether, I find among his papers six essays which are certified to have gained first prizes; besides a great number of disquisitions on divers subjects, literary, theological, and philosophical, prepared either for college use or for the sake of the intellectual exercise of composing them. All these are singularly free from bombast and juvenility; and both in thought and style are ripe and clear. From the beginning of his college life, the winters of which were spent at St. Andrews, and the summers, apparently (with the exception of one during which he lived in a family at Exeter), at or near Tweedmouth, he had the habit of keeping commonplace books—of which several remain,—their contents bearing witness to an unusual amount of solid reading, and a still more unusual vitality and vivacity of intellect. In the absence of any other record of his life in these years at college, some extracts will be interesting :—

"*Feb.* 5, 1828.—Intend to study more closely this winter than I have done hitherto. I believe my quick talents are a snare to me. If I took more time to learn my lessons I should certainly succeed better at last. Half the session is past, and I shall certainly gain far less honour than I have ever yet done.

"But is honour worth attaining? No: but knowledge is.

"The following plan must be tried :—To rise always before 8 A.M., and walk till 9. From 9 till 10, breakfast and preparation for Dr. J. From 10 till 1, at College.

From 1 till 3, mathematics. From 3 till 4, class. From 4 to 5, walking. From 5 to 6, engaged with M., H., &c. From 6 to 7, Greek. From 7 to 8, with Ferrier. Always to return home at 8, and study mathematics for two hours till 10. Then natural philosophy till 12. After that always read a chapter of the Bible and pray. *Deus adsit.*"

This exhaustive programme (afterwards repeated with some modifications), in which time is not even left for dinner, does not seem to have been thoroughly carried out; but it evinces a resolute intention of hard study. The whole tone of these commonplace books shows that mental work absorbed in winter, at least, almost all his time and interest. While he is at St. Andrews there are but few entries of a lighter cast, although we have heard that in those days he was rather a dandy, and not insensible to the allurements of society. Only once or twice, a passing reference shows that he occasionally gave an hour or two to the fascinations of golf;—(and indeed the student who won't or can't play golf, should matriculate at some other university.) And once or twice, too, there is some such entry as this:—"Have not studied much this week: too much out: 'verbum sat.'" But such entries are rare.

Probably no young man whatever, certainly no young man of genius, ever kept a journal or commonplace book without registering in its faithful pages a few, at least, of those tender experiences which seem to be inseparable from the earlier stages of manly life. This part of the record generally bursts the bands of honest prose, and effloresces into metre. Our student's chronicles are remarkably free from these passages, but still here and there we find an allusion, now in prose, now in verse, to some name which had its spell then, long blotted out—Ah me!—by what waters of oblivion!

One can note in one or two places his early sympathy with the devotional feeling so richly expressed in the hymns and prayers of the Latin Church. He copies out, for instance, Hildebert's beautiful *Oratio ad Dominum:*

"Tu intrare me non sinas
Infernales officinas," &c.,

saying, "This, though in rather dog Latin, contains so much piety, such an exalted devotion, that it ought to be committed to memory by every one who understands the language in which it is written."

He was evidently a diligent student of Principal Campbell's works; and their influence in shaping and confirming his critical habits of approaching and investigating Scripture, can be traced in his extracts and remarks, *e.g.*, "Dr. Campbell's Preliminary Dissertations certainly exceed anything of the kind I have as yet read; and from the perusal of them I have derived information which will enable me to peruse the Greek Testament, the Septuagint, and even the Hebrew Bible, with great advantage. 18th December, 1828." The candid and critical bent of his mind is seen in such entries as this—"The word ὁ, 1 Tim. iii. 16, was altered to Θεος at Constantinople in the beginning of the 6th century. The true reading, which is visible in the Latin and Syriac versions, still exists in the reasonings of the Greek, as well as of the Latin, fathers; and this fraud, with that of the three witnesses of S. John,* is admirably detected by Sir Isaac Newton."

A great part of his time during his later years of college life was spent at Mount Melville, where he was tutor to Mr. Whyte Melville's eldest son, who has since won his spurs in the fields of literature, as the author of many popular, fashionable, and historical novels—"Digby Grand," " The Interpreter," " The Queen's Maries," and several others. "In consequence of this," says one of his fellow students in S. Mary's College (the Theological College of St. Andrews), the Rev. T. J. Crawford, D.D., afterwards his colleague in the University of Edinburgh, " we were not much thrown together. Still I had sufficient opportunities of appreciating his pre-eminent talents and attainments, of which I entertained then, as ever afterwards, the highest admiration. Of the students of his year he was by far the most distinguished. His brilliant appearances in the Literary Society gave promise of that remarkable power and readiness in debate which he afterwards evinced. His warmth of heart and generosity of disposition secured for him in a remarkable degree the esteem and affection of all his fellow students."

Lee left the University in 1832, and was licensed† to preach the gospel early in that year. "This University," wrote Dr. Haldane, then Principal of S. Mary's, "has not for many years sent forth a more distinguished

---

* Is it fair that this avowedly spurious text—1 John, v. 7—should continue to be quoted in the Shorter Catechism as a "proof" of the doctrine of the Trinity?

† This "licence," according to Scottish use, does not confer any ecclesiastical order, but is simply a permission to "preach the word" in the congregation. A licentiate is, by courtesy, styled The Reverend, but is in the eye of the law and of the Church still a layman.

student. He has gained during a succession of years the highest honours which the University can award." His style of preaching seems to have been interesting and effective; and in the Scottish Church, in which preferment depends too much on preaching, he was not likely to remain long without a charge. In the beginning of the next year, 1833, he was elected to be minister of a chapel of ease at Arbroath. His friend and colleague, Dr. Stevenson, now Professor of Ecclesiastical History in the University of Edinburgh, has kindly noted down some of his reminiscences of the period during which he and Lee were at Arbroath together, and these (other materials being very scanty) opportunely help us here.

"It was," says Professor Stevenson, "at a meeting of the Presbytery of Arbroath, convened within the parish church there, about the middle, as I think, of March, 1833, that I saw the late Dr., then Mr. Lee, for the first time. Recently, before the date which has been named, he had been declared the successful candidate for the charge of the S. Vigean's chapel of ease, subsequently called Inverbrothock Church, vacant through the translation of the Rev. Mr. M'Culloch, now Dr. M'Culloch of Greenock, to the parish of Kelso; and he was present at the presbytery on account of some formal step in the process of his settlement. His term of probation as a preacher had been unusually short, comprehending not more than a few months. It was as one of the defeated candidates that, at the meeting referred to, I was introduced to Mr. Lee; and naturally, in such circumstances, I regarded him with some special curiosity and interest. My first impression, as I still recollect perfectly, on being told who he was, surprised me; for he seemed older than I had anticipated, or than I believed him really to be; an impression which came afterwards to be explained by the fact that years produced less change on his personal appearance than on that of almost any other man with whom I was ever acquainted. The same compact, vigorous, and singularly active figure, which I had keenly observed in the old church of

Arbroath so long ago, continued till the spring of 1867 to be presented by Dr. Lee to the eyes of his friends, with almost no perceptible alteration except the silvering by time of his originally fair hair.

"The mutual acquaintance thus begun soon ripened into a warm and familiar intimacy, which suffered no abatement so long as opportunities for its indulgence lasted. I might venture to affirm that no jealousy had poisoned the disappointment of my defeat; but even if the case had been otherwise, the morbid feeling must have vanished at once in the society of my new friend, whose superiority I cheerfully acknowledged. And for a few years after our first meeting, we were, by force of circumstances, thrown very much together. Immediately after the result of the competition for the S. Vigean's chapel was declared, I had entered on the duties of assistant to the Rev. George Gleig, the aged minister of Arbroath. We were thus settled, temporarily at least, as fellow-labourers in the same town; and my appointment as successor to Mr. Gleig, shortly after Midsummer of the same year, gave our relations the aspect of considerable permanency. We were both of us fresh from college, neither conceited nor presumptuous, I trust, though sufficiently conscious of having earned some academical distinction, whether at St. Andrews or at Glasgow; we were both of us merely beginning our public life, and we were strangers alike among the members of the two large congregations which looked to us for our best professional exertions; we were both hopeful and aspiring enough, though consciously ignorant of many things that nearly concerned our duties and prospects, so that I think such young ambition as we ventured to indulge was at any rate free from arrogance; further, we had some controlling tastes and pursuits in common, fondness for music, love of books, and a consuming desire to write better than we were able to do; and finally, we had our lodgings not only in the same street, but within two doors of each other. Under conditions like these, nothing but some personal aversion could have prevented the growth of a very hearty friendship; and as no such ungenerous feeling existed on either side, our intimacy became familiar, confidential, and to me, at least, as profitable as it was happy. We frequently met in the afternoons, at the tables of kind people who were pleased to entertain their new ministers, and whose hospitality was apt, even to us who were no ascetics, to prove at certain seasons of the year rather oppressive. These social gatherings, however, at their very best, yielded no more than a little passing amusement. It was in our almost daily walks—mostly along the cliffs—and in the quiet evening hours spent at the lodgings of one or other of us, that the charm and the solid advantage of that remote and memorable intercourse lay. There the results of our reading were discussed as if they had been common property; plans of future study were projected; grave consultations were held concerning our professional work, its incidental difficulties or eccentric disclosures, and the best methods of securing its success; our sermon-writing, whether actually in hand or still merely prospective, was talked over, and at least one of us received many a valuable hint from those frank and genial conversations; while, finally, the rivalry which, as we well knew, existed between our respective congregations, our poor selves, our public appearances and deportment generally, being the cause of it, furnished us with an inexhaustible subject of gossiping anecdote and good-humoured raillery.

"On looking back over the preceding sentences, I am half ashamed at the apparent egotism which they betray. Yet I feel that this vice exists only in appearance; since it was impossible for me to express what I know respecting Mr. Lee's manner of life, at the period and in the matters referred to, otherwise than as I have done. We had, no doubt, a considerable number of friends among the laity of the town and neighbourhood, many of them common; but although at certain seasons of the year the fashionable hospitalities became somewhat burdensome to both of us, my distinct recollection is that Mr. Lee's attractions of manner and conversation entangled him in a wider social circle than that with which I was familiar. We had our professional intimates also in the rural manses; with these, however, our intercourse was much impeded by distance and indifferent roads,—restricted, therefore, chiefly to the long summer days.

"No one who ever knew Mr. Lee as intimately as I then did, will wonder that his company was much sought and warmly welcomed at the dinner-tables and in the drawing-rooms of all who were capable of appreciating it. Well informed for his time of life, he possessed, in a very remarkable degree, the unembarrassed frankness and the mental vivacity which enable a man in society to avail himself easily and promptly of all his intellectual resources. Acuteness, point, and wonderful readiness characterized his conversation; the same qualities, in short, which at a later period secured and sustained his well-earned distinction as a debater. But he was then practising, so to speak, in a prolusive way, and with the foils merely. The hour for serious polemics and the use of naked weapons had not yet struck; nor was it even so much as anticipated.

"It was only after the passing of the Chapel Act by the General Assembly, or about midsummer 1834,* that Mr. Lee became a member of the Presbytery of Arbroath. But for some time he seldom, or almost never, appeared in the presbytery; nor do I remember a single appearance of his, during the ensuing autumn and winter, in any of the church courts, which could be looked on as prophetic of his future eminence in that arena. But we had other prognostics to the same effect, and these neither rare nor of dubious import. I refer to Mr. Lee's occasional addresses, regarding which, in general, I need say no more here than that, whatever may have been their subject, they were always easy, graceful, and effective, as well as directly to the purpose. Two distinct examples of this kind, however, deserve, as I think, some more special notice. The first of them, indeed, may be easily disposed of, for the details, long forgotten probably, are already on record. I allude to the pamphlet entitled, 'Account of a Meeting held at Arbroath, on the 16th April, 1834, in Defence of Church Establishments,' &c. Of this publication the editorial charge was devolved on Mr. Lee, who accordingly drew up the 'introduction;' and I need only refer to the *brochure* itself for the proof of all that I have said or surmised. The other example must be briefly rehearsed, since it cannot be otherwise known. Mr. Lee and I had arranged to have some kind of missionary meeting, in the old or parish church, on the Monday evening after our communion, in the beginning either of October, 1835, or of March, 1836; I rather think the latter is the true date, but am uncertain. The late

---

* An Act, afterwards decided to be illegal, admitting ministers of chapels, *i. e.* the non-parochial clergy, to the same status and privileges in the Church courts as the parochial.

Dr. Ferrie of Kilconquhar was his assistant, and the late Mr. Doig of Torryburn was mine. We had apprised these gentlemen that we wished them to address our meeting, and, without having obtained their formal consent, had intimated to our congregations that we expected them to do so. Mr. Doig dined with me, and Mr. Lee along with his friend joined us at tea, shortly before the bells began to ring. But what was my consternation on finding that Dr. Ferrie was in one of his surliest humours? He scolded us—that is, he scolded Mr. Lee directly and me by implication—for intimating a meeting without due pre-arrangement, and declared that he would have nothing to do with it. Mr. Doig followed suit, not in the scolding certainly, but in the refusal to speak. To my dismay, Mr. Lee replied in his blandest manner: 'Pray, Dr. Ferrie, give yourself no uneasiness. We certainly wished you and Mr. Doig to help us in a good cause; but do not discompose yourself; we can do all that is necessary without you.' Then, turning to me, he said in a whisper, 'You open with a psalm and prayer. By the time these are over, I shall have considered what to say, and you will be ready to follow.' In a most unenviable state of mind I accompanied our friends into the church, and there, noticing that an important functionary had failed to appear, I said despairingly to Mr. Lee, 'the precentor has not come; what are we to do?' 'Never mind,' he answered quickly, 'sing yourself.' This intrepidity of self-possession was contagious. I proceeded accordingly; and when Mr. Lee's time came, he delivered, to a large and obviously delighted audience, one of the most effective addresses I ever heard from his lips. Anxiety regarding the success of our meeting was at an end, and when I rose to speak, admiration of Mr. Lee stimulated me to do my poor best. When we returned to my parlour, where some frugal refreshment was—after their patient fatigue in listening—duly provided for our two friends, it was amusing to observe the change which they had undergone; Dr. Ferrie, in particular, had become bland and complimentary, giving Mr. Lee no more than his due, and frankly confessing his regret at not having taken some part in what he was pleased to call a most interesting and successful meeting.

"I have nearly nothing more to say, unless it be that, in those days, Mr. Lee was a diligent and an eminently acceptable preacher; that he was, moreover, a laborious pastor, devoting much of his time to household ministrations; and that he was a zealous supporter of all the missionary enterprises which had then been undertaken by our Church. Although, therefore, his appointment to the parish of Campsie, which took place early in the year 1836, was felt to be an instance of well earned promotion, still his removal from Arbroath was generally and very deeply regretted. I was present at his induction at Campsie, on, as I think, the 8th of May; and remember perfectly the sense of personal bereavement with which I contemplated his hearty reception by his new friends in the West."

He does not seem to have kept many of his Inver-brothock sermons.* Among his MSS. are some communion services, including "Table Addresses," and "Fencings † of the Tables," in the style common in those days, but now found chiefly among the older clergy, of considerable length, and somewhat sermonic in their tone. He had already however begun to display those qualities as a preacher which strongly marked his preaching afterwards: a thorough logical analysis of the relations and meanings of his text; a clear and systematic order; a keen incisive criticism; and a love of practical rather than doctrinal discourse, with an unconcealed contempt for those who hid a dislike of practical appeals to

---

* In his Journal, of date 13 August, 1842, he writes: "Reading some old sermons, I find them full of quaintness and witticisms; a style of composition into which I was led by the example of T. Guthrie, now of Edinburgh, then my neighbour, but which I now condemn as bad taste."

† An address delivered before the act of communion—"fencing the table" —i. e. from the intrusion of the unworthy. Recent usage, in accordance with a juster devotional feeling, has much modified the character of this part of the communion service. Left entirely to the judgment of the minister himself (for in this, as in many other instances, the practice of the Church has set at nought both early usage and the recommendations of the Directory) the "fencing" was sometimes, one may say, profanely absurd: e. g., on one occasion an old minister wound up by saying, "And finally, brethren, I debar from this sacred ordinance any man that puts twa fingers into his neighbour's mull, and but one into his ain."

their consciences under the veil of a professed desire to have nothing but "the Gospel," "the sincere milk of the Word," preached to them. In a sermon on Rom. xiii. 8, which followed one or two discourses on Civil Government, delivered in 1835, he says, "But some will say, 'Why discuss such subjects from the pulpit? What have questions of civil polity, what have smuggling and defrauding the revenue to do with the Gospel?' I do not take upon me to answer this question. I send him who asks it to S. Paul, to learn from him why the Holy Ghost has spoken on this subject, which many think is no part of the Gospel. If any ask, 'Why preach on such points?' my answer is, 'S. Paul hath written on them,' *i.e.*, the Holy Ghost hath decided that such doctrine is part of the Gospel; and whether we must be guided about such a matter by the wisdom of God or the foolishness of man, is a question not very difficult to be solved. 'Owe no man anything.' This is another duty which many people would fain persuade themselves is no part of the Gospel. For it is often easier to be high professors than honest men; to make long prayers and pious speeches, than to make restitution of unjust gains. You will excuse me if I take S. Paul's word for it, that the precept, 'owe no man anything,' is part of the Gospel, and quite as necessary to be preached and insisted on as any other precept whatsoever."

He had begun then what he continued to the last, to the great advantage of his hearers—the habit of delivering courses of sermons or lectures upon special subjects. He always insisted on the higher benefit and interest of this than of preaching on detached topics. I remember his saying to me, after reading and laughing over " Salem

Chapel," "Depend upon it there's nothing like Tozer's plan of giving 'a *coorse*.'"

Prefixed to a series of lectures on Christian Evidences, begun in September, 1833, he has on the fly-leaf written the following prayer;—"Me adjuva, precor, O Domine Deus, in hoc incepto opere. Spiritus tuus sanctus in veritatem ducat; eamque ita exponam ut illam videant homines, percipiant, recipiant, et per has lectiones Christiani fiant, non solum nomine sed re; quique nuncupati sunt fideles, fideles vere sint per Jesum Christum, Salvatorem nostrum. Amen."

The deficiencies of our Scottish service in the matter of devotional forms, and of due reading of the Holy Scriptures, had evidently wrought upon his mind, even during his first incumbency.

A member of his congregation in Old Greyfriars, and one of Dr. Lee's closest friends, told me that when [he was taken as a boy to the church at Inverbrothock, what impressed him most was the minister's copious reading of the Scriptures, and his repeating of the Lord's Prayer, a rare formula which this youthful worshipper had never heard used in any other church. And when the deputation from Campsie came to hear Mr. Lee preach, with a view to his becoming minister of that parish, they were greatly influenced in his favour by the impressive manner and well-chosen language of his prayers.

Under his able and faithful ministry the church at Inverbrothock increased and multiplied. "There is not an unoccupied pew in the chapel," say the managers in one of their minutes, recognising the proof of success, to which the minds of managers are most sensitively alive. And in consideration of the ability with which Mr. Lee had discharged all the duties of his office, they recommend, and the proprietors of the chapel agree, in November, 1834, that his stipend of 150*l.* should be raised to 175*l.*, no very extravagant remuneration, after all, for the best educated and hardest worked man in Arbroath.

In 1835, the parish of Campsie, comprising a large village, and a quiet pastoral valley between green hills, and lying in the Presbytery of Glasgow, became vacant, by the transference of the Rev. Dr. McLeod (father of the editor of "Good Words") to S. Columba's church, in the city of Glasgow. After some debate, Mr. Lee was chosen by the " Heritors, Kirk Session, and Male Communicants " of Campsie, as the clergyman whom they should petition the crown to present to the benefice. The crown assented, and he was accordingly transferred from Arbroath to this large and populous parish, in 1836. " The numerous and ample recommendations forwarded in favour of Mr. Lee," wrote Dr. McLeod, "led to his appointment. These recommendations were of no ordinary character. Language could not express in stronger terms the high opinion which the writers entertained of his natural talents and literary acquirements, his varied accomplishments as a scholar and divine, and of his character generally as an able and impressive preacher, and as a faithful, laborious, and acceptable minister of the Gospel." One of the " recommendations " is before me now. In the light thrown back on it by the subsequent relations of the writer to him of whom he wrote, it assumes that air of half-pathetic irony, which too often, in the history of men's lives, comes to enwrap a kindly memory, or to blur the features of an ancient friendship.

The recommendation was from the pen of the Rev. William Muir, D.D., minister of S. Stephen's church in Edinburgh. Dr. Muir was a divine of high repute for piety, for earnestness, for zeal. Though in his Church policy he took the side of the "Moderates," his theological bias was strongly evangelical. At this time, and for many years afterwards, he was much consulted about the qualifications of applicants for vacant parishes ; and the youthful probationer or minister, who was lucky enough to secure the expression of Dr. Muir's approbation or interest in his behalf, felt that half the battle was won. Dr. Muir writes to Dr. McLeod :—

"Mr. Lee was introduced to me by a friend on whose judgment of character I have great reliance, who expressed a high opinion as to his talents and zeal in the objects of our profession. What intercourse I have had with him has given me sufficient proof that the opinion was well founded. I regard Mr. Lee as a person of well-cultivated talent, possessed of no small degree of mental energy, zealously interested in the duties of the ministry; and both from conversations I have had with him on the subject of the care of souls, and from what I have heard of his professional labours in Arbroath, who is willing as well as able, to do the work of an Evangelist. I had the satisfaction of listening to two sermons given by him in my church, which were sound in doctrine, distinguished by acuteness and ability, well sustained by scriptural proofs, and practical. I have no doubt as to his personal piety."

One other letter from a friend of these early days, afterwards widely severed from Lee by the estranging discords of the Church, and this chapter may be closed. It is from the Rev. Thomas Guthrie, who was then minister of Arbirlot, near Arbroath, afterwards famous for Free Church oratory, and some other better things.

"Many, many thanks for all your kindness to me. I have

enjoyed much pleasure in your friendship, and am sensible of no little profit from it ; and you carry my respect, my affection, and my very best wishes along with you. I could almost play the woman while I write this farewell note. Fare thee well, my good friend ; again I say, fare thee well. May the Lord bless you, and make you a blessing, and I have now only to say that at the very sight of you my door shall swing wide open on its hinges, and that I am, and ever will be,

"Your most affectionate friend,

"THOMAS GUTHRIE."

"MANSE OF ARBIRLOT,
  "*April* 18, 1830."

CHAPTER II.

LIFE AT CAMPSIE.—" NON INTRUSION " AND ANTI-
PATRONAGE AGITATION, ENDING IN SECESSION OF
1843.

" The guilt of schism is where each party, instead of expressing fully his
own truth, attacks others, and denies that the others are in the truth at all.
Avoid the cursed spirit of sectarianism : suffer not yourselves to be called by
any party names. . . . Let each man strive to work out, bravely and honestly,
the truth which God has given him ; and when men oppose us and malign
us, let us still, with a love which hopeth all things, strive rather to find good
in them—truths special to them, but which, as yet, they perhaps unconsciously
falsely represent."—F. W. ROBERTSON, *Lectures on Corinthians*, iii.

THE time of Mr. Lee's settlement at Campsie was one
in which the religious world was much stirred and shaken.
In Germany, Strauss had just published his " Leben
Jesu." In England, Dr. Pusey had but recently joined
himself to Newman's movement, and associated his name,
"clarum et venerabile," with the Anglo-Catholic reaction.
In Scotland, the immediate interest and excitement
attaching to the deposition of Mr. Campbell and Mr
Irving had subsided ; but had left, in the minds of many
liberal and thoughtful men, a sense of dissatisfaction
with the course which the Church had followed in dealing
with these two ministers. That course had begotten a
doubt of the justice of her policy, a distrust of the
soundness of her Evangelicalism. Chilled by this doubt
and distrust, the love of many had waxed cold. Simultaneously there had sprung up within the Church, mainly

under the influence of Dr. Chalmers, a strong (so called) "evangelical" reaction against the long predominance of the "moderate" party. This reaction expressed itself, in the parochial ministrations of the clergy whom it moved, by a praiseworthy amount of pastoral activity; and still more in a kind of preaching more direct and earnest than had been common, but imbued in many cases with the rigid and narrow Calvinism of Jonathan Edwards.

In the general good works of the Church the new life showed its young vigour by an increased interest in missions to the Heathen and the Jews, and in Church extension at home. In the Ecclesiastical Courts it inspired a policy whose design, no doubt, was to cut off abuses, to render the Church more popular, and to extend her usefulness by removing causes of offence—especially the most notable cause, an ill-administered patronage. In the evangelical movement there was thus—as in all movements—a mingling of bad and good. There was much, in its activity and Christian earnestness, that good and wise men could not but admire and respect. There was much also in the cast of its theology with which these could not agree. There was a great deal in its public policy that did not fail to estrange the sympathies of those whose minds were not heated by excess of zeal, or warped by passionate attachment to their own theories. Unfortunately—as time passed on —agreement with this public policy, in all that related to the vexed questions of patronage and "spiritual independence," was adopted by the Evangelicals as the one test by which a clergyman's worth, or right to be associated with them in any good work, was to be tested.

Unless he assented to their policy, they would have nothing to do with him. Thus choosing a false bond of union, it was natural that the unity of their own party should soon come to assume the character of a political combination, more than of a spiritual concord ; and that their contendings for those principles, which they maintained all the time were purely spiritual principles, should often in temper be but carnal, and in tactics worldly. It was natural also that those who differed from them, being men of like passions with themselves, finding themselves opposed and thwarted at all points at which opposition was possible, and seeing every Church court, committee room, and platform made the arena of a strife the end of which no man could foretell, should either gradually drift into a like hostility of feeling and intent, and engage in the warfare with corresponding earnestness, or should, in weariness and disgust, hold themselves aloof from the wranglings of the Church courts, and from all public connection with the two great hostile camps into which the Church was ere long divided. " We have discussion on discussion here," writes a well known member of the constitutional party in the Presbytery of Edinburgh in those days, " and all manner of violent agitation. Our Presbytery is really a bear-garden ; and such is the ferocity of the attacks which are ever ready to be made, that though I do not *feel* the thing, yet to save the occasion of sin in others, I have almost formed the resolution (if I continue to frequent the Presbytery) never to utter a word . . . . I am well-nigh brought to the resolution to quit and forsake all Church courts for ever." This expressed a common feeling. The violence of language indulged in by fiery popular leaders ; the bitterness of spirit evinced ; the quick development of a grasping love of ecclesiastical power veiled under the *nom de guerre* of "Spiritual Independence ;" the rude abuse of the constituted tribunals of the country, to which the Church had herself referred her disputed claims ; the heated denunciations of their impartial legal judgments ; the obstinate refusal to recall unlawful acts, or to quit false positions ;—all these characteristics of the "Ten Years' Conflict" were enough to scandalize and grieve sober-minded, charitable, and sagacious men.

Mr. Lee seems to have looked on the progress of the internal war with sorrow and indignation ; but he did not mix himself much in the melley.*　He was averse to squabbling and dispute.　"No employment," he writes in 1838, "is more hazardous than controversy ; for it tends to inflame the passions, and to cover them under the decent cloak of zeal for truth.　And of all sins those are the most dangerous which may easily be passed off as virtues, to which they have a kind of resemblance."　I find the expression of a sentiment akin to this on the first page of one of his common-place books of the same period.　"Let this be my ambition—to be known *in* my parish, to be unknown out of it ; *i. e.*, to be known for use and edification, to be unknown to fame and men's speeches."　Accordingly his name does not figure in the annals of that stormy time.　It does not occupy the exuberant pages of the "Ten Years' Conflict ;" or of the other histories of the agitations which preceded and accompanied the secession of 1843.　A certain sympathy,

* I adopt the spelling vindicated by so great a master of the English tongue as Mr. Kinglake, "Invasion of the Crimea," vol. iv. chap. v.

perhaps, with the principles, though not with the policy, of the "Non-Intrusionists" in the earlier stages of their agitation, forbade his opposing them actively. His near relation also to one of the foremost agitators in his own Presbytery, the Rev. Robert Buchanan, D.D. (whose sister became Mr. Lee's wife in June, 1836), may have partly served, as some of his friends think, to repress any desire he may have felt to hasten to the fray. He could not agree with Dr. Buchanan, and he was, probably, averse to open and constant disagreement. But, no doubt, that which governed him most, in his abstinence from Church battles, was the sentiment which marked him to the end of his life, and which the necessities of his position in later years cruelly wronged,—a dislike of feud and controversy. It is probable also that, like several other earnest men, while he generally disapproved of the conduct of the revolutionary party, he could not altogether sympathize with the principles and doings of the extreme "Moderates;" and thus found himself occupying that middle place from which it is ever difficult to give a thorough support, or a thorough opposition, to either of two hostile parties. Thus in the Assembly of 1841, of which he was a member, we find him speaking and voting in support of the Duke of Argyll's bill—a bill in its principle identical with the Church's veto law, and the approval and adoption of which was proposed in the Assembly by Dr. Candlish.* The bill never passed the House of Lords; but it was believed that, had it been carried, it would have healed the troubles of the Church, as far as any enactment could heal them. "They were all agreed," said Mr. Lee, "that nothing could relieve

* See "Robert Story, of Rosneath," p. 260.

them from their difficulties except a legislative enactment, and he could not conceive any enactment adapted
to that purpose if not some such one as this . . . .
This bill was the only modification of patronage the
House would get." "With the honourable exception of
Mr. Lee," says Dr. Buchanan, "no member of the
moderate party gave anything better than smooth words
as their response to Dr. Candlish's appeal." * As a body,
the moderate party, somewhat obstinately, voted against
the Duke's bill.

Mr. Lee's keen intelligence and sober judgment, however, left him in no doubt as to the inherent wrongness of
the ultimate principles and proceedings of the revolutionary, or " Non-Intrusion," party in the Church.

It was right and just, and in accord with the ancient
theory and practice of the Church of Scotland, that no
minister should be settled in a parish against the reasonable wish of the parishioners. Such "intrusion" is
necessarily offensive to Christian feeling and opinion;
but it had become too common under the policy of
Principal Robertson and those who carried down the
traditions of his "moderate" rule. The act of Queen
Anne, restoring their powers to lay patrons, and putting
an end to the popular patronage of the heritors and
elders of the parish, made these discreditable settlements
possible. †

* "Ten Years' Conflict," vol. ii. ch. xiii.
† In the Second Session of the Revolution Parliament of 1690, among other
acts affecting the Scottish Church (one rescinding the act of royal supremacy
adopted in 1669 ; another restoring the Presbyterian ministers who had been
ejected from their churches after 1st January, 1661 ; another ratifying the
Westminster Confession of Faith, and settling Presbyterian Church government) an act was adopted transferring those rights of patronage, which were
coeval with the Reformation, from the ancient patrons to the *heritors* and
elders of parishes. But it is very remarkable to find that in the claim of right
and the articles of grievances drawn up by the Convention, and in all the

The Church had long protested against that act, but at last had sullenly or apathetically acquiesced in it.* Time passed; and enforced settlements, now and again occurring, wrought much mischief in estranging the affectionate loyalty of the people from the Church, and in breeding dissent. It was not, however, until the year 1834, that the Church took any direct step towards remedying the evil. And then, under well-meant but unsound advice, she took a wrong step. Instead of going to the legislature, as her position as an Established Church obliged and entitled her to go, and seeking the co-opera- tion of the legislature, she took the question into her own hands. She broke the terms of her compact with the State, and strove to evade the grievance of an act of Parliament, by passing a law of her own, which trenched on those debatable rights which are inevitably involved in the union of Church and State. She did this, first, in promoting the non-parochial to the full rights of the parochial clergy, whereby all the acts of the Church courts, to which those ministers were illegally admitted, were vitiated. She did it also in passing the "Veto Law," of 1834-5, which enacted that the opposition (without any assigned reason) of a majority of the male

public addresses and papers of the Presbyterian ministers at that time, there is not one word to be found complaining of patronage in the Church as a grievance, or pointing to any claim of popular election as a *divine right* inherent in the people of Scotland. We find, indeed, in the more occult documents of the period, indications of a desire for the abolition of patronage; and it is understood that it was Principal Carstares, acting at Court for the Presbyterian aristocracy and clergy of Scotland, who overruled the strong objections of King William to the course which was adopted, by assurances that, politically, it was indispensable for insuring the permanency of his throne. See M'Cormick's *Life of Carstares;* and *The Constitution of the Church of Scotland*, a pamphlet by A. Peterkin, 1811.

* For seventy years after the restoration of patronage the Assembly had protested against, or the Commission of Assembly had been annually instructed to petition for redress of, the grievance. In 1784 this protest, which had become a mere form, was dropped.—See CUNNINGHAM's *Church Hist.*, ii. 12.

heads of families in communion with the Church should warrant a Presbytery in refusing to ordain or "induct" a presentee.*

This may have been a desirable solution of the problem of patronage. Many people, Dr. Lee among the number, had no special aversion to the veto law in itself. But it was, unless ratified by Parliament, an illegal solution of the problem; and its illegality was proved as soon as it was challenged—as in the case of Auchterarder—and referred to the judgment of the Court of Session and of the House of Lords. All the long contests, and the final rending of the Church, the protracted struggle and agony which no one can think of without pain, or wish to have told over any more, followed unavoidably from the refusal of the popular party to acquiesce in the legal decision, and to begin their campaign against patronage in a legitimate way.

Mr. Lee, before the contest had reached its height, saw clearly enough its essentially dangerous character, as the Non-Intrusionists carried it on; and not all the thunderous eloquence of Dr. Chalmers, nor the sledge-hammer violence of Dr. Cunningham, nor the adroit force of Dr. Candlish, nor the bland subtleties of Dr. Buchanan, availed to shake his conviction that they and their followers were in the wrong, and were ruining the Church. He detected also in the movement a tendency which he always held in abhorrence,—the tendency of strong-willed and domineering ecclesiastics to grasp at

* In Scotland the person presented by the patron to a benefice is called the "Presentee." If he has been already ordained, the Presbytery "induct" him to the charge; if he has not been ordained, the presentation is held to be the warrant for his receiving ordination, provided he is found, after due examination, properly qualified.

exclusive power; to erect an *imperium in imperio*, to claim a high spiritual jurisdiction, and the right to define what is spiritual; to draw their own narrow circle, and within it to deal, without appeal or challenge, their anathemas. Against this he ever raised his voice, recognizing in it one of the worst foes of rational Christian liberty. He thought that, as it was, the democratic constitution of the Scottish Church gave too much room for the play of this hurtful tendency. Long after this time, in an article on the collected works of Edward Irving,[*] he writes, " Among the many striking differences which separate our two venerable establishments, perhaps this is the most important of all, that the laws of the one are interpreted by lay, of the other by clerical judges; from which it follows that the one Church tends more and more to liberality and expansiveness, while the other degenerates more and more to narrowness and isolation, taking the place of a sect rather than of a Church catholic and national."

One of the few speeches which can be traced to him in the debates of those angry years, was spoken in the Presbytery of Glasgow on December 16, 1840. By that time the cry for " Non-Intrusion " had changed into a whoop for the abolition of patronage. Mr. Burns, the minister of Kilsyth, proposed an " overture " to the General Assembly for this abolition. Mr. Lee moved an amendment, but his motion was lost by a majority of 50 to 12. His speech, however, seems to have made a pretty strong impression. Dr. Muir read it in Edinburgh, and wrote to a friend, "The speech of our friend Mr. Lee was quite original in its arrangement of thought, most pointed

* *Scotsman,* Feb. 29, 1864.

in expression, and telling with prodigious strength and acuteness." It has many of the characteristics of the style to which those who heard him in later years were accustomed; the happy originality of treatment, the close logic, the sagacious prescience, the clear common-sense, the disregard of the bugbears of tradition and authority, the sharp yet airy satire.

A few extracts will give an idea of the question and of his handling of it :—

"I have heard it supposed that Providence, having obstructed the Church of Scotland in her efforts to obtain a settlement of this question another way, means now to direct her to take the course which our friends opposite are pursuing; which means, that because the Non-Intrusion agitation has failed, the Anti-Patronage agitation should commence. The ways of Providence are a great deep. Another interpretation has suggested itself to my mind, namely, that that course should be relinquished on which Providence has so remarkably frowned. Two circumstances dispose me to think this interpretation may be correct,—one is, this lesson seems to be needed; the other is, it is not likely to be taken. For Providential warnings, however much they may benefit others, seldom instruct those more immediately concerned. We are told that lay patronage is contrary to the constitution of the Church of Scotland, that it is contrary to Scripture, and most mischievous in its operation. These are dreadful charges. And we naturally turn to ask who makes them? To our amazement we find that they are the very persons who have sanctioned patronage in their own persons, by *accepting* presentations, and by sustaining them as members of Presbyteries. But it seems they are not implicated, because, as they say, *patronage is not embodied in the constitution of our Church;* and, because *they have lately protested against it.* But they omit what would be the only really important condition, namely, that they have no connection with it—make not themselves parties to it—and above all, *do not profit by it.* If they do the very thing against which they protest, or aid and abet those who do it, why, whom does their protest condemn but themselves ? . . . . Our friends need not blame us for reiteration of this charge of inconsistency. Let them cease to reiterate *their* charges, and we shall instantly cease *ours*. This quarrel is not of our seeking. . . . . I don't know any of the Reformers who dissented, as we have been told some of them did, from the Roman Church *because liberty to protest was denied them.* It was not Luther or Melancthon, Zwingli or Calvin, Cranmer or Ridley, Latimer or Knox. All of these dissented on quite different grounds. In point of fact, at the period of the Reformation, and immediately before it, a remarkable liberty was allowed, in the Roman Church, of censuring both opinions and practices. This the writings of Erasmus, and many others, clearly prove. After the establishment of the Inquisition, indeed, and the first sitting of the Council of Trent—especially after the elevation of Cardinal Caraffa to the Papacy—this liberty was repressed. And then the Reformers justified their separation by pleading that liberty of protest was denied them in the church of Rome. But, sir, let our friends remark that those Reformers *did not desire, like them, liberty to do a thing, and then protest against it.* Luther did not desire first to recognize the Pope, and then to protest against the Pope—to use mass, and then to protest mass was an idolatry. This is a stretch of ingenuity left for reformers of a more enlightened age. If lay patronage be unscriptural—being either forbidden or discountenanced in the word of God—*is it sinful?* and the statements constantly heard show that our friends opposite consider it so. They say it involves a defrauding the Church of her liberties, so that it is not only theft but *sacrilege.* If so, *all* the parties concerned in this system are implicated in this awful guilt—the legislature which enacted the law, the patron who issues a presentation, the preacher or minister who accepts it, and the Church courts who sustain it and give effect to it. All these are *participes criminis.* 'But what can we do?' You can at least *protest.* We hear what a salvo for wounded consciences *protesting* is. But no protest is heard. *Vastum ubique silentium.* We should *rebel*, indeed, by refusing to sustain a presentation! But what then? The divine right of resistance is now well understood, though we could not comprehend the doctrine at all, some time ago, when others attempted to teach it us. Thus you are bound to act if you will be consistent. Your conduct then would be intelligible. But to reconcile your present course with your professed opinions would exhaust all the subtilty of all the schoolmen; Aquinas and Scotus, with Bonaventura, Lombard, and Hales at their elbow, would confess themselves puzzled. This problem would put all the doctors, 'irresistible and irrefragable, angelical and seraphical,' to flight.

"Sir, I can hardly persuade myself that my brethren are serious when they assert that patronage is contrary to the word of God. For if they felt the truth of their own assertion, I cannot persuade myself they would, or could, act in relation to patronage as they do. Another thing which tempts me to doubt whether they are serious is this:—that almost all of them —I may say all of them—are willing to submit to patronage, *if properly limited*, though they cannot agree among themselves what is a proper limitation. Now, in this, my brethren themselves must admit, they are glaringly inconsistent. For if this system of patronage is indeed forbidden by Scripture, or contrary to it, *all degrees of it are forbidden alike, the least as well as the greatest;* even as the commandment which says, 'Thou shalt not steal,' forbids the unjust taking of one farthing as much as of a hundred; and, therefore, on their own theory, they are not at liberty to tolerate patronage at all, however limited it may be. No addition of what is right can ever make what is wrong cease to be wrong. . . . . . .

"As to the contrariety of patronage to the constitution of the Church of Scotland, it has been asserted, but not proved. It has always been the practice in the Church, with the exception of a few years. We hear much of the great improvement which has taken place in the Church during the last few years. I hope those pleasing pictures are correct. I hope ecclesiastical zeal has not been mistaken for spiritual zeal, to which it is as like as party spirit is to patriotism. We are not, indeed, disposed to consider self-applause as the most unequivocal sign of growth in grace. But, admitting this improvement, which in part I do admit, has it not taken place under the law of patronage? So that, after all, patronage must not be so very inimical to the Church's constitution. If you saw a man partaking of a certain kind of food every day, and yet growing every day more strong and robust, you would suspect the doctors had made a mistake who pronounced that food mortal poison. It will not help you to say he grew strong *in spite of what he ate*, for it showed this at least, that that food was *innocuous*, as it did not hinder his possessing strong health. But suppose patronage *was* contrary to the ideas of John Knox and Andrew Melville, and all the rest, have not we as much right to form our own judgment as they had? And have we not much more abundant means of doing so correctly? I do not admire the Popery of those who set up the authority of some few men, and are ever denouncing us because we will not fall down with them and worship it.

"But patronage is condemned in Scripture! Where? Let us have the chapter and verse quoted. 'He gave some to be apostles, and some evangelists,' &c. This is nothing to the purpose at all, for it only tells us that Christ instituted a ministry, and what the ends of that ministry are. Profoundly mysterious it is that so monstrous a conception as patronage should never be once described or alluded to in that volume which was written for all time! My friend Mr. Burns, of Kilsyth, told us just now, that, by merely looking on a well-known engraving of the General Assembly as it appeared last century, he was able to discover what formed the subject of conversation among the members there represented. I don't wonder that persons endowed with such creative optics as his are able to discern the condemnation of patronage in the Bible, for they can find in it not only all that is there, but all they wish to find; while we, poor souls, who can see nothing but what is to be seen, must take our information touching the hidden doctrines from such gifted seers. Before the examples of election of office-bearers, mentioned in the New Testament, can be shown to bind us in all particulars, it must be shown that these examples are *so fully and clearly set forth as to direct us*, that *they agree one with another*, and that *some intimation is given that we are bound to follow them.* None of these three things can be shown. But if we must form a judgment in the matter it would be this : that as the apostles, or their delegates, seem to have uniformly nominated all ministers of the Word in the New Testament Church, the patronage now should be vested in Presbyteries, where no man of common sense would wish to see it vested. Surely, sir, we may safely conclude that, if one particular system of appointing ministers had been constantly obligatory on the Church, it would have been fully unfolded and distinctly enjoined in the Word of God. I cannot assent to the position that all Church practices of the Apostolic Church are necessarily binding on us, or that nothing is lawful in the Church but what is expressly enjoined or exemplified in the New Testament. . . . . 'The apostles knew nothing of patronage.' Well, neither did they of tithes, teinds, Church-rates, annuity-taxes, endowments, stipends, manses, or glebes. Shall we reform away all these clerical comforts and appliances? 'They were all unconscious of a presentation, and all innocent of it.' So they were of a benefice, of which the presentation is an accident. How, on such ground as this, can we ever defend our position as a civil establishment—which, though there be principles of reason and Scripture out of which we can maintain it, is never commanded in the Bible, and never exemplified there, for the Mosaic institute was not a union of Church and State, but *an identity of the two*—the Church being the State, and the State the Church—its God being its king, its civil law being its religion, and its synagogue its courts of law? The matter is not mended by saying the New Testament at least informs us that the appointment of office-bearers *was within the Church.* Where else could it be, when all external institutions, all the governments of the world, had arrayed themselves against the Church? Does it follow, as a consequence, that a State in union with the Church must be excluded from all influence in its affairs, because another State, hostile to its very existence, neither sought nor could be permitted to exercise any? Men don't generally treat their friends and their enemies in exactly the same way. All unions imply some abridgments of liberty, submitted to in the prospect of greater advantages. . . .

A great deal is said of the consequences of patronage during the last century. Without inquiring whether those representations be correct pictures or gross caricatures, I may be permitted to remind those who love this dark subject so well, that the only question for us now is—what are the effects of the system *in the present state of society?* It might be easy to draw an argument which would prove monarchy an intolerable evil out of the same materials out of which that argument against patronage is manufactured. Institutions are often dangerous, even ruinous, in one state of society, which in another are innocent, or even highly beneficial; and we may well conclude that, if gentlemen opposite could find those evils they seek in the living actual world, they would not thus constantly resort to charnel-houses of the past to raise up those dead mischiefs out of their graves. But I cannot admit those evils, whatever they were, to be truly attributable to patronage.

"They seem rather to be chargeable on the church courts, and on them alone, for *they* always had the power to prevent that kind of intrusion which has done harm—the intrusion of unholy and inefficient ministers. To hear our friends talk, one would suppose that the *patron*, and not the Presbytery, had the charge of judging whether the presentee was learned, holy, apt to teach, and suited for the charge! While the ill consequences this law may have produced are dwelt upon and magnified, those which it has prevented are entirely overlooked. Is this a fair method of judging? We should hold him uncandid who described a man's faults only, and gave us these as a complete character. I must add that instead of comparing the system they denounce with other systems actually existing, or which have been tested by experience, it is their constant practice to compare it with an *idea* which has never been exemplified or reduced to the test of experiment. No institution in the world can stand, if judged by such a criterion as that. Our difficulty, however, they cannot meet. What is to succeed the present practice? Strange that a model should be held up in the New Testament, and no two of you can agree what it is? Our friends say it is their wisdom not to tell what they would substitute. It is their wisdom, for they cannot speak on the subject without contradicting one another. It becomes the anti-patronage party to tell the people what is the object at which at present they aim. Is it to obtain the repeal of the Act 1711; in which case the Act 1690 becomes law, and the heritors and elders are constituted the patrons? This change, instead of satisfying the people, would be much more unpopular than the present system is. For the nearer power is brought to men's hands, without being actually possessed by them, the more they feel aggrieved. We envy that only which is a little above ourselves. In the meantime the law of patronage is rapidly repealing itself. The people, if you will only let things take their course—if you will only not insist on being made martyrs—will soon possess the whole power in this and many other things. We need not regret what cannot be prevented ; our duty is to prepare them, as much as we can, for using what all events are conspiring to give them. If you will not render the stream muddy by your grotesque attempts to hasten it, you may stand quietly on the banks and see patronage make its grand plunge into the abyss of things that were ; and then, if you will reserve as much breath, you may sing its '*fuit*' as lustily as you like. Your noise, then, will do no harm.

" Allow me to say, sir, I feel as much concerned for the good of the people, and for their liberties too, as they can do who speak so much about them. My opinion is, however, that the liberties of our people are increasing faster than their knowledge and their grace are. And I cannot judge them friends of the people, however friendly their intentions, who are lending their efforts rather to increase the people's power, than to qualify them for exercising the power they have, and that greater power which they must soon possess. They have read history to little profit who have not learned that the interests of liberty itself have been so much injured by almost no cause as by a premature assertion of liberty, or by conferring power suddenly on those who were not prepared to use it. Time, I believe, will settle this question much more satisfactorily—much more safely —than those hands which are now busy with the work.

" I conclude with remarking the effects of this agitation. Our nobility and higher gentry, you have heard, are not generally of our Church. Let me ask, will this agitation tend to conciliate them ? A large, intelligent, wealthy, and influential class of the community are notoriously cooling rapidly in their attachment to the Church of Scotland. Let that pugnacious temper, that debating and disputatious agitating humour, be indulged in a little longer, and they will be lost for ever to the establishment. And, then, it may be worth your while to foresee the influence of your arguments on those who receive them most willingly, and are most convinced by them. (Who can be expected to resist reasonings which pay a perpetual compliment to himself ?) They will be thoroughly convinced that patronage is repugnant to the Word of God, even though one verse to that purpose cannot be quoted to them. And they will rid themselves of it either within the establishment or without. There is not the very slightest probability of the law in question being repealed at present ; and the people, not able to comprehend that subtle logic by which their ministers can do what they condemn, will feel themselves driven to dissent. *Their* consciences will tell them this is their only course. I cannot join in this agitation. I cannot sympathise with it. I think it has done, is doing, and is still to do, infinitely more harm than the success of it could ever do good. It is my opinion that as a Church we should be stronger, and as ministers more respected and more useful, if we could contrive to be more peaceable and retiring, and imitated less the politicians and agitators of this world." *

It is fortunately unnecessary to follow out in these pages, the history of the contest which, after raging for about ten years, was brought to its baffled close on the 18th of May, 1843, by the secession from the Church of 289 of her parochial clergy, with 162 of the non-parochial, followed by a large body of the laity. It is irksome to renew the unprofitable and grievous strife, " *infandum renovare dolorem:*" it has been chronicled so often and so fully, that it ought now to be pretty well understood in Scotland ; out of Scotland it is not likely it will ever be understood.†

In November, 1842, Mr. Lee wrote to a leading non-intrusionist as follows :—

" I believe, and I say so from considerable observation of the opinions of various people who naturally speak more unreservedly to me than they would do to a more determined partisan, that if you go out of the Church, your honesty will be much less commended than the theory which drives you to such

---

* *Glasgow Courier*, Dec. 19, 1840.
† I may refer those who wish the Seceders' own account of it to Dr. Buchanan's " Ten Years' Conflict ;" others to Dr. Turner's " Scottish Secession of 1843 ;" to " Robert Story, of Rosneath, a Memoir :" Macmillan, 1862 ; and to Dr. Charteris' " Life of Robertson :" Blackwood, 1863.

a course will be condemned. The whole Presbyterian and Independent ministers conformed to the Episcopal Church in England in 1662, except about 2000 (under one-fifth of the whole), and when the conditions imposed were palpable and grievous; and not more of the Episcopal clergy were expelled and sequestered during the Commonwealth, the conditions being equally grievous and tyrannical.

"Let the non-intrusionists say what they will, they cannot make their grievances appear to be anything like the same in point of magnitude, besides being of their own creation entirely. And I am disposed to consider human nature very permanent in its workings. The cost to you and a few others will be easily counted. You will prosper much better in your worldly interests after the change. But what will be the case with the country brethren?

" These are considerations which will occur to even the most spiritual and conscientious men, and will weigh with them in settling the questions whether they should relinquish a position in which they are permitted to preach the Gospel and administer discipline among their flocks without interference; and to refuse to ordain any man to the ministry of whose qualifications, after hearing and weighing all that the people of the congregation can allege, they are themselves not fully satisfied. And I with many others consider that they who have driven so many men to this pass, have been guilty in many ways of a great iniquity. I have no faith in bonds and engagements. From the Solemn League and Covenant down to the bond against using the Glasgow Railway, they have afforded no guarantee of the manner in which the parties should afterwards act. The people almost universally seem to consider your secret convention,* which is the last, also the greatest, of your errors; and of this I am certain, nothing could have been devised less likely to produce any impression either on the country or the Government. It must, I think, injure your prospects exceedingly.

" You do not seem to be aware of a feeling extensively prevailing among the moderate party, and which seems to me not without reason, namely, If you remain in the Church much longer and proceed as you are doing, you will inevitably expel

* The " Convocation " held in Edinburgh in 1842.

them in detail. They will refuse to enforce the veto against the decision of the civil law, and you will depose them for that refusal. It has therefore become war to the knife. Maintaining their present position, the moderate party have an interest in your expulsion ; they feel it essential to their own safety. This they have long felt, and this explains their determination not to help you. All propositions to this effect are neutralized by that feeling, and by exasperation at the tyrannical manner in which they conceive they have been used.

"I do not apprehend matters are destined at present to come to extremity. The Government doubtless will pass a law next session. Whether it comprehends what is now held to be non-intrusion or not, I have not the least doubt a very large proportion of the 550 you mention will find it makes such concessions as will enable them with tolerable consistency to remain in the Church. A few perhaps may not submit, but as to the Church as a Church breaking off her connexion with the State, it seems to me a strange imagination, which, notwithstanding all you say, I cannot persuade myself is likely soon to be realized. I may be wrong, I am not in the middle of the strife, and various causes hinder me feeling that deep interest in it which others feel. If it is the will of God that the Church of Scotland should now be overturned, I doubt not God has purposes to answer which none of the instruments have in view, and that another Church will succeed it founded on more comprehensive and Catholic principles, of a less sectarian character and spirit, and better adapted to the present state of society and the wants of men. These defects in our Church are becoming more and more apparent ; they are felt by many of the best ministers in the Church, and by more of the people, and they will prove fatal to the Church of Scotland at no distant day. I am thankful for this controversy, in that it has tended to inspire this feeling in many quarters and to deepen it. The discussions about spiritual independence have to many men who have not yet avowed it, suggested that the Church of God has sinned in binding herself to relinquish her liberty to interpret the Word of God otherwise than as God himself shall give light ; and that to cause her ministers to swear they will never hold or teach otherwise than as they may believe when they swear, is to tempt them to swear they will refuse any new instruction

God may give them ; that they will be obstinately blind, and that the Church shall, century after century, refuse to become wiser or to understand the Word of God better than she did at a given period. And it excites my wonder that a Church can talk of spiritual independence in a trifle and deem it essential, when she has relinquished her independence in that capital and essential affair of the interpretation of the Word of God itself.

"If you do secede in numbers, and frame a Church on truly Catholic principles, many will join you whom you do not now count on; but I repeat I do not anticipate any such result. I know you are perfectly sincere in your professions, and earnest in your purposes, but I feel equally confident the result will be such as I have here predicted. At all events I have no power to influence any party who might influence the course of events, and I wait the result, knowing that whatever happens will eventually contribute to the glory of the Church of Christ, and the advancement of His kingdom on the earth."

I may fitly introduce here, as mainly referring to the period during which the revolutionary movement was in progress, the following letter which has been kindly addressed to me by the Rev. W. G. Smith, minister of Ashkirk, then minister of Fintry, one of Dr. Lee's most intimate friends. Mr. Smith says :—

"It is now a long time since Dr. Lee and I were ministers of adjoining parishes, but the period was in some respects a marked one, and I remember it well.

"My intercourse with him began soon after my settlement at Fintry, in the end of 1840. He was then in the prime of life, and full of vigour and activity. With the frank and ready kindness which at all times distinguished him, he took a friendly interest in all his neighbours, and I had the happiness to be very soon admitted to his intimate acquaintance. I found him uniformly anxious, even then, to impress upon his younger brethren the necessity both of diligent study and of careful attention to all parish work. And his own example on those points was most instructive. While reserving ample time for thorough pulpit preparation, he applied himself assiduously to every branch of professional literature. He was a great economist of time, so that, while doing full justice to the many claims which a large parish had upon him, he still commanded leisure for his favourite pursuits. The consequence was that, even before he left Campsie, he had acquired a very great store of that theological and critical knowledge which he afterwards turned to so much account. He was at the same time very earnest in his searching after truth. With pains and *prayers* he strove to find it, and to hold it, for himself. And to no less worthy motive than that innate love of truth must be ascribed whatever views he held, which some might think peculiar. But the fact is, that to all the leading doctrines of the Bible I believe he was sincerely and devotedly attached—and to the many conversations which I had with him about them I shall ever feel indebted, under God, for much enlightenment, in regard both to the fulness and the freeness of the Gospel.

" In his influence with his people there was something very striking. It was shown very notably at the time of the secession. In the movements and discussions which preceded that event, he took, as you may well suppose, a very keen interest, and he bore himself through all with characteristic independence. But although, in common with many others on that occasion, he had to mourn the estrangement of some valued friends and brethren and co-presbyters, his parishioners adhered to him with a marvellous unanimity. Every effort was of course made, from Glasgow and elsewhere, to persuade them to withdraw from the Church of their fathers, but in vain. In that large parish, of some 6000 people, to the end of his incumbency, and for several years thereafter, there was not only no Free Church, but scarcely even a Free Churchman. I question much if such another case occurred throughout all Scotland. And the result was mainly due to the ability and the honesty and the manliness with which our friend explained the points at issue. In his sermons, and by lectures, and in private conversation, he took pains to set the thing in its true light before his people, and he had the satisfaction of succeeding with them perfectly. When he left, and though the country, near to Glasgow more especially, was still tossed with all the tumult of the recent agitation, there was not the least secession in that very populous parish.

"I may add that, while undoubtedly that was owing in the first place to the special efforts made by Dr. Lee for the purpose, the success of these may also be ascribed indirectly to the standing which his general ministrations had obtained for him. In his preaching he was then, as ever, able and most acceptable. I may give a little anecdote which serves to illustrate that. He was going through the parish, taking leave of the people, on the eve of his removal to the church of Old Greyfriars, when a worthy parishioner took occasion to suggest that they would all greatly like to have a volume of his sermons to remind them of himself and of his ministry among them, and he specified a certain course of lectures on the Hebrews, which would seem to have been listened to with great satisfaction. " Oh, but, John," said the minister, "those lectures are not extant; they were preached by me from notes, which I have since thrown aside." 'Weel, sir, it's a pity,' was the answer, 'they would have *immortaleezed* ye!' In his other parish work, too, he was faithful and laborious. I remember the astonishment which I felt on one occasion, when I saw him for some purpose turning up a large folio, in appearance not unlike a very portly merchant's ledger, which was filled from end to end with an account, in his handwriting, of the names and all particulars which a minister cares to know, of all the families in that large and somewhat shifting population. He kept that record for his guidance in his usual visitations, which were frequent and minute, and always highly prized and welcomed by all classes and by all denominations in the parish.

"I should have mentioned, as one way in which he tried to be of use, that he arranged with some of his younger clerical neighbours to have monthly meetings at each other's manses, for prayer and the critical study of the Scriptures, with a view to mutual improvement, and it was only from his efforts in that direction not being zealously seconded that the plan was after a time given up.

"Of Dr. Lee in private intercourse, I need to say but little. From the very first, and through all my long and close friendship with him for more than seven-and-twenty years, I found him ever the same—cheerful and kind and affectionate. For

ignorance and bigotry he had little toleration, and his caustic
way of speaking was at times more plain than pleasant ; but,
even to those from whom he had the bitterest opposition, I
believe he never cherished any feeling of ill-will ; while, by all
who had the privilege of his intimate acquaintance, he was
known, beloved, and trusted as a most sagacious counsellor, a
most delightful companion, and a warm-hearted, constant, and
most valuable friend. Such was *my* experience of him in an
eminent degree."

CHAPTER III.

"Not slothful in business; fervent in spirit; serving the Lord."
S. Paul's Epistle to the Romans, xii. 11.

His life, during these years at Campsie, was singularly active, bright, and happy—shining with a clear light of heart and intellect,—full of well-done work and of kindly affection and friendship, with the sacredness, then as ever, of a real and quiet piety pervading all.

His heart rejoiced in his home, more almost than that of any man I ever knew. And his home was just beginning then to brighten into beauty and echo with music. His marriage was a most happy one; and he delighted in his children. He always seemed to stand entranced before the innocent beauty—the "sancta simplicitas" of childhood. "People generally do not consider how great a boon and help a child is," he writes to a friend. "I have found them so in a degree which I had no conception of." "May God bless the mother and child," he wrote to me long afterwards—in 1866. "It is the beginning of a new life to you both; 'the perpetual Messiah,' as the Chelsea Prophet has spoken—ὡς ἐκ τοῦ Θεοῦ." "The affection of parents," he says, in one of his common-place books, "comes down upon their children in floods. It ascends from children to their parents, but in *drops*, like the descending cataract, which sends nothing back to the mountain whence it pours, but some exhalations and mists."* Those who knew him well know how his life was bound up in his family, and how amidst all his troubles from without he sought and found rest and gladness there.

In his general activities—in his own parish and elsewhere—his influence was most wholesome and invigorating. "You never find Mr. Lee *flat*," said one of the most intelligent of his parishioners, agreeably stirred by his ceaseless mental energy; and again, "I never met with any man who read so much that remembered so much." "My recollections of him are of a most delightful kind," writes a friend who met him first in 1841. "He came over to preach on the evening of the first Communion Sunday I had been in Scotland, and spent a considerable time with us after the service. I can never forget how refreshing his conversation was to us,—he seemed so thoroughly to enter into and enjoy the truths he had been preaching, and he appeared to me one of the most spiritually-minded men I had ever known. It was about that time, I think, he began to dwell much upon the extent of the atonement, *for all men*; and this was the more striking because at that time this great truth, now happily so generally taught, was considered almost a heresy. I remember his writing several letters to my husband on the subject,—and little short notes—with just a thought that seemed to have occurred to him at the moment. He was anxious that we should enter as

* I suspect this must be an adaptation, or possibly an unconscious reminiscence of Jeremy Taylor, who says in his "Duty of Nursing Children in Imitation of the Blessed Virgin-Mother," "If love descends more strongly than it ascends, and commonly falls from the parents upon the children in cataracts and returns back again up to the parents but in gentle dews, &c."

fully and warmly into the subject as he did,—and you know how energetic he always was."

His minute and anxious care of his parishioners and all their interests—especially their highest concerns—was never interrupted. While it was too common for the champions of "non-intrusion" and "spiritual independence" to be careering over the country, emitting windy speeches and rousing an irrational agitation, he set an example of zealous devotion to his appointed work and steady shepherding of the flock over which the Holy Ghost had made him overseer. He tolerated no lax or slovenly idea of what his duties as a pastor and teacher were. With a reference to the Episcopal pretensions urged in those days, and indeed at all times, in Scotland, he says: "I am a bishop of a diocese containing some twenty square miles and some 6000 souls. This is surely oversight enough to constitute any one a bishop . or overseer, or if any one thinks this too little, all I can say is, he has a very extraordinary idea what oversight means. Surely he must understand the word to denote looking over everything and looking into nothing; and he must have a wonderful taste for charge, and a most voracious and false appetite for responsibility."

In November, 1842, he lays down in his diary the following programme for Prayer Meetings :—

Mr. Marshall, my worthy assistant, and I, this morning, considering in what way we might best promote the glory of God in this parish, resolved to commence a prayer meeting next Thursday evening, in Lennoxtown, to be continued weekly. The chief aim and end of this meeting is to promote among the people a spirit of devotion, and to impress on them the importance of that temper and exercise. We think the following order may advantageously be observed :—

1. A short introductory prayer, confessing our great unworthiness to approach the Divine presence, and imploring grace to offer an acceptable sacrifice.
2. Singing.
3. Psalm—one or more, in the prose version. The reading may be accompanied with a word or two as to the character, design, or supposed authorship of the psalm.
4. Prayer. The longest prayer shall now be offered, in which the minister shall embrace as many topics as may be, making this prayer as comprehensive as possible: adoration of God our creator, preserver, redeemer, sanctifier, father, and portion.

> Confession of sin against God, against our neighbour—personal sins—supplication for ourselves—for pardon, peace, illumination, faith, love, zeal—to walk holily, wisely, and kindly towards our fellow men.
>
> Intercession for all men—for the whole Church—for heretics and erroneous—for inconsistent Christians—and the coming of Christ's kingdom,—for the sick and afflicted—the dying—and poor.
>
> That we may walk in all purity, sobriety, patience, and humility—and may be salt and light in the world.
>
> That we may constantly live in preparation to die, working out our own salvation "with fear and trembling," daily hoping and desiring to meet our most blessed Lord.

5. Singing shall follow. This exercise shall always be performed by the congregation standing.
6. Next shall follow a lesson out of the Old or New Testament, or both if there shall be time, and the officiating minister shall, if he thinks proper, follow the reading of such lessons with what exposition, remark, or improvement he may judge suitable, taking care to turn what may be said as much as may be to the use of edifying.
7. Prayer. Which shall consist chiefly in thanksgiving for God's great mercies to us, and prayer for grace to live suitably. This prayer shall conclude with the Lord's Prayer.
8. Psalm.
9. Benediction.

It is judged proper, to avoid tediousness and prolixity, which are great and manifest lets to devotion, that these meetings do not ordinarily exceed an hour.

O Lord, let thy blessing follow this and every other design to promote thy glory and to build up the souls of thy people: And for this end give to us the grace of perseverance, that we may continue in this and in every other good work, to the glory of thy holy name, through Jesus Christ our Lord.   Amen.

The following letter written to a parishioner who had been led away by the Mormonites—who have had some success in Glasgow and its neighbourhood—illustrates his wise and dutiful watchfulness over those for whose souls he felt he must render an account.

"CAMPSIE, April 4, 1842.

"DEAR THOMAS,

"I am much grieved to learn from your family here that you have been persuaded to join yourself to a set of men calling themselves 'Latter-Day Saints,' and that your eyes are so blinded that you are even become zealous to make proselytes to that delusion. As I can have no motive but your good in writing you this letter, I hope you will give what I shall write an attentive perusal; for if you perish in your delusions, remember you yourself will be the sufferer; and I pray God that He would open your eyes to the enormity and absurdity of this wicked imposture of which cunning men have made you the victim, that before it is too late you may be brought to the knowledge of the truth and to repentance. And I beseech you, instead of taking this letter and showing it to any of your seducers, take it and read it yourself with serious prayer to God, and no doubt, if you do so, He will lead you out of this palpable delusion. You are bound to use your understanding, and if you perceive that this pretended revelation has evident marks of forgery, you are bound instantly to reject it. Let me entreat your attention to these arguments :—

"1. The Book of Mormon has no appearance or semblance of being an inspired book. It is a heap of puerile and absurd stories from beginning to end, not only unworthy of God, but of which any man of common abilities would be ashamed. Your brother George or John could write a wiser book, and more accurate, for there is not a page of it but is full of the grossest blunders in grammar and sense.

"2. You will remember that the Books of Nephi profess to have been written before the Captivity. Now, they contain numerous plain proofs that they were written at least a thousand years later, and by a person who, so far from being a Jew, was even ignorant of the plainest principles of the Jewish law. For example : (*a*) Nephi tells that he and his family were of the tribe of Joseph, and yet he represents them offering sacrifices and acting as priests, which was death for any to do who were not of the tribe of Levi and the family of Aaron. See 2 Chron. xxvi. 16—21 ; and Numb. xviii. 1—7. Now, can you believe a Jew of the days of Zedekiah so ignorant as to commit such a gross blunder as to represent his father and his family—these, too, favoured by God—doing what their law punished as a capital crime ?

"(*b.*) Nephi speaks of *genealogies,* though none such are ever spoken of by the Jews except in the books composed after the Captivity, as for example, Chronicles, Nehemiah, and Ezra. Is not this a plain mark of forgery ?

"(*c.*) But the most glaring absurdity of the whole is the mention of the mariner's compass a thousand years before it was invented. They say, indeed, this compass was miraculously provided; which is most absurd, and that for many reasons. First, because Nephi and his friends evidently did not understand the use of this compass; secondly, it was not necessary for them, as they are said to have been under a divine guidance, and apparently did not know where the land was to which they were going ; and, thirdly, because Nephi does not speak of the compass as then a new discovery, but as a thing with which himself and his friends were familiar. This mark of forgery is so gross that, considering it, any person of common sense will allow it proves the Book of Nephi, instead of being written by a Jew twenty-three hundred years ago, was composed very lately.

"I might instance many other examples which show this Book of Mormon to be a manifest forgery. But let me draw your attention to some of the doctrines held by these people and taught by them, which you must have surely consented to put out the eyes of your mind entirely before you could swallow.

The 'Voice of Warning' (pp. 14, 16, 17) tells you that all prophecies which have been fulfilled have been *literally* fulfilled. Are you so ignorant of your Bible as not to know that this is flatly contrary to the truth? The prophecy of the seed of the woman (Gen. iii. 15) has been accomplished, but not literally. (I am aware of the childish attempt to apply this to the literal serpent, p. 162.) Balaam's prophecy (Numb. xxiv. 17) has been fulfilled, but not literally. The same is the case with Daniel's prediction (ix. 24—27), and Joel's (ii. 28—32), which St. Peter (Acts ii. 14—21) expressly says received a fulfilment, not literal at all, on the day of Pentecost.

"In the 'Voice of Warning' the ridiculous proposition is frequently stated (pp. 159, 162, 170, 194) that there was no ocean anywhere but in the north till sin brought it from the north and divided America from the other continent. And, what is more amazing than even the doctrine is this—that the text (Gen. x. 25) which means that the earth was divided among the different nations or families (as you may plainly see by looking at the 1st, 5th, and 32nd verses), is brought to prove that the different parts of the earth—the two continents and the islands—were divided from each other by the sea (p. 163). Dear Thomas, can you persuade yourself that those men are sent by God, and inspired to communicate a new revelation, who thus fall into blunders of which even a child might be ashamed? In p. 179 (at the bottom) of the same book, you will find a reference or rather allusion to the ancient of days (Dan. viii. 9—14). Be pleased to refer to the passage, and you cannot doubt who the ancient of days is. If you now read the 'Voice of Warning,' pp. 179 and 180, you will be amazed to find that 'the ancient of days' means '*Adam*,' and, what is equally astonishing, that Adam, in the millennium, is to be worshipped as God, and that Jesus Christ our Lord is a very inferior personage to him. I wonder your feelings of reverence, of which once you were not destitute, are not revolted by such blasphemous absurdities as these.

"I might multiply examples to almost any amount in which these men, claiming inspiration, have committed the grossest and most ridiculous blunders as to the meaning of passages of the English Bible. Now *one* such blunder is as conclusive a proof of their being impostors as a thousand would be, for the

Spirit of God can no more err once than he can a thousand times. But I hasten to remind you that the system has no evidence whatever to support it. I do not say it is deficient in evidence, but it has no evidence whatever. Its only proof is the word of Joseph Smith—a man whose word is worth nothing—telling a story which carries falsehood on the very face of it, and of some other eleven persons who are evidently Smith's accomplices in trying to cheat you and other simple people out of your money, and don't care, though they ruin you soul and body, provided they can succeed in plundering you. Just ask yourself these plain questions:—Was anyone with Smith when the angel discovered the golden plates to him? How did Smith know they were Egyptian characters which were engraven on the plates, seeing Smith could not read, at least could not write, his own language? If Smith was inspired to translate the plates without knowing the original, what was the use of the plates? Has anyone seen the plates who knew anything of the Egyptian language? If such plates exist, why are they not produced? Copies of them are said to have been submitted to one learned man (though whether they were copies in truth nobody knows), and he said he knew nothing about such characters—in short, that there were no such letters in the world, so far as he knew. Do you not observe that while Moses and our Blessed Lord wrought many unquestionable miracles *publicly*, and in the presence of enemies, Joseph Smith and his accomplices have nothing to allege that is unquestionably miraculous, and that their wonders, such as they are, are all said to have been done in private, and when any witnesses are said to have been present, these were always partisans? *This is no doubt a cunningly devised fable, for all these things were done in a corner.* Finally, do you not see that *money* is the end and aim of the whole imposture? Have you not seen the Books of Ordinances, or, at least, the last pages of the eighth number of the ' Millennial Star?' Care of your purse should quicken your conscience, if concern for your soul will not. I hear you are gone so far in this delusion as to propose joining that herd of dupes who are suffering themselves to be transported to Nauvoo, the New Jerusalem in Illinois. Now, dear Thomas, let me tell you, you will probably never reach Nauvoo. Your bones will probably lie among the swamps, or be rolled down the waves of the Mississippi, through whose pestilential marshes you must pass to your earthly paradise; but your money (if you have any) will reach the New Jerusalem in safety, for the elders into whose hands you have resigned it, will take good care it shall pass into the hands of Joseph Smith, 'who is sole trustee of all the property of all the saints'—into whose society, if you ever have the misfortune to come, you will discover that they are a parcel of savages, and that they are 'saints' who are intolerable companions, even for this world, much less for eternity. I pray that the Lord may give you repentance of your great sin in resigning yourself to so wicked and gross a delusion before you are ruined in soul and body, which you will soon be, unless you turn your feet to the good ways of the Lord.

" I am your sincere friend,

" R. LEE."

We are not told what was the effect of this re-monstrance.

The following extracts from his diary record a trip to Tweedmouth with his wife, about 1841 or 1842 :—

" Thursday was a day of mishaps. We lay too late. The clouds lowered threateningly on the Lammermoors. My wife said I hurried her so as to prevent her eating her egg to break-fast. We got to Haddington—thanks to an active horse—without much rain, and on as far as Dunbar; but there it came down in earnest. My poor wife, uncomforted by her egg which she had not eaten, and her thick boots which she did not put on, had to brave it as best she might. I could only comfort her by holding up the umbrella as best I could to save her, and wet the elbow of a good old gentleman, who took it patiently. At last it cleared, in time to afford us a view of the lofty rocks above Burnmouth, and of the expanse of the German Ocean. Berwick appeared cold and damp; the first impression was not good. Met our friends with great joy, which, however, was sadly damped by dear Anthony's appearance, and yet more by a doctor's opinion of his case.

" *Sunday the 8th.*—Assisted to-day at the dispensation of the Sacrament in Tweedmouth Chapel. The chapel was full of people, with many of whose faces I had been familiar even from child-

'hood. Time has sadly blanched the heads of most of them, and the boys and girls had all grown into staid men and women; *douce* papas and mammas; which changes are very affecting and melancholy, though instructive withal. Verily good, worthy, religious people, many of these Tweedmouthites. A great crowd of them going to Heaven, I verily believe, less corrupted than most populations in these wicked times of the world. We have been observing those people with both our eyes since we came among them, and we are not a little interested in their peculiarities. First, their dialect is most amazing and unique! unlike anything to be heard within the bounds of the solar system; and then the people seem a lively, vivacious, and somewhat quaint race of mortals, evidently not disposed to die of grief, having, it seems to us, a good dash of the Irish in their composition, and a different sort of animal from Sawney altogether. We often peep into their cottages too. Green paint is in great request outside, and brisk chat within. A cleanly, tidy race. No Chartism here, but much church going, though no church, or as good as none. On the whole, our impressions are very favourable. It would be a good region this if it were planted with trees."

"*22nd.*—I attended Tweedmouth Church this morning, and again was edified with that impressive Liturgy. The sermon on Confirmation was somewhat sapless, though not without points out of which edification might perhaps be extracted. How delightful a service would this be if so good prayers were followed by good preaching. Heard Mr. Grant of the Meeting in the afternoon; a good man, not judicious.

"Went with Isabella to hear the funeral service, which we felt to be most affecting and impressive."

The following letter was written to a younger brother, Anthony, who took orders in the English Church, and died early in January, 1842, aged 25. This letter was never read by him on earth. He was dead before it reached him.

"MY BELOVED BROTHER,

"The letters we have received from your friends regarding your health have greatly distressed us, the more so as we cannot be near you to comfort you. Yet 'you are not alone, the Father is with you,' and your Elder Brother also, more faithful and loving far than your elder brother on earth. And yet I have loved you tenderly, my dearest Anthony, and the prospect of a separation is more bitter to me than I can express. And yet it may, by the mercy of our God, not be everlasting or long. You, I feel assured, when you have the victory over the last enemy, will enter into peace and eternal joy; and oh! may I, unworthy as I am and polluted, be permitted, through the blood of Jesus, who died for each of us, to join you there, though it be to occupy the lowest place, of which I know I am utterly unworthy. Ah, my dear Anthony, you have many dear friends beyond that flood! Your sainted mother is there, and many others, who will be filled with joy that you have been redeemed from the earth. If the glorified saints pray for those on earth who are still militant, you will remember your elder brother, who, though most unworthy and compassed about with many temptations, loves you as his own soul, that he, and those who are his, may, when it shall please the Father of our Spirits, be united with you in the eternal rest. I feel some of us should have been with you, and I hope Isaac may have reached you by this time. My most dear Isabella joins in deep sympathy for you, my dear Anthony. And now I commend you unto God our Father, and Jesus, that Lamb who taketh away our sins. May His Spirit be your strong support, and ever present comforter; living or dying, you, I believe, will be the Lord's. I have written you with an aching heart, and many tears, feeling it may be the last of our intercourse on earth.

" Your ever affectionate Brother,

" ROBERT LEE.

" *20th January*, 1842."

Large numbers of his sermons preached in those days are extant. Many of them were preached again in Edinburgh, one or two as late as in 1864. Though not so broad and ripe in tone and sentiment as most of his Edinburgh sermons, and though more " evangelical," in the ordinary sense of the term, they exhibit the identity

of his mental powers in their careful execution, and
frank, searching, and practical reference to duty and
conduct. They are often more full of a free, bold
criticism, and of a forcible and well connected reasoning, than one would expect an ordinary country congregation to relish or easily follow. But no doubt
he educated his congregation—as any able preacher
will—to the requisite measure of sympathy and understanding. "If the strain of his sermons," says one
of his friends, perhaps a little anxious to vindicate his
often impugned "soundness" in doctrine, "was largely
of a practical nature, it was from considering that such
instruction was apt to be overlooked in recent times,
and not by any means from undervaluing Christian
doctrine as the foundation of personal godliness." His
preaching, however, even then, by no means satisfied a
taste accustomed to the full flavour of Calvinistic dogma
and "evangelical" discourse. The effect which it produced on minds trained to relish this, and to look in all
preaching for certain doctrinal Shibboleths, which were
the proofs of "soundness," is illustrated by the words
of a kind and excellent correspondent, one of his
parishioners at Campsie, who writes : "——'s remark on
his preaching I thought very just. 'The Apostle Paul
says with the *heart* man believeth unto righteousness;
Mr. Lee says with the *head*.' . . . . He roused indignation by falling foul of the Shorter Catechism in the
pulpit ; even his criticisms on the Bible were injudicious.
* * * Yet his self-denied diligence and zeal gained
him the respect of many."

He sometimes used, like S. Paul, "great plainness of
speech," and where he saw a crying evil, attacked it

openly.*   In a sermon on Preparation for the Communion, from 1 Cor. x., 1—12, preached at Campsie twice within three years (for he had none of the nervous hesitation some men feel about repeating a good sermon), he says:—

"Some of you may be guilty of the same sin with which in the next verse they are charged, '*Fornicators.*' Yes, the holy people defiled themselves. So many in the Christian Church are constantly doing—being sensual, not having the spirit. How many are constantly—to their own shame and the scandal of the Church, compelled to make confession of this gross iniquity; and of how many is there reason to fear that their repentance is a cloak put on for the occasion, and their sorrow is for their shame and their punishment, rather than for their sin? But God seeth as man seeth not. And doubtless hundreds, against whom no human being can bring any charge, are pronounced fornicators by Him who looks upon the motives and desires of the heart, who says 'out of the *heart* proceed evil thoughts—murder, adultery, fornication;' and 'he that looketh on a woman to lust after her is already an adulterer.' Neither let us commit fornication as some of them committed, and there fell in one day three-and-twenty thousand."

Again, in a sermon on the " Necessity and use of Good Works," from Ephes. ii. 10, he says, referring to the notion that good works are chiefly valuable as the evidence of Faith.

" A more absurd reason was never, perhaps, assigned for anything. If good works be needful to evince the reality and genuineness of faith, it is obvious that faith must be the *principal* thing, and righteousness or good works subordinate. For when we say that the use of one thing is to manifest or prove the existence of another, we mean to intimate that the thing manifested or proved to exist is of greater importance than is the thing

---

* He reproved very directly any inattention or indecorum in church. A parishioner tells of his once saying, with his eye on a prominent member of the congregation who was dozing in the front gallery, " I am now coming to an important point, so I hope those who are sleeping will awake, and those who are awake will pay attention."

which manifests it. So when the *use* of good works is said to
be the manifestation or proof of faith, the notion is inevitable
that compared with faith they are of small value or of none.
Yet how does this view of good works comport with that
estimate of them furnished in the text, which speaks of them
as the very things God creates men anew that they may
perform. 'We are created in Christ Jesus unto good works?'

"As a man is created naturally that he may live and work
naturally, so God creates us spiritually, that we may live and
work spiritually. . . . . . Faith is the opening of the
eye of the mind to behold, to converse with, spiritual objects.
Now would it not be absurd to say a man does all the actions
which he performs (and which can be performed only by one
whose eyes are open) in order to show that his eyes are open?
And if any one were to ask you why you walked about and
worked at your employments, and read and wrote, and did the
other acts which no blind man can do properly, if at all, would
you ever think of replying, 'I do all these things in order to
prove that my eyes are open?' . . . . . A man opens
his eyes that he may see to walk and work. He does not walk
and work to prove that his eyes are open. So the spiritual eye
is opened, *i.e.*, faith is given to the soul, that it may see to walk
in God's command and to work the works of God; but it is
absurd to say that the use of the spiritual works is to certify
the openness of the spiritual eye."

In another discourse, from Acts xix. 1—7, drawing
the lesson that a man is not necessarily a Christian
because his life is outwardly reformed, he says :—

"Although the exterior of the life be garnished, what will
it avail if you stop here? It will now indeed be a whited
sepulchre, but still a sepulchre, more accessible and less loath-
some without, but not less filled with the foul tokens and effects
of death, and as little a temple of God as ever it was. Therefore, dear brethren, be equally anxious to have reformation
produced upon your lives, and not to rest satisfied with that
reformation. With equal zeal go to hear John the Baptist's
sermon, and look whither he directs you. He invites all men
to come to him, but he will suffer none to remain with him.

‘ I am not he, I am not the Light ; I am come to bear witness of the Light.’ If John says to Jesus, ‘ *I have need*, I ’ (the ascetic and righteous John whose holiness extorted reverence even from an abandoned people and their abandoned king) ‘ have need to be baptized of thee,’—if John felt that he required for the purification of his heart the gift of Christ, the fire of his spiritual baptism, who else can be indifferent or presume he needs it not ? ”

Another extract—from a sermon on the Parables of the Tares in the Wheat—shows how he tried to inculcate those broad principles of liberality and charity which were peculiarly dear to him, and, as he thought, far too little understood in Scotland :—

“ If all Christian Churches should act on the principle of admitting none to Church privileges but those of whom they felt assured that they were really and in truth the children of God, it might happen, and it would probably happen, that some of the children of God would be for ever, on earth, excluded from the Communion of Saints. For, without question, many are worshippers of the Father in Spirit and truth, whom men know not of. ‘ Many shall come from the east and west, and sit down with Abraham and Isaac and Jacob in the kingdom of God, while the children of the kingdom are cast out.’ That never can be a proper principle for conducting the discipline of the Christian Church, which might, and probably would, perpetually keep many true Christians out of it. And surely it is better to exceed on the side of lenity, or even of laxity, if you will, than of exclusiveness ; better a thousand inconsistent professors should come in, than that one child of God should be kept out,—as it is better that ten criminals should escape punishment than that one innocent person should be punished.”

He published, while at Campsie, a few discourses in the pages of the “ Scottish Christian Herald ”—a religious periodical begun in 1836, and coming to a close in 1841 ; and whose contributors were chiefly ministers of the “ Evangelical ” party. “ An Address to People who seldom or never go to Church" was issued separately, and reached its second thousand. He also published a Catechism "intended to assist young persons in becoming acquainted with the truths of Christianity. It is divided into seven sections— treating, lucidly and scripturally, of—1. God the Creator; 2. God the Redeemer; 3. God the Sanctifier; 4. Good Works; 5. The Christian Church; 6. The Dispensations of Religion; 7. The World to Come.

Although delighting in his parish work—and especially in visiting and going about among his people *— the bent of his mind was so strongly towards theological study and exposition, that he naturally looked to a professorial chair as his proper sphere. In 1840 the Chair of Theology in Glasgow became vacant, and he proposed himself as a candidate. Dr. Chalmers was also in the field; but against Chalmers was arrayed all the influence and policy of the constitutional party in the Church, which urged as preferable to his the claims of the Rev. Dr. Hill. With two such rivals—each regarded as representing a powerful

* "In speaking of him as a country parish minister, his visiting of the people should be specially dwelt on, as I believe there has been an unfounded impression that such work was distasteful to him—the very contrary being the fact. I have myself heard him say how much he liked, when in later years spending his holidays in the country, to supply the place of the minister, when absent, and to engage in those services which had been a labour of love in former days."—*Letter of Rev. D. Aitken, D.D., formerly Minister of Minto.*"

"I met," he writes, in November, 1842, after he had been visiting his people, "a man who seemed to me a perfectly consistent Calvinist. He asked me whether, if he was one of the reprobate, he could possibly go to Heaven, do what he might? and if he were one of the Elect, whether he could possibly go to Hell, whatever he neglected? and, whether God would not, on the latter supposition, arouse him and sanctify him in his own time? Calvin, of whose writings he had read a good deal, and Toplady, had been his teachers. He refused to go to Church, saying he had done so for many years without profit, and he now began to conclude he was one of the reprobate."

Again—referring to his prayer-meetings he says, on one occasion, "I had not had time to compose the second prayer, but I think the service was edifying. As little exciting it was as possible. It is useful to feel that prayer and praise are the main matters for which people assemble.'

party—Mr. Lee had no chance of success. "I do most sincerely regret"—Principal Haldane writes to him in September—"that I was engaged to do everything in my power for Dr. Hill before I received your first letter." On that occasion, as on some more recent occasions, the choice of the electors (who in this case were the Senatus of the University) was ruled, less by the theological attainments of the candidates, than by personal and party considerations. The chair was given to Dr. Hill. Sir James Graham, then Lord Rector, travelled from London to record his vote against the brilliant leader of the Evangelical agitators; and "the same University, which had refused the Chair of Logic to Edmund Burke, refused that of Theology to Dr. Chalmers." *

Mr. Lee still continued his early habit—always a very useful one—of recording his stray thoughts in a commonplace book. "A Trap for catching stray Thoughts," he inscribes one of these volumes; and from its registers we can see what he was thinking about in times of which we have but little other chronicle; for it has been difficult to recover any of his correspondence. He never was a great letter-writer, and always preferred speaking to writing. These stray thoughts range over a great variety of subjects. We see in some places the germs of thoughts and opinions afterwards more fully developed; in others we trace a wide divergence from the later workings of his mind. A few extracts will be interesting :—

"An argument which shows demonstratively that Jonathan Edwards' notion of freedom of will is utterly wrong, is that the liberty which he allows man is exactly that which a horse or a

* Hanna's " Life of Chalmers," vol. iv., ch. 13.

dog enjoys. The horse or the dog does as he wills, but his will is irresistibly determined by circumstances; so, says Edwards, is a man's will. Therefore, on this supposition, the freedom of a man is of no higher a kind than that of the dog or the horse. The advocates of Jonathan Edwards' liberty, *i. e.*, the Necessitarians, allow that if their theory were carried out to its consequences and acted on, the result would be the same which Fatalism has produced in Mohammedan countries, and must everywhere produce when fairly acted on, the suspension of all activity and energy.

"But this difficulty they seek to surmount by saying the *practical* result of the *doctrine is not such*, that men do and should *forget* the doctrine; that it is necessary they should, and act as if all depended upon themselves. Now this apology seems *fatal to the truth of a doctrine;* for God, the God of truth, never can require man to act on a false supposition. Neither can he require him to act in forgetfulness of the truth, nor in a manner inconsistent with what the fullest conviction and remembrance of the truth would dictate. The Bible represents holiness as the necessary and natural result of knowing the truth ; and therefore holiness is styled by S. John, 'doing the truth.' But if a man must hold necessity to be true, and yet act as if it were not true, he must do, not 'the truth,' but falsehood. This is, I think, an objection utterly fatal to the doctrine.

"The general notion of liberty is that it is identical with the possession of political power—the power of making the law. If this were so, then under the Theocracy, the freest of all commonwealths, men could not be free, for they had no power of making laws or of altering them. Neither could women be free if that be the definition of liberty. But surely the essence of liberty is to live under a just and equal law, whoever makes it."

On Dr. Arnold's Lectures on Modern History :—

"I have read few books with more interest or instruction than this most delightful volume, which is full of the best philosophy and the best learning, combined with an exquisite judgment and a refined taste. How delightful to see a man unmistakably loving and seeking truth, and evidently superior to that party bigotry which leads many even strong minds astray.　God grant unto me to love the truth!　How excellent is truth!　How miserable to be deceived, and how wretched to love and court deception and darkness.　Surely this makes men like devils whose element is darkness, and whose whole existence is one great lie.

"Hundreds of passages I should like to quote, but time permits not.　*Church controversies are political* is a truth I am glad to have confirmed by so great an authority.　He that is a Tory in a State will be in a Church, &c.　This is a rule; exceptions do not invalidate this rule.

"With what freedom of spirit and superiority to party spirit these great Englishmen write.　It is refreshing in this narrow-minded country, amid the din of Controversialists, furious in proportion to their ignorance, to read such writings as these of Whately and Arnold."

"This morning (August 12), I found a beautiful butterfly in my dressing-room when I entered.　The creature kept flying against the window, and would by no means come from it into the darker part of the room.　But I reflected that this was a child of the sun, whose light was her life, and that she was but seeking her native region to bathe again in her father's beams and rejoice in his smiles.　So let me be a child of light and of the day, and then shall I not willingly fly towards the darkness of this world, but shall draw as near as may be to that light which is my life.　And tho' God, my Father in Heaven, and the Father of lights, has given me to see as yet through a glass darkly, through that glass let me continue to gaze, that when His gracious hand opens the casement, I may be found ready to fly direct to Heaven."

"When I read the philosophers and their tenets,—thus Plato taught, thus Aristotle; Pythagoras held this, and Epicurus that; Plotinus reasons in this manner, Proclus in the other; this notion was maintained by the Stoics, this by the Sceptics, this by the Eclectics; the old Academy was distinguished by these tenets, the Middle by those, and the New by a third set; and when I turn to all the prophets, evangelists, apostles, by whom the Sacred Books were composed, and find them all agreeing as one man, I am forced to remember that truth is *one*, and ever consistent,—the dictate of one spirit and that of God. And I am compelled to conclude that those philosophers were inspired by that demon whose name is legion, and who was a lying spirit in the mouth of all the priests and prophets of Gentile philosophy. Give me, O Lord, meekly and humbly to sit at the feet of thy dear son, Jesus Christ, and hear his words."

"It is a huge misfortune when he has much wealth who has not also much discretion; for a poor foolish man can only *talk* his folly, whereas a rich fool can act his."

"I find very few men agreeable companions. Sometimes this makes me suspect myself of misanthropy. Yet I feel I am no misanthrope. This rather I take to be the reason: most men live in the present,—the last meeting, the next scheme, Mr. So-and-So's speech, such an article in the *Times*, the prospects and doings of the ministry, &c., &c., &c.—all of to-day, all of the *peritura* species. For myself, I live but little in the present. Though of necessity I must speak of it (with those whose thoughts are absorbed in it), yet by thoughts and by musings my spontaneous contemplations almost altogether turn towards the men and times that have disappeared. I like the society of those who will go back with me, though not travellers on that road themselves. There is a pleasure even in visiting the sepulchres of the dead in company."

"The *consistency* of theological systems is generally regarded as a powerful evidence of their truth. I believe it is a sufficient argument of their being ill-founded. For, seeing only a part of the moral system is revealed to us in the Bible—a fact which no competent judge will question—any system which harmonises these parts so as to give them the completeness of a finished and consistent whole, must misrepresent the parts and force them into combinations not natural,—as if a person should attempt to form a complete map when some of the sections into which it had been cut were awanting."

"That orthodoxy has commonly been error is plain from this, that orthodoxy is another name for the opinion of the majority;

and in religious disputes the majority has for the most part been wrong. And this is only saying in other words that truth has commonly been known and believed by a few.

"Besides, orthodoxy does not always mean what the majority really believe, but only what the majority find it convenient to profess. It is a startling and an alarming fact that so many of those men who have thought independently regarding the doctrines of Christianity, and whose abilities and impartiality entitle their judgments to respect, have formed what we reckon erroneous opinions regarding them ; or, in other words, have been *hetero-dox*. This circumstance cannot but teach a lesson of circumspection and also of candour. Origen was as great a neologist as Strauss, quite as great as De Wette. Milton, Locke, Sir I. Newton, Chillingworth, J. Hales, Cudworth, all were unsound regarding the doctrine of the Trinity. Paley was so probably, and how many of the more learned and thoughtful clergy no one knows, as they had good and sufficient reasons for concealing such opinions if they entertained them."

"It is often difficult to allow that persons are truly Christians who hold opinions different from our own regarding either the more external or more obscure and metaphysical doctrines of Christianity. Nothing can more clearly betray the general feebleness of love in the modern Church. For if we had not both lost, in great measure, the genuine spirit of the gospel, and the faculty to discern it in the pages of the New Testament, we should instantly discover that the way to judge of others and ourselves is rather by our tempers and deportment than by our *opinions*. For the correctest tenets afford no security that the individual holding them is a true disciple of the Lord Jesus ; whereas holy dispositions and righteous conduct demonstrate that every one who has these, and nameth the name of Christ, is a genuine believer, however erroneous his judgment may be as to many doctrines of the Christian faith. What sensitiveness, *e.g.*, our own and other Churches manifest as to the *orthodoxy* of ministers, and what callousness as to their *spirituality*, though the latter is of infinitely greater importance than the other. For an orthodox carnal pastor will do little or no good—perhaps much evil (such being commonly bigots, and who make the people bigots like themselves)—whereas a truly spiritual minister will assuredly be the father of many children who will be to Christ a crown."

"There never can be peace in the Church so long as the different forms of Church government are held as being of *Divine appointment.* For, on this supposition, to persevere in adherence to a wrong form is to persist in rebellion against the declared will and institution of Christ; and persons who are regarded as doing this never can be viewed but as (so far) enemies and rebels against the Lord's authority.

"All those who contend a particular form of Church polity is laid down in Scripture, assert it is there *plainly* laid down; and all who, instead of apprehending its plainness, cannot even discover its existence, will inevitably be looked upon as persons who close their eyes against the clearest light. Mutual tolerance, mutual love and peace, never can grow in such a soil as this. The *jure divino* Prelatists and the *jure divino* Presbyterians appear to me men of the same class, and subject to the same delusions, and both of them infected with the temper which that delusion creates."

"It is vain to expect that those whose incomes are provided independently of the people among whom they minister will ever, as a body, cope in point of attention to their flocks with those whose livings depend upon the people; for how many motives to diligence soever may actuate the former, the latter have always *one additional.* And this one, it is not unworthy of being remarked, acts most powerfully upon those persons who are least sensible to the higher motives. Hence a grossly careless minister, not a very uncommon phenomenon in Established Churches, is very rare among dissenters. For among them the carnal restraint comes in to check the carnal indulgence. On the whole, however, I suppose more may be lost than is gained by the strength thus allowed to so inferior, not to say culpable, a motive; which, if it hinders bad men appearing to be so bad as they are, also tends to prevent good men becoming so good as they might."

"The care of the sick in hospitals, which in Great Britain is procured only by high payment, is in France performed by the

Sisters of Charity, who expect and receive no reward on earth. Whence it is to my mind clear as day that the Catholics understand at least one part of the Gospel better than Protestants do. For that must be the most correct theory of Christianity which is most successful in producing those duties which Christianity requires. Indeed, considering the common opinion of the use and value of good works which Protestants hold, my wonder is not so much their good works are few as that they are any."

"Catholics, when they object to Protestants their want of unity, are frequently answered that their unity is in truth greater than is that of the Catholics themselves. And this assertion is sought to be supported by showing how many and important are the Christian doctrines on which Protestants are agreed, and on how many considerable questions Catholics are at variance with each other. But this defence, if rightly considered, involves the Protestants in greater condemnation, and is the strongest objection against themselves and their principles. For, the more they show their agreement, the more emphatically do they condemn their separation from each other, which must be more unjustifiable in proportion as the grounds of it are less. If a husband and wife should separate, would they defend and exculpate themselves by proving that there were very few things indeed about which they did not coincide in opinion, and that these things were of very small importance? On the contrary, could it ever be with reason alleged as a crime against another married pair, that they persevered in living together, and on the whole in very great harmony, though they had some serious differences of sentiment. Surely this would be esteemed a high commendation.

"We have Churches of England and Scotland, Episcopal and Presbyterian, Independent, Baptist, Relief, Established Churches, Secession Churches, and Churches with old lights and new lights. In the New Testament there is but one Church—the Church of Christ—'the Church of the living God.' The Apostles knew no more of two or three or four Churches than they did of as many Saviours. In their idea there can no more be two bodies than two spirits, and it would have seemed to them as monstrous to have two Churches of God as for a man to have two distinct bodies.

"There is 'the Church of God,' and the 'Synagogue of Satan,' which is to be excommunicated and avoided. Most Protestant Churches excommunicate *each other*, for they refuse mutual communion and recognition, and yet all or nearly all their members admit that those societies are Churches of God. The Episcopal Church has its basis of union in its Thirty-nine Articles; the Church of Scotland in the Westminster Confession. Their schism, however, arises, not from the differences of opinion there set forth, so much as from what neither symbol embraces, viz., Church Government. This is in fact the Shibboleth; and so of the rest. Some minute point, such as infant baptism, the obligation of the Covenants, or some such obscure and tenebrious point, is the basis of their Church. Alas! what a basis of a Church!"

"Very often when I have a great many things to do, and a very oppressive sense of the number and urgency of them, I can do no one of them, for going from one to another; I have this book to read, that and that to write; I have several matters of business and out-of-door duty to attend to; when I take up one book and cast it down—it is too light, take up another—it is too solid, and requires more leisure than I can spare at present. I try to write, but then I should be about my out-of-door duties. I go out accordingly; but then I am grown good for nothing but walking about the world and talking in it,—I am ceasing altogether to be a studious man, and should get home again without delay, to apply to reading and meditation and prayer. When one is in such humours, the attempt to study is almost a certain throwing away of time. It were better to dig in the garden, or hear music, or talk to a friend, or ride, or go out and scold any of one's neighbours whom one has met drunk yesterday, or in short engage one's self in anything that will exercise the body and not vex the mind.

"I find it impossible to study on summer evenings or almost at any time in summer except the morning. The sun, and the sky, and the earth, and every shrub and flower, seem to upbraid me with deserting their society, and every breeze appears to murmur a gentle complaint against me that I will not be found when they are at the pains to breathe so sweetly. In one word, when God's book is opened so wide, my taste for men's books decidedly abates, so that my mind is the reverse of the bear's body; for he subsists, during winter, on the fat with which he has clothed his bones during the summer, but I live all the summer upon the stock of ideas I have been able to lay in during the dark and gloomy months. Though fond of books, I cannot say I am a determined thorough-going reader. My eyes will not permit it. Did I attempt the thing, I should soon finish my reading for ever. Neither, in truth, will my *patience*. My curiosity generally outruns the writer's pace, so I take the liberty of out-going my guide. Unless in literary works of art, such as poetry, oratory, &c., when the *very thought* depends upon the words, I should much prefer to have the notes and memoranda from which the book was composed than the book itself. Very few books are worth reading quite through. Most authors give you all the thoughts that they have to give, I mean that are peculiarly theirs, long before the end of their work is reached. Yet I deeply blame my want of application; I am sensible that it is a fatal habit; and I deeply reverence anyone who has fairly mastered a huge tome of solid matter. Such a person, I think, might have been a builder of pyramids, and would have been, if he had lived soon enough and in the proper country, and had been born of suitable parents. I never judged myself a great man but once. It was when I had finished 'Hooker's Ecclesiastical Polity,' but that sentence has been long ago and frequently reversed, for, since then, not only Ralph Cudworth and Thomas Aquinas have absolutely routed me, but my march has been stopped by far less formidable opponents. With shame I confess it, but confess it I will, the truth constraining me, that Basil and Cyprian, Raleigh and Milton, yea, Burnet himself, have all of them, as well as numerous others, decidedly forced me to lay down my arms.

"I will confess further, as I am got into a humour of confessing (a fact for which I feel somewhat at a loss to account), that my patience wears much better upon dull and dry authors than upon such as are professedly written to amuse. With Chillingworth, or Butler, or Hooker, I really proceed with a respectable pertinacity, but 'Hudibras' foiled me in two readings. Smollett, Fielding, Sterne, have all gained easy triumphs, while 'Don Quixote' so frightened me at the first onset that I was discomfited almost before the encounter began. I say I feel shame in making these acknowledgments, which I consider really humiliating, and which I am quite at a loss to account for. Looking at my library, I see the tomes of Jeremy Taylor, T. Aquinas, and Laurence Sterne. I believe, if spared, I may go quite through the 'Ductor Dubitantium,' into which already I have made considerable inroads. I think it possible I may peruse the most important questions in the 'Summa Theologiæ,' but I feel a strong prophetic impression that my patience will never carry me through 'Tristram Shandy.'"

These extracts extend, in date, from about 1836 to 1842.

A project, which he shaped in writing, and laid before some of his friends, in the latter year, was the establishment of a Brotherhood, a kind of Reformed and non-celibate Order among the clergy of the Church. His Catholic sympathies and wise discernment suggested to him the advantages of such an institution. He saw how much effective strength was lost to the Church through lack of fellowship and conference among those who sought her spiritual growth and good, and held themselves aloof from her political strifes; and he knew what vast benefits had been wrought in other Churches through combination of conviction and force.

He sends the following sketch of his plan to one of his correspondents :—

"AD majorem Dei gloriam.
"An Order :—
"I. Objects :—1. Stricter life. 2. Increased ministerial fidelity. 3. Mutual intelligence, communion, and admonition.
"II. Members :—Ministers and preachers, &c., who hold that the Gospel is a message of peace to all men, and who appear in earnest to save their own souls and those of other men.
"III. Constitution :—1. The Order shall be governed by a General, who shall continue in office for a limited period or for life, as may be agreed. 2. A General Congregation of the Order

shall be held annually, at which much time shall be spent in devotion, and conference on a discourse by one or more of the members. The Eucharist shall also be dispensed. 3. Members shall furnish to the General monthly or quarterly Reports, touching the matters to promote which the Order was instituted. Of these Reports the General shall communicate as much to the general Congregation as he may judge prudent and edifying. And he shall freely admonish and reprove the several members. 4. As one object of the Order is unreserved communication, the members shall understand that they pledge themselves to absolute silence regarding what may be transacted at its meetings."

In reply to some criticisms on the scheme, he writes, in November, 1842 :—

"Perhaps all conditions of admission had better, at least in the first instance, be omitted ; though I did not intend the phrase, ' Peace to all men,' in the absolute sense in which you have taken it. For many think (however inconsistently) that, though atonement has been made only for some, the Gospel is yet a message to all ; and on this latter truth their whole preaching proceeds. A General for life would, I think, be an imprudent step, at the beginning at least. Indeed I have serious doubts whether any of us possess all the qualities which would perfectly qualify him to exercise functions so important and delicate as those assigned to that office, which yet, in my mind, is the very spine of the whole affair. These things I write hypothetically, for I suspect the order will never prove anything more than an hypothesis.

" Our worthy friend, W., has, I see, at heart, no stomach to this diet."

The Order does not appear to have been initiated; but his devising of it shows how anxiously he was then searching for the means of stimulating the life of the clergy and promoting the good of the Church.

The following entry in his diary illustrates the same

thing, and the earlier workings of his mind towards reform of the Church :—

"The Christian Church has greatly lost its influence through neglect of those obvious arrangements—those obvious adaptations of itself to the circumstances of the Church and the world which the merest prudence might suggest. So that while different parties have wearied themselves and the whole world with disputes regarding a true model of a Christian Church, as displayed in the New Testament, they have unanimously consented to reject some of the most obvious provisions of the New Testament. 'He gave some Apostles and some Prophets, and Evangelists, and Pastors and Teachers' (Eph. v.; 1 Cor. xii. 28; Rom. xii. 6). And lo, the Church, instead of retaining them (all of them, exclusive of *Elders*, if indeed Elder be not a common name for them all), 'till we all come, in the sincerity of the faith, to the stature of a perfect man,' has rejected every one of them, except the Pastor, whom, for greater simplicity, it confounds with the *Teacher*.

"One great reason, unquestionably, why the modern minister so often spends his strength for nought and in vain, is this—that he must do so many incompatible things. Doing everything, he does nothing. In a parish with a large population, when a field is open and wide enough to employ them, the following arrangement or something like it, might perhaps, by the blessing of God, tend to prevent the growth of wickedness, and hinder members of the Christian Church from falling away :—

"1. Pastor.
"2. Evangelist.
"3. Catechist or Teacher.
"4. Elders.
"5. Deacons.
"6. Deaconesses.
"7. Singers.

"All these, except the last, have express warrant in the New Testament, and all seem absolutely necessary. They all, except the last, should have some form of ordination or solemn appointment, so that the Church may recognise them as its officers appointed for various purposes.

"I. The Pastor. His proper province is *the Church*,—the *bonâ fide* communicants, whom he must often visit, and exhort and take care of, endeavouring, if possible, to speak to each one of them before every communion.

"He presides in the meetings of Kirk Session, as well for discipline, with the Elders, as for care of the poor, with the Deacons.

"Under his authority also are the Evangelist and Catechist, whose operations he must direct.

"He preaches to a congregation, in which he may also receive assistance from the Evangelist and Catechist.

"In short, the Pastor is the Head of the Church officers in every parish or church.

"II. The *Evangelist* has a most important duty. His work is to labour among those who have no profession of religion, or have fallen away—to persuade them to reformation, and to come unto God and believe in Jesus Christ. He is to go from house to house, even as many as will receive him. And to hold meetings with as many as may be willing to attend them—of those especially who are without the pale of the Church. When any are brought to the profession of religion, and so become members of the Church, they then cease to be the care of the Evangelist; and become the care of the Pastor and Elders.

"III. The Catechist. His duty is to instruct the young and ignorant. To prepare persons, by a long course of instruction, for the Holy Communion. To superintend all Sunday-schools, and to organise them. To give instruction to the teachers of these. When persons apply for baptism who, in the judgment of the Pastor, are not sufficiently instructed, it is the duty of the Catechist to instruct them.

"IV. The Elders we have already, but the uniting of their office with that of Deacons has marred it greatly. Their duties are :—

"(1.) To assist at the Holy Communion. (2.) To assist the Pastor in the discipline of the Church. (3.) To visit the members of the Church and their families in their afflictions. (4.) To take a fatherly and godly charge and care of them.

"V. The Deacons have in general the charge of all the pecuniary affairs of a Church. They make all collections in the congregation. They collect from the members funds for supporting public worship—paying ministers. They distribute to the necessities of the poorer brethren. In all their meetings the Pastor presides. They pay for educating poor children.

"VI. Deaconess. This office was in the Apostolic Church; and has an obvious and important use now. (1.) They attend to the sick poor, especially those who are members of the Church. (2.) When necessary, and when they are qualified, they in some cases are employed to instruct those of their own sex who are ignorant.

"VII. Singers. These are the only Church officers for whom there is no warrant in the New Testament. They should be pious persons, if possible, with good voices, who, in a decent and decorous manner, will assist the Precentor in leading the music of the public worship."

It does not appear that Mr. Lee attempted to carry out, in Campsie, this theory of the Church. The difficulties of realizing sections II., and III., would have been insurmountable.

On the 13th January, 1843, when the threatened secession was impending, he writes to his friend, the Rev. Robert Paisley, minister of S. Ninian's, "Will you meet our friends Story and Wylie* on Friday, the 20th, at 87, High Montrose Street, Glasgow, at 11 o'clock? The purpose is to consult and pray together regarding our prospects and duty at present." And again, on the 17th, he says :—

"If you are the least dubious about the meeting on Friday do not come. But I wonder you should fancy *I*, at least, should propose joining any party or making any public movement.

* The late Rev. Robert Story, of Rosneath, and the Rev. John Wylie, D.D., of Carluke. In a letter, referring to a proposed transfer to a parish near his friend Young's, he says, "Alas, dear Young. Let Story remain at Rosneath ; far better he is neath roses, than above sand and rocks and peat moss. Why banish that fine soul to the South, toward Gaza, which is desert ? I could not be accessory to the fact."

I have no feeling that way, and I can see no end to be served by it. My wish is, that as many of us as are of one heart, should join together in praying for *direction*, and strengthening each other.

" Within the last eight days I have carefully read through the Confession of Faith and the Larger Catechism, &c. They are stronger than ever I imagined on the points of which we have sometimes spoken. Chapter v. 4, contains a distinction which my friend Aquinas invented and worthy of his subtle genius,—' God has ordained all acts—sins and all, and is the author of all alike. But he has ordained sinful acts, not as sins, but simply as acts. Thus God ordained, and is the efficient cause, that Ravaillac should put a piece of iron into the body of Henri Quatre, by which this monarch should die ; but that this act should be a crime, a murder,—*that* part of the business Ravaillac must look to,—that is not God's !' Is not this brilliant ? Yet you see it in the latter clause of the section referred to. Be pleased to refer to the 109th question of the Larger Catechism, where you will find a statement which puts the principles of the Assembly regarding toleration beyond question, especially where the *proofs* are referred to. I have been much edified by reading ' The Lives of Eminent Christians.' They are very instructive—especially as showing us that the same afflictions to which we are called, were accomplished in our brethren who formerly were in the world. Dear Paisley, I request you will pray for me,—for I feel that I am ill prepared to be a witness and confessor for the truth. May the Lord pray for us who hath bought us with his blood, that in the time of trial our faith may not fail."

The day of trial came and passed. The 18th of May, 1843, saw the Church rent by the greatest of the secessions which have weakened her and marred her beauty. It saw discord and estrangement enter many a hitherto undivided parish and family and circle of friends. To many it was hard to quit the Church. To many it was scarce less hard to abide in her.

It was a time of sorrow and bitterness throughout

Scotland, such as a stranger to Scottish thought and feeling could not understand. But those who had felt it their duty to remain in the Church turned themselves to the task, almost hopeless as it seemed, of repairing the breaches that had been made in her bulwarks. Among these, Mr. Lee was not idle, and his high character, his energy, and his recognised intellectual power soon marked him for a higher post than that of minister of Campsie. He was first offered, but declined, the parish of Cramond, near Edinburgh.

The storm which had ravaged the Church had been wildest in Edinburgh.

The Presbytery of Edinburgh which, from its metropolitan position and prestige, had always held the foremost place among Presbyteries, had been swept of its most distinguished members. Chalmers, Cunningham, Welsh, Gordon, Candlish, Guthrie—all were members of the Presbytery of Edinburgh,—and all, with other useful and influential men, had left the Church, and had thrown all their weight and strength into the cause of the schism. It was necessary that the places through secession left empty should be filled, and that, if possible, by men who should be able to maintain the Church's cause with a zeal and vigour fit to cope with the aggressive force and stress of her assailants. It was difficult to obtain such men; and the Town Council, in whose hands the patronage of the City churches was vested, and which was composed in large measure of Dissenters, was not the best instrument of discovery and selection. One or two wise selections were, however, made; of these the wisest was the selection of Mr. Lee. His repute as a scholarly, zealous, and active clergyman, and an able (though not in the vulgar sense "popular") preacher, was enhanced by the strong recommendations of Dr. Muir and other eminent divines ; and on the 29th of August, 1843, he was appointed to the Church and parish of the Old Grey Friars, vacant by the secession of the Rev. John Sym.   He left Campsie amid many expressions of his parishioners' affection and respect ; one of these taking the substantial form of a cheque for £110, which the principal heritor in his parish, Mr. Kincaid Lennox, enclosed to him, at the request of the subscribers, on 16th November, " as a mark of their esteem and regard."

On 5th November, he preached his last sermon in Campsie, from the text, " Work out your own salvation." In the course of it he tells his people with a frank honesty, in pleasant contrast to the unreal talk about "providential calls,"* so common on such occasions, that one of his reasons for leaving them is that with his growing family he cannot afford to live among them as their minister should.

"A bishop, says S. Paul, must be given to hospitality, and though he may innocently dispense with this duty when he finds it impossible to perform it, there is surely no reason why he should continue in those circumstances when he may relieve himself from them. A minister who has not a shilling to give to a poor man is justified in withholding it; but it is not desirable he should be in those circumstances if he can help it."

Towards the end he says :—

" My brethren, it will comfort my heart if you continue as heretofore a united people. If murmurings and disputings and

* " It's weel kent," said a shrewd parishioner to a friend of mine, "that the Lord never gies a ca' to a puirer steepend."

separations take place among you I shall be truly grieved and humbled—for then I shall fear that my labour among you has been in vain. I have laboured to impress on your minds the doctrine that schism is a sin most solemnly condemned in the New Testament; whereas the things on account of which the late painful separations have been made, are mere *opinions*—erroneous opinions I think them—but even if correct, nothing but opinions, never expressly laid down, much less enjoined in the Word of God. And I do hope it has been your apprehending this, that your separating yourselves from your brethren would be a sin, a sin against Christ, because of His Body, and no mere feeling or custom which has kept you together in one body. . . . . .

"Brethren, I thank you for all your kindness to me and mine. From many I have received much substantial kindness, and kind wishes from many more. The Lord reward it. And I ask forgiveness of those whom I may have offended in any way. I may have done so in many cases of which I am not aware. For my own part, I feel it very easy to pardon anything which any one has done amiss toward me. I rejoice to do it, and I do it from the heart. Let us bear each other on our hearts when we approach the Mercy Seat. So let us continue for ever united, for our separation will not be long. Soon we shall meet in the world of spirits to give account of the things done in the body, according to that we have done. Oh, let this deeply affect our hearts ! Work out your own salvation."

In November he quitted his pleasant country manse on the green slope of the Campsie Hills, within sound of the burn dashing down Campsie Glen, and full of life and hope took up his residence and work in Edinburgh.

CHAPTER IV.

OLD GREYFRIARS.—CHURCH COURTS.—ERASTUS.—CORRE-
SPONDENCE.—HERIOT'S HOSPITAL.

"Vulgus hominum existimat, se non frustra vixisse, si per fas nefas-que
congestas divitias relinquant morientes. At Cato ideo non putat se frustra
natum, quod integrum et sanctum civem præstiterit reipublicæ, quod in-
corruptum magistratum, quod posteritati quoque virtutis et industriæ suæ
monumenta reliquerit."—*Erasmus: Convivium Religiosum.*

THE Church of which Mr. Lee now became the minister
was a plain and heavy edifice, built in 1612, within the
enclosure fronting the Castle Rock, which had formed the
gardens of the old Monastery of the Grey Friars. Under
its roof, in February, 1638, THE COVENANT was produced
by Alexander Henderson and Johnston of Warristoun,
and after a prayer by Henderson and an exhortation by
the Earl of Loudon, was solemnly signed by the assembled
multitude of nobles, gentry, clergy, and burgesses. The
crowd was too great for all to enter the church, and the
document was afterwards carried out to a flat stone in
the churchyard, and there signed until night fell, and
men could no longer see to write their names. Again,
in 1679, the churchyard of the Greyfriars was the scene
of another act in the tragedy of the Scottish Church
history of the seventeenth century. Through the summer
and autumn of that year it was thronged with the
prisoners taken at Bothwell Brig, whom no jail in
Edinburgh could contain, and who were kept there

under the open sky until the paternal Government of Charles II., having executed some, and shipped others off to be sold as slaves at Barbadoes, released the broken remnant.

The Church had been served by several distinguished ministers—by Principal Robertson, Dr. Erskine, and Dr. Inglis, among others.* The parish embraced a very poor and squalid district in the region of the Cowgate. The congregation had been much crippled by the secession in May, 1843, and when Mr. Lee began his ministration in November, was weak in numbers and influence. The walls of the old church looked down on a very different scene from that which was to be witnessed in the restored church on any Sunday during the last nine years of his incumbency. The minister himself was, in some respects, a very different man then from the man he afterwards became. The liberal and rational element, which subsequently marked his character and ministry so strongly, was then only partially developed. The process had been going on, but it had not reached its height. He, as yet, had a cautious aversion to several principles and measures which he afterwards came to adopt and advocate. His preaching, while free and full in its declarations of the gospel, was more tinged with what is popularly called "Evangelicalism" than it afterwards was. He still was half inclined to look askance at *advanced* Liberalism. A lady, who valued his advice, remembers being reproved by him in those days for reading "so ungodly a paper as the *Scotsman*," though the *Scotsman* then was in

---

* Sir Walter Scott attended it in his youth and describes the service there in Dr. Erskine's time, in "Guy Mannering," chap. 37.

point of piety much what it was afterwards, when Dr. Lee was a frequent contributor. He was disposed to oppose secular education, as he had been in Campsie, where Mr. Robert Dalglish (now M.P. for Glasgow) had adopted that system, rather than leave the Roman Catholic children in his works without education altogether. He was not at first prepared in the Church courts to go as far as his friend Dr. Barclay, who in the earlier years of Mr. Lee's Edinburgh career was the most advanced Liberal, and consequently the " best abused " man in the metropolitan Presbytery. He was, however, moving on. His intellect was too keen, and his sympathies were too generous, to allow of his acting, for any length of time, along with the advocates of reactionary policies, or the supporters of inert and effete systems, and doctrines that through long misuse had lost their meaning and living force. Among his later readings before quitting Campsie, he had given much attention to Carlyle,—to " Sartor Resartus," "the French Revolution," and some of the "Essays and Tracts." This had its proper influence, which is traceable. No reasonable man can read Carlyle, and not grow into a deeper apprehension of the solemnity of duty, and of the necessity of testing all doctrines and systems by their moral worth, and into a stronger reverence for the rights of men, as men.

Mr. Lee brought to the extended arena in which he had now to work, and in which he must needs encounter a greater variety of intelligence than is usually presented to the influence of a country minister, a mind thoroughly well furnished with its own stores, naturally open and receptive, and candid in meeting the opinions of others. For the last few years he had been reading and studying pretty hard. His bulky, common-place books bear witness to a remarkable amount of reading and of thoughtful use of what was read. They embrace not only the lists of the books perused, but careful abstracts of most of them, with criticisms of their style, arguments, and tendencies, On a page by themselves, and prefaced with the title "The Teachers," he has written the names of Bacon, Burke, Butler, Shakspeare, Milton, Locke, J. Taylor. But from 1840 to 1843 his general reading included, among many others, Coleridge, Thierry ("Norman Conquest"), Spenser ("Faëry Queen"), Clarendon (History), Cicero (Treatises), S. Bernard, Justin Martyr, Whately, Neander, Bishop Bull's Harmonia Apostolica, Cook Taylor's "Natural History of Society," Ranke, Carlyle, and Emerson ("Essays"), of whom he says, "This wild American has been introduced to the British public by T. Carlyle, whose shadow and child he is. . . . . That he has deep insight need not be denied, and that he truly sees truth is manifest, having looked at it with his own proper eyes, yet from strange positions. . . . I know not whether to call him very religious or very profane. I suspect he is at heart the former, though a weak brother would shudder at many of his expressions, which indeed are quite unjustifiable."

He also reads and comments on A. J. Scott's "Social Systems,"* saying, "This book must be read again. The profound and ingenious author is full of subtlety and thought."

* "Social Systems of the Present Day, compared with Christianity," by A. J. Scott, formerly Principal of Owen's College, Manchester, originally Irving's assistant in London.

These are re-published, along with other selections from the writings of this singularly profound Christian thinker, in a volume entitled "Discourses."— *Macmillan & Co.*, 1866.

He quickly adapted himself to the duties and habits of his new sphere and of town life, and began his labours in his Church and parish with energy and zest. He conducted public worship after the usual fashion, and did not at this time attempt any of those restorations of the earlier and better order of Church service which were effected in later years. He adopted the custom of delivering a sermon in the afternoon, and in the forenoon a lecture, or exposition of a passage of Scripture. In these lectures he confined himself rather to a critical explanation of the meaning, than to an inculcation of the lessons to be deduced. He began with Genesis, went regularly through the historical books or portions of books, and then took the Psalms. To many of his congregation these elucidations of Scripture were fully as interesting as the more elaborate sermons in the afternoons. He visited the parish regularly. When he went to the worst parts of the "closes" and stairs with which it abounded, he occasionally was alone, but he frequently took an elder or deacon with him. None of the elders had seceded with Mr. Sym, and he found in them zealous and intelligent assistants. Up to the time of Dr. Inglis's death, in 1834, the order of deacons had been preserved in the Greyfriars' Church. After that it had been allowed to lapse. Dr. Lee restored it, according to the original idea of the Church,* and the wise practice of the congregation. He assigned a deacon to each elder, and expected that he should assist the elder in the management of the affairs of the Kirk Session, and in the superintendence of the district of the parish allotted to his charge. This arrangement subsisted throughout his whole incumbency.

* See 2nd Book of Discipline, chap. 8.

His first impressions of the religious world of Edinburgh were not favourable.

"From what I observe" (he writes in his diary on 2nd December, 1843), "I am led to conclude that true religion is at a very low ebb in this place. Controversy, I fear, has in the Scottish capital done its usual and deadly work. The parasite of religion, it seldom, almost never, fails to kill that goodly stem, round which it twines itself so closely, and which it seems only to strengthen and decorate. For how can men breathing habitually the atmosphere of controversy preserve alive in their own breasts the spirit of Christianity? And how can they diffuse among the people a purer spirit, a more heavenly temper, than their own? Doubtless the Lord has a great work to do in this place; and he will find or make proper instruments to accomplish it. Oh, Lord, make me willing in the day of Thy power. Fill me with the spirit of love and meekness, of power and zeal. Preserve me from all anger, bigotry, spite, party spirit. May I love Thee, O my God and Saviour, with all my might and strength; and my brother may I love with a pure heart fervently. And in love may I ever hold the truth. Bless me in my soul and body; in my studies and preaching; in my pastoral labours and common intercourse with men. Let my family be a Bethel—a house of God. Hear and answer me, oh, most merciful and holy Lord God, through Jesus Christ our Lord. Amen."

He had been engaged for some time on a work which he was able to put into the printer's hands soon after coming to Edinburgh. This was a translation of "The Theses of Erastus touching Excommunication." He translated these from the Latin, and wrote a preface; and the book (a small 8vo) was published by M'Phail, Edinburgh, in 1844. He was moved to this undertaking by the desire, not unnatural in a so-called "Erastian," to expose the error of applying the name of "Erastianism" to the principles and policy of the constitutional party in the Church. An "Erastian and residuary establishment," was one of the favourite epithets in vogue among the Seceders, whereby they strove to express, with fitting scorn, the idea of a despicable ecclesiastical remnant, trodden under the iron heel of the "civil magistrate."

"Multitudes in Scotland, at this moment," says Dr. Lee in his preface, "regard 'Erastian' as a term expressing, in a compendious way, whatever is most heretical and apostate in the Christian Church ; and Erastus as some heresiarch so abandoned that men may not permit themselves to say more respecting him than merely to utter his name.* And in their notion it settles the whole question regarding any opinion, any man, or any Church, if to that man, that opinion, or Church, the word Erastian can with any show of plausibility be applied. . . . . Surely if any of the seceding ministers had known what Erastianism truly was, he would not have permitted either himself or his brethren to style a Church Erastian, which neither now holds, nor has ever held, any of the distinctive principles of Erastus ; and which cannot be shewn ever to have acted on any of them."

He then goes on to sketch the theory of Erastus, as set forth in his Theses ; and sums up thus :—

"This, then, is properly Erastianism ; to wit, that excommunication" [which is the proper subject of the treatise] "is not a divine ordinance, but a device of men ; in other words, that the sins of professing Christian people should be punished by the Christian magistrate with civil penalties, not by pastors and elders denying them access to the sacraments. In the whole treatise there is not one word of those questions which have distracted the Church of Scotland of late years."

---

* My father used to relate that in a house which he had gone to visit, ecclesiastical division had separated a venerable grandmother from the other inmates. They had seceded. She had stuck to the Church. Her presence being desired in the parlour, one of the children was sent to call her down from her room. The messenger went to the foot of the stairs and shouted, "Granny, come down !" No answer; then, after a pause, "Granny, come down. Come down, ye auld Erastian granny."

Again, in the same preface, he proceeds :—

" Without meaning anything offensive, it may yet perhaps be permitted us to question whether (Erastianism being rightly understood) the persons who now glorify themselves under the name of the ' Free Church of Scotland' are not at this moment more Erastian than is the Church which they have left. That they are not less so, no honest man will, I think, attempt to deny. For however open, or *lax*, if you will, admission to the sacraments at any time may have been in the Established Church—that is, however *Erastian* may have been the practice there—none will pretend that the terms of admission in the Protesting Church are *less* open or lax. The ministers, elders, and members who seceded, were, *en masse*, included in the New Communion. The very fact of secession, indeed, may have been regarded as of itself a sufficient evidence of grace ; but, on reconsideration, this mark will perhaps appear not perfectly decisive ; and certainly it is *not* included among those tests which are prescribed in the Word of God, Gal. v. 22-26.

*   *   *   *   *   *   *

" It may, perhaps, surprise the reader to be informed that, in the writings of Erastus regarding Church government, occupying a quarto volume of near 360 pages, all that can, by any interpretation, be referred to the general question, is included in a very few pages, even in which no mention is made at all of that matter of ordination of ministers, concerning which our controversies have chiefly been ; and that it is not absolutely certain whether, even in that one passage, he is arguing the question of Church power further than as it relates to the matter of excommunication, which is the subject of both his treatises. This, at least, is certain, that some of his expressions, which, taken by themselves, might bear the most general meaning, are by himself restricted, in the context, to the particular question to which his argument had reference.   .

*   *   *   *   *   *   *

" Erastus nowhere puts the authority of the civil magistrate in competition with that of our blessed Lord ; but everywhere he insists that all men, as well magistrates as ministers and people, should be subject unto Him who is King of Kings and Lord of Lords. So that, if it should be proved (which it never can) that we are Erastians, it would be proved that, as such, we hold, instead of denying, the 'headship of Christ.' Certainly no man ever recognized that doctrine more distinctly than Erastus did. He may, indeed, have misinterpreted the command of Christ; but surely it is one thing to misinterpret a command, and another to question or deny the authority from which it proceeds.

    *   *   *   *   *   *   *

The peculiarity, or error, in the doctrine of Erastus (his language being understood, as it has generally been) is this, that the magistrate holds the same relation to religion, and the ministers of it, as he holds to secular affairs, and those who manage them; so that, as these are the province of the magistrate in whose name they are done, and who does not perform them himself, only for this reason, that it is more convenient to perform them by proxy, so the government of the Church is part of the government of the State, and is conducted in the name of the magistrate; and, though God has appointed that he may not perform the functions of the ministry himself (except, perhaps, in cases of absolute necessity), yet he must see that it be done, and that it be rightly done. And whatever authority may be exercised by ministers, in any way, there cannot be two magistracies in the State, at once distinct and supreme, nor two supreme legislatures. This seems the general theory, which Erastus produces in defence of his particular doctrine, but· regarding which very little is said in his works."

The whole preface is very instructive, and elucidates, with great distinctness, not only the tenets of Erastus himself, but the general idea of the Reformers of the sixteenth century regarding the union of Church and State.* Closing with a reference to the hard names used in the unhappy strifes of "Moderate" and "Non-Intrusionist," he says :—

"In the meantime, all that are children of God have mutual

<hr>

* Mr. Macaulay, then Member for Edinburgh, to whom he sent the book, writes, "I have only had time to look very rapidly over the interesting account of Erastus, which contains much that is new to me."

bonds which even their estrangements and separations cannot break. Whether they will acknowledge each other in that character or not, all believers in Jesus Christ, the Head of the Body, are members of one holy, Catholic, and Apostolic Church, and members one of another. Let us fear, lest we sin against Christ by sinning against those whom He may recognise as His members, though we will not."

Another volume which he had on hand about this time, and for which, indeed, he had long been amassing materials, was his "Handbook of Devotion." It was the first of the many books of prayer which he contributed to our devotional literature, and was finally completed and published in 1845.

His Alma Mater, the University of St. Andrews, conferred on him the degree of D.D. in 1844.* He liked distinction, when honestly won, and this recognition of his merits pleased him. He has wafered on a blank page of his diary the letter from his kind old friend, Principal Haldane, which announces the degree. " I trust," says the Principal, " you may long live to enjoy your well-merited honour, and to reflect lustre on your Alma Mater, as you have already done."

In this same year his father died. A visit to Tweedmouth, and a few days with his father and the old friends there, had been one of the rarest pleasures of his life ; and he heartily enjoyed the boating on the Tweed, and the simple recreations of early days brought back again, for a little, out of the fading distance. " Had a kettle with father and all his family," he records on one occasion, " at New Water. Had a nice sail beforehand

* "D. D.—Decent Debility,"—he used to say when scandalized, as he occasionally was, at the facility with which this distinction was permitted to grace obscure names and mediocre talents.

up the lovely Tweed; and sat down on the grass, and ate salmon in the genuine fashion, with much comfort and love." But now the old links were broken at last, and the central figure of the familiar Tweedmouth landscape disappears. "His children," writes Dr. Lee, "must ever cherish his memory with tenderness, and think of him with veneration and gratitude. A more affectionate parent never was, nor could be. His last letter to me is very characteristic of him. 'What can I give you? What can I do for you? Is there anything I have that you need?' This was his constant feeling. May his children follow that example of piety and integrity and benevolence which he left us, and which was left us also by our saintly mother."

On 19th January, 1845, an event occurred, which had a great influence on Dr. Lee's future career. But for it, his energies might, not improbably, have fastened on some other labour than the reform of the Church's worship. For this catastrophe led to arrangements being made, which, while they relieved him from the weekly pressure of having to prepare for two services, subjected him to the necessity of witnessing, generally every Lord's-day, the celebration of public worship, as well as of himself conducting it, and thus tended to fix in his mind the deficiencies of the ordinary Scottish ritual. It also led to the congregation of Old Greyfriars being ultimately provided with a Church which offered great facilities for the realization of enlightened ideas as to the adornment proper to a house of prayer. The fire which consumed the old building, therefore, though regarded as a mere deplorable accident at the time of its occurrence, did not burn in vain ; and from its ashes sprang a goodly Phœnix.

Dr. Lee writes in his diary on 19th January :—

"This morning the venerable Old Greyfriars caught fire by the flue being overheated, and now lies a ruin. Thus has come to an untimely end a church which is associated with the names of more great men than any in Scotland : Principal Robertson, Dr. Erskine, Dr. Finlayson,* and Dr. Inglis, are among my illustrious predecessors.

"When I saw the roof fall in, which had so often resounded to their voices, I said to myself, Is this prophetic ? Is it the foreshadow that the Church, of which these men were the pillars and ornaments, is about to be consumed ? This event will form a serious inconvenience, I fear, and may involve us in considerable trouble. But I desire in patience to possess my soul, and to be warned by this event that the end of all things is at hand, and to gird up the loins of my mind. Lord, quicken me that I may discern all things as foreshadows of Thy coming, in flaming fire, to judge Thine enemies. May I, and my beloved people, then be safe under the covert of Thy wing."

The congregation, thus unhoused, was, after some little negotiation, accommodated in the Assembly Hall, in which the congregation of the Tolbooth parish met for worship. The latter congregation was a very small one ; and the large and handsome hall (built for the use of the General Assembly) was able to take in both. This arrangement lasted until the restoration of Old Greyfriars Church in 1857.

For the first year or two, Dr. Lee does not appear to have taken much part in the meetings or business of the

* Professor of Logic and Metaphysics in the University of Edinburgh, and Minister of Old Greyfriars from 1793 to 1799, when he was transferred to the High Church.

Presbytery. The atmosphere of the Presbytery Hall did not suit him.

"New experience," he says in 1845, "again begins to convince me of what I felt so strongly in the Presbytery of Glasgow, that 'defective sympathies,' as Charles Lamb calls them; or hatred of party spirit; or a contempt and hatred of the conduct of men, who are continually doing things from motives altogether different from those palpable; that these causes, or some of them, render me unfit for Church Courts, as one who cannot be led unless I think the matter right, and cannot lead those who are asking only what is expedient."

"The *Edinburgh Review* says the English Convocation was a stage which served no other purpose but to afford the clergy an occasion to make fools of themselves. So our Church Courts do, most lamentably. The intercourse of ministers with ministers seems much less useful, and even pleasant, than that of clergymen with their people, and with laymen generally. I should consult my own dignity and usefulness, and peace too, I think, by going no more to Church Courts than absolute necessity demands."

The line which he took, when he did attend them, was sure to lead him farther and farther away from the sympathies of his brethren. Dr. Barclay* was then the only Liberal in the Presbytery. Almost all the rest were of the most Conservative type in mind and policy; not a few of them, "Moderates" of the old school. Some of them were men of real ability and high personal character and influence. Others were men of very small ability, and, from no fault of theirs, but from lack of force of character and mental power, of no social or public influence or weight whatever. The Metropolitan Presbytery had ceased to control, or even sensibly to

* Then Minister of Currie, now Principal of the University of Glasgow.

affect, public opinion. The dullest adherence to the *status quo;* the most dogged resistance to any liberal measures in politics ; and the most unreasoning dread of and opposition to the modern spirit of critical inquiry and quest of less absolute dogma, always found ready exponents in the Presbytery of Edinburgh. With all this Dr. Lee had no sympathy. The basis of his mind was essentially liberal and rational ; and he had nothing in common with the illiberal, the intolerant, the obstructive. He was too sagacious not to perceive that the Church was entering on a region of political and ecclesiastical change ; and that if she would be safe and useful, she must make ready to meet and acquiesce in many inevitable alterations and reforms. " I apprehend," he writes to his friend, Mr. Paisley, in 1845, " that we are approaching great changes in the relations of Church and State, and in all ecclesiastical affairs. The relations of the clergy to the people, the power of Church Courts, and the relation of the Church to the government of Christian countries, are all unsatisfactory."

With such views as his, he naturally found himself—even at this early date—in pretty constant opposition to the majority of the Presbytery on all general questions.

We find him—for instance—in May, 1845, speaking in favour of Lord Advocate Rutherfurd's Bill for the Abolition of University Tests, then before the Legislature. The Church clung with desperate tenacity to these useless badges of her connexion with the Universities, and imagined securities for "religious education." " Do not the tests," says Dr. Lee, " keep out many that are Christian ? Do they not let in many that are not ?

Where then is the use of them as securing a religious education?" And he argues against them at considerable length. Dr. Simpson,[*] when he had finished, rose to "dissent from every point, every view, and every doctrine laid down by Dr. Lee." Dr. Muir prophetically foresaw in the abolition of tests, "the separation of our schools from Bible influence and Bible teaching, and the approach of a time when we should have a country without a God."

One sees in this debate the dawn of the disastrous light in which Dr. Lee was afterwards regarded by so many of his professional brethren. We meet with also one of the first expressions of that recognition of his superior enlightenment and practical sagacity, by the general impartial public, which increased year by year, and did much, in the end, to strengthen his position and influence in the Church.[†] " Accustomed as we are," says

---

[*] Minister of Kirk Newton, and one of the Clerks of the General Assembly.

[†] Mr. Macaulay writes to him as follows, in reply to a letter which, of course, cannot be recovered :—

"ALBANY, *May* 23, 1845.

"DEAR SIR,

"I thank you for your friendly and interesting letter. On one point my mind is, I think, unalterably made up. I never did vote and I never will vote for any test of which the object is to exclude any man on account of his religious opinions from any office not religious ; and I do not conceive that a professorship of surgery or of chemistry is a religious office. At the same time, if the bill can be carried only with the amendments which you have suggested, and if Rutherfurd and my other friends think that, even so amended, it may be useful, I will accept it, that is to say, I will not oppose it on the third reading. Further than this I cannot go. And I am truly concerned to think that when the Tories are founding colleges without any tests in Ireland, the Whigs should be compelled by the prevailing fanaticism to devise new tests for the colleges in Scotland.

"As to the argument drawn from the Articles of Union, I need not remind you that, if Episcopalian professors are admitted, that argument falls entirely to the ground. For it was undoubtedly against Episcopacy chiefly, if not solely, that the Act of Security was directed.

"I shall be most happy to hear from time to time what your views are on this very important subject.

"Believe me ever,

"Yours very truly,

"T. B. MACAULAY."

the *Scotsman*, " to narrow sectarian views, affected scruples, and false alarms in Church Courts, we felt it quite refreshing to read a speech like Dr. Lee's—liberal, straightforward, and full of common sense."*

At another meeting of Presbytery he opposes a movement less directly supported by the majority; but support of which was considered to indicate a commendable warmth of evangelical feeling—a movement in favour of what was somewhat vaguely called " Ministerial Communion "—*i. e.* interchange of pulpits with the ministers of dissenting sects.

The General Assembly of 1799, in the dull strength and anger of its moderatism, passed a Declaratory Act,† to the effect that no person save an authorized licentiate or minister of the Church should be suffered to officiate in any congregation ; and that no minister should hold " ministerial communion " with any person not qualified to accept a presentation to a charge in the National Church. A Pastoral Letter also was prepared by the polite pen of Dr. Blair, and read in all the churches, to warn the faithful people against giving heed to certain itinerating and innovating " missionaries," who, " in the fields or in places not intended for public worship, gather crowds ; while pouring forth their loose harangues, they frequently take the liberty of censuring the doctrine and character of the minister of the parish,"‡ and commit other reprehensible irregularities.

This Act and this Letter were aimed at Robert and James Haldane and Rowland Hill, who had been going

---

* *Scotsman*, 24th May, 1845.
† *i. e.*, an Act declaring the Law of the Church to be, &c.
‡ Acts of Assembly, 1799.

through Scotland, scattering tracts, establishing Sunday-schools, preaching, and holding what would now be called "revival meetings." All this was extremely irritating to the moderate ministers, who regarded everything like zeal with Talleyrand's aversion. Their irritation was not lessened by the free and all too candid criticisms of their lives and doctrines vented by the "missionaries," and especially by Rowland Hill.* The Assembly expressed their wrath, and took its revenge, by issuing the Letter and passing the Act.

When the evangelical movement, which owed a good deal of its vigour to these very "missionaries," had pervaded the Church, this Act became unpopular; and the revolutionary Assembly of 1842 rescinded it. But the proceedings of that Assembly were vitiated by the fact, referred to in a previous chapter, that men sat in it who had no legal right to do so (because they were not ministers of parishes). The law, as declared in 1799, therefore resumed its sway, on the Church obtaining again a constitutional Assembly, through the elimination of the illegal element at the secession of 1843.

The Act of 1799, however, has never regained its original respect in the eyes of the Church. It has been popularly regarded as an instance of illiberal and arbitrary legislation, unworthy of the catholic spirit of the National Church. Clergymen, anxious to be considered liberal, and to be able to save a sermon occasionally by exchanging pulpits with a dissenting brother; and laymen, unacquainted with, or careless of, the

---

* Lives of the Haldanes, p. 228 (3rd edition).

Church's peculiar constitution; and both, unconscious or forgetful of the fact that the law they decry is to be found in some form, in the statute book of every National Church, and greatly mistaking the true conditions of communion (ministerial or any other), have made it a kind of fashion to advocate, with pseudo-liberality and pseudo-charity, the repeal of the Act of 1799.

The Rev. Dr. Simpson, of Kirk Newton, who had been a keen ally of the "Non-intrusionists," and a member of the "Non-intrusion Committee," in the rough days before May, 1843, but who had not considered it necessary to carry out his principles by secession, seems to have been desirous to save his somewhat faded reputation for Evangelicalism, by making a little innocent agitation about the obnoxious enactment. He accordingly brought an overture, in favour of its modification, before the Presbytery. Dr. Lee opposed his motion, or the making of any new enactments to regulate, under the name of "ministerial communion," the occasional admission of dissenters to the pulpits of the Church. He said:

"Before proceeding to make laws regarding ministerial communion, it might be desirable to know what this ministerial communion is, what it declares, and what purposes it serves. On all these important points, however, the reverend doctor has given us no light; they seem never to have occurred to him as questions at all.

"Is ministerial communion the exchange of pulpits by ministers? Then the great majority of ministers in the Church of Scotland have no ministerial communion, nor can have; for they do not and cannot exchange pulpits. Even were it desirable, it is not possible. Our unity is neither declared nor promoted by this means; it has another foundation altogether. If Dr. Simpson and I were to exchange pulpits every month, nobody could understand that there was on that account any greater unity between the Church at Kirknewton and the Old Greyfriars than there is now. They could only gather from the fact that between Dr. S. and myself there existed a particular friendship or a great congeniality of sentiment. The unity manifested in this way is not the unity of different Churches, but the unity between different individual ministers.

"I don't find in the New Testament that *ministerial communion* is even mentioned as the way, or as one of the ways of signifying to the world or each other the unity of a Church. So far as I see there is another way of indicating that unity, namely, communion in the *sacraments*.

"'There is one Lord, one Faith, one Baptism, one God, one Father of all, above all, through all, in all.' And so of the other sacrament. 'We being many—though many individuals—are one body and one bread, for we are all partakers of that one bread.' If any Church wishes to have communion with us, or if we wish to hold communion with any, I apprehend the proper way to indicate or ratify this unity is, not by ministers exchanging pulpits, but by a common participation in the sacraments, which, however they have been made the means and the badges of division and sects, were yet designed as the means and expressions of *unity* among all the soldiers of Jesus Christ.

"Another method of indicating unity or having communion is that mentioned in 2nd Cor. viii., 4, and Ep. to Phil. i., 5, '*ministering to the necessity of saints.*' These are the only ways of indicating the unity of Churches, so far as I can see, in the New Testament. And therefore in the early Church the expression which signified the unity of Churches was *communicating* with such a Church.

"The only thing in the New Testament that bears the least resemblance, or gives the least countenance, to this notion about ministerial communion is the passage, Gal. ii. 9, when James, Cephas, and John gave to Paul and Barnabas the right hand of fellowship. But observe they were not the leaders and teachers of different sects coming forward and consenting to preach for each other while they maintained different and protesting societies, and different communion tables; but it was an acknowledgment of each other as true apostles, and as having a different vocation, the one to the Jews, the other to the Gentiles, and an agreement (not to preach for each other but) to confine themselves to different spheres of labour.

"I have serious objections against any overture regulating this thing, 'ministerial communion,' and for these reasons.

"1. I do not know how to make laws regarding a thing unknown in the New Testament. *It* affords me no light. I do not know how, on New Testament principles, we can regulate our relations with other sects, while the New Testament condemns all sects and divisions as scandals. 2. Because the existence of the sects or parties to whose ministers this overture has reference is a great sin. It indicates that a great sin has been committed, either by them or by us. If we were such that they had just cause to separate themselves from us, then are we guilty before God, and should deeply repent and humble ourselves before those whom we compelled to leave us. This I submit is the proper attitude for us under that supposition, and not making laws about ministerial communion with them, which would indicate that we thought lightly of a sin. If, on the other hand, we gave them no just cause of separating themselves from us, then the sin of erecting hostile churches and communions is *theirs.* And is it a small sin? And can the Church, with common consistency or common sense, by a law about ministerial communion, recognise them as true ministers of Christ, whom she has pronounced no longer ministers, and whom, if she had been consistent, she should have deposed ? What, sir! men cannot hold communion with us in the sacrament, but must set up separate places of worship What communion requires a less agreement than this ? And yet we shall make laws implying that they have, or may have, a far greater agreement, namely, such an agreement as would qualify them to teach our people, or we theirs !

"Why is this proposed ? To exhibit the unity of the Church ? What does this phrase mean ? That there is unity among all the protestant sects—Episcopalian, Presbyterian, Independent? If they *are* united in all matters of importance, why are they yet separated ? why are they sects ? If they are not united in all matters of moment, then this declaration of their unity is a declaration of a thing that does not exist. It is therefore an act of hypocrisy or an illusion. Is there not something incongruous in our making laws declaring persons to be ministers whom our Church holds *not* to be ministers ? 'Ordinary and outward *calling* has two parts, *election* and *ordination*.' The ceremonies of ordination are 'fasting, earnest prayer, and imposition of hands of the Eldership.'* There can be no 'calling' in this sense among the Congregationalists, for they have no *Eldership* in our sense, and they deny any right of any person out of a particular congregation to exercise any power or jurisdiction within it. I neither discuss nor blame their theory at present, but I say this: It seems very strange that you should make laws recognizing persons as duly qualified ministers, who, according to the legislation of your Church, want *one* essential qualification at least.

"I don't comprehend how, under this law, you could prevent the lay members of your own communion preaching if they chose. . . . . These reasons persuade me that you should make no law admitting dissenting ministers.

"I see no reason for making any law on the subject, for,

"1. Nobody is wishing admission, and there is no likelihood of ministerial communion taking place to any great extent.

"2. Because it is a fact that under the most stringent laws it has taken place, and I believe in certain cases (few in number), it will take place. I would, therefore, rather not make a law which will not be enforced.

"3. It appears to me not necessary to make a law to admit; neither do I see any necessity to make any law to exclude. For foreign Churches stand on a very different footing from the Dissenters at home. . . . The individual discretion of ministers may, I think, be safely trusted in this matter. . . . ."

One of his principal correspondents in those earlier years at Edinburgh was the Rev. Robert Paisley, of S. Ninian's, and his letters to this valued friend are the only ones—with hardly an exception—that have been obtained, out of his correspondence from 1844 to 1847, or so. These letters are interesting ; for, writing to one

* See 2nd Book of "Discipline."

well able to sympathize with his intellectual pursuits and his earnest search for truth, he enters freely on the questions and studies which were engaging his mind at the time.

"Though probably I differ from you," he says, in one of his letters, "in many particular opinions, there are few persons with whom I have a more perfect agreement as to the true notion of what Christianity is, and what are the evils of the Christian Church, and of the world around us.

"*March* 15, 1845.—This morning I had a party of thirteen divinity students at breakfast, who presented me with Arnold's Thucydides and his Lectures on Modern History, as an acknowledgment of their gratitude for my poor prelections on the New Testament. . . . . I think, with you, this disruption* an awful event; but the spirit which produced it, and which has been exasperated by it, seems to me much more awful. One sees in their organs little but fulsome self-praise, and virulent abuse of their opponents. I am no idolater, as you know, of the Kirk as it is now, but no man of common candour will deny that in bigotry and virulence the Free Church men have outrun us immensely.

"I am, with modifications, an admirer of Edward Irving. But I fear his vanity was too decided to be made an historical question. I should be most happy could I be brought to doubt it. But I admire him as a great, and venerate him as a good man, notwithstanding. For what man has no imperfection ? And if any one were perfect, our judgments are so perverted that we should pronounce him the contrary.

"Arnold has interested me profoundly, though I think he was too restless in his spirit, too full of plans and schemes. Curiously enough I had just been resolving to recommence Aristotle, and Thucydides also. They are so little known, to our great cost.

"Do you know Gillies' Translation of the Ethics and Politics ? It is an excellent book, and very good to read after one has got at one's own interpretation of the text. There are several Bibliothecas of the Fathers. I would not give fourteen guineas for them all together. They are all, so far as I know, disagree-

* Secession of 1843.

able books, the Greek authors not being given in the original, but in Latin translations, and closely printed, with no notes or other apparatus. Indexes are essential in works of such magnitude. I agree with you in thinking Warburton was much more clever and learned than wise, and his insolence is insufferable. Mosheim I respect much more. Maclaine caricatures him sadly. Still he is a hard, or rather a cold man. I suppose his idea of Church and State agrees substantially with Arnold's. Write often, my dear Paisley. It is a real refreshment to me to exchange thoughts with you, having, I may say, no person here among the ministers who seems to know or care about any of the things of which we love to think and speak."

"*September* 11. Little is passing at present in general, and in Edinburgh less than elsewhere, except railways, and the pullings down and buildings up which they occasion—except the Free College, for which they are making preparations by knocking down houses at the head of the Mound. These people are as much alive ecclesiastically as we are dead; the spiritual somnolency in both, I fear, is about equal. . . . Much need have we to work, my dear friend, for I am more and more persuaded that this in which we dwell is a dry and barren land."

He adds, at the corner of his paper,

" Custodi me ab omni peccato, et non timebo mortem nec infernum; T. A'Kempis—a brave thought,—and yet I think most of us have so thought many times."

"*October* 9, 1845. . . . I have been painfully and profoundly interested in reading the Autobiography of Blanco White, a most curious psychological study. I think it is most useful to consider the views of men like him; men, I mean, who have adopted views which the great body of Christians consider unsound and dangerous. I wish you could see the book. I have the loan of it from a Free Church man. I am making a little progress in German, but the way is toilsome. Have you seen De Wette's Introduction to the New Testament? A translation of it by an American, Theodore Parker, has come into my hands, and I feel, afresh, how immeasurably behind the Germans we are in the science of literature. Questions which among them have been fully discussed and settled, and which are looked upon as settled even by the most orthodox, are hardly known among us as questions. Many years ago, I got a friend to translate for me passages of Eichhorn's Introduction, and what was my amazement to hear of the Elohistic and Jehovistic documents, out of which the Pentateuch was composed, treated as admitted facts! . . . . The Rationalists are very wild, probably, but they must be understood and answered. It will not do to answer them with exclamations of horror. My good old professor, Haldane, had one comprehensive refutation of all their theories, or all he chose to notice, or all he knew, perhaps, ' Absurd, absurd, quite absurd!' He measured accurately the understanding of his students, for most of them appeared satisfied."

His commonplace book at this time bears witness to a most careful and anxious study of German. He evidently felt its indispensable value for his biblical researches. German criticism, and De Wette in particular, had their proper share in that liberalizing process which his mind was undergoing.

" *Oct.* 23, 1845. . . . . Rosenmüller is very valuable, so far as I have seen, the best of German commentators. . . . I should like Eichhorn's ' Einleitung' translated, who is one of the ablest of critics, and one of the most learned of men, as is Gesenius. I hope soon to read German for myself, but as yet my progress is not very great.

" I am sorry Origen is not more studied and known. A passage of his, ' Contra Cels.' i. 42, seems to lay the foundation of all the fabric of Rationalism. He expresses the same thought in several other parts of his writings, especially in his commentary on Abraham and Abimelech. Indeed, few truths or errors are new. I am doing very little of anything that is useful. May God help me, for I feel I am a most unprofitable servant."

" *Nov.* 14, 1845. . . . . Burke is an old favourite of mine ; none ever pleased or instructed me more. Aristotle, Bacon, and Burke, to whom I should not much object to add Locke, and Harrington, and Arnold, are sufficient instructors in the science of politics. I am ever more convinced of the soundness of Arnold's maxim that politics and religion are the only subjects worthy of the serious consideration of a rational being—all else is secondary. . . . . Have you seen Martineau's 'Rationale of Religious Enquiry?' It is rhetorical but very clever and acute, and contains, in my opinion, much important truth. Blanco White set me to read him. I am ashamed to say it is the first Unitarian book I ever read—except White's Life, and Taylor's Retrospect of the Religious Life of England—though this last is not a Unitarian book, though written by a man who holds those opinions. May God guide us through this sea of notions! I verily believe, at the same time, that something may be learned from all men and from all parties in the Christian Church. May God guide and bless you, my dear Paisley."

"*Dec.* 6, 1845. . . . . The Bible, so far as I can understand, cannot, properly speaking, be considered as an object of Faith, being not the Truth itself, but merely the vehicle of its conveyance ; besides which, we can imagine many other vehicles. What was not an object of faith when Christianity was first preached can never afterwards become a necessary object of faith, unless Christianity has since acquired some new doctrine. Also, the whole question regarding the books of the New Testament is historical merely ; it is *probability*, therefore, and probability in different degrees regarding the different books ; quite sufficient regarding most of them,—perhaps regarding all, but surely not a proper foundation for divine faith,—if this be not the admission of an historical probability—but of the Divine testimony.

"I think the Quakers are clearly right in saying that the ultimate ground of faith is the witness of the Spirit in our hearts, and nothing else, unless faith is our receiving and resting in the testimony of men. I therefore look with more and more aversion on the Bibliolatry which is probably the weak point of Protestantism. None of the ancient Fathers ever thought of putting into their creeds, 'I believe in the Holy Scriptures.' True, the ancient councils investigated and settled (after their fashion) the canon, but they never put the canon into the Creed, any more than they put the

Christian ministry into it, which the Liverpool Unionists have sufficiently done. It is sickening to see men running continually round in the same circle of errors, and so many set up to teach who need so much to learn.

"I think almost all these people who are talking of union, advocating and opposing it, are unconscious of the distinction between that truth which is necessary for a man himself, and that which must be required by him of his neighbour. What I know and believe, is all of it essential truth *to me*, and I can no more relinquish or deny it, or hold any part of it unessential, than I can deny the Lord that bought me. But I have no right to demand that my neighbour receive my opinions, or admit my interpretation of the words of our common Master. If he profess to receive the doctrines of Christ, and to believe them in the sense which seems to him their true one, I may think him wrong, and labour to set him right, but, unless I deny to him that liberty which I claim for myself, I do not see how I am justified in refusing to acknowledge him as a Christian, unless I assert my own infallibility and consequent authority over his faith. This ultra protestant doctrine, and the purely popish doctrine are, I think, the only ones that are consistent or will hang together. I do not understand what is meant by assemblies determining. controversies of faith ' *ministerially.*' It either must mean *authoritatively*, or that their decisions are mere counsel or advice. The latter no true blue Presbyterian and no genuine Episcopalian would admit.

"The Morrisonians are regularly preaching here. The Free Church has published a catechism on ' The Headship of Christ,' full of Popish doctrines. I had a bad cold, and all the children have been afflicted in the same way. We live very privately, and the longer the more so. Do you ever see Mr. Wylie? He seems to have forsaken us utterly; for what reason I cannot imagine. The oracle of Mochrum is also dumb.*

"I am, my dear friend,

"Truly and affectionately yours,

"ROBERT LEE."

---

* The late Rev. Alexander Young, M.A., Minister of Mochrum, Wigtonshire, a man of deep piety, sound learning, and great and original force of character.

"*Edinburgh, Jan.* 1, 1846. . . . . Mrs. Lee unites with me in the compliments of the season, and in sincerely wishing you many happy new years. May God make us all to dwell in Eternity, for dwelling in time we inhabit a tottering and falling house. I am (*inter nos*) writing a review of the Liverpool Conference for M'Phail's Journal, which will appear in the beginning of February. I have no idea what kind of thing it will be; but S. is also at work, and if I find any measure of good in it, or that others will tolerate what one may write, I shall go on—if not, I will cease. I feel more and more separated from all around me almost—whether the fault is theirs or my own, I do not know. I hope you will contribute to M'Phail. It is of consequence, if possible, to give it a tone; though I fear anything really good will not be endured. The more I see of them, the more I fear that the majority of our brethren are men prepared to resist any truth that coincides not with their prejudices and worldly interests. It is a sad conclusion, but I cannot deny I can form no other."

It was one of his projects to make M'Phail's "Ecclesiastical Journal" a liberal and catholic organ of theological and literary criticism, and of sound Church principles; but though his connection with it continued, with more or less closeness, for some years, he never saw his idea of what it ought to be, realized. There were difficulties in the way; among others, a limited number of subscribers, and these, for the most part, hostile to liberal opinion in matters ecclesiastical and theological. This magazine struggled on till 1862, and then succumbed.

The Liverpool Conference which he refers to, was the conference held in that town in October, 1845, preparatory to the organization of the abortive "Evangelical Alliance." The "Free" Kirk* having successfully con-

* Sundry critics of a previous work of mine, in which I spoke of this body always as the "Free," objected strongly to the inverted commas. I cannot

summated a violent schism, and sundry other dissenters having been much edified and encouraged thereby, it was thought a fit time to set about the glorification of Unity and the promotion of Union. A volume of eight essays by ministers of as many different communions, and with an introduction by Dr. Chalmers, was issued to the "Evangelical" world, pleased, but somewhat perplexed, with this novel Propaganda. The Liverpool Conference followed, and the "Alliance" was finally hatched in the summer of 1846. Dr. Chalmers' plan of what it ought to be was certainly not a very catholic one, though vastly more practical than the designs of his coadjutors anticipated, or their skill could conduct. It is difficult to understand what amount of unity he could expect to be reached, through the Alliance "standing forth" as he proposed—"in the character first of a great anti-popish association, and secondly of a great home mission." *

The Alliance, erected on a narrow basis, and controlled chiefly by sectarians, has long sunk into its natural barrenness and obscurity. Dr. Lee refers to it again in another letter—" I am going on with De Wette's Introduction to the Old Testament, and gaining much knowledge. The more I read, I am the more persuaded of the absurdity of making the books of Scripture an Article of Faith. You observe the Liverpool Unionists have done so. The French (if you remark the pro-

---

see the justice of the objection. In writing history, on ever so small a scale, one must be careful only to use and perpetuate names for which there is a moral ground of truth. Because this estimable body calls itself *the* Free Church, I am not bound to admit it is exceptionally free, or to use language which would corroborate a fact which I deny. It is no freer than others. If it had called itself the "Holy," or the "Infallible," would those who had nothing to do with it have been bound to call it so too?

* Hanna's "Life of Chalmers," vol. iv., c. 20.

ceedings of the French Protestants at Lyons) understand the matter more accurately."

He enters in his diary on 1st January, 1846, the resolution, "To avoid, as much as possible, Presbytery and Church Courts' business, which consumes much time and has little profit." We find, however, that this resolution could not be altogether carried out. He began to see that he must take some part in these affairs. He could not stand aloof and let narrow policy and officious incapacity have it all their own way. He already saw what a fine future the Church everywhere, and especially in Edinburgh, had before her, if now, when delivered from the broils and fanaticisms of the "Non-Intrusionists," she would only adapt herself to the growing liberality of thought and culture of feeling which were pervading the best intelligences in all ranks of society. But this was a movement with which—if indeed the presbyters perceived the possibility of it at all—the Presbytery of Edinburgh could not be expected to have much sympathy. And Dr. Lee, who was very impatient of dulness and mere unintelligent obstructiveness, was therefore all the more stirred to forego the abstinence from public ecclesiastical business which was congenial to his own nature. Besides, he began to know his strength in that arena in which he afterwards bore down all rivals.

"I have lately," he says, in March, 1846, "made two speeches in the Presbytery. My power of speaking is, I think, improving, though still it has many defects. Indeed the Presbytery is a bad audience, in many respects—impatient, prejudiced, and narrow-minded in a high degree. I speak of the members generally. And from this reason, as well as from the narrow and technical grounds on which matters are commonly argued, it is one of the worst audiences. Still, practice is essential to success, as eloquence is an art as much as it is a science; and men make themselves speakers, commonly, at the expense of their audience. Sometimes I doubt whether I do wisely in withdrawing so much as I do from public life, and the means whereby one might move other men's minds. Perhaps it is wisest and safest not to seek either publicity or privacy,—but to enter on that path which may seem to be pointed out by the necessities of society, or one's own peculiar position or qualifications. In short, let us seek to serve God, and not indulge our own humour or inclinations. 'God forbid that I should glory,' &c."

There are in Edinburgh no fewer than eight* hospitals for the maintenance and education of the young. The city clergy, besides the general interest in these institutions which their office gives them, have a special connection with the greatest of them all—Heriot's. They, along with the Town Council, are the governors, and, as such, have the control of this magnificent establishment, with its revenue of more than £15,000 a year. Annually, on George Heriot's day—the 1st of June—a part of the commemoration consists in the governors, the children, and their friends attending public worship in the New Greyfriars' Church, and hearing a sermon preached there by one of the ministers of Edinburgh.

On 1st June, 1846, the sermon was preached by Dr. Lee. He took for his text Psalm cxxvii. 3, 4, 5, and, much to the annoyance of some of his hearers, but to the great satisfaction of others, he proceeded to enlarge on the twofold advantage of the family relation, of the blessing of the parents to the children, and of the children

---

* Heriot's; John Watson's; George Watson's; Trades' Maidens; Merchant Maidens; Orphans'; Donaldson's; Stewart's;—all, under varying conditions, for boys and girls.

to the parents,* in such a strain as to indicate an opinion distinctly unfavourable to the character and tendencies of such institutions as Heriot's Hospital, under its existing management. He had not examined the system of the hospital without detecting its liability to abuse, through the selfishness and indolence of parents anxious to transfer from themselves to it the duty of bringing up their children. He had also discovered the mischief done to the children by their withdrawal from all connection with the home circle during their six or seven years of monastic residence. On each of these points he spoke out plainly, and concluded with a practical advice both to parents and to the governors of the hospital.

"The first conclusion I would suggest concerns *parents*. If what has been said contains any truth, it follows, that parents should be very averse to permit their children to be separated from them—to be removed from under their roof. And this reluctance they should cherish, both for their children's sakes and their own. It is, on the one side, vain to expect that any person will perform to a boy or a girl the part of an affectionate and faithful father and mother. However willing others may

---

* "What renewers of our existence—what fresheners of our life are children! When all things begin to grow stale upon us, as they presently do, and our wearied senses ache with the repetition of the same sights and sounds; and this world is felt to become a flat and tedious thing, which we are ready to call a bleak and sterile promontory, whose fruits are turning to 'bitter ashes;' and when we are tempted to steel our own hearts against other men, with the same selfishness which we witness in them, and to take refuge ourselves in the same low passions with which they assail and disgust us; and the more clearly-discerned baseness of mankind renders ever more a bondage that duty, Thou shalt love thy neighbour as thyself;—how delightful, how precious, to see the fresh tide of life rising around us in our children, watering and rendering verdant and fruitful again that soil which the scorching rays of time were quickly turning to barrenness and desolation—to feel the tide of their young existence washing the old waste places and renewing their withered affections —to behold in them divine wonder, the parent of both knowledge and worship —to witness the charm and zest which novelty gives existence to in them; and to observe how their unsubdued intellects rush headlong upon those deep mysteries of our being, those unsolved problems and unanswerable questions, which we have learnt to put away, because we have interrogated all things in vain for an answer, the sea and the earth, the heaven and the grave having each confessed, 'It is not in me!'"—*Sermon*, p. 20.

be, they cannot do this. In the nature of things it is plainly impossible; and notoriously so in institutions containing so many young persons as this does. But it is equally needful for the parents themselves, that they retain their children under their roof, if they can. For in their anxiety to get them otherwise disposed of, they are seeking to deprive themselves of what is to them a continual lesson, and a powerful motive to well-doing. I should say a great deal more on this important point, unless I feared it might not be profitable to a part of my present audience. But I hope what I have hinted at, may be considered by those for whom it is intended. The vast number of applications, indicating the excessive anxiety, so generally felt by parents, to obtain admission for their children to the different hospitals of this city, shows how imperfectly many parents understand their own duties, and how miserably blind they are to their own privileges in connection with their offspring.

"My second remark, arising from the considerations already offered, applies to *governors*. I would most respectfully remind the honourable and reverend governors of this hospital, and all others similarly situated, that the relation of parent and child is an ordinance of our all-wise and bountiful Creator; and as the wisdom of this relation is both most manifest, and as it is most important to the well-being of families and society, of parents and children, so we cannot disregard it, we cannot trample upon it, without convicting ourselves of unpardonable presumption, and bringing down upon us tremendous penalties.

"This begins to be seen even in quarters where the true light of Christianity has been little heeded. In France the state of society has for ages been wrong, uneasy, bad—things have been all out of order—people hardly knew why. Reflecting men have of late years begun to ask, What ails us? what is the matter? Something is very wrong in this great nation of ours; there is some terrible disease in our social system, which produces this incessant fever. What is it that is wrong? Christianity would have told them what was wrong; but they have got the answer from bitter experience—they have bought at a dear price what they might have had for nothing. 'Our family life is all wrong.' So confess the French observers and philosophers, 'We are ruining everything—our public security and peace —our social comfort, our domestic happiness—all is going to wreck, by separating children from their parents—secluding the girls in convents, the boys in schools. This tearing from the mother those children who are as necessary for her, as she is for them, first weakens the tie between the husband and the wife, and ends at last in the virtual dissolution of the family.' 'This,' say those French inquirers, 'is the radical disease which preys upon the vitals of our social system ; and till this be corrected, amelioration of our other evils is impossible, for they spring from this.'

" It is, I humbly submit, the imperative duty of the governors of George Heriot's Hospital to adopt such regulations as may prevent any mischief of the kind now alluded to, from arising in the management of this institution—an institution of the greatest importance, and which we fondly hope has been, and is the means of great good to many individuals, and which ought to be a mighty instrument of social improvement, if administered in consistency with the constitution of human nature, in harmony with and in maintenance of that family life which is the genial soil of human virtue.

" Let us, the governors of this institution, be ever impressed with the solemn fact that the connection of parents and children is one which God has established, and which man cannot break without guilt and danger ; without deep injury to both parties, as well as to society. And, I sincerely hope it will be felt by the governors to be a sacred duty, to adopt and maintain such regulations regarding the boys educated here as may preserve inviolate the family tie, as shall keep alive in freshness and vigour the mutual love, and interest, and sympathy which should unite them with their fathers and mothers—their brothers and sisters—and that we shall feel that we are really betraying our trust, and violating the true intention of the venerable founder, if we shall order matters so that that sacred bond shall be virtually broken—that these boys shall become estranged from the homes, the habits, the interests, the sympathies of their parents : and that, by this means, we should inflict an injury on all parties, far greater than any benefit of another kind, which we have it in our power to confer.

" I will only add that it is of great importance that the officers in this institution, and all employed about its affairs, should be impressed with these truths (for such I persuade myself they are), and that they labour zealously and habitually to carry them out in regard to the inmates. To many of these young persons, they must stand in the place of father and mother—to all of them in some degree. How necessary they should carry a parental mind toward those children ! that they should feel that concern and interest in them, that watchful authority, that considerate kindness, that sympathy which may in some measure make up for the want of their natural parents. This is, no doubt, a somewhat difficult task ; it requires much love and great self-denial. To interest children and young people, to hinder their life hanging heavy upon them, to render them good, not by the lazy, absurd, and cruel system of forbidding everything to them, and taxing them with work to prevent them being troublesome, but by enabling them to use and enjoy everything—in short, by labouring to render them good by making them happy : this is an enterprise which demands great self-denial, and much patience ; but no other method will prove effectual ; and it has great reward. They who thus sow in tears, shall return rejoicing, bringing their sheaves with them." *

The sermon was published, with a preface, in which the preacher more fully explained his ideas on the subject of it, and suggested a change in the regulations of the hospital, which, after several years of opposition, has now been recognised as a wise and sound innovation, and carried into effect.

"It appears to me that the governors have in their hands a very simple remedy, and one which should hurt the prejudices of very few, and the consciences of none, while the ' will of the pious founder' would rather be obtempered by it than frustrated.† By all means let the fatherless boys, and the motherless boys also, remain inmates of the house, as they now are. I would go farther, and admit, that it might be expedient to retain in the same position those of the boys whose parents are

---

* The substance of this sermon is reprinted in the " Family and its Duties," No. I.

† The will designs the hospital for the maintenance of poor fatherless boys.

notoriously drunken, or otherwise immoral. But surely no evil could arise from permitting those of the boys who have parents —and very many of them have—who are sober, industrious, well-conditioned people, to go home every evening and lodge with their parents. They may receive from the funds of the hospital the same education, food, clothing, and all the other privileges to which they are now entitled ; and if the parents should grudge to furnish them a bed—for it is impossible to say how far the spirit of selfishness, nurtured by this eleemosynary system, may carry some congenial tempers—a sufficient sum may be paid them for lodging their own flesh. The better class of the parents, however, so far from regarding the change as a burden, would hail, as a valuable boon, any arrangement which afforded them daily opportunities of seeing their children and holding intercourse with them. Saying this, are we supposing more than that men and women are not generally destitute of natural affection—that the love of their offspring, which animates even the irrational creatures, is not wanting in the breasts of human beings?" *

* "The plan of boarding and educating young persons of either sex in large beneficiary establishments has latterly attracted much serious consideration in Edinburgh, which possesses a number of institutions of this nature. The more closely the working of these institutions has been examined, the less reason is there to be satisfied with the principle of seclusion inherent in their arrangements, and it is now a pretty general belief that it would be a blessing to the country if they were all abolished, and their funds appropriated to general purposes of education.

* * * * *

"Another matter demands consideration—the expense. Laying aside the initiatory expenses in building hospitals, and taking the mere cost of sustaining them, the outlay, even under the best management, is extravagant. The ordinary expenditure for Heriot's Hospital, including salaries for general management, was £10,748 for the year ending December 31, 1857—the number of boys in the hospital being 180. The annual cost per boy was therefore very nearly £60. The disbursements for Heriot's foundation schools, for the same period, amounted to £4323—the number of pupils attending these schools being 3022. The annual cost per pupil, therefore, was little more than £1 8s. 6d. Such, without going deeply into particulars, is the remarkable difference between the cost of hospitalising children and of simply educating them at school. It is not too much to say that, for every child reared in a hospital, you might give elementary instruction to thirty, or a liberal education to twenty, boys or girls. On turning to the account of general expenditure of the Merchant Maiden Hospital, you will see that for 96 girls the cost of each is on an average £40 per annum. I am confident, however, that in any part of the United States, the cost of hospitalising girls would be considerably above £40 or 200 dollars per head per annum. The shabby accommodation, the breakfast of oatmeal porridge, and the mean uniform garb of the Edinburgh hospital girls, would never be tolerated in America, where an annual cost of £80 or 400 dollars each would scarcely suffice to render a hospital popular or endurable."—*Letter from W. Chambers, Esq., to W. Wilson,* (*New York*) 1858.

The hospital system, as a whole, appeared to him unsound. He held that it was bad for body, mind, and morals.

"I long ago remarked" (he says in a letter to Mr. G. Combe in 1855) "depression, languor, and listlessness, as characteristics of hospital boys. . . . Those children want most of the things which tend to render children happy. They want the wild freedom which is so natural to the young, and *their affections are entirely unexercised.* Can a man in jail be happy? How, then, can a boy in jail be so ? No physical improvements can ever cure this. It is the cursed spot on the system which all the waters of improvement, feeding, ventilation, temperature, and all the rest—important as these are in themselves—can never wash out. . . . . At Heriot's Hospital the boys are fat and flabby, but not muscular, for they are much fed and little exercised."

At this time, and for the first six years of his Edinburgh life, he occupied a house in Lauriston Place. "I used to be a good deal at Lauriston Place," writes a member of a family who were amongst his most cherished friends, "about 1846. Dr. Lee was not such a public man then, and his home was full of happy children, whom he adored, and he used to sing to them and study their ways. He certainly was a most lovable man in private. A young lad, from America, Willie Duncan by name, boarded with them, and used to have private theatricals, or shows, which we all enjoyed.* . . . Dear Dr. Lee was a true friend and teacher to me, giving me books and directing my reading, and encouraging me to cultivate my mind and to *enlarge* it, and to be dutiful and womanly in my character. On one occasion at A., when

* In his diary Dr. Lee has written out, in verse, a kind of burlesque, "A Scene to amuse a Children's Party"—*Dramatis Personæ:* Queen Victoria; An Astrologer; Maids of Honour.

he was visiting us, and I had some sick-nursing to do, I remember his encouraging me by repeating the text, ' The Son of Man came not to be ministered unto, but to minister.' His visits to me were always charming." This lady has kept the following letter, written to her in 1846—a memento of a kindness and friendship which continued uninterrupted to the end :—

" MY DEAR I.,

" I am very sorry to hear from Mrs. Lee that you have been so unwell. I hope when you breathe the pure air of home you will soon be well again. I feared you had been working too hard. I am sorry to hear also that you will be disappointed this week in some sights you wished to see. But, my dear young friend, if you are enabled with patience to bear the disappointment—to take it as a part of the loving chastisement of God our Father, it will do you far more good, and will even give you far more pleasure than the things would have done which you have been prevented seeing. We have a great deal to learn before we are perfect and complete in all the will of God, and the giving up our own will in all things is the hardest lesson, but it is also the most valuable. May you learn it perfectly ; and then you will be perfectly happy, in whatever outward condition you may be. Let us pray that God would teach us thus to walk in the steps of his dear Son. If we are not seeking and attaining to this, all outward religion is vain and even delusive. We hope to have the pleasure of seeing you when you return. Make my very kind regards to your dear parents and Miss E——, and all the young ones.

" I am, my dear I.,

" Truly and affectionately yours,

" ROBERT LEE."

This summer he took a walking excursion through the Highlands with Mr. Smith (Fintry) and another younger friend. " I shall never forget," says Mr. Smith, " the light-hearted enthusiasm with which he yielded himself to the exhilarating influence of the scenery and air and

exercise.   He was full of buoyancy and wit and repartee.
At Fortwilliam we booked by the coach for Inverness,
and, having breakfasted in a leisurely way, we strolled to
take possession of the box-seats, which we had made a
point of securing, when, lo! we found ourselves fore-
stalled by no less a personage than the redoubted Dr.
Candlish, and with him Dr. Beith, of Stirling. Of course
we remonstrated against the *intrusion*, but at first to no
purpose ; and it was only on appealing to the civil powers
(in the coach-office) that we were restored to our status.
"Sorry to *depose* you," said our friend to Dr. C., as he
unwillingly dismounted. But I am happy to say that
the affair passed off good-humouredly, and with no worse
results to the two reverend Free doctors than their being
relegated to the dignity of a post-chaise to themselves."

In September, the Rev. Dr. Bennie, minister of Lady
Yester's Church, in Edinburgh, and one of the Deans of
the Chapel Royal, died. He was succeeded in Lady
Yester's by the Rev. John Caird, who in that Church
commenced his distinguished career as one of the most
eloquent of Scottish preachers.

Other changes consequent on Dr. Bennie's death had,
as we shall see, an important relation to Dr. Lee's future.

CHAPTER V.

CHAIR OF BIBLICAL CRITICISM.—CHURCH COURTS.— PRIVATE LIFE.

"We live in the midst of religious machinery. Many mechanics at piety, often only apprentices and slow to learn, are turning the various ecclesiastical mills, and the creak of the motion is thought 'the voice of God.'"—THEODORE PARKER, *Ten Sermons*, No. VIII.

THE Royal Commissioners, appointed in 1827 to inquire into the state of the Scottish universities, had recommended, among other beneficial measures, the institution of a chair of Biblical Criticism in the University of Edinburgh. The government of Lord Melbourne had, in 1841, resolved to carry out this recommendation, and to appoint the Rev. R. S. Candlish, minister of S. George's, Edinburgh, to the chair, which was to be endowed with a part of the revenues of the Chapel Royal. These revenues had hitherto been divided into three portions; and with the title of "Dean of the Chapel Royal of Holyrood," been bestowed on clergymen of eminence. The rapacious spoliations to which the ecclesiastical property of Scotland was exposed at and after the Reformation, had robbed the Church of every other distinction and emolument with which merit might be rewarded or energy stimulated. So niggardly, however, was the Liberal government, and so apprehensive of the jealous opposition of the dissenters, that it dared not venture to endow the new chair, except by

appropriating to it some of the funds connected with
the deaneries. The appointment of Mr. Candlish would
have taken place in 1841, had not Lord Aberdeen
induced the government to postpone it, in consequence
of the large share which that reverend gentleman had
taken in the ecclesiastical troubles of the time. He
had, in particular, broken one of the interdicts of the
Court of Session by preaching in the parish of Huntly ;
—no offence in itself, but a violation of the law of the
land, in the circumstances unhappily existing. Lord
Aberdeen forcibly pointed out the impropriety of nomi-
nating so keen a controversialist and partisan to be the
first professor of Biblical Criticism. "This reverend
gentleman," said his Lordship in his place in the House
of Lords, "this professor of Biblical Criticism, if dealt
with by the Court in the same way as any other person,
would be immediately sent to prison, where he would
have leisure to compose his first syllabus of Lectures."*
No other appointment had been suggested at the time ;
and Dr. Bennie had, as dean of the Chapel Royal, drawn
the revenue destined to endow the chair, until his death
in 1846. Now, however, the government of Lord John
Russell resolved to carry out the postponed intention of
the government of Lord Melbourne. Dr. Lee's friends

* "Ten Years' Conflict," chap. xiii.; "Hanna's Life of Chalmers," vol. iv. chap.
xiii. It must be explained that the majority of the Presbytery of Strathbogie
(within whose bounds Huntly lay) had proceeded with the settlement of
Mr. Edwards as minister of Marnoch—he having been "vetoed" by the
parishioners, and the Assembly having confirmed this (be it remembered,
illegal) "veto." The Presbytery acted in accordance with the law ; the
Assembly in defiance of it. For this offence the Assembly first suspended, and
then deposed, the seven ministers who formed the majority ; and sanctioned
Mr. Candlish and other members of the revolutionary party proceeding to
Strathbogie and preaching in the parishes there, as if they were legally vacant.
Against this invasion of their parishes the seven ministers had tried to protect
themselves by obtaining from the Court of Session an "interdict" prohibiting
these irregularities.

at once busied themselves in securing the appointment for him. There is no doubt that there was no clergyman of any mark in the Church better fitted for the office than he. His scholarship, though not profound, was exact; he had studied theology with thoughtful care; and his theological reading had been judicious and comprehensive. His mind, moreover, was inquisitively critical in its tone; and all his sympathies went out towards liberty of thought and rational progress in science. Higher qualifications than these were not to be found in the Church. The poverty of the Scottish Church; the lax and variable entrance examinations; and the absence of any sinecures or wealthy prizes among her offices, have operated disadvantageously against the learning of the clergy.* With the exception of Principal Campbell, (whose treatise on Miracles was translated into three continental languages)—and should we add, Dr. Macknight?—the Scottish Church had, since the revolution, produced few theologians notable either for great learning or original genius. The literary activity of the "moderate" era did not seek its outlet in theological research or dissertation; and the "evangelical" revival was not favourable to learning and culture. The standard of qualification for a theological chair was, thus, not a high one at the time of Dr. Lee's appointment. He did more than come up to it; and that it has since

* The sagacious eye of Dr. Chalmers saw this evil. In his evidence before the House of Commons' Committee on Sites, he says:—"It struck me that there was a vulgarizing process going on, by the alienation of cathedral property; and I endeavoured to point out what I thought a better direction for this property, and this was turning each cathedral institute into a theological seminary or college. I am very friendly to what may be called ecclesiastical sinecures, not that I mean that they should be sinecures, but that there should be a certain number of persons of learning maintained at leisure, and endowed for the purpose of contributing to theological literature."—HANNA'S *Life*, vol. iv., Appendix K.

that date been raised higher, is in no small degree owing to his own labours in the cause of theological education.

He writes in his diary : "Nov. 8, Sunday evening. I feel this an evening of peculiar solemnity. To-morrow, if spared, I am to have an interview with the Lord Advocate, when I shall know the result of all that has been said and done regarding the professorship. In the hand of God all things are safe, and they are truly blessed that trust in Him ; " and then follows an earnest prayer for the divine guidance and "the Spirit of *Love*." He was duly appointed to the professorship and conjoined deanery, and to the office of Her Majesty's chaplain, which also Dr. Bennie had held.* "I have no doubt," wrote Mr. Macaulay, who had used his strong influence in Dr. Lee's favour, "your important duties will be well performed, and that I shall always remember with satisfaction the share, small as it was, which I had in your appointment." In acknowledging the letter in which the Lord Advocate announces his appointment, Dr. Lee says (and the reference reveals his apprehension, as a professor, of that clerical interference with his liberties, of which he was to experience the full activity, as a minister) : "I take it for granted that no provision will be introduced into the constitution of the new professorship, which will expose the holder of it to any disqualifications, except those to which all other professors holding parishes may be made subject by the laws of the Church ; or which will recognise that jurisdiction of the Church courts over the

---

* There are six royal chaplains in Scotland. Formerly, when the Sovereign never required their services, they had a modest salary of 50*l.* a-year ; now, when the Queen resides annually in Scotland, the honour of the office seems to be considered sufficient remuneration.

universities, which all who advocate a repeal of the present test-law are so much concerned to deny."

He anticipated annoyance from a party in the Church opposed to pluralities. It had been forbidden by the General Assembly* to hold a professorship and a parochial charge, unless the two were in the same city. And there were many who were anxious to cancel even that exception, and to prohibit absolutely any union of offices.† His anticipations were realized. On various occasions the general question of pluralities was bandied about in the Church courts; and his tenure of his church and chair was covertly or openly attacked. In 1847 it was discussed both in the Edinburgh Presbytery and the Assembly. He writes to Mr. Paisley in reference to the former: "The debate in some hands, and these much more burdened with plurality than mine are likely ever to be, made it really a personal and most spiteful attack on me. I shall not be sorry to have it discussed in the Assembly, where I predict we shall have the best of the argument, whatever we may have in the voting." In the Assembly there was a long debate, virtually ending in nothing. In 1852 the old subject was revived again; and in the course of a somewhat personal debate, one of Dr.

---

* Act vi. of Assembly 1817.

† "Yet pluralities exist. In the Church one or two remain, the last memorials of palmier times; but in the faculties of law and medicine they are rife. There are professors in our universities who work as hard in the Parliament House as any minister in his parish. There are surgeons and physicians who hold academic seats with distinguished honour, and yet manage an enormous practice. Neither the university nor the city complains; neither the lecture-room nor the sick-room is neglected. If lawyers and doctors can do this, why should not ministers? Is their work necessarily heavier? Are their energies necessarily less? Why, in short, should not the same rule be applied to all the faculties? But the Church of Scotland has ever been a self-denying community. It might have had episcopal revenues, and it refused them. It might have had seats in Parliament, but it declined them. It had professorships and principalities, and it threw them away."—CUNNINGHAM's *Church History*, vol. ii., p. 615.

Lee's co-presbyters, with what must be called unwarrantable rudeness and vulgarity of feeling, adverted to the income which he was believed to derive from his two offices.

Dr. Lee rose, and with warmth and skill, argued for the connection of academic chairs with parochial charges, as, in reality, beneficial to the Church. "If his professional income," he added, "was much more than it was, he would feel no shame in accepting it, for he had been neither sluggish nor inefficient in the discharge of his duties; and in his conscience, and before God, he could declare that the professorship which he had the honour to hold had never proved any impediment to the discharge of his ministerial functions." The debate ended in the question of pluralities being consigned, as it had been before, to that vague limbo, a committee ;— in whose custody it is to be presumed it still remains, as it has not been much heard of since 1852.

Dr. Lee was installed on 30th January, 1847, but did not lecture till the session of 1847-8. What follows is from his diary.

"This is one of the most important events of my life. One in which I have seen most distinctly the good Providence of God, and one certainly which will involve the greatest amount of responsibility. How great the effect may be on the condition of the Church of Scotland by the efficient occupying of such a chair, it is impossible to say, for to a great extent, it affects the sentiments of the clergy in the first place, and through them of the whole people.

"O God, Father of lights, fountain of all wisdom and all grace, I humbly implore thy mercy and grace to forgive my manifold offences and all my unworthiness, and to fill me with the gifts and graces of thy good Spirit. Especially, O Lord, I beseech thee to confer upon me the gifts of wisdom and prudence, that I may avoid all occasions of unnecessary offence, and may discern what my duty is, and how I may best perform it.

And do thou give me a spirit of love, and oh, Lord, that I may truly seek the good and honour of all around me, and may rejoice in their welfare and reputation. Endow me also, Almighty God, with the spirit of power, that I may effectually and successfully instruct others in the true knowledge and understanding of thy holy word. O Lord, do thou teach me, and I shall be taught myself, and qualified also to instruct others. May thy grace be sufficient for me, O Lord, and may thy strength be made perfect in my weakness, through Jesus Christ our Lord. Amen."

On November 11th, he writes as follows :—

"This is my forty-third birthday, and it is to me probably the most important day of my life, as on it I propose commencing my duties as Professor of Biblical Criticism, &c. All men, no doubt, have, but it seems to me as if I had, above all men, reason to praise and bless God Almighty, for his mercy and loving-kindness. For I cannot look back on my past life without acknowledging that He hath loaded me with his benefits. And when I reflect on my unworthiness and sinfulness, I am humbled in the dust before God, my Heavenly Father. Unless I quite deceive myself, I am conscious of a desire to glorify God, who has redeemed me with the precious blood of Jesus Christ his Son, so that I might enjoy the liberty of doing His holy will in my body and spirit. And in humble faith in His promise, I would now implore of Him to baptize me with His good Spirit, that I may be filled with wisdom, love, and power ; and may obtain a victory over all my corruptions and enemies within and without, and may prove the *perfect* will of God.

"I remember with thankfulness, on this day, my dear, pious, benevolent, and excellent parents. If I may not pray for it, I may yet hope in God, that they may sleep with the saints, whose dust is precious in the sight of the Lord, and may obtain a joyful and blessed resurrection. I remember in like manner my dear brother Anthony, who lived the life and died the death of the righteous. I remember all my departed friends. And I humbly pray that God, my loving Father in heaven, would pardon all my sins against them.

"I bless God that I am not alone and desolate in the midst of the earth ; having the most affectionate and prudent of wives, and one who perfectly sympathizes with me in all good things ;

and having children who are now, and promise to be yet more,
a comfort to us.   Also, for our dear adopted mother, Miss
Napier, who loves us, and whom we love, with the strongest
affection : and for all our friends, and all our other mercies.
Bless the Lord, O my soul!

"I am not forgetful of the dark and cloudy day.   Whether or
not I improve it, the thought of it is habitually present with
me.   But I fear no evil, for Thou art with me.   I endeavour to
remember that death as well as life is the property of the
children of God; and that tribulation and distress shall not
separate them from the love of God in Christ Jesus our Lord.

"Let me therefore not cast away my confidence, which hath
great recompense of reward.   In Thee, O Lord, have I trusted ;
let me never be confounded.

"Let me remember these things :—

"1. To be more earnest and frequent in prayer.

"2. To read the Scriptures with a view to edification.

"3. To be slow to speak, and slow to wrath.

"4. To judge not ; and to speak evil of no man.

"5. To labour with the students, to free them from superstition, fanaticism, and bigotry ; and to instil into their minds, as I
may be enabled, principles of true wisdom, piety, and charity.

"O God, give me grace ; that what I intend piously, I may
perform effectually, to the honour of Thy name, through Jesus
Christ our Lord.   Amen."

"I got through my trial," he writes in the evening,
after delivering his inaugural lecture, "I hope so as
to create, at least, a favourable impression.   I do not
attribute much importance to the compliments and kind
expressions of friends ; but the terror of the undertaking
is past—now let me work with fear and trembling, for
God worketh," &c.

Again, on the 19th November, "I have finished my
first week's work.   I am thankful to find the matter not
so formidable as I had pictured to myself.   Finding how
little some of the students know, I feel the greater cou-

fidence in my own resources. May God give me grace to be faithful, and wise, and energetic in this work which I am called to do."

In his inaugural lecture, he defines the business of his class as embracing Criticism, Hermeneutics, and Biblical Antiquities; and proceeds to enforce, especially, the importance of accurate textual criticism, as the basis of all sound theology.

Adverting to the Rabbinical dogma that every word and letter of the Scriptures was a gift of God, and dictated by the Holy Spirit, and the congenial inference that what had been thus supernaturally given must be supernaturally preserved and transmitted, he says—

"These were the views with which the great body of Churchmen were actuated, in the second and third centuries, and, indeed, through the whole patristic period, down to the time of Gregory the Great. These sentiments prompted them to misrepresent the enlightened diligence of Origen, the father of Biblical Criticism; who, like most men who are before their age, and who labour to make things in the Church better than they found them, was, during his whole laborious life, a special mark of theologic hate and misrepresentation. Strange to say, the seventeenth and even the eighteenth century found the Church no wiser in this respect. With this prejudice, all the earlier editors, both of the New Testament and of the Old, had to contend in their attempts to improve the received text. In this particular the Protestants were generally not a whit more enlightened than the Catholics. Robert Stephens, who was compelled by the bigotry of the Papists to flee from Paris on account of his audacity in presuming to correct the text of the Latin Vulgate, was the victim of the same blind zeal which actuated the Protestants in their attacks on Mill and Wetstein, at a later period. So strong, in fact, was the conviction in the minds of Protestants generally that the Jewish dogma was undoubtedly true, that, down to near the conclusion of the last century, it was found to be impossible to introduce into the printed text of the New Testament, even those alterations, in favour of which all MSS. of any value, as well as the ancient versions concurred; or to remove from the text even those clauses, in support of which there existed no MS. authority whatever. And, even at this day, there are not wanting men who prefer their own opinions to truth in such a degree that they are not ashamed to maintain the genuineness of certain passages, in defence of which little else can be alleged than that they seem to prove doctrines which they regard as true, and in support of which they are anxious to find as many testimonies as they can in the Holy Scriptures. . . . . . .

"The injudicious zeal of the great body of Churchmen, both in ancient and modern times, affords a lesson of the greatest importance to their successors; a warning by which we should be studious to profit. There are few greater temptations to the presumption and self-confidence of men than the identifying *objective* Christianity with Christianity as it may exist *subjectively* in themselves: feeling confident that their views, on all points, must be infallibly correct; and that anyone labours to overturn the Gospel who opposes any of their cherished opinions respecting it. Many others besides Whitby, yea thousands of sincere and earnest Christians, both in the ancient Church and in modern times, were confident that the stability of the Christian faith would be utterly destroyed if the opinion were admitted that the text, whether of the Old or the New Testament, did not exist in immaculate purity. This opinion is now, however, an admitted, an indisputable truth: and yet Christianity is not subverted; nay, none of its doctrines, none of its precepts, none of its ordinances, are sensibly affected in consequence. In no line of inquiry is it more necessary than in the different departments of theological study, to refuse being so alarmed by the supposed consequences of certain doctrines, if admitted, as not to allow ourselves to inquire, in *the first place*, whether or not those doctrines be true. In this, as in all the other departments of study, *truth* must be our first object; and that which is true will always, in the end, vindicate itself as that which alone is safe. . . . . ."

Going on to speak of Interpretation, he says :—

"Every student of theology should master those hermeneutical principles which ought to guide him through various passages which he must constantly encounter, and ignorant of which principles, he is as unfurnished with the instruments of his art as a physician would be who commenced medical practice without any theory of pathology or of therapeutics, and who treated every particular case as it occurred *empirically.* The practice of such a man could be only one heap of contradictions. And the labours of such a preacher can only perplex and confound his hearers.

"Before proceeding to the work of exhibiting the sense of Holy Scripture, with the view of assisting those who are less favourably circumstanced for ascertaining it than we are, it becomes us to have investigated various questions which must be settled, before systematic and consistent interpretation can proceed :—such, for instance, as the relation in which the old dispensation and its Scriptures stand to the new? What, among the various contents of both Testaments, are to be regarded as incidental, and what we should consider as Divine teaching, for the sake of which the former was introduced? On what subjects we ought to recur to such a book as the Bible for information? whether its statements regarding physics, for example, such as cosmogony, astronomy, natural history, theology, are to be understood by us as the dictates of the Spirit of God, or only as made in accommodation to the popular opinions prevailing in the times of the writers, whether those opinions were true or false? On these, and many other kindred questions, it is indispensable that the expositor of Holy Scripture, (and every preacher of the Gospel is an expositor of Holy Scripture, and must be, if his preaching be anything better than vapid declamation), must have arrived at some satisfactory conclusion. . . .

"If we would appreciate the spirit in which the apostles of our Lord addressed the ancient Romans and Greeks, we must have made ourselves familiar with the mental and moral condition of those great peoples, when the apostles addressed them; and this can be done only by a diligent and critical study of those great works which themselves produced, and in which they have drawn for us their own spiritual portraits. How much illustration, for example, have the works of Plato already afforded to innumerable passages in the New Testament, particularly in the writings of S. John; and I am persuaded that the productions of that remarkable man, who is indeed the type rather of the Oriental than of the European mind (which latter his great disciple, the Stagirite more truly represents), would furnish still an abundant harvest to any qualified person who should seriously set himself to study them with this view. Indeed, without competent classical scholarship the work of sacred interpretation cannot be successfully carried on. It affords the very rudiments of this kind of knowledge ; and this, irrespective of the fact that the New Testament itself is written in Greek ; and a very large proportion of what is worthy of being read regarding the criticism and interpretation of it exists in the Latin language.

"Every conscientious person among you (and I hope you are all such) would shrink from being the instrument of distorting the rays of divine truth. I have no doubt you are sincerely desirous of conveying its lessons to men in the true spirit in which they were intended to be received. But the qualification to do so is neither an instinct nor an inspiration. It is the result of laborious study, of well directed labour, accompanied with that purifying and enlightening grace, which the Father of Lights has promised to humble and faithful hearts. Let us, therefore, gird up ourselves for this important work. Let us labour to strip ourselves, as much as may be, of those prepossessions and prejudices, with which education, common opinion, authority, worldly interest, may warp our minds and let us, in the spirit of faith and love, look up to God with this desire stronger than all within us, that we may be enabled truly to know what He hath revealed, that so we may be qualified to prove channels of His truth, and instruments of His mercy to our fellow-men.

" Which of you would not shrink from becoming, through his own ignorance, sloth, or worldly passions, the means of increasing, in any degree, that spirit of contention, rancour, and uncharitableness, which is so palpably opposed to the true spirit of the Gospel, and by which the Christian Church among us has been brought to the very verge of ruin, and Christianity itself, at least in its highest form, ἡ ἀγάπη συντέλεια τῆς ἐντολῆς, is in danger of perishing from the earth ? In proportion as you are enabled to enter into the true scope and spirit of the New Testament, you will be the less capable of fomenting evils on which the Head of the Church cannot look but with displeasure, which scandalize the weak and wavering, and grieve all truly Christian hearts. For my part, I can see no hope of any reconcilement among Christians, till the New Testament shall become the *bonâ fide* text-book, from which all parties shall be content *immediately* to draw their theology. In that case, a general agreement is conceivable, and would be possible, which now it is not, when each sect makes its own system, written or unwritten in creeds, its hermeneutical code. In such a state of things agreement is hopeless—it is inconceivable. . . . .

" I am resolved, in the strength of divine grace, to spare no pains or labour in discharging, to the best of my moderate abilities, the trust I have received. And however I may fail in the opinion of any of you (for that I shall not realize my own ideal I am well prepared to expect), I hope and pray that God may preserve both you, gentlemen, and me, from failing through want of the will to do well, and from erring through lack of love of the truth. In faith, therefore of his promise, ' Who followeth *me* shall not walk in darkness,' let us lift up our hearts unto God, praying that he would cleanse and enlighten our minds, and make them receptive of His spirit, in all truth, holiness, and power, to the glory of His name, through Jesus Christ our Lord."

Thus he started on his career as professor—a career peculiarly congenial to him, and which he regarded as his chief avenue of practical usefulness. In accompanying him to this point, we have, however, passed over some events in this year, 1847, to which we must now look back.

One fact in the history of Scotch dissent, giving rise to a new body and a new name, is passed over by Dr. Lee, as far as can be traced, in total silence. In May the Secession and the Relief bodies coalesced into one aggregate, and assumed the name of United Presbyterians, a title vulgarly shortened in common parlance into U. P.*

* The Secession Kirk originated in 1773, when, aggrieved at high-handed patronage, Ebenezer Erskine and three other ministers seceded from the

A rather noteworthy fact in the political annals of Scotland he comments on however with some force. "July 30, 1847. To-day the electors of Edinburgh disgraced themselves by electing Mr. C. Cowan, a person whom nobody knows about, instead of Mr. Macaulay, one of the first statesmen and writers of the age. Such is the mutability of popular favour, and the ingratitude of masses of men. Whisky-sellers were Mr. Cowan's chief supporters ; then temperance men, free churchmen, and voluntaries, tories and ultra-radicals composed this unholy alliance." *

He appears once or twice in the Church courts during this year, steadily advocating the liberal principles to which he was becoming more and more attached. The only exception to this is at a meeting of Presbytery near the end of the year, when the question of Jewish Disabilities was discussed. Dr. Muir had at a previous meeting been arguing, with all the impracticable rigidity of evangelical intolerance, that it was the duty of the British constitution to "maintain, acknowledge, and defend the Christian religion according to the evangelical peculiarities of it ; in the declaration of the doctrine of the glorious Trinity ; in devout acknowledgment of Christ as God, and of His precious sacrifice." Dr. Lee, although not probably swayed by this exposition of principles, yet announced

National Church. In 1747 the new body split into two (on the question of the burgess oath), the Burghers and Anti-Burghers. These again threw off two lesser sects, the Old-Light Burghers, and the Old-Light Anti-Burghers. The Burghers and Anti-Burghers came together again in 1820. The Relief sect originated in 1752, on the deposition of the Rev. Thomas Gillespie, and, as its name suggests, was the result of oppressive exercise of patronage. The U. P. body formed from this union has adopted voluntaryism as its distinctive principle. It numbers, in Scotland, about 480 congregations.

* Mr. Macaulay, writing to Dr. Lee in 1849, says, "I have every reason to be grateful to your fellow-citizens. If they had not dismissed me to my library, I should have been unable to complete my two volumes till 1850."

that, " though considerably liberal upon many points, he thought the Jewish Disabilities Bill warranted neither by justice nor policy," and he went away before a vote could be taken. No vote was necessary, as Dr. Barclay found no seconder to his motion, " That in the opinion of this presbytery no British subject ought to suffer either forfeiture or abridgement of his civil rights on account of his religious opinions, and that the civil disabilities at present affecting Jews being unnecessary, impolitic, and unjust, ought to be removed." *

On other occasions, however, Dr. Lee was staunch and consistent.

The question of running railway trains on the Sunday was at the time engrossing much attention.

In 'Scotland the Lord's Day has generally been regarded in the light of the Jewish Sabbath. And while individuals have commonly been lax enough in their interpretation of the clause of the Jewish law, " Thou shalt do no manner of work therein," and have required their servants to serve them on the Sunday as on other days, public companies have been always much vilified if they attempted to serve the public on that day, even to a small extent. No one could value more highly than Dr. Lee the rest and sanctity of the Lord's Day as consecrated by immemorial Christian usage; but no one could hold more cheaply the Pharisaic formalism which prided itself on the strictness of its Sabbath-keeping, and neglected the weightier matters of the law. He equally disliked the false importance ascribed to the outward observance of the fourth commandment, and the essentially immoral policy which, finding that certain persons

* *Scotsman*, Dec. 22, 1847.

or companies would not keep the letter of that commandment in the Puritanic way from principle, essayed to make them do it by force. He accordingly always protested against enactments in favour of " Sabbath Observance," and against the Judaism which denounced Sunday trains, or the opening of gardens or galleries on the first day of the week, as violations of the eternal behests of the moral law. Dr. Muir had a committee on Sabbath Observance, of which he was perpetual convener, and brought up, in its name, wonderful reports to the General Assembly. In these he charged against divers forms of " Sabbath desecration," and specially against Sunday trains, in a style with which it must have been difficult for any intelligent man, unless he were a Jew, to agree. The Sabbath question has cropped up again and again, in many a Presbytery and Assembly ; but it never was more keenly canvassed than in 1847. The great mass of the clergy jumped with Dr. Muir. A very few, among whom the late Dr. Anderson of Newburgh, and Mr. Cochrane, minister of Cupar, deserve honour for manly frankness of speech, took a similar wise and Christian view of the relation of the fourth commandment to Sunday trains, to that taken by Dr. Lee. In opposition to Dr. Muir's denunciations of these impious vehicles,* he insisted that, as the railway companies had practically usurped control of the usual means of conveyance, they were bound to afford the public opportunities of travelling on Sunday. Whether these were to be used or not, was for the conscience of the public to decide. " The question came to this," he said, in the Assembly,

* See Report of General Assembly's Committee on Sabbath Observance 1847.

"whether he was to determine on his own conscience, and under the guidance of the Word of God, if he should travel on a Sunday or not, or whether that question should be left to be determined by a set of railway directors, of whom he knew nothing, who might or might not be religious and enlightened men, and who were to decide whether his errand was or was not one of necessity and mercy. He would ask the members, as reasonable men, whether this was a power which was to be entrusted to any body of men whatever. . . . . . If no manner of work was to be done on the Sunday, how could they excuse the large amount that was done in every household?　If works of mercy were not forbidden, why should they, of their own accord, put the rest of the one day in seven above the works of mercy?"

Eighteen elders voted with him in opposition to the Jewish view of the question; but only three ministers were found bold enough to go along with them. "Alas, poor Robert Lee!" wrote one divine to another, after the debate—into what latitudinarian seas was this rebellious brother drifting!

We find him at the Presbytery advocating the system of "denominational grants," in aid of education, which was brought forward by the Government in the session of 1847. He moved that the Presbytery should express its approval of the government scheme, being "deeply impressed with the importance of connecting moral and religious instruction with secular education." In supporting his motion, he said:—

"I am happy to think that after the vote—the triumphant vote of the House of Commons last Thursday* (372 to 47), the great

* 21st April 1847.

question of National Education may be regarded for the present as settled in the affirmative. This is a result, sir, which every enlightened lover of his country must rejoice in. For, in opposition to this measure I think little can be heard but the angry voices of religious bigotry or sectarian jealousy, sensitively alive to the supposed interests of little factions, but dead to the great evils which afflict society in this country.

" There are men who tell us indeed that the people are sufficiently educated already; that voluntary exertions at least are sufficient to overtake all that is necessary. It surely requires no little hardihood to venture on such a statement in the face of the facts that out of 132,249 marriages performed in England in 1844, 42,912 men and 65,073 women could not write their names ; and that a very large proportion of prisoners in a gaol in England were found who were ignorant of the name of the reigning sovereign, or even of the Saviour of mankind. We are not so bad in Scotland as this comes to, but I will assert that in spite of our parish schools, and all other additional means, there exists in this country also, especially in the manufacturing districts, an amount of ignorance which is astonishing, not to say deplorable. I say this not from any one's report, but from my personal knowledge. Having had two large manufacturing parishes under my ministerial charge, I can vouch for the facts, which astonished myself and every person to whom I mentioned them. Let us remember the *Mormonites* a few years ago. In the spring of 1842, the apostles of Mormonism appeared in the west of Scotland, and many families are now expiating their folly on the wilds of south-western America. This is a parallel to the mobs in Kent, who received Thom as the Messiah.

" I need not attempt to trace the connection of ignorance with popular discontent, tumult, and crime. That has been done by many writers, and it has been done in the late debate on this question by that great master of historical wisdom, Mr. Macaulay, with a breadth, a fulness of proof and illustration which in my mind leaves scepticism on this point inexcusable and even incomprehensible. I need not in this place labour to prove that it is the duty of the State to educate the people. An ecclesiastical system is founded on that idea. Nor need I attempt to show that that power which is ordained of God to protect our lives, properties, and reputation, reaches its end more legitimately, as well as more effectually, by cutting off the sources of crime than by punishing crime ; that man has a strange notion of the functions of government, who holds that the State may not teach the people their duties, and yet should punish them for transgressing them."

I find in one of his note-books, another short speech —given evidently at some public dinner—but which I have been unable to trace to an exact date. It must, however, I conclude, have been spoken about this period ; and it is inserted as a specimen of his after-dinner oratory, a species of discourse to which he, like all wise men, had no favour :—

"The toast I have been requested to give contains a sentiment of much importance. 'Religious Progress hand in hand with Religious Liberty.'

"Religious liberty has been much discussed since the days of Jeremy Taylor and of Locke. I doubt if even now it is well understood. Everybody, indeed, now-a-days, condemns religious persecution, or rather irreligious persecution on account of men's religious opinions ; all the world are unanimous in saying that to incarcerate or burn a person because he does not believe as we do, is monstrous. We should be glad the world has come so far as to acknowledge this. And we may wonder that it should have been so long in perceiving that a pain of the body has no connection with a conviction of the mind ; and that the most any bodily suffering could do, was to make the subject of it, not a believer, but a hypocrite—could make him profess with his mouth, but not believe in his heart.

"But most Christians still appear not to apprehend this, that uncharitable censuring and judging of each other, calling all heretics and enemies of God who don't think of God as we do, denying that they are Christians who are not Christians after our fashion,—that this spirit of hatred, and malice, and uncharitableness, is as much persecution, as hateful, and as cruel, as the burnings and tortures of our less refined forefathers were. In this point of view we may very reasonably desire the advance of religious liberty.

" The advancement of this is essential to true religious progress. If there be liberty to speak, men will be encouraged to speak what they think, and to think for themselves. But when they dare not speak, they soon lose the liberty of thought. Thought, like air, grows putrid by confinement. What we want at present is the exposition of men's honest thoughts; this would help us hugely.

" None will doubt that religious progress is possible, and, therefore, desirable, who consider how few of the genuine fruits of Christianity appear in Christian countries in the abundance they ought. Our *parties* prove the same thing. There are always parties and sects in sciences till the true principles of them are generally understood. Only when men shall come to see that Christianity is neither a set of dogmas, nor an external regimen or ritual; but a set of rules of life founded on and animated with the purest and strongest motives ; that its object is to make us not hate each other, but love each other ; to pity and help, and not to curse and vilify those whom we think in error, and to manifest our own superiority rather by good deeds and kindly tempers than by supercilious conduct and pharisaic speeches,—in short, sir, when people shall go back to the beginning, and learn what their religion is from the precepts and example of Jesus Christ, casting their doctors over-board, who, under pretence of explaining His words, have so often contradicted them, only then will they come to a better understanding with each other, and make that progress which is truly valuable—progress in real wisdom and substantial goodness."

The years 1848 and 1849 seem to have been, outwardly, uneventful in his life. I have discovered hardly any of his correspondence of that period ; and the entries in his diary are few and far between. There is no entry, for instance, from 31st March to 9th November, 1848 ; and there are only three between that and August, 1849. He seems to have been working steadily in his church, parish, and professorship. He frequently preached, it is true, an old Campsie sermon ; throwing in, however, new thoughts and illustrations as he spoke, for it never was his habit to adhere closely to what he had written. In his parish he was diligent in visitation. It was what Dr. Chalmers called "a very beautiful field"—that is to say, one of the most degraded quarters of Edinburgh, where want and vice cohabit in a squalor rarely seen in any other European capital. It is no disparagement to Dr. Lee to say that he was not very well fitted to deal with the worst aspects of such a parish. There are diversities of gifts; and his gift was not that tact and force which endow some men, like George Whitefield, and some women, like Elizabeth Fry, with an almost magical influence over the ignorant and outcast. His nature was too sensitive to carry him, without a certain shrinking, through the filth and brutality of the Cowgate wynds; and the people, with whom one has to do in these haunts, are quick to discern and resent any symptom of repugnance—merely physical though it may be—on the part of a visitor. Dr. Lee never gained the hold over the Cowgate that Dr. Guthrie had. Still he went through his parish dutifully; though the duty was to him a very different one from what it had been in rural Campsie. To all the wants of his congregation, as distinct from his parish, he was sedulously attentive; and soon gained no ordinary share of their love and reverence.

He devoted much time and study to the duties of his chair; and there was no work he loved better than this. "I feel my duties pleasant, and I hope useful," he says in a letter to Mr. Paisley in February, 1848. "I think my students *cannot* preach many things which are commonly proclaimed as gospel. You may observe that Mr. Stevenson of Leith has given notice of a motion regarding the Biblical Criticism class, with the view of rendering it imperative."* Again : "My students and myself have the best possible understanding ; and this has gone on increasing. I pray that God's blessing may rest upon them, and that every one of them may prove a burning and a shining light in his generation ; and may they be to me, the unworthiest of the servants of God, a crown of joy in the day of Christ."—(*Diary.*) He did not find the attention he gave to his students conflict with that which was due to his parishioners. "At no time, I think," he says, after beginning a new Session, "have I done so much ministerial work (within the same number of days), as during the ten days since the Session commenced." One often finds that when there is most to do, one works at a higher pressure, and does most.

"I resolve this year," he writes in 1846, "to avoid buying books as much as may be consistent with duty and the improvement of my mind." It is a resolution often repeated, and yet again and again broken. Though by no means so ubiquitous and omnivorous in his seeking and acquiring as his namesake, the Principal,† he still suffered from the restless acquisitiveness of the book-hunter. "Now that I have access to the College Library," he says on another occasion, after blaming himself for "the enormous folly" of a heavy outlay on books—"and my room is full, I hope I shall be able quite to lay aside so destructive a folly." "How much money is it prudent in me to spend in books ?" he asks in his diary again,

---

* This was afterwards done, and attendance on that class required of theological students as part of their regular curriculum. A chair of Biblical Criticism now exists in each of the Scottish Universities, to the great advantage of the Church.

† Sketched with affectionate fidelity in the "Book Hunter" of Mr. Hill Burton—himself an erudite and skilful Nimrod in the same wide field.

and gives himself the very indefinite reply :—" If any
book is wanted, it should be bought, provided the price
is not extravagant, and it cannot be kept out from the
University Library." The struggle against the bookshops
is recorded in the diary with an amusing earnestness. In
December, 1847, he writes, " I am amazed to discover
that since the beginning of August I have spent 20*l*. on
books alone. This is my great expense. I am sufficiently
saving and prudent in everything else. But this folly
must not, and by the grace of God shall not, be repeated.
There is no reason why I should heap up books . . . .
Too much has also been expended in wine ; a considerable folly also, inasmuch as no man knows what shall be
on the morrow, and this looks like making provision for
the flesh to fulfil its lusts." Again : " My resolution
against buying of books I have rigidly kept so far as this
year has yet gone "—5th February, 1848. " Yet herein
am I not justified ; neither do I feel confident that I may
not again fall into the same weakness, or perhaps some
other that is less excusable."   His objection to book-buying was founded on a serious consideration of the real
evil of the tendencies which it gratified. " Few follies,"
he says, " are greater than that of book-buying.   I
know no weakness of which so many, otherwise sensible,
men are guilty. It is a species of avarice or covetousness, and arises from the same causes, and is covered
over with the same disguise, as the more vulgar avarice
of money. The books are desired, in the first instance,
as means of knowledge ; as money is, in the first place,
coveted, because of the things which money can buy.
But gradually, because of this close association of money
with these objects, the money *itself* gradually becomes

an object of distinct regard and appetency, and this is covetousness in its grossest form. So do *books;* and by a like association of ideas ; because themselves objects of covetousness,—*to have them,* satisfies the collector, for that he ever can or will *read* them, is what we cannot obviously suppose : as instead of doing so, his thoughts and time are taken up in hunting after more. Of all the books in his library, a bookseller's catalogue is to him the most interesting and engrossing. Surely this is the folly of wisdom, or the ignorance of knowledge : it is to mistake the means for the end."

"Among the best gifts which God gives us in this world, is the love of those who love Him and are loved by Him. This I and my family enjoy in an eminent degree in the warm attachment of our most dear friend Miss Napier."—(*Diary.*)

This name often occurs in his home records for several years, and among his papers I find multitudes of notes and letters from the old lady to him, her "dear son," as she calls him. There is a vein of fine, tender-hearted, delicate romance, one might almost call it, in the affection she pours forth on him and his. There was in her, too, a constant open-handed kindness, thoughtful and prompt, a little wilful perhaps in its determination to express itself in its own ways ; and withal, a cheerful practical piety, always beautiful, specially in old age.

Dr. Lee had found this friend after he came to Edinburgh. She was at first attracted to him by his preaching, then by his character, and by that capacity in him to meet the affection that she felt, which rivets love. She was descended from the chivalrous old family of Napier of Merchistoun, whose watchword, " Ready, aye ready," has been made good on many a field of fame. She had the keen intellect, the warm heart, and the strong will which are thought to mark the members of her ancient house.

"To-day Miss Napier, who is indeed a mother to us, put into my hands 50*l.* for one of the children. I am ashamed of so great kindness; but I must take it or offend her." (*Diary*, 29 Nov. 1847). Entries like this occur from time to time. She seems to have adopted, as it were, him and his family, and found her chief pleasure in their intercourse, and in loading them with kindnesses. Beautiful as Dr. Lee's relations to his own family circle were, this tender friendship and confidence add a ray to these of kindly light shining from without, and mingling lovingly with the brightness of his own fireside.

His reading in 1848 and '49 seems to have turned very much to the subject of the Westminster Assembly and its Confession of Faith and Directory for Public Worship. He studied the history of them minutely, and has entered, for reference and after-use, careful abstracts and notes of his reading in his commonplace-book. Among the books he comments on, are Aiton's Life of Henderson, the appendix to which contains the celebrated correspondence between Henderson and Charles I.; Rutherford's Lex Rex; Baillie's Letters; Rapin's History; Neal's History of the Puritans; Hume's History; Walker's Sufferings of the Clergy; Nichol's Arminianism; Records of the Kirk; Whitelocke's Memorials; Milton's Tractates; besides pamphlets and minor works, bearing on the ecclesiastical affairs of the 17th century. Some of his comments are interesting enough, but we can extract but a few.

"The great idol of the *Scotch* Presbyterians especially was *uniformity*, not *unity*, for they would neither acknowledge nor tolerate any that differed from them in Kirk government . . . . They attached an exaggerated, not to say absurd, importance to external arrangements . . . . Their blind attachment to the intended uniformity is a remarkable instance of a national monomania.

"The Covenanters—a term which describes the Church of Scotland at this period—were a politico-religious party. Acting under the conviction that the kingdom of Christ is a kingdom of this world, they were necessarily led to identify politics with religion, and their discussing politics in the pulpit was a necessary inference from that opinion; an obvious duty in those who regarded the nation and the Church as one subject, viewed in two different relations. The consequence of this confounding these two elements should have opened the eyes of these zealous men to its true character. Instead of spiritualizing politics, it secularized religion. It involved the ministers of the Gospel in unholy intrigues; led them to look too much to these worldly causes, to look beyond which it was their business to warn their hearers; and it tempted them in preaching to exceed their commission, publishing their own views (generally narrow and often erroneous) of temporal politics, thus prostituting their power and desecrating their office. Though the ministers themselves were slow to discern the danger of that practice so flattering to their vanity and unworthier passions—of praying and preaching against their enemies—the people (there is every reason to believe,) were not equally obtuse. And the ministers paid the penalty of their presumption, in the gradually lessened esteem of the people, who, having the New Testament in their hands, could not fail to remark that it breathed the very opposite spirit to that exhibited by those who expounded it to them.

" It is wonderful, when the Covenanters were so sensitive as to the breaking of the Covenant in so many other respects, their consciences were not wounded at all by that most glaring violation of it, viz., their not defending the king with all their power, venturing their estates, lives, &c., in his defence. Many men, and bodies of men generally have a squinting conscience, a microscopic conscience, not able to perceive large objects, but grossly enlarging the small.

" As bearing upon the true meaning of the 23rd and 31st chapters of the Confession of Faith, the sense in which these chapters were understood by the Westminster Assembly, from which they emanated, and by the Church of Scotland, whose commissioners assisted in drawing up these propositions and approved of them, it is very important to observe that that same General Assembly of the Scottish Church which gave the Confession of Faith that public approval and ratification by which it became, from that period, the symbol and standard of the Church, has distinctly and emphatically entered its protest against toleration of any but Presbyterian worship and government, and has solemnly declared *this* is its faith,—that the civil magistrate may, and ought to, persecute all who cannot acquiesce in this form of Church regimen. S. Thomas Aquinas himself is not more clear on this point than the General Assembly of 1647.* It is fortunate for the interests of truth that their deliverance on the 111 propositions embodies their sentiments on this important point with a clearness which admits of no evasion. When these men have been at such pains to hinder their sentiments being mistaken, can we but wonder at the temerity of those who now presume to deny that such were the sentiments held by the Church of Scotland in the 17th century, or (what is little less amazing) who affect to doubt whether they were or not ?

" The Westminster Assembly is another instance of the futility of attempts to secure unity of the Church by insisting on uniformity of creed and ritual. Not only have all such attempts hitherto proved utterly futile, but they have, without exception, been attended with the most deplorable consequences; involving the stronger party in the guilt of persecution and oppression, and of depriving others of those very rights of conscience, which they so clamorously demanded on their own behalf : and tempting the weaker party to elevate minuter points of doctrine and ecclesiastical polity to an importance which the party itself would never have attached to them, unless they had been found necessary to be so exaggerated in

---

* See Acts of Assembly, 1647 ; " Act concerning the CXI. Propositions."—
" Constantly to endeavour in our place and callings . . . . the *extirpation* of heresy, schism, and whatsoever shall be found contrary to sound doctrine. . . .
The civil magistrate ought to *suppress*, by corporal or civil punishments, such as . . . dishonour God . . . and disturb the peace of the kirk."

order that they might form their shibboleth, both a bond to unite them together and a badge to distinguish them. So that both parties in these unhappy collisions were equally injured, and the grand truth and spirit of Christianity received, between them, a death wound. ' By this shall—&c.—*if ye have love one toward another !* '

" It is especially worthy of observation that Nye, Goodwin, Sympson, and Burroughs, leading Independents of that time in England, were all of them men who had been driven to Holland, whence they returned on the downfall of Episcopacy in England ; and whence, in all probability, they derived those ideas of toleration which honourably distinguished them from their Presbyterian coadjutors in the Westminster Assembly.

" The Covenant bound those who signed it, to extirpate *Prelacy*, but not *Episcopacy*. Baxter, for example, and Reynolds, who afterwards accepted a bishopric, which Baxter refused only that he might (as himself states in his letter to Clarendon) the more effectually promote the cause of peace, were favourable to a moderate and limited Episcopacy.

" The Synod of Dort, or rather the British Calvinists in that Synod, long before Laud's advancement, had maintained that the Pope ought not to be called anti-Christ, till it had been fully proved in that Assembly by what right the epithet appertained to him or his office. Yet the ignorant represent Laud as the first and chief patron of that opinion.

" The unquestionable antipathy of the papists to Laud, forbids the supposition that he meditated bringing the Church of England under the papal power. In fact, Laud and many other eminent men in the Church of England, as well as men in the Church of Rome, such as Cassander, Erasmus, and others, aimed at a *catholicity*, which, rejecting the extremes, both of Popery on the one hand and Puritanism on the other, might yet acknowledge those ideas and practices which were common in the first ages, though not expressly sanctioned by Scripture, and might be acquiesced in by moderate men as well Romanists as Protestants. We know not whether to wish such compromises as that proposed by Melancthon and Bucer had succeeded. No doubt God has his wise purposes to answer by all events. Yet we may perhaps be permitted to desire, that since the mischiefs of division have been so awfully illustrated, the Church should now attempt the opposite principle. It is, I think, very hard to imagine that any sacrifices of opinion could be demanded, in order to the establishment of a catholic unity, which would be equally detrimental as those schisms have been, which have left the Church little else than a name, and have exhibited Christianity to the world as little else than a subject of contention.

"As for most of these unions which have recently taken place (among Presbyterians), they are only schisms uniting to render the joint body more schismatic than it was. For on examination it may perhaps be found that the excess of the antipathy against some common adversary has proved the real cause of union.

"The circumstance that rendered Presbytery intolerable to the English was not so much its persecuting principles,—for these the Church of England had always shared with it; nor yet its strict discipline in cases of overt crimes,—for the propriety of a Church exercising that kind of control over its members, could not be questioned. But what made the platform odious to the English was its perpetual petty interference with almost every action of life ;—its intrusion into all affairs; its meddling, and thrusting its officious counsels and reproofs into everything ; so that even the sanctity of domestic life could not escape its inquisitorial impertinence ; so that, to quote the words of a contemporary observer, 'a nurse shall not dare to quiet her child but with a psalm, and you must not presume to ask what o'clock it is, without a text to prove that the question tends to edification.'

"It was fortunate for the Presbyterian party that the government of the country was never in their hands, that civil dominion, though always eagerly grasped, was not at any time wielded by them ;—so that their persecutions were only in will and intention. They could only express their approbation of imprisoning and killing men for religious opinions, by their petitions and remonstrances to the Parliament, for its laxity in permitting such criminals to escape ; and in their sermons, which, with a painful uniformity, breathe the same spirit.

"Parliaments were popular, because Parliaments never had power. Whereas kings had frequently abused the power which no party possesses long without frequently abusing. Ten years of rule have damaged the popularity of the Whigs to a degree which forty years of previous eloquent declamation in favour of liberty, &c., goes no way to counteract. If the experiment did not cost too much in the meantime, the most effectual way of destroying Chartism (the present form of turbulence), would be by permitting the Chartist Convention to have one year's licence to misgovern the country."

This chapter may close with one or two extracts from his diary.

"*March* 29, 1849.—I have been of late a good deal annoyed by reports and whispers respecting the sayings and doings of a co-Presbyter, who is very wishful to make me a heretic. Whether the matter is now over I cannot tell; but I pray God to keep me from evil. It is true, as John Milton says, I think it is he, that he who signs a formula subscribes himself 'slave.' And every bigot and ignoramus has the power to insult and malign him—perhaps to bring him into great trouble. Yet 'Magna est veritas et prevalebit.' 'Have faith in God.'"

Dr. Lee wrote at last to the worthy representative of the bigot and ignoramus, to ask if it were true that he had imputed to him "unsound and heretical doctrines." His co-Presbyter, in reply, denied that he had. A correspondence ensued, which led to nothing, except to the conviction in Dr. Lee's mind that there were clergymen in the Church, some of them very near him, who, out of dislike of him and his views, or their hot zeal for what they thought to be orthodoxy, were watching him jealously, and would be well pleased to be able to arraign him on any charge. Perhaps the conviction was of use in making him more careful than he would otherwise have been, of his mode of expressing his opinions.

"*7th May*, 1849.—Plans cannot be carried out absolutely or uniformly, unless men were monks, with whom a *regula* is turned into the first thing. But this is to lose the end of life for the sake of the means. Many things occur that should put all plans aside for the time. Yet a rule is good. I am always busy, yet I never could study on a plan, or do anything on a plan, which is probably the cause why I have done so little. I am disposed, however, to make another plan (to be broken I do not doubt), and to mark to what extent it may be observed : 1st, To study daily at least three hours. 2nd, To visit at least two hours five days in the week."

"*31st August*, 1849.—Returned all of us in health from Innerleithen, where my family have rusticated two months, and myself a month, enjoying its streams, and hills, and breezes exceedingly. After all, home and its duties have the greatest and purest charms ; and recreations are chiefly useful and pleasant, as disposing one again to return to these with relish and strength."

"*3rd September*.—This day concluded an important engagement, viz., to take Mr. David Duncan into our family for three or four years. It is a serious matter to have children of one's own, much more to take charge of other people's. May we have grace to discharge this duty faithfully, that God may in all things be glorified through Jesus Christ. It is most gratifying to learn that our good friend Willie* is turning out a good and worthy man. I am most thankful for this."

* An elder brother who had been with Dr. Lee previously.

CHAPTER VI.

PAPAL AGGRESSION. — " THOU ART PETER." — SMALL LIVINGS.—UNIVERSITY TESTS.—RAGGED· SCHOOLS.

" To all Popes and Popes' advocates, expostulating, lamenting, and accusing, the answer of the world is,—once for all your Popehood has become untrue. No matter how good it was, how good you say it is, we cannot believe it ; the light of our whole mind, given us to walk by from heaven above, finds it henceforth a thing unbelievable."—CARLYLE, *Lectures on Heroes*, iv.

THE Pope's Bull, dividing Protestant England into Romish bishoprics, Cardinal Wiseman's Pastoral from the Flaminian Gate, and last, not least, Lord John Russell's letter to the Bishop of Durham, kindled a roaring fire of anti-Popish zeal all over Britain towards the close of the year 1850. Though Scotland was not to enjoy the blessings of the restored hierarchy, the heat and the tumult of the conflagration raged north of the Tweed as violently as in the south. Pamphlet and petition flew about ; and platform, pulpit, and Church Court rang with the war-cry " Papal Aggression." The government sought, feebly, to give expression to the indignant sentiment of the country by the " Ecclesiastical Titles Assumption Act." This piece of legislation was hailed by those who felt themselves aggrieved by the Pope's new invention of titles, as a proper, though, perhaps, inadequate vindication of the rights of the Church and of the Crown. The Presbytery of Edinburgh could not allow

the opportunity of demonstrating the healthiness of its
Protestantism to pass unimproved, and accordingly sent up
a petition in favour of Lord John Russell's bill. The resolutions in favour of the bill which the Presbytery adopted
on the occasion do not need to be further described
when it is mentioned that they were proposed by Dr.
Muir. Dr. Lee opposed them, and took exception to the
Ecclesiastical Titles Bill, for this reason, among others,
that it forbade one class of dissenters to do in England
that which it allowed another class of dissenters to do in
Scotland. The third section of the bill exempted the
bishops of the Scotch Episcopal communion from the
operation of the act; providing, however, that "nothing
herein contained shall be taken to give any right to any
such bishop to assume or use any name, style, or title
which he is not now by law entitled to assume or use."
Accordingly, while the law demanded from the Rev. Dr.
Wiseman 100*l.* of penalty if he used his title of Archbishop of Westminster, it charged the Rev. Dr. Trower
nothing for the use of the title of Bishop of Glasgow
and Galloway. This seemed, and was, unjust. The
offence in each case was the same. It was the assumption and use of territorial titles unknown to the law, and
unbestowed by the Sovereign, the fountain of honour.
That these titles were, in the case of the Roman
Catholic, conferred by a foreign ecclesiastic, though it
made their illegality more glaring, did not make the use
of them a whit more illegal than in the case of the Scotch
Episcopalian, whose misdemeanour lay in the resumption
of titles expressly abolished by Parliament. Dr. Lee
held the opinion expressed by Sir George Grey, who,
during the debate on Papal Aggression in the House of

Commons said,* "Those bishops have no shadow of right whatever to assume or use titles drawn from Scottish dioceses. There are those who think it against positive law, the Act of Union embodying the Act of Settlement. That may involve a nice question, but, at all events, they are without law, I believe, in this."

Apart from his strong disapproval of the doctrines commonly held by the Scotch Episcopalian clergy (which he believed to be deeply imbued with what was in those days called "Tractarianism" or "Puseyism"†), he, as a clergyman of the national Church, resented what he considered the childish impertinence of the parade of Episcopal titles, "my Lord Bishop," "the Very Rev. Dean," and so forth, by men who were almost all English, and in a country where there were no bishoprics, no deaneries, no chapters, none of the substance which alone could give reality to the empty names, and where the adherents of their "lordships" the bishops were very few in number, and the believers in their titles, fewer still.

The clause which, though it did not sanction, pre-

---

* March 7, 1851.

† The strange bigotry and unchristian feeling towards the Church of Scotland evinced by that party in England with which the Scotch Episcopal Church seems to have most sympathy, may be understood from the following extract from a journal supported by the High-Churchmen and High Tories:—"We wonder who the scribe can be who at present furnishes the information for the Court Circular. Among other absurd and incredible records which he chronicles, is the attendance of Her Majesty and Prince Albert at the 'Parish Church of Crathie.' The Court Circular's informant does not appear to be aware that the Queen is a member of the Episcopal Church of England and Ireland, and that the 'parish Church of Crathie' is a Presbyterian place of worship. Common sense might have taught him that Her Majesty, who views episcopacy as a divine ordinance, and has received her solemn consecration to the kingly office at the hands of the Archbishop of Canterbury, is not likely to attend the worship of a body whose distinctive tenet is, that Episcopacy is 'a rag of Popery.' Besides, if he was not utterly uninformed, he would know that Her Majesty, when in England, scarcely ever attends the public worship of her own Church; which makes it all the less credible that she should attend the public worship of a communion whose creed is an insult to her faith. Really the Lord Chamberlain ought to see to this, and to take care that Her Majesty's subjects are not misled and offended by misrepresentations of so palpable a character."—*John Bull*, Sept. 21, 1850.

served to them the cheap indulgence of their love of titular glory, grated on his fine sense of justice. It dealt out one measure to the Catholic—another to the Protestant. Dr. Lee took further exception to Dr. Muir's resolutions on the ground that they contained no recognition of a Roman Catholic's right to equal toleration with a Protestant. But Dr. Muir and his friends had no notion of a Roman Catholic being tolerated at all. To grant the same rights to a Papist as to a Presbyterian was, in their view, an act of grievous wickedness.

At a later meeting of Presbytery, the reverend brethren got on the Maynooth Grant. Dr. Lee said he had been in favour of the grant as a matter of policy. He was bound, however, to admit that the policy had failed. He found the priests no better than they were before— obstructing the useful career of the Queen's Colleges, and resisting the progress of education and knowledge. The grant had become a grant in aid of the spread of Ultramontanism. He thought, therefore, it might very well be withdrawn. Dr. Muir could not let this pass. He rose to deprecate any opposition to the Maynooth Grant on the worldly ground of "policy." The grant was to be opposed only on the ground that to continue it was a breach of Protestant principle, and a "flagrant sin." *

It was of little use to discuss Papal Aggression in the very home of such sentiments as these. Dr. Lee made his contribution to the universal theme in the shape of a " Discourse on Papal Infallibility," † in which he tried

---

* *Scotsman*, Feb. 28, 1852.
† " Thou art Peter : a Discourse on Papal Infallibility and the causes of the late Conversions to Romanism. Edin. 1851."

to turn the present engrossment of the public mind with the Pope and Popery, to good account, by some rational argument on the leading Papal dogma.*

Examining, first, the scriptural foundation for the dogma, he undertakes to show that the words of our Lord, "Upon this rock I will build my Church," refer not to Peter himself, but to his confession, "Thou art the Christ, the Son of the living God." He interprets the gift of the "keys of the kingdom of heaven" to mean that, inasmuch as Peter was the first who preached the Gospel both to Jew and Gentile, he opened "the door of faith" to both, and especially to the Gentiles. (Acts, xiv. 27.) "What could the key be for but to open the door; to admit into the house of God, first the Jews who were already in his vestibule, and especially the Gentiles, the human race, who were quite excluded by the great middle wall of Jewish ordinances, but who in Christ were brought near?"† "As to those keys of *discipline*, of which Romish and other priests talk so much, whatever may be their uses or their necessity, authority for them must be found elsewhere; for the keys which our Lord gave to S. Peter, on the occasion in question, were for no purpose but to open to mankind the door of faith."

After an interesting exegesis of the sentence "whatsoever thou shalt bind on earth, &c.," tending to show that these words refer to the teaching of Peter upon the *restraints* of the Gospel on the one hand, and its *liberty* on the other, he goes on to examine the argument from tradition, "the mainstay of the Papal advocates." If tradi-

* "The supremacy and infallibility of the Pope may be said to be the hinges on which the whole body of modern Popery turns."—*Discourse*, p. 1.

† "Discourse," p. 29.

tion really affirm the supreme jurisdiction and infallibility of the Pope, then he declares, "in the judgment, I will not say of every rational person, but of every man who is persuaded of the inspiration of the Apostles, the only result would be not to authorise the Papacy, but to condemn tradition." But he refuses to admit that the pure voice of tradition makes any such affirmation.

In a third chapter—in which there is, as, indeed, in all the four, a great deal of curious information and acute criticism—he maintains that Papal infallibility is contrary to reason and to fact; and finally, in chapter fourth, he discusses the causes "why so many Protestants have lately joined the Church of Rome." This question is not of less interest now than then, and the answers given are probably not less applicable. These secessions, "all or almost all, on the part of members of the Church of England," he traces, partly, to the latent sympathy with Romanism fostered in the Anglican mind by the influence of what Lord Chatham called the Church's "Popish ritual;" partly to the reaction against liberalism and rationalism,* driving the Anglicans towards tradition. Towards that venerable harbour of refuge he held they were also urged by the presence and aspect of English Dissent. When an Anglican "priest," devoutly believing in the pleasant "figment of an apostolical succession," † looks at a dissenting "teacher" on one hand, and a Roman Catholic priest on the other, he naturally feels more closely allied to the latter than to the former, for does not he, too, share in that ineffable and mysterious

---

* Since then, we have seen the truth of this borne out in the wonderful and pathetic pages of the "Apologia pro Vitâ Suâ." See *e. g.*, p. 240 (1st edition).

† Dr. Chalmers, before the Committee of the House of Commons on Sites, in 1847. See "Hanna's Life," vol. iv., chap. **xxiv.** (1st edition).

gift which links the dullest curate, in spiritual generation, to S. Peter and S. Paul? Nay, the Roman priest
possesses the gift by a more undoubted title than the
Anglican, for "in the Church of Rome alone can an indisputable apostolical succession be acquired, without
which there is no priesthood, no sacraments, no food for
Christ's flock. Thus, again, the Anglican finds himself
entangled in a net of his own spreading, and which inevitably lands him on the banks of the Tiber." *   He
concludes with an earnest condemnation of Tradition, a
thing for which truly he had no respect ; respect for
which, or for any authority that was not a rational
authority, was alien to the whole constitution of his
mind. " Tradition is, so far as it goes, the denial of the
authority of Christ, and also the denial of liberty of
thought, and of responsibility to every Christian man.
It is the substitution of human opinions and commands
in place of the authority of God, on one side, and in
place of our reason, conscience, and responsibility on the
other."

The "Discourse," though really much more to the
point of the existing controversy about the Pope and his
bishops than half the pamphlets of the day, did not
obtain so wide a circulation as might have been expected.
The following note from Dr. Lee's great colleague, Sir
William Hamilton, acknowledging the copy which had
been sent to him, deserves a place in our pages.

" MY DEAR SIR :
        "I ought before this to have thanked you for your able
discourse on Papal Infallibility, which I have read with much
interest. It seems to me a curious instance of hallucination

* " Discourse," p. 114.

that in this country there should be found so many who stand up for the personal infallibility of the Pope, as this Ultramontane doctrine is not only no principle of the Catholic Church, but by that Church itself has been virtually condemned as heretical. (By-the-by, do you know who Thomas the Abbas Scotiæ (head of the Scottish Cistercian Monastery at Vienna) was, who makes so distinguished a figure in the Council of Basle in vindicating the superiority of a Council to the Pope? I have not been able to ascertain this on a hasty and superficial inquiry in the books I chance to have at hand. It would please me much to know that he was a native of Scotland.) I have no doubt that your theory of the late conversions to popery has a great deal of truth, and I have been long surprised that no one has been found to vindicate the pure catholic element against the corruptions by which it has been overlaid through the personal interest of the Roman bishops. Catholicism seems to me a respectable doctrine, popery utterly contemptible.

" Believe me, my dear sir,

" Very truly yours,

" W. HAMILTON."

" 16, GREAT KING STREET,
July 11th, 1851."

In one of his note-books he has the following thoughts on " Popery and Protestantism : "

" The question at issue between these two parties is sometimes represented as lying between the divine word and human authority; the one contained in the Bible, the other speaking through the Church, *i. e.*, the Churchmen of the Romish communion. This, however, is not at all the true issue; the question, indeed, is, between *the Bible* on one side and the Church on the other—which, as of these two, should have the first place yielded to it in determining points of Faith; for no Catholic denies that the divine word should be preferred to any human word whatever. But he maintains that the Christian Church is the organ of that divine word as well as the Bible, and in a higher sense than the Bible. The controversy, therefore, lies between the claims of the living Church in all ages and this dead Book. It is true the Bible is, or rather contains, the Word of God : as such it is entitled to most reverent regard. But the Church, also, is a divine institution ; and, whereas, very little is said in the New Testament of the Scriptures, and hardly anything at all of the New Testament Scriptures, as teachers and guides of Faith, *the* Church is perpetually spoken of there in the most emphatic manner, and is declared, besides other attributes, to be the "pillar and ground of the truth." So that, looking at the matter from the New Testament point of view, the Scriptures and the Church being both of them divine ordinances, and both in some sense organs of the Holy Ghost, and the Church being always spoken of as an *inspired body* not less (or rather much more) than the Bible as an inspired book, it will not do to ignore the Church in favour of the Bible any more than to suppress the Bible, that the Church, under claim of inspiration, may teach for gospel whatever it pleases. For, if the inspiration of the Apostles and that of the Church be the same, (reasonable allowance being made for the distance of time and modes of thinking), the teaching of the Church and that of the Book must coincide, at least in substance; else we must conclude that there are two Spirits suggesting the ideas and feelings of the two. Also the Church with the Bible means something. Thus Christianity would at least live and propagate itself; but without the Church the Book were nothing ; barren, dead.

"But while the Romanists have witnessed for an essential element of Christianity in upholding the claims of the Church, they have quite misinterpreted the thing they upheld. For they understood by the Church, not the enlightened and sanctified body of Christians—all whose reason and conscience were cleansed by the Holy Spirit, and so were taught of God— but only the clergy of one communion, multitudes, not to say the majority, of whom were actuated by an unholy spirit, pride, ambition, fear, misled by prejudice, led blindfold by authority, and who no more were guided by reason and conscience, than if they had not been endowed with such faculties.

"This doctrine of the Holy Spirit guiding the Church comes very near the Rationalist notion of Reason being the supreme judge and ruler in all matters whatever, even religious matters

For, he that is spiritual judgeth all things, even the contents of a Book claiming to be inspired.

"Very strange, too, is the proceeding of those who, first having exalted the Book at the expense of the Church, and made the latter a footstool for the Book; yet presently are found composing creeds which express the sense and judgment of the Church, or their section of it; and exacting of all who enter their pale that they shall subscribe to this judgment of theirs respecting the sense and meaning of what is written in the Book. Thus they advance under cover of exalting the Book the very same arrogant claims which made them so angry when advanced by others.

"Thus we all, whatever we may pretend, can admit in Scripture only so much as we see to be reasonable and feel to be right. Our creed, in spite of ourselves, constantly shifts with our advancing reason. The page is the same, the words continue, but we read under new lights, and we discern something new or different.

"It matters not how infallible the Book may be in itself; it is to us just as wise and infallible as is the interpreter. 'If the eye be single, the whole body is full of light.'"

Dr. Lee was a member of the General Assembly of 1852. He did not take any leading part in the business or speak often.

He met, as we have already mentioned, a rude attack about his "plurality," and repelled it. He spoke also, shortly, on the question of "Private Communion," which was brought before the House by Colonel Dundas, of Carron Hall, who desired that this should be permitted. By an Act of Assembly* the private administration of the Lord's Supper and of Baptism is forbidden; but the usage of the Church has long allowed private Baptism. Usage, which is more respected in the Scottish Church than law, has, however, never sanctioned private

* Act x., 1690.

communion; and those clergymen, who, in case of necessity, have celebrated the Lord's Supper privately, have done so at the risk of ecclesiastical censure. Colonel Dundas sought to have this risk removed. The opposition to his proposal was led by Principal Lee, who argued against it with all his usual wealth of recondite lore, and maintained that the "ordination vows taken by all the ministers of the Church of Scotland," forbade their entertaining such a proposal. This assertion, so often made in answer to any suggestion of reform, was one the force of which Dr. Lee never could perceive. He advised Colonel Dundas not to press his motion in the meantime, as he thought the question was hardly ripe for discussion; but he added what was very indicative of the spirit in which he was prepared to discuss any change of the usages of the Church. "The practice," he said, "should only be revived" (for in almost every case he considered "innovation" to be only a wrong name for resumption of disused practice) "after the general feeling and sense of the community had been expressed in its favour. At the same time he wished to enter his dissent against Principal Lee's doctrine that the sending down of the overture would be a violation of their ordination vows." *

His principal work in this Assembly was his bringing forward, for the first time, a subject of great importance :—the small livings of the clergy.

---

* In the Scottish Church Courts legislation proceeds by "overtures,"—a term derived from the French law. If a proposal is made in an inferior court, an "overture," or draft of it, is sent up to the Assembly. If the proposal is made in the Assembly, a similar draft is prepared and sent down to the Presbyteries for their consideration. The "Barrier Act" prevents any overture becoming law till it has had the sanction of a majority of the Presbyteries and of the Assembly.

The country clergy, throughout Scotland, only enjoy a small portion of the Church's ancient revenues. Knox's statesman-like conception that the "whole rents of the kirk, abused in papistry, should be referred again to the kirk, that thereby the ministry, schools, and the poor may be maintained within this realm," [*] was too noble for the men with whom he had to deal.

They, the greedy barons and poverty-stricken lairds, cared but little for religion, education, and the poor. The division of the Church's revenues among these three was, according to Lethington, a "devout imagination." The laity had not lent a hand to, the overthrow of the old Church without making sure of a substantial recompense. Many a lord and laird in Scotland would be a very small man indeed to-day, but for the comfortable share which his forefathers "greedily gripped," (as John Knox frankly says) out of the property of the Church.[†] The allotment of one-third for education, and one-third for the poor, was never effected. One-third was, however, nominally assigned to the clergy; but as the funds were in the hands of "modificators," who were required to make over a certain portion to the Crown, the stipends provided for the ministers were miserably poor. Their position did not improve during the reign of James VI., who laid hold of all Church lands not already filched by laymen. The tithes, or "teinds," were not, however, meddled with. Charles I., in this a true friend, as in other matters a bitter enemy, to the Church, settled the stipends at last on their present basis. He devised

---

[*] First Book of Discipline, section 17.

[†] Knox's History. The subject recurs in many passages in the 3rd and 4th Books. Hill Burton's "History of Scotland," chap. xli.

a plan, ratified by Parliament in 1633, whereby the teind, being valued at a fifth of the rental, might be purchased by the heritors, subject to the payment of such a stipend to the minister of the parish, as should be assigned to him by the commissioners of teinds.*

The only way of adding to these stipends is by obtaining an "augmentation" from the Court of Teinds. It is the duty of the Court, if the existing stipend of a minister is held to be inadequate, to decree that it shall be increased out of the teinds in the hands of the heritors, these being only held, subject to this burden. As an application for increase can be made but once in twenty years, and as the heritors have the power of making objections, which the Court may sustain (a power used often, and as zealously as if the ministers, and not they, were the parties trying to appropriate what was not their own), augmentations do not go far to enrich the clergy. The stipends vary annually in amount, being paid according to the prices of grain in the year in which the stipend falls due.† The repeal of the Corn Laws, cheapening grain, had necessarily a disastrous effect on the stipends. It lowered their value materially, and it offered no compensation to the clergy for their loss. On this ground Dr. Lee dealt with the question. He brought up a report which illustrated the serious diminution of income which the clergy had suffered, through the operation of that beneficent measure ; and which they had borne, to their honour, without complaint or agitation.

---

* Cunningham's "Church History," vol. ii. chap. 2. Connel, on Tithes, vol. i.

† Called in Scotland "Fiars' prices," the values being officially ascertained and declared in February or March in each county separately.

In one case in the Presbytery of Annan the stipend was in 1839 323*l.*, and in 1846 407*l.*, while in 1849 it was reduced to 214*l.* Taking the average of the nine years preceding 1847 in this case, the stipend amounted to 294*l.*, while in the four succeeding years the average was 231*l.*, making a difference, owing chiefly to the repeal of the Corn Laws, of 63*l.* per annum. In another case, in the Presbytery of Kirkcudbright, the average stipend for the seven years prior to 1847 was 261*l.*, and for the four years subsequent to that date 204*l.*, making a difference per annum of 57*l.* The highest stipend obtained during the period was in 1846, when it was 347*l.*; and the lowest in 1849, when it was only 187*l.*, or about one-half. The return stated that the same applied to almost every parish in the Stewartry. The population of the parish in question was about 3000. In a third case, in the Presbytery of Hamilton, the highest stipend paid was in 1846, and the lowest in 1849, the sum for the former year being 394*l.*, and for the latter 168*l.*, making a difference of 226*l.* In a parish in the Presbytery of Meigle the stipend was in 1846 243*l.*, and in 1849 only 107*l.* Taking the average of four years prior to 1847, it was 182*l.*, and for the four years subsequent the average was 127*l.* In one of the parishes in this Presbytery the stipend was in 1838 302*l.*, in 1846 336*l.*, and in 1849 only 168*l.* For the ten years prior to 1857 the average stipend in the parish was 257*l.*, and for the four years subsequent it was only 198*l.* In a certain parish in Perthshire, the stipend was 169*l.* in 1837, 217*l.* in 1846, and only 106*l.* in 1849—the average of nine years prior to 1847 being 159*l.*, and of four years subsequent to that period, 122*l.* For this small remuneration, the clergyman had to attend to a parish 18 miles long, and from two to three miles broad, with a population of 2700.

These returns Dr. Lee gave merely as specimens, and they were not selected as cases of particular hardship. The repeal of the Corn Laws had in fact taxed the Scottish clergy in the amount of from 60,000*l.* to 70,000*l.* a year. The stipends they were now drawing were a third less than they had been before 1848. Dr. Lee was cordially thanked for the care he had taken in presenting the grievance forcibly and clearly; and a committee was appointed to consider and devise measures for its abatement.

We may vary these somewhat dry details of public business with one or two extracts from his diary. At the close of his third Session of College, he writes :— " There is something pleasant and congenial to my mind in thus quietly and unobserved working with a few young men, instilling truth into their minds from day to day. May God prosper the seed sown !"

In May, 1850, he removed from Lauriston Place to the house in George Square, No. 24, which he occupied till his death.

May 26, 1850.—This is probably the last night I shall spend in this house, which has sheltered us the last six years—a long portion in the short life of man. During this time much temporal prosperity has visited us, and little adversity ; indeed none, except the long sickness of our dear Maggie.* Outside our house, indeed, Death has picked off many of our kindred and friends; particularly my father and Isabella's, who yet had served their generation, and were gathered to their fathers in peace. May they, and our mothers, and all our other friends

---

* His eldest child.

sleep in Jesus, and obtain a glorious resurrection! Miss Rennie, also, who was so active at our last removal, is now cold and silent in the dust. Since removing to this house I have acquired a station of high importance, and considerable wealth with it. May God enable me to be faithful in the use of these talents.

"How solemn an event is a removal of this kind! how full of suggestion and of warning! Soon must I vacate this clayey tenement; it is to be taken down, and I must quit : so the builder and proprietor has determined. Soon must I go elsewhere, and be lodged in very different quarters; changing this warm and living world for the narrow house—for the clay, corruption, and the worm. Yet, 'when the earthly house of this tabernacle is dissolved, we have a building of God, an house not made with hands, eternal in the heavens.' This is the irrepressible longing of man's nature; and they who labour to destroy this hope would cheat us of our most precious consolation, and our strongest support. 'Now is Christ risen from the dead, and become the first fruits of them that slept.'

"Alas! I have to lament that I still lag behind in the race of wisdom and virtue. I reach not forth as I should, to lay hold on things before. 'My soul cleaveth to the dust; quicken me, O Lord, according to thy word.' Amen."

"15th August, 1850.—Returned this evening from a tour which I have had with my son George, to Berwick, Newcastle, Carlisle, Preston, Ambleside, Patterdale, Keswick, Penrith; and which has occupied a fortnight. It is delightful to see the general prosperity, happiness, and refinement of the English people. Their lakes far exceed my expectations; and I shall be anxious to visit them again in company with my wife, whose relish for fine scenery is so exquisite."

"3rd March, 1851.—This Session I have committed an error which I thus record to prevent its repetition ;—I have been too late in asking the students to breakfast, so that that personal acquaintance which is so necessary for effectually teaching a class is too late of being attained. In future, if spared, I will begin to ask them at the very commencement of the Session; and I shall also endeavour to employ them about my parish, and to keep them about myself. In this way much more can be done to leaven and enlighten young men's minds than even by public lecturing.

"Ignorance is the great mother of assurance and undoubting confidence ; and if comfort were preferable to truth—as many think it is—I should certainly recommend a proposition which was once made by a clergyman who himself acted on it, ' Go no farther than the shorter Catechism.'

"*23rd Nov.* 1851.—This day I finished the Pentateuch, in correcting and improving the marginal references of the English Bible, which I began in August, but laid aside till the 18th September; so that the fifth part of the whole has been completed in somewhat more than two months. It is astonishing how steady perseverance gets one on.

"*Jan.* 17, 1852.—This winter has been less pleasing to me than usual ; arising from this partly, that I have had more work and less (not leisure exactly, but) quiet study, which I find is needful not only for the progress and health, but even for the quiet of my mind. I feel some return of that feeling of *agitation* and *anxiety* which troubled me much some few years ago, and which is very difficult to be controlled.

"It is difficult to be calm and quiet sometimes. May God give me grace to be so. *Irritation* is my besetting sin : I have probably temptations to it, but let me do my own part. Our dear children are loving and obedient hitherto. May they so continue. I feel I am much more happy when in the bosom of my family. My desire is to enjoy this oftener in quiet. It is difficult to be a perfectly good and wise man : dissipation is surely the sin of this time. God teach and guide me : uphold my goings in Thy paths that they slide not. Amen.

"*13th July.*—To-day returned from Arbroath, whither I went to re-open the Abbey Church, which has been closed since the disruption in 1843. I never preached to such a crowd, and almost never saw such a crowd in a church. I was told that five or six hundred people went away from want of room.

"*27th July.*—My great fault has ever been a want of self-conversation. I have retired too little within myself, and communed too little with my own heart. Most of my outward faults and sins, which have been many and great, have sprung from this and the self-ignorance which this produces. I have consequently not been so familiar with my besetting sins as to guard against them habitually.

"Lord have mercy upon me. Teach me Thy will: teach me
what I am, and what I should be.

"*Sept.* 24.—I would exercise a greater inspection over
myself, *especially in speech.* God teach me to keep the door
of my lips that I sin not with my tongue. I have often no call
and no right to judge others : and when I should and must, it
is generally neither necessary nor expedient that I should
express my judgment to any one, much less proclaim it to
every one. God be merciful to me a sinner."

One of the questions pre-occupying the public mind in
Scotland at this time was the repeal of the University
Tests. These tests bound the professors to subscribe the
Confession of Faith, and, by implication, to be members
of the National Church. The greater power of the Church,
and the tenacity of conservatism in England, have preserved similar tests in the English Universities till this
day. But in Scotland the Church was not strong enough
to retain them in spite of the liberal opinions which
demanded their repeal ; and the liberal opinions were
backed by all the force of dissent, which, though bigoted
and somewhat intolerant in principle, hailed the repeal
of these tests as a blow to the supremacy of the Church.
The solution of the question was hastened by the action
of the Town Council, which, before the reform of the
Universities, held the patronage of most of the chairs in
the University of Edinburgh. On the retirement of
Professor Wilson, in 1852, the Town Council, to the
surprise of the educated world, elected as his successor,
neither Professor Ferrier, of St. Andrews, nor Mr. Scott,
of Manchester, but Mr. McDougall, Lecturer on Moral
Philosophy in the Free Church College. The leaders of
the Free Church had decided that it was impossible for
their students to study Moral Philosophy under Professor

Wilson, or Metaphysics under Sir William Hamilton, and had therefore instituted a professorship of each of these sciences in the "Free" College. It was surmised that the professorships had proved expensive and rather unprofitable luxuries, and that the Free Church was warmly interested in getting its professors transferred to the dignified chairs of the University, as soon as these should fall vacant. Whenever one of their own lecturers should be installed as Professor in the University, it would become possible for youthful Free Kirkmen to receive their intellectual nutriment within its walls without mental or spiritual injury. Accordingly, as soon as the highly intelligent and disinterested patrons had nominated Mr. McDougall to the vacant chair, the Professorship, which he had hitherto occupied, ceased to exist,* and the embryo moral philosophers of the Free Kirk migrated from the Head of the Mound to the old College. Mr. McDougall, naturally enough, feeling himself pretty safe from the interference of the law, would not take the test; but was, nevertheless, formally installed as Professor, and prepared to deliver his lectures. He was to begin in November, 1852. The Commission of Assembly, on a requisition from the agitated Presbytery of Edinburgh, met in October to contemplate this horrid spectacle of a full-blown Free Kirk Professor sitting in the seat of Dugald Stewart and Christopher North, and to devise means whereby he might haply be driven from that " coign of vantage." The spectacle, coupled with the simultaneous abolition of the Free Professorship, and the general exultation of the Dissenters at the feat of the Town Council, was certainly irritating to the eccle-

---

* The same thing was repeated on the appointment of Mr. Fraser as successor to Sir W. Hamilton.

siastical mind; but that mind could devise no remedy, beyond a silly recommendation to the students who had intended to take Moral Philosophy that session in their ordinary course of preparation for the Theological Hall, that they should not enrol themselves in Mr. McDougall's class.*

This recommendation was regarded only by the timid, and came to nothing. The debate waxed keener and keener however over the tests in the Church courts, the more distinctly it was seen that their days were numbered, and that the Government was prepared to abolish them.

"A great debate," says Dr. Lee, on March 16th, 1853, "in the Presbytery on the subject of University tests; when I made a long speech, and one which I persuade myself cannot be answered. I do not think the brethren ever heard before the arguments which may be urged, and have been, against their opinions."

Dr. Muir, in the van, as usual, proposed a set of resolutions roundly condemning any interference with the tests. He was followed by a man too gentle, too kindly, for the strifes of Church courts; full of a genial piety and old-fashioned culture and courtesy, whose name no one can recall without affection and respect, Dr. Hunter, of the Tron Church. Dr. Hunter's politics did not fit so good a man; and his professional prepossessions led him into the company of the narrow-minded, to which his Catholic spirit was really alien. On this occasion he contrived to express a good deal of illiberal opinion; and with a strange ignorance of what he was talking about, uttered

* A student preparing to enter the Theological Hall, must attend Lectures in the Faculty of Arts for four Sessions previously, and in his penultimate Session attend the Lectures on Moral Philosophy.

this sentiment, which seems to have been received without protest, that " if they placed a Carlyle in the Moral Philosophy chair, they would have an utter subversion of the very first principles on which true religion and genuine morality stood."   After Mr. Veitch* had spoken in a similar vein, concluding by an appeal to the Church to " stand firm by her principles, in the present critical position of evangelical religion throughout the world, and in the downward progressive tide of innovation and revolution," Dr. Lee spoke. . He said :—

" I shall not be deterred by the solemn adjuration which has just been uttered from stating here what appears to me to be the truth.   Remembering my own vows, having, I hope, some regard to the welfare of society and the progress of religion, I am conscientiously of opinion that the course advocated in the resolutions laid on the table is not a wise or a right one for this Presbytery to take, and, therefore, I take the liberty of now moving as an amendment that these resolutions be not entertained.   A very great deal has been said, and has been said, I acknowledge, with great ability, particularly by the last speaker, on this important question.   But it appears to me that the point sought to be proved has all along been taken for granted, while the point so taken for granted was the very one which ought to have been proved.   That we ought to be careful for the religious training of youth, that we should be anxious that none but godly men should occupy any public office, are principles so clear that no one here will call them in question.   But the point which should have been established, and which the speakers have signally failed to establish, is that the present test is conducive to that end, or that it has succeeded in any considerable degree to secure that end.   Now, let me say in the outset that I cannot understand how any member of the Church of Scotland can desire the continuance of the law in its present state.   It has been in operation now for more than one hundred and sixty years, and what have its results been ?   Has it resulted

* Now Rev. Dr. Veitch, one of the ministers of S. Cuthbert's.

in securing to the Universities only members of the Church of
Scotland as Professors? On the contrary, is it not the fact that
there have been introduced into these Universities a number—
a continually increasing number—of men who are dissenters
from the Established Church? And is it not perfectly evident
that if the present state of things remain, the result will be that
this number shall still farther increase, till for aught we can
say, under the operation of that system of which many gentlemen have so great an admiration, the whole of the Professors
together may be dissenters? For my own part, if I entertained
the views which have been expressed by many of my brethren,
my course would be quite different. Instead of petitioning
Parliament that the present law should continue, I should petition Parliament that, as the present law proved utterly ineffectual, additional and more stringent laws might be enacted,
bestowing upon the Church plenary powers to require subscription of every Professor at his admission, to insist on conformity
ever after, and finally to dismiss him from his office if he were
either guilty of nonconformity, or of questioning any tenet of
that law which he had subscribed to. All this is indispensable
for the object in view ; but to beg Parliament to preserve to us
only what we have now is poor beyond expression ; for in fact
we have nothing—no power, and I maintain, no real security
under the law as it now stands. It must also appear evident
that the lapse of a very few years will render the present law
practically null and void in all the Universities, as it has been
during a century in the University of Edinburgh. For it cannot
be disguised that men have begun to sign the Confession merely
as articles of peace, and to make the declaration merely as a
promise that they will not act so, in their professional capacity,
as to injure the Church of Scotland. Now, this view of the
subject is one which I do not defend ; it is one, on the contrary,
which I think is wrong. At the same time we cannot shut our
eyes to the fact that this doctrine has received the sanction of
many able writers, not only casuists and jurists, but moralists
and divines. And what is more, it received a certain degree of
judicial sanction in the case of the Presbytery of Aberdeen and
others. Professor Blackie, in 1839, having declared that he had
signed the Confession of Faith in his public capacity, the judge,
so far as he spoke at all, sanctioned the view that this was

sufficient. Now, if this notion, which undoubtedly is entertained, should become established, dissenters will gradually in
greater numbers become Professors in our Universities; and the
door, if once opened, can never be shut again, because, should
one or two respectable men show the example, everybody else
will walk through. So that if you should unhappily succeed in
keeping matters upon their present footing, your success would
be fatal to your wishes, for the law would in time effectually
repeal itself; and that time would be a very short one, considering the ever-growing strength of public opinion. I am
therefore not a little surprised that any resolution should be
proposed here which expresses approbation of the law as it now
stands; for that law appears to me not only unfavourable to the
interests of religion and morality, of literature and science, but
even to those of the Church itself, rightly understood.

" There are several grounds on which those who would maintain
the present law seek to support their opinion. They sometimes
are alarmed lest the ingenuous youth should be corrupted by
the flood of irreligious Professors who would thenceforth fill the
chairs. This would deter many parents from sending their sons
to these seats of learning, and so the Universities themselves
would be ruined by this innovation. At other times the interests and security of the Church are dwelt upon, and always the
Treaty of Union and Act of Security are appealed to, as afford-
ing an argument against repealing the present law, which
admits no reply. As we have had this argument urged to-day
with the usual confidence, and, I must add, the usual want of
discrimination, I shall take the liberty of discussing this point a
little more minutely, with the view of showing that the case for
them is not so clear or strong as some gentlemen suppose, and
that they rest upon a very sandy foundation indeed.

"In the year 1707, the kingdoms of England and Scotland
thought proper to enter into a union by which thenceforth they
were to constitute one kingdom, reserving to each certain rights
and privileges. The most prominent of these reservations were
the Churches of the two kingdoms, which were declared unal-
terable for ever. And particularly regarding the Church of
Scotland, it was enacted that ' it should continue without any
alteration to the people of this land in all succeeding gene-
rations.' A similar stipulation was enacted for security of the

Church of England. From this text many conclusions are drawn. Among others, that to take away what was thus secured, or change what was thus established, is illegal, immoral, a breach of faith, &c., &c. Such censures, however, will, on examination, perhaps, be found to be too precipitate. Before running into them so fast several things need to be considered. In the first place, if these conclusions be sound, it must follow that the Scotch and English Parliaments in 1707 came somehow to be possessed of an authority which belongs to no succeeding Legislature; and that sovereign authority does not belong to the British Legislature now, nor ever will. Is this, then, a sound conclusion? On the contrary, I suppose every juridical authority, from Cicero downwards, will denounce this as a constitutional heresy. Let us hear what the oracles of the law have to say on this point. Blackstone says:—'Acts of Parliament derogatory from the power of subsequent Parliaments bind not. Because the Legislature, being in truth the sovereign power, is always of equal, always of absolute, authority; it acknowledges no superior upon earth, which the prior Legislature must have been, if its ordinances could bind a subsequent Parliament. And upon the same principle Cicero, in his letters to Atticus, treats, with a proper contempt, these restraining clauses, which endeavoured to tie up the hands of succeeding Legislatures. "When you repeal the law itself" (says he); "you at the same time repeal the prohibitory clause, which guards against such repeal."' Now, that is the judgment of the highest authority in English law; and he is more precise even than this, for in a subsequent passage of the same introduction, he speaks of this very subject, the Union of England and Scotland—and after reciting the principal conditions of it, he adds the following note:—'It may justly be doubted whether even such an infringement (though a manifest breach of good faith, unless done upon the most pressing necessity) would, of itself, dissolve the union; for the bare idea of a State, without a power somewhere vested to alter every part of its laws, is the height of political absurdity. The truth seems to be, that in such an *incorporate union* the two contracting States are totally annihilated, without any power of a revival; and a third arises from their conjunction, in which all the rights of sovereignty, and particularly that of legislation, must of necessity reside (see Warburton's Alliance, 195). But

the wanton or imprudent exertion of this right would probably
raise a very alarming ferment in the minds of individuals ; and,
therefore, it is hinted above that such an attempt might
endanger (though by no means *destroy*) the union. To illustrate this matter a little further; an act of Parliament to
repeal or alter the act of uniformity in England, or to establish
Episcopacy in Scotland, would doubtless, in point of authority,
be sufficiently valid and binding ; and, notwithstanding such an
act, the union would continue unbroken. Nay, each of these
measures might be safely and honourably pursued, if respectively
agreeable to the sentiments of the English Church, or the Kirk
in Scotland.' Now, you will observe that, according to this
great legal authority, the whole question turns upon this—
Whether the people of Scotland desire, or whether they do not
desire, such a change as even that contemplated ? But not to
detain you with many authorities, I will only quote another.
I shall refer you to the author of one of the ablest works on
jurisprudence in the English or any other language. Discussing
the principles of Legislative supremacy, Mr. Austin, in his
'Province of Jurisprudence,' lays down the same doctrine, and
declares that to deny that the Legislature has the right to
interfere with the Act of Security and with the Act of Union
is not only incorrect but even an absurdity. I presume these
are sufficient authorities to show that the British Parliament
is warranted on every ground of legality, morality, and every
other consideration which should affect a Legislature, to open
up this question, and to alter, amend, or abrogate these laws, in
part or in whole, as they shall see fit, any enactments of 1707,
and any ideas then prevalent, notwithstanding. A multitude of
considerations might be added to the same purpose, but I shall
now only draw your attention to this fact that the British Legislature itself has already decided the question of its own rights
in this matter, and that not only so far as the Act of Union is
concerned, but even in regard to the Act of Security. It has
indeed been confidently maintained, and that in our Church
courts, that the Act of Security stands to this hour untouched
in any of its provisions by any act of the British Legislature.
But I shall allege much better authority than mine for the
opinion that the Act of Security has been infringed on several
occasions by the Imperial Parliament. I shall instance two of

these infringements. The first was committed by the act tolerating the Episcopal worship in Scotland ; the other by the act
restoring lay patronages, passed both of them in the year 1712.
Every one knows that during the Episcopal establishment, from
1662 to 1688, the Presbyterian worship was prohibited under
penalties ; and that after the Revolution, and the re-establishment of Presbytery, the Episcopal worship was in turn subjected
to legal penalties. In this position of affairs the Act of Security
was passed ; in which it was provided that, as in England none
but the Episcopal worship should be legally allowed, so in Scotland none but the Presbyterian should be legally allowed. It
was accordingly provided, not only that the Presbyterian Church
Government, which had been established at the Revolution,
should be maintained in Scotland, but that the 'said Presbyterian government shall be the only government of the Church
within the kingdom of Scotland.' These words probably convey
to most persons who read them now a very different sense from
that intended by their authors. They meant by them, not only
that the Episcopal worship and government should not supplant
the Presbyterian in the Established Church, but that no other
than the Presbyterian worship should be at any future time
permitted, or legally tolerated in Scotland. We are apt to be
quite misled in reading those statutes by our different positions
and ideas. The Church of Scotland then regarded itself as the
only Church of Christ in the land. Those without her pale she
stigmatised as either Papists, Malignants, or Sectaries, who were
to be punished and prohibited by law, as well as refuted by
Scripture. Now, these being her views, it was not wonderful
that the Church should consider the toleration of the Episcopal
worship as 'a manifest and ruinous encroachment' on 'that
plenary security in law which she had for her present Church
government and discipline.' Accordingly, if you will look at
'the Humble Representation,' &c. of the Commission of the
General Assembly, 1711, which was approved by the Assembly, 1712, you will find ample confirmation of all I have
now asserted. You will find bitter complaints against the proposal then before Parliament ' to allow the Episcopal Dissenters
liberty to meet and assemble for the exercise of their own worship, and to use the Liturgy without any disturbance, and that
no person shall incur any penalty for resorting to said Episcopal

meeting.' These seemed monstrous and impious proposals to the Commission of 1711 and the Assembly of 1712. But they denounce the proposed toleration specifically on this ground, that it was *illegal*, being a violation of those acts from 1690 downwards, by which Presbytery had been established, and which were ratified by the Act of Security. Now, I presume those Assemblies understood very well what were the meaning and intent of the Act of Security, and when it was infringed, for they were themselves the very parties at whose instance that act was made and enacted. We have, then, the authority of the Church of Scotland herself for holding that the Act of Security has been infringed by the British Parliament. If, therefore, the British Parliament shall repeal the provisions of that law regulating the admission of Professors, they would not be the first to invade its sanctity. One precedent at least exists to encourage or to warn them.

" Now, let me propose a question. Do we approve or disapprove of the conduct of the British Parliament in passing that act? If we do not, we approve of persecution. If we do, we approve of the violation of the Act of Security. But another instance of the violation of the same Act of Security was the act restoring lay patronages. That this was a violation, the Church has emphatically declared again and again ; indeed, the thing is too manifest to be denied. The Church of Scotland's Humble Address of 1712 says, ' Which act, we conceive, is contrary to our Church constitution, so well secured by the Treaty of Union.' Lay patronage, then, is a violation of the Treaty of Union and of the Act of Security; and yet, strange to say, there are gentlemen, here and elsewhere, who defend lay patronage, and yet plead the inviolability of that Act of Security in violation of which lay patronage was restored. How they can justify this inconsistency I cannot imagine. If the Act of Security be of right inviolable, then lay patronage is now, and has always been since 1712, a legal wrong, and should as such be denounced. If, on the contrary, lay patronage be good, expedient, and defensible, then a breach of the Act of Security is good, expedient, and defensible. The present law must, therefore, have some better defence than an act which the British Parliament has already dealt with according to its sense of duty, and which it was in the judgment of the best authorities entitled, and even bound, so to deal with. I deny that there is any bar, legal, constitutional, or moral, which hinders the British Parliament from proceeding to legislate on this matter. They have as absolute a right to repeal the Act of Security, in whole or in part, as the Parliament of 1707 had to enact it. Nay, I go farther, and maintain that they are bound to do so. The very considerations which dictated that act should now require its abrogation. It was originally enacted on the demand, and for the supposed protection, of the Scottish people. Gentlemen have spoken here to-day, and elsewhere, as if the change which is contemplated by the bill now before Parliament had been some spontaneous act of the British Legislature, or something thrust upon us from without. It is not so. It is Scotland itself which is the moving power in this matter. It was Scotland which called for the Act of Security, and it is Scotland now —Scotland immensely more enlightened, with a population far more numerous, more moral, and I hope not less religious than Scotland in 1707—which is calling for a modification of the present law respecting University Tests. If it be not so, whence the movement? Am I to remind you that at this moment the law exists in spite of the votes of the Scotch members in Parliament, that it is by the votes of English and Irish members that it now remains on the statute book? On every occasion that a bill somewhat similar to that now proposed was brought before Parliament, two to one of the Scotch members voted for it. The voice of the people of Scotland therefore, so far as that goes, is distinct enough. And where, excepting in the Church courts, can any assembly of educated Scotchmen be found who are not of the same opinion? Is there any public body, any Town Council, is there any collection of men in office in any burgh in Scotland, who can be found holding the opinion of our Church courts? No, sir. Is it not certain that, within the bounds of the Church of Scotland itself, a very large number of the most enlightened and educated members—men most eminent for intelligence and impartiality, and let me tell you, not less attached to the best interests of the Church of Scotland than we are—hold that it is not expedient, that it is not right nor consistent with the interests of morality or religion, that the present tests should exist? But 'the Church of Scotland,' it seems, 'is opposed, remonstrates, protests.' This I deny. The clergy of the Church of Rome may call themselves ' the Church,' but it is not the theory or language of the Church of Scotland that the clergy or the Church courts are the Church. Our definition or idea of the Church is the whole body of the faithful people. In some respects, indeed, Church courts and ministers may be called the Church, as being an *ecclesia representans*. But they are rather an *ecclesia misrepresentans* if they hold opinions— as they notoriously do—which the whole body of those whom they pretend to represent join in repudiating. And let me draw attention to the fact that the acts which I have been referring to are not in favour of the Established Church as against Presbyterian Dissenters; they are in defence of the whole body of the Scotch Presbyterians in opposition to Papists and Malignants or Episcopalians. I maintain, therefore, that the true representatives of the Church in Scotland in 1707 are the great body of Presbyterians now existing in the country. The whole question then turns upon this—Do the people of Scotland—do the Presbyterians of Scotland, or do they not, wish the present law to continue ? If they do not wish it to be altered, then, according to the judgment of Blackstone, which I think is plainly sound, it would be wrong to alter it. If the great body of the religious people of Scotland, especially the Presbyterians, are opposed to the change, then it would be wrong in the Parliament of Great Britain to force that change upon them; but if, on the contrary, which is notoriously the fact, the Presbyterians of Scotland, and a large majority of the people within the Church itself, are desirous of the change, then the Legislature are, by the same principle which warranted them in enacting the law in 1707, now warranted in abrogating it.

" We have heard a great deal to-day about the rights of the Church in this matter ; and not only the reverend mover of the resolutions, but others who followed him, spoke as if the rights of the Church over the Universities were the same as their rights over the parish schools. Where will you find legal authority for this ? It will not do to quote to us Acts of Assembly; we must have Acts of Parliament; and I should like any gentleman here to put his hand on an Act of Parliament telling us that the Universities are subject to the Church in the same way as parish schools are to Presbyteries. Every one who knows anything must know that this is a complete mistake ; and surely the judgment of the Royal Commission of 1830, to the contrary,—and the only two cases which have come before the courts, that of the Rev. W. Browne, of St. Andrews, in 1756, and that of Mr. Blackie in 1839,—should satisfy gentlemen that the Church has at least no power whatever in the matter of University Tests, except to receive the subscription when it is offered. This decision, indeed, has been often murmured against, but has been acquiesced in, and no one has thought of appealing it to a higher court. The power of Presbyteries over parish schools stands on quite a different footing; it is arranged by an express Act of Parliament.

"And now let me observe that, if the maintenance of the present law as to tests be favourable to the rights of the Church, I can only say that, in my opinion, and in the opinion of the great mass of our countrymen, and, what is more, in the opinion of the great majority of the Professors in the Universities, it is not favourable to the interests of morals and religion. I should be sorry to believe that the interests of religion and the interests of the Established Church are opposed to each other; but I cannot permit myself to believe that a law which seems to me to put a stumbling-block in the way where it ought not to lie, is a law required for the security of the Establishment. Can it be doubted that the present law is such a stumbling-block; for if it be not so, why the evasions which have been devised to get rid of it? Have we forgotten that, instead of seeking to perpetuate a temptation, or a stumbling-block, we are commanded by that faith which we preach, 'to take heed not to put,' and of course not to continue, 'a stumbling-block or an occasion to fall in our neighbour's way.' Now, there can be no doubt that this test has proved a stumbling-block to many, and if continued, it will to many more. If, therefore, I should lend my feeble hand to uphold it, I should feel I was not innocent of the sin, because I had been instrumental in maintaining 'the stumbling-block and the occasion to fall.'

"We have heard a great deal about the dreadful effects which are sure to follow if the present law is removed, but I do think that the pictures which have been put forward owe their existence very much to the warm imaginations of the gentlemen who have drawn them. Schools have had tests long ago removed. In the High School there is no test, in the New Academy there is no test, and yet we send our sons there to be taught by masters who have signed and been asked to sign no test whatever. In like manner do we not send our daughters to boarding and other schools, the teachers of which have. never been required to sign any test ? Do we take the Confession of Faith in our hand, and say we will send our son or daughter, or pupil to the school, if the teacher will sign the declaration ? Gentlemen speak here as if they would not send their sons to the University unless the Professors signed the tests, and yet they send them without scruple to all other schools, taught by masters who have subscribed no declaration. The picture, therefore, which has been drawn is totally imaginary ; because, if the non-operation of the tests produced such dreadful effects as had been described, these must have been seen in Edinburgh University, where practically tests have been in abeyance for one hundred years. Between 1756 and 1852 there were admitted to that University 113 Professors ; of these only 20 had signed the test, while 93 had not signed it ; and these 20, with one or two exceptions, were members of the Theological Faculty or ministers of the Church. Upon this point I beg to draw your attention to a declaration made in an address to the students of this University a few years ago by my friend Principal Lee, who, as you know, has always been a zealous advocate for the existence of tests. He says— 'There had been times when the ensigns of infidelity had waved over the academic walls ; he might safely assure his hearers, however, that now not even a whisper tending to unsettle the foundations of the Christian faith would be heard from any of the chairs. On the contrary, every fitting occasion would be seized to render philosophy and literature subservient to inspired truth, and the purifying influences of our most holy faith.' Such is the condition of the University which is singular in Scotland in having practically abolished the tests."

Dr. Lee then proceeded to deny that the spread of Neology and Pantheism in Germany was attributable to the want of a test, inasmuch as subscription to the Augsburg Confession was required at the Universities when this great corruption of doctrine took place, while it was a notorious fact that some of the leading Neologians were most zealous for the maintenance of that Confession. The abolition of this test, therefore, he contended, was not the cause of the corruption of opinion, but it was the corruption of opinion which led the way to the abolition of the tests. Referring to some remarks by Dr. Muir upon oaths, he observed that the tendency of modern legislation was to abolish these as much as possible, and expressed his surprise at hearing gentlemen speak in such a way as to indicate that they were unacquainted with what had been going on in the world during the last twenty or thirty years. To know modern things, and to sympathise with modern ideas, might be denounced as liberalism or by any other name ; but he thought that if they attended to the course of legislation, they would make certain discoveries which would be of no small use to even ministers of the Gospel.

He then proceeded to reply to another argument. "It has been argued again," he said, "if tests are not enforced, where is the grievance ?   Now, I have to say, in reply to this, that the non-enforcement of the law is a grievance, and it is not right that any law should be maintained which is not enforced. 'It is not wise,' says Burke, 'to maintain a law which it is not wise to enforce'—for it might be enforced partially, and used as an instrument of oppression. But there is one thing in which I perfectly agree, the impossibility of having any other test but the present, and yet if the present law continue I think we shall lose not only the lay but the clerical chairs too. To me it appears that the attitude which the Church Courts have taken in regard to this question is most detrimental to the interests of the Church. Either the bill now introduced, or some similar bill, must inevitably pass, and that soon, because such is the will and resolution of the people of Scotland. Our opposition, therefore, will have no effect, except to put the Church courts and clergy in a wrong position with the body of the people. This course will give occasion for our enemies to represent us as men who are careless of all interests, except the preservation of our own privileges and powers, or what we imagine to be such. If my counsel might be listened to, which, of course, I know it will not, I should advise that we should make a virtue of necessity ; and as our opposition can only expose our weakness and damage us otherwise, we should frankly accept the bill for abolishing tests as regards lay chairs, and should, regarding the others, make the best bargain we can for securing them, with the principalities, for the Church.   This flat opposition will deprive the Church of all influence in the settlement of this great question." Dr. Lee concluded by moving a negative to the resolutions of Dr. Muir.*

Dr. Muir's resolutions, of course, were carried. Twenty-three voted for them, and five against them, Dr. Lee, and the Rev. R. W. Fraser, of S. John's, being the only clergymen in the minority.

The question engaged the reverend brethren yet once more. A bill, abolishing the tests in the non-theological chairs, was carried by the government of Lord Aberdeen in the session of 1853; and in February, 1854, the indefatigable Dr. Muir made a last attempt to revive the " cold obstruction" of his defeated and hopeless policy. He calmly proposed in the Presbytery of Edinburgh, that the Church should agitate for the rescission of the Act of 1853, and if unsuccessful, should establish separate colleges of her own. Said Dr. Muir, " The facts of this case do form, undoubtedly, one of those peculiar sections in modern public history, the reading of which will ever touch—yea, pungently affect—the hearts of all who, venerating and loving the Church of Scotland, seek to promote her credit, and honour, and prosperity. For the Act, recently passed, breaking the connection of the Church with her own colleges, is an Act that has evidently done a wrong—has inflicted an unmerited grievance—was a glaring and studied injury," and so on, and so on : one can fancy the impotent reclamations. The proposal of establishing separate colleges was, however, a little too wild, even for Dr. Muir's usual supporters. Dr. Simpson and some others rebelled ; though, strange to say,

<hr>

* *Scotsman*, March 19, 1853.

Dr. Grant,* a clergyman whose "moderate" proclivities allowed but inadequate scope for the exercise of his admirable talents, yet were not always strong enough to warp his excellent common-sense, was content, on this occasion, to adhere to this ridiculous device.   Dr. Lee said :—

"I could not have believed that such a proposal should have been made in this Presbytery, or in any other court of the Church of Scotland ; because I could not have supposed that any of her ministers could have been so blind to her interests as to follow the very course which the enemies of the Church, if consulted, would recommend. Such an overture, so violent and reckless, is indeed a strange phenomenon. Complaints are sometimes made that the Established Church is styled a sect. But this is just a plan for making ourselves a sect, as far as we can. We have lost something, as we hold, and it is proposed to remedy that by throwing away everything, and abandoning all connection whatever with the Universities. If you do so, I forewarn you that you will do a thing at which your adversaries will greatly rejoice, and for which they will heartily thank you. You will then have done your best to bring the Church to the same level—in regard to the Universities,—which the Dissenting Churches hold, and they can hardly fail to admire such disinterested generosity.

*   *   *   *   *

"But the gentlemen who support this overture can, I think, hardly wish to succeed in their petition. For the repeal of this Act by our means would, if it were possible, bring down a storm of obloquy and reproach upon the ministers and elders of the Church of Scotland, which I should not like to see added to all the unpopularity they have already gained by their conduct in this matter. I do not say that the conduct was wrong because it was unpopular ; but surely there is no reason in pursuing a course which will have no effect but to incur unpopularity and increase it. The conduct of the legislature in passing the late Act, and that of the government, has been

---

* Rev. James Grant, D.C.L., Oxon., D.D., Minister of S. Mary's—a prominent member of the Moderate party, and Moderator of the General Assembly of 1854.

severely censured. But why have the government and the legislature so acted ? Simply for this reason, that they could not help it. In this country, governments and legislatures are, in a great measure, the organs of the opinions and wishes of the people. And if a conservative government—such as the present may be considered to be—felt itself unable to resist the measure complained of, can we expect less compliance from a more radical government? This provision of the Act of Security was repealed, because the people of Scotland, in whose interest it was passed originally, wanted the security no longer. They felt, or they fancied, that the security was really an impediment and an injury, and the legislature could not resist their almost unanimous demand. No doubt that Act of Security was passed to protect the *Church* as well as the *people* of Scotland. But if the people and the Church should happen to differ respecting what is proper to be enacted or repealed, whether is it reasonable that the Church shall yield to the people or the people to the Church ? Surely the more comprehensive interest cannot be expected to yield to the less—the whole to the part. But who are the Church of Scotland ? Is it the ministers and elders assembled in a Church court? Are these few individuals to be reckoned the Church of Scotland, whose interests were contemplated in the Act of Security ? The last time this subject was discussed in this court, a majority of twenty-three individuals (unless my memory fail me) resolved to petition Parliament against the passing of the Act now complained of. And within the bounds of this same Presbytery are some 200,000 individuals—the great mass of them Presbyterians. Now, who authorised those twenty-three men—only about one-third of the members of this court itself—to represent and speak for the 200,000 persons living within the bounds of this presbytery ? Who authorised that small number of men to speak for the Church and people of Scotland in Edinburgh and its neighbourhood ? On the contrary, who does not know that the laity of the Church are as generally favourable to the repeal of the Test Law as the clergy are otherwise; and that the true Church—that is, the members of the Church—coincide with their fellow citizens in approbation of what the legislature has done in this case ? Your petition can succeed only by a complete revolution in the opinion of the whole Scottish people

—whose understanding and conscience were offended by the law as it stood—and who have not yet discovered any impiety or any danger in the law as now amended. Is it not a fact sufficiently significant that this bill passed almost unanimously? What was the reason that no statesman of name, and particularly that no Scotchman could be found to offer opposition to the measure? Is it not ominous that the defence of your position, and the expression of your sentiments, should have been left for Lord Redesdale in the Lords, and in the Commons for Sir Robert Inglis—the representative of the University of Oxford—that last refuge of exploded bigotries, that congenial sanctuary of opinions and theories which can find no shelter anywhere else? This very extraordinary fact that the supposed rights of the Presbyterian Church could find no person to maintain them except the representative of the High Episcopal, almost Popish University, is a sufficient commentary on the character of your ideas and claims. No politician of any liberality of mind, or any largeness of view, could be found to defend our grievances or plead our cause. No Scotchman, no Presbyterian, would indorse them."

Dr. Muir, no doubt to his profound astonishment, found himself in a minority. An amendment, proposed by Dr. Simpson, was carried, "Dr. Muir protesting."[*] University Tests had now got their *quietus*.

On another question—also connected with the educational problems of the day—Dr. Lee was as widely separated from the mass of the clergy as on that of the Tests. He had come to see the impracticability of giving, in a mixed school, such religious instruction as should be acceptable to all. He did not undervalue religious instruction,—though he held that the usual reading of the Bible and learning of the Shorter Catechism by rote, little deserved the name; but he saw that it could not be given in common. Children of one Church or sect

---

[*] *Scotsman*, Feb. 11, 1854.

could not, or rather would not be allowed to receive this instruction from a teacher of another Church or sect. Although, practically, Presbyterian children were sent to Church, or Presbyterian dissenting, schools, as convenience rather than as principle dictated, yet the very existence of dissenting schools proved that the theory of their education was that it should be always conducted by a teacher of their own "persuasion." In the case of Roman Catholics, of course, the theory was the same, but the practice was much stricter. As a general rule, a Roman Catholic child would not be allowed to attend a school, where he was obliged to listen to Protestant religious instruction. Dr. Lee thought that a system, to be truly national, should recognise the rights, and provide for the case, of all alike. He, therefore, was prepared to advocate the "conscience clause;" or the system of combined secular and separate religious instruction. The advantage of this system had been specially presented to the people of Edinburgh in the management of the "United Industrial School," of which Dr. Lee became an ardent supporter, and whose cause he took every opportunity of advocating. The history of this school is an instructive one.

Ragged schools, originally invented by John Pounds, a shoemaker at Portsmouth, in 1819, first gained a local habitation and a name, in 1841, at Aberdeen. Mr. Watson, the sheriff there, opened a school in which he offered teaching and food to poor and vagrant children. The plan succeeded, and was adopted in other towns. In 1847, Mr. Guthrie, then minister of Free S. John's, in Edinburgh, published his first "Plea for Ragged Schools." It justly produced a very strong impression;

money poured in plentifully, and an association for the establishment of a Ragged Industrial School in Edinburgh was formed. "All men," says Dr. Guthrie, "were ready to sing over the birth of this Christian enterprise. They hailed the proposal to establish it on a broad unsectarian basis."*

It soon appeared, however, that the basis was neither to be "broad" nor "unsectarian;" inasmuch as Roman Catholics were to be excluded from any share in the management, and religious instruction by a Protestant teacher, and with the use of the authorized version of the Bible, was to be compulsory. "We insisted," says Dr. Guthrie, in 1861, forgetting his earlier professions, and glorying in an exclusiveness which necessarily barred Roman Catholic children out of the school, "that every child in our school should read, and be instructed daily in the word of God, without asking the priest's leave, whether he would or would not. We held *that* to be the really sectarian school that excludes the Bible from all or any." †   But the question was not, is the Bible to be excluded?   It was, are Catholic children to be compelled to receive Protestant religious instruction?   And this question the leading promoters of the school could only answer in the negative; the more so, as the secretary of the Association avowed, in a correspondence with Mr. Hill Burton, that the religious instruction was not even to be confined to the reading of the authorized version of the Bible.   It was to embrace "explanations" of the Bible.   On Sundays the children were not only to

---

* In a paper in " Good Words," for 1861, p. 5, which never should have been admitted into that Magazine, the account given of the question raised being grossly unfair.
† " Good Words."

receive religious instruction in the school, but were to attend a Protestant service. The only exception to this rule was to be in the case of any children whose parents should " satisfy " the strictly Protestant Committee of Management that their children would be properly looked after during the " hours of worship," in which case the pupil should be exempted from attendance at the Protestant Church.*

It was felt that to insist thus on religious instruction of a purely Protestant character, and to refuse a place in the board of management to Roman Catholics, was a breach of faith with the subscribers to the Schools. Mr. Guthrie had implored universal aid, on the ground that the cause was, in the true sense, Catholic ; and that the work to be done belonged " to all denominations and all parties." Mr. Fox Maule, in advocating the cause of the schools at a great public meeting in Edinburgh, on the 7th of May, 1847, had said, amid the applause of the audience, " I do hope and trust, on this question of education, we may not hear, in these Industrial Schools, of the appearance of sectarianism at all." The liberal and rational position recently taken up by the Free Church Assembly as to national education, also seemed to indicate that Mr. Guthrie, and those at least of his coadjutors who were members of that sect, would act on the principles which it had publicly avowed.† "At none of the meetings which I attended," wrote Professor

---

* " Explanations regarding the Establishment of the United Industrial Schools: " W. Blackwood and Sons. 1847.

† In the Free Church Assembly of 1847, Dr. Candlish moved, and the Assembly adopted the motion,—" That this Assembly agree in the propriety of opening all public schools to those who wish to avail themselves of the merely secular part of the instruction embraced in them, without requiring attendance at any religious service or exercise either on week-day or Sabbath-day."

Gregory, " was there a whisper of such a thing as an exclusively Protestant character being given to the schools ; and I feel convinced that had such a principle been suggested, it would have been scouted by a large majority, the fact being quite notorious that the children of Irish Catholics constitute a very large proportion of the destitute children of this city . . . . . I desire nothing more earnestly than that the children should be instructed in practical Christianity, but I cannot see the justice of excluding, by the compulsory teaching of doctrinal Protestantism, any part of those who are the proper objects of the institution."*

The unsectarian party among the subscribers were anxious to settle the difficulty, by having it arranged that the Protestants and Roman Catholics should receive their religious teaching apart, and from different teachers. But Mr. Guthrie and his friends, insisting that they stood *in loco parentis* to the children, and were bound to teach them the Protestant religion, or none at all, would not accede to this reasonable proposal. The Roman Catholics, to show their desire to give and receive fair play, then held a meeting, at which they resolved to open a ragged school on their own resources, but in which Protestant children should be enrolled, and be permitted to receive Protestant religious instruction. Among other Protestants, Mr. Guthrie was invited to act on the Committee of the proposed school, but he refused to do so. To bring the matter to an issue, a meeting of all the parties interested was finally summoned to be held in the Music Hall on the 2nd of July.

* " Explanations," &c., pp. 29 30.

The debate which then ensued between Protestant sectarianism and Christian charity, is fallaciously described by Dr. Guthrie in the paper in "Good Words" already quoted, as a dispute between him and his party on the one hand, and those, on the other, who fought "for Popish intolerance." The verdict of the meeting was, as might have been expected from an Edinburgh crowd, in favour of the sectarianism which embodied that Anti-popish mania to which the Scotch mind is liable. But though the hands of the meeting were held up on the wrong side, the heads were on the right. Almost every man, whose support gave weight and credit to the movement, now drew back from alliance with Mr. Guthrie. Those, whose names were connected with the honourable traditions of free thought and liberal principles, in the better days when these reigned in Edinburgh, and made their sway to be felt throughout Britain, could no longer identify themselves with an institution which was avowedly sectarian and intolerant. Lord Jeffrey, Lord Murray, Lord Dunfermline, the Earl of Stair, the Gibson-Craigs, the Chamberses, Mr. J. H. Burton, Mr. George Combe, Mr. Charles Maclaren, Professor Pillans, Professor Gregory, Mr. Adam Black, Dr. John Brown, and many others, went heartily together in repudiating the principles which won a poor triumph in the Music Hall.

Lord Murray, in an admirable speech, explained the views of the liberal party as to these schools. His lordship, commenting on the statement of the Acting Committee as to the religious instruction to be given to the scholars, said:—

"It is said that it will be 'effectually secured by the superintendence of a Committee impartially selected from the various leading religious bodies composing the great bulk of the community.' There could not be a better mode devised of securing freedom from sectarian bias than that of selecting from all the religious bodies composing the great bulk of the community persons for the committee of superintendence. So far, we are perfectly agreed. The only question comes to be a question of fact—a question of fact which I never anticipated—and it is, have persons been selected from every religious body composing the great bulk of the community, to be placed on this superintending committee? If they have been so selected, all is well; I have no objection to make."

He then went on to show that one body—the Roman Catholics—had been excluded.

"I have no sympathy," continued Lord Murray, "with the Roman Catholics in religious views. I differ from them entirely. I regret our religious differences, but still I must acknowledge that they are a religious body; and why should they not have the same security against sectarian bias which is given to every sect of Protestants? Are they not exposed to greater risk? Do not we Protestants differ from Catholics more than we differ from one another? I hope that we agree better with each other in our religious views than we do with them; and yet security is given to every sect of Protestants, and no security whatever is given to Catholics in regard to these Schools. . . . . . . I know that many of my friends think that the Catholics have no right to complain—that they are very unreasonable. It may be difficult for me and my friends to bring ourselves to think that Protestants are ever . wrong, or that Catholics are ever right; but in order to come to a right opinion in this matter, I must reverse the case, and, putting the Catholics where the Protestants are, I suppose the Protestants to be in the same condition as the Catholics are here. Now, I will suppose that, instead of this occurring at Edinburgh, something similar to it occurred at Dunkirk—that there was at that place a great number of wretched children, in a deplorable state of ignorance and destitution—that a great many of them were Protestants, who, with their parents, had flocked there from various States of Protestant Germany—and that an amiable Roman Catholic clergyman, of great genius, who united the eloquence of Bossuet and Massillon with the benevolence and enlightened principles of Fenelon—and I assure you I cannot allude to Mr. Guthric, and say that he does not unite these excellences to all the graces of a Protestant clergyman—had published a most impressive and admirable discourse addressed to the public of Dunkirk, pointing out the misery and destitution of these children, and calling on all the inhabitants to unite, in order to give them education, religious instruction, and food; and a committee is appointed on the most liberal principles, to carry his views into effect. Well, the Fenelon of Dunkirk goes to Paris; and, in his absence, the committee proceed to make their selection. Whom do they select? They select a committee from all the various classes of Catholics; but they cannot find one single Protestant in Dunkirk to put upon the committee of superintendence. Nay, although a most respectable individual expressed his opinion that there should be a communication entered into with the Protestant clergy of Dunkirk, yet no communication was made to the Protestant clergy there, with regard to any one of the arrangements. They were treated as if the Protestants had no clergy. I put it to all Protestants present, if in these circumstances we had been at Dunkirk, and there was such a school proposed, whether any Protestant could possibly approve of sending his children to these schools, more especially since it was declared that religious training was to form an inseparable condition of his children receiving instruction and food. I put the case to all Protestants present—would they submit to their children falling under the domination of Catholics who refused to give Protestants that security, which they gave to every other sect of their own persuasion, that the schools should be free from sectarian bias? If that be the case—if no Protestant would submit to that—can we be surprised, when we reverse the case, that the Catholics who are here excluded in the manner which I have supposed the Protestants to have been excluded at Dunkirk, and which would not have been submitted to in any kingdom of Europe—can we be surprised that they object to it? They say, 'You give security to every other religious body, but you will not give security to us; you give religious instruction as part of the education, but you allow us no control—no share in the superintendence or management of the school;' and, therefore, (just as I put the case of the Protestants of Dunkirk,) the Catholics of Edinburgh, in conclusion, say, 'We will never submit to it.' . . . . . . I observe an express reference to what has been done at Aberdeen.   Now, I was surprised at this reference to Aberdeen.   Aberdeen was referred to as clearly establishing that in ragged schools religious instruction might be given free from all sectarian bias, and so as to excite no jealousy in any part of the community.   I have long taken a great interest in the schools at Aberdeen; but I happened to hear, with great sorrow and distress, that there was an entire split in these schools, arising, not from a religious dispute between Roman Catholics and Protestants, but between Protestants, the very persons whom we should have expected to agree among themselves—for the girls' school in Aberdeen was conducted by most zealous Protestants on both sides; but notwithstanding this, they have all split.   The Free Church children went to one side, and the children belonging to the Establishment went to the other, and there was an entire difference.   If, therefore, two bodies so nearly allied as they are—differing only on the point of Church government, but agreeing in the Westminster Confession of Faith and the Larger and Shorter Catechisms—cannot give religious instruction in the Ragged Schools of Aberdeen without coming to a rupture, how can we expect that Roman Catholics—from whom we differ so much—whose religious opinions we consider to be erroneous, and whose worship we consider to be somewhat tinged with idolatry—can submit to Protestants giving religious instruction without having some security, some share in the management, which may control a zeal for making converts which some persons may possibly have.   No doubt, while the war rages between Protestant and Protestant, the Catholic may feel a temporary security; when he sees them in violent collision about their own small differences, he may expect that they may forget their greater differences with him.   But if means have been taken, as it is supposed they actually have been taken, to avoid such differences here, he has not even the safeguard of a certain or probable conflict between these two bodies, who are supposed to be placed in a state of neutrality, by the selection of this committee of superintendence. The case of Aberdeen, therefore, satisfies me that such schools are not the least exposed to danger from sectarian zeal, which, if it rages among Protestants, is still more likely to prevail between Protestant and Catholic. I am far from wishing to avoid the question as to the instruction that is to be given. I have the misfortune to differ from Mr. Guthrie as to the possibility of giving religious instruction to Protestants and Catholics in the same school, free from sectarian bias. Let me put this, the simplest possible case. Phelim O'Shaughnessy comes up to the teacher:—'Please your honour, you have agreed to teach me the Word of God direct and free from taint;—you are acquainted with the whole Word of God.' I presume the answer would be, with due humility, in the affirmative. 'Then, may a poor boy, who is very ignorant, ask your honour's reverence a question?' Could any Protestant teacher refuse to answer the poor boy's question? 'I am very ignorant,' says Phelim; 'but your honour knows that good Mrs. Smith killed a baste last night, and sent the head to the school—and an iligant head it was; and this morning, being Friday, it has been cut down to be made into soup for us. Now, will your honour tell me, is there anything in the whole Word of God against my eating a small bit of that head this day at one o'clock?' Could any honest Protestant refuse to answer that there was nothing in the Word of God, so far as he knew it, against eating a bit of the cow's head? Yet a Protestant teacher, by giving this answer, would sanction what, according to the Roman Catholic faith, would be the commission of a religious offence. How can a Protestant give religious instruction to the children of both creeds, without being often obliged to say what must offend the faith of the opposite sect? If you do not give that instruction honestly, your Protestantism will be good for nothing. If you do so, you must express your own religious feelings, although you may wish to avoid doing so in an offensive manner. . . . . . .

" Fifteen Catholic children are said to have come to these schools, while there are at least five or six hundred who ought to attend them. If the mess of porridge and the good education are sufficient to overcome their objections, they will attend the school and say nothing. If they think that they have done what is against their faith, they will make no complaint to the

Protestant, but ask for comfort and consolation from those of their own sect; for it is from them alone that they can receive it. I trust that schools will be established which will give the best religious instruction to Protestants, without interfering with the religious opinions of Catholics—that the Scriptures will be read more regularly and frequently than they have hitherto been usually read in any Protestant schools in this country—and that the religious instruction thus given to Protestants will be better than it could be if any restraint were imposed upon it. I am not qualified to judge how religious instruction should be given to Catholics; that is a matter for Catholics alone to judge of and determine—both Protestants and Catholics keeping in view, in all instruction, the same principles of Christian charity which they both acknowledge. Catholics are as much entitled to judge as to the religious instruction of their children as Protestants : religious instruction ought to be as free in the one case as in the other. Protestants should see that good Protestant instruction shall be given to all the Protestant children; and it ought to be left free to the Catholics to do the same. I do trust that it will be given to both with a spirit of Christian charity which Protestants and Catholics both acknowledge ; and the children having received such religious instruction to its fullest extent, I see no reason why they may not afterwards read, write, cipher, or engage together in any branch of industry which may be thought advisable."

Lord Murray concluded as follows :—"I have no wish to divide the meeting. I am far from saying that these schools, conducted by zealous Protestants, will not do good, but they will not do the same good which I was so sanguine as to expect they might accomplish. I am perfectly satisfied that this meeting cannot alter the constitution of these schools : it is fixed, and, so far, must remain ; at least I will not attempt to disturb it. I wish these schools, though under a system of which I do not approve, every possible success. I acknowledge that there is a difference among my friends, not in principle, nor in the application of the principle, for we are perfectly agreed that religious instruction ought to be separated from ordinary education, and that industrial schools for destitute children form no exception to the application of that general principle. Some of my friends, however, will not agree to give any aid to any schools in which that principle is not recognised and carried into effect. I do not, however, consider myself precluded, after asserting that principle in its fullest extent, from contributing in some measure to the Protestant schools conducted by my zealous friends."

I have thought it worth while to make these extracts from Lord Murray's speech, which, wise and liberal as it is, at once explains the attitude assumed by those who opposed Mr. Guthrie, and rebukes the unworthy and ungenerous misrepresentations with which, after the lapse of fifteen years, that reverend philanthropist thought it proper to darken the aims and designs of those who drew back from his sectarian enterprise.*

The non-sectarians immediately set about organizing a school upon the principles which Mr. Guthrie and his friends had renounced. The "religious difficulty" was avoided by the simple expedient, which only fanaticism could reject or misrepresent, that the religious instruction should be distinct from the ordinary education given to the children. Protestant children, it was fixed, were to receive their religious instruction from Protestants only, and Catholic children theirs from Catholics only, and in separate rooms.† In this way the religious con-

* In the article in "Good Words" referred to above, Dr. Guthrie talks of his opponents as the "tools of Rome"—"those who fought for Popish intolerance"—"those between whom and us there could be no concord;" and makes merry over the "ludicrous" figure which their supporters cut in the Music Hall; although he admits it "would be unseemly to exult over their defeat."

† The rules laid down were, and are, the following :—

The Religious Instruction given in the Schools shall be exclusively and entirely under the direction of two separate Committees of Religious Instruction, namely, a Protestant Committee to be chosen by and from the Protestant members only of the General Committee; and a Catholic Committee to be chosen by and from the Catholic members only of the General Committee. In both cases the Committee of Religious Instruction shall not consist of less than three members, of whom one shall act as Secretary to the Committee, and also be a member of the Finance Committee.

The Protestant Committee of Religious Instruction shall have the entire management of the religious instruction given to Protestant children; as a

victions of parents, guardians, priests, or pastors, could not be offended ; and that kind of proselytism which, combining food and teaching, appealed to the starved stomach more directly than to the easy conscience, could not be practised.

"In all matters save detailed or dogmatic religious instruction, the children are provided for in company and from a common fund ; in that one department, the Protestant and the Roman Catholic children are taught separately, and from funds provided respectively by Protestants and Catholics; every child is bound to attend one or other of the religious classes ; and in those cases where the absence of any natural guardian, or the want of any former training, leaves a doubt as to which Church the child belongs, it is assigned to Protestantism, as being the prevailing faith of the community and of the subscribers and managers. In this way, no subscriber to the general fund of the United Industrial School, whatever his religious opinions, is asked to contribute either to the promotion or the assailing of any faith different from his own—either to the teaching of what he does not believe, or to the bribing of others to the profession of what *they* do not believe; while every subscriber has the means placed before him, by contributing to one of the religious instruction funds, of teaching his own faith to all save those who, by parentage and past training, are marked as of another Church."*

The institution opened suitable premises in the Old Town, in November, 1847, and took the name of the

part of which instruction, the authorised version of the Bible shall be read every day.

The Catholic Committee of Religious Instruction shall have the management of the religious instruction given to Catholic children, subject to the direction and control of the Catholic Bishop of the district. The reading of the Sacred Scriptures shall form a part of the daily religious instruction.

The Protestant Committee shall receive instructions from, and be reviewed in its proceedings by, the Protestant members of the General Committee only.

The Catholic Committee shall receive instructions from, and be reviewed in its proceedings by, the Catholic members of the General Committee only.

* "Edinburgh United Industrial School," 1851 : a valuable pamphlet by Mr. J. R. Findlay.

“ United Industrial School ;” Mr. Guthrie’s calling itself the “ Original Ragged School.” It was soon amply attended ; and its three branches of instruction, ordinary elementary education, religious, and industrial training,* were in full operation.

With this school, at its commencement, Dr. Lee had no connection. But as his opinions on education expanded, in view of the hopelessness of obtaining a national system which should overcome the religious difficulty and the jealousies of the sects, he grew more and more interested in it. He saw in it the only practical solution of the problem which legislators seemed to regard as insoluble; the diffusion of instruction both secular and religious, without introducing sectarianism into schools. Here the secular instruction was common to all ; the religious was given apart ; the common funds paid for the one, the special funds, specially subscribed and managed for this end by the parties interested, paid for the other.† He saw in it, also, a noble practical rebuke of the heresy, always too prevalent in Scotland, that a particular species of dog-

---

* Under the four classes of carpentry, tailoring, shoemaking, and book-binding.

† “ In any national system of education, the State ought to give secular, and ought not to give religious instruction. This opinion is clearly gaining ground, and as I never doubt that the truth will prevail in a country where there is free discussion and a free press, so I do not doubt that in the result there will be a system of National Education established, based on the principle that secular instruction is the duty of the schoolmaster, and that religious instruction is the duty of the parents, and of the Pastors of the parents. Until that principle is established under proper regulation, we shall have neither religious peace, nor the people so instructed as to enable them to exercise their civil rights usefully and with intelligence. The country cannot be in a safe state unless intelligence keeps pace with the extension of civil rights, and of political power conceded to the people. Secular instruction, when taught according to the models which experience has approved, inculcates and enforces by reverence for religion those moral principles and virtues which are common to all sects, leaving only to parents and their pastors to train their children in the tenets of that religious creed to which they belong.”—*Lord Dunfermline to Lord Murray*, 1847.

matic opinion can be more religious than justice, mercy, and truth.

The first time he spoke in public in support of the school, was at the Annual Meeting of the Subscribers, on 27th December, 1853.

In seconding one of the resolutions, he said :—

"You have begun by removing the temptation of *hunger*. You have followed the example of our blessed Saviour, who instead of questioning the multitudes that followed him, fed them. So have you done. Instead of asking the children how much they believed, or what they believed, or what their parents believed, you have begun by feeding the hungry, on which act, unless I very much misread the New Testament, a blessing has been pronounced .... Here you find going about the streets children of different religions, some of whose parents profess, but don't practise our own religion. Well, we feel a call upon us to instruct these children ; but there are other children whose parents profess a different religion. Shall we throw them out ? Shall these children not be taught to gain their bread, and do justly, and love mercy, because they are not prepared to receive all the instruction which we perhaps would like to convey to them ? Can these boys not learn to steal ? Can they not learn to rob ? Can they not learn to take our property, or perhaps our lives ? Are we to be interfered with in our efforts to defend ourselves against this, or in teaching them as much as they can be taught without involving the violation of any principle which we ourselves hold ? It seems to me the plainest thing in the world that if we cannot do all the good which we would like to do, or impart all the instruction we would like to impart, we should at least do all the good we can, and impart all the instruction which the parties concerned are willing to receive consistently with their own convictions, which we are bound to respect because they are their convictions. . . . . . A great deal is being talked and written, and a great deal for many years past has been talked and written, about national education. I think that till this hour I have never opened my lips in public on that subject. The reason was that I was not very clear on some of the points involved in it; and I wish that a great number of people who are equally in the dark with myself had imitated the same example, and kept silence until they had something to say. There is one thing, I think, which everybody must see—that in this country education, in the true sense of it, is only beginning. With all our boastings, and all our national conceit, I say, with perfect assurance of truth, that education is only beginning. There is a great body of people, indeed, who know a great many things, but how many people are there who have learned to think, and to think for themselves? It appears to me that a very great proportion of people in this country do what a certain animal does; when one animal of the species, in much authority, has taken a certain leap, a very large flock are always prepared to do the very same, even though that into which they leap may be a most unaccountable and dangerous position. And I do think that if to be educated is to acquire the power of observing and thinking for ourselves, the foundations of national education are still to be laid. I think, therefore, we are much obliged to any Institution which shows us that something is practicable which had been doubted before. Now, I consider that this Institution is in the way of showing that something is practicable, the practicability of which a great many people have very confidently doubted. Several years ago, when this institution was set agoing, people said it was impossible to do this. 'You can't do it,' said they—'you can't do the thing.' But it has been done; and I think, without much presumption, we may maintain that what has been done must be a thing possible, and that what is shown to be practicable must also be possible. The practicability of the thing has been demonstrated by this school, and I therefore draw the very profound inference that the possibility of the thing may be looked upon as established. This morning I have gone over the whole of this Institution. I have seen all the departments in operation, and I take the liberty of saying that, having considerable experience in the management of schools, there is a great deal indeed besides the matter I have alluded to in this school which should be an example to all schools in this country. A great many things are taught here which are not commonly taught in schools, but which would be a great advantage to be there taught. I may also add that the management of the school—and I may say this, not having any hand in it myself—appears to me a perfect model of accuracy, order, economy, and intelligence."

He followed his speech with a sermon, preached on the 8th of January, 1854, and which was afterwards published for behoof of the funds for the religious instruction of the Protestant pupils.

It is republished in "The Family and its Duties," under the title "On doing Good without seeking to promote Sectarian Interests." He expresses frankly his opinion about secular and religious education :—

"But some one will ask," he says, "'Do the children in this school not receive a religious education?' Now, suppose I should answer, 'No; they do not receive any religious education'—do you think it is not an immense step towards a religious education, that a person has been taught to read, and so is qualified to read the Bible, which, we Protestants say, contains the whole Christian religion? If this be no part of a religious education, strictly speaking, it is at least a great help towards it, and an indispensable qualification. Again, *cleanliness* is no part of a religious education, strictly speaking; yet wise men and pious have insisted that *cleanliness* is next to godliness, and is at least *half a virtue*. Truth-speaking, also, unless I mistake, is part of Christianity, for we are told, 'Lie not one to another,'—'Speak every man truth with his neighbour.' *Obedience*, in like manner, is a Christian virtue, and as such is solemnly enjoined in the New Testament; for there, children are charged to obey their parents; wives their husbands; servants their masters, and, in general, all of us those who are invested with lawful authority over us. Finally, *honesty* and *industry* are among the requirements of our holy faith, which charges us to be 'not slothful in business ;'—'let him that stole steal no more, but rather let him labour, working with his hands, the thing which is good. I ask, then, Whether children who have learned these lessons have learned no part of Christianity? whether in these acquirements (if they have made them) they have not acquired some elements at least of religious and Christian education; especially when, at the same time, they have been carefully instructed, from day to day, that they are the creatures of God, who is almighty, just, wise, and good, —who preserves them, and sees them continually,—to whom they are responsible for all their conduct,—whose favour is their life, his displeasure their destruction ? Without having received any special religious instruction, they would, I presume, in these general ideas and in those habits, have acquired a very momentous part of a Christian education.

"The branches, or subjects, now mentioned, most people would perhaps class under the general description of *Secular Education*. It is an opinion which seems to prevail very generally, that secular education, without religious education, would prove not only *useless* but *pernicious*. This opinion is constantly repeated; but it has never been established by any proof, so far as I have heard. Till it be proved, I shall take the liberty to question the soundness of that opinion—to pronounce it false, chimerical, childish, contrary to all reason, inconsistent with all fact and experience. This subject I cannot discuss at present. I shall only stop to remark that we may understand secular education to comprehend that knowledge of the works of God and the works of man, which we possess apart from revelation; and I should like to know which of these it is, the understanding of which, the contemplation of which, exercises a depraving effect upon the human mind ? Is it the heavens, which declare the glory of God—or the earth, which is full of his riches ? Is it our own bodies, which are fearfully and wonderfully made by Him ? Is it History, that solemn voice sounding throughout all ages and all climes, which is now, and has ever been to mankind, the living witness that God not only exists but reigns—that He is a Ruler whose righteous laws cannot be violated without entailing tremendous penalties, whoever the transgressor may be ? Which of these departments of secular education is it that is to do the mischief that is so perilous ? I hold that religious education should be united with secular, because man has eternal interests as well as temporal; but I hold, also, that secular education is *good* so far as it goes—that it is *profitable* so far as it goes, and that the possession of it is incomparably better and safer for all parties, than the want of it; and, therefore, if any impediment should prevent our communicating a strictly Christian education, it would be our duty to give a secular education; because this would prove beneficial, so far as it went. And I shall hold this opinion until some reason to the contrary shall be produced, which, so far as I have observed, has not yet been done."

CHAPTER VII.

REPUTE WITH THE RELIGIOUS WORLD AND RELATION TO
THE CLERGY.—LORD MURRAY'S ADVICE.—SERMONS
ON LAWS OF NATURE.—REFERENCE BIBLE.—DIARY.

"Mean men, in their rising, must adhere; but great men, that have strength
in themselves, were better to maintain themselves indifferent and neutral."—
BACON: *Essays—Of Faction.*

BY the time of which we have been speaking, Dr.
Lee had become almost entirely isolated from the most
of his fellow-clergymen in Edinburgh. They had no
sympathy with him; he had none with them. He could
not stand what appeared to him their narrow-mindedness
—their dull and supine conservatism. They could not
stand his liberal views—his love of progress—his indiffe-
rence to the shibboleths of party, and the time-worn
dogmas of the current interpretations of religious truth.
He could not be troubled with their little gossiping
interests, and with their peddling ways of managing the
general affairs of the Church. These affairs are very much
in the hands of certain ministers and elders in Edinburgh.
The Church has six chief missionary schemes — home
and foreign—and all the head offices of these were at
this time in Edinburgh. Instead of a Central Board of
Missions, with a paid Chairman, there are six Committees, with unpaid "Conveners," charged with the

management of the schemes. The convener, with a few dexterous friends, practically controls each scheme. A bustling clergyman, with a love of committees, is frequently a member of half a dozen at a time, and scuffles about from one to another with an air of "general missionariness" very impressive to the beholder. Much eloquence is poured forth over these committees' tables; and the cleric, who expends the greater portion of his time beside them, is generally himself under the impression—and persuades his admiring friends, in word or print, that he is "doing a great work," and that his shoulders bend beneath "the care of all the Churches."

Dr. Lee had no taste for this sort of thing. He was too sharp a man of business not to see that the committees were in general no models of intelligence or dispatch; but he had not patience enough to give that attention to the details of their transactions, and to their little arts and jobberies, which alone could have enabled him to control them. Besides, it was very uphill work to fight single-handed against a compact committee, and he honestly did not think it worth his while. On one occasion he attempted to alter the policy of a committee, and being steadfastly opposed, he completely failed; and thereafter he almost entirely withdrew from any interference, and his name was soon dropped out of the lists of committees. This was to be regretted. He ought to have taken a more patient interest in the schemes of the Church, even although he disapproved of their management. The majority of the six chief schemes did not recommend themselves to his co-operation. He had grave doubts about the scheme for the "Conversion of the Jews." He did not like the "Endowment" scheme, advocated with such noble enthusiasm by his great-hearted colleague, Professor Robertson. The design of this scheme—to provide a parochial endowment of £120 a year for every unendowed chapel and district—appeared to him to be practically the creating of a set of poor incumbencies, of which there was already plenty. To create these with one hand, and to collect funds for enriching impoverished livings with the other, seemed to him folly. He would have preferred a scheme for endowing a few large prizes in the Church, the effect of which, he believed, would be to elevate the general standard of clerical income, and the whole status of the clergy. He sympathized with the objects of the "Education" scheme, but felt himself hampered in his support of it by its necessary adherence to the principle of religious instruction. The "Home Mission" and the "Colonial Mission" were more to his mind. But as regarded the Home Mission, he thought far too much money was spent on stone and lime, and too little on providing suitable evangelists and teachers for the half heathen masses of our towns and large mining and manufacturing populations. He really felt also that the Church did not offer to the ignorant at home, in whose behalf the "Home Mission" laboured, or to the pagans abroad, to whom the "India Mission" devoted itself, such unexceptionable instruction or so pure an example of high and united Christian life, as to make it worth a man's while to give her much aid in her enterprise, in Scotland or in India. He writes in February, 1854 :—

"I confess I have little sympathy with their schemes of missions, education, and Church extension. The things to be propagated are so poor, narrow, and ineffectual, that I cannot feel zealous to extend them. To multiply preachers who are no true ministers of the Word, who fancy there is no Word of God but in the Bible, and show daily that they have no faculty to find it even there—who have the word neither in their mouth nor in their heart—who preach us farther and farther away from the true and living God, and send us out of the Church with even less faith than we carried into it—to multiply such preachers till they cover the land is, I think, a very small benefit. Should we not have more religion if half the preachers whose sermons we now suffer were sent to honest mechanical trades, which, no doubt, they might exercise powerfully and profitably for the community and themselves also—with pleasure, too, and good conscience?

"A man who does not know more and cannot see farther than common men, why should he be elevated in a pulpit and be the only man in a whole parish authorised to teach in the name of the Lord? Infinite controversies have been how ministers should be *appointed?* But the great question is how, being discovered to be no ministers, they should be *removed?* Is there no remedy for this sore evil under the sun? Shall a whole generation be starved because a patron or a bishop, or a set of pew-holders, or a Kirk Session, made a mistake, wanting the gift of discerning spirits, and sent a man to minister who wanted inspiration like themselves? Would people submit so tamely to any other grievance of so huge a magnitude?"

Again he reverts to the same subject, in connection with the evils of sectarianism : —

"People are discouraged from missionary enterprise by the sectarianism which prevails. They doubt whether the Christianity which is current is worth sending to the heathen; whether that which sows such seeds among us is worth labouring to diffuse among other nations. The same that makes Christianity less worth to ourselves renders it less worth the sending to others. If we feel little the better, no wonder if we ask, Why should we make sacrifices to diffuse this? And when we have made it as worthless as possible at home, we have supplied the strongest objection against transporting it abroad. Moreover, we have prepared the most formidable obstacle against its success abroad, if we do attempt to plant it among heathen nations; for we have provided an objection for the heathen: Why ask us to embrace a religion, respecting whose nature you, who profess it, maintain fifty or sixty different theories? Who are the authors of this evil? The clergy. Generally speaking, they,—their ignorance, pride, intolerance, &c., &c., have produced very much of this directly by themselves— indirectly through the Governments. And who are to remove it? Not they. If the people wait till they agree in making a religion for them, they will wait for ever. Let the people know they need not wait till their clergy shall concoct a religion which may unite them."

The open expression of these opinions vexed the clerical mind, and did him harm in the esteem of those good people who are apt to judge a clergyman's worth and usefulness by the exactness of his conformity to the ordinary professional standard, and by the amount of work which he performs in the accepted routine. Dr. Lee might extend the Church's influence to persons whom it had not before reached, and might enforce the great duties of charity, and liberality, and tolerance, and admirable lessons of moral purity and social wisdom, upon those who had been unaccustomed to hear these from the national pulpit; but all this availed him little, if he dared to disbelieve in the Church's missions, or to express a doubt of the wisdom of the " conveners."

About this period also, evil tongues were wagging scandalously over his alleged heterodoxies. We have noticed how he had seen cause to charge a co-presbyter with traducing him in 1849. Since that time, the dirty work had had no need of a co-presbyter's help or con- nivance. His honest frankness of speech, his sharp satiric power, his practical preaching on moral and social questions, and his political liberalism, all loomed before the leaden eye of the religious world of Edinburgh—one cloud of darkness. He was a moderate,—he was a rationalist,—he was a Unitarian! The last especially was a favourite charge. It was alleged he had emptied the Unitarian chapel. "That is a fault!" said he. "I should have thought people would have been glad to hear it."

Unitarianism has never been strong in Scotland; but its preaching has always been intellectual and interesting to educated men. Many who had been attracted to the Unitarian chapel by this magnet, came over to Dr. Lee's church when they found there what interested and instructed them. That he allured them by preaching Unitarianism was untrue. Like every thoughtful man, he felt the difficulty of pronouncing dogmatically upon the mysterious doctrine of the Trinity; and he could sympathize with those who looked in vain for any practical benefit or spiritual light in the popular expositions and illustrations of that doctrine. He held, too, that Christ being "the one mediator between God and man," it was out of place to address prayer to him, in public worship, instead of to God *through* him. This created a marked difference between his prayers and those of others, accustomed to mingle addresses to the Father with addresses to the Son, in the same act of public worship. But nothing, in his belief or in his practice, ever derogated from the loving reverence due to the divine Son of God.

"I had few opportunities of hearing him preach," writes a lady who knew him well, "but after being told by many people that he had become a Unitarian, and denied altogether the Divinity and Atonement of our

Saviour, I determined to satisfy my own mind by telling him what I had heard, and asking him to tell me frankly if he had so changed his views. I shall never forget the expression of his face as he stood still—(we were walking in the Square garden at the time)—and looking at me almost with tears in his eyes, he said, 'Those who charge me with such opinions little know me. My entire trust for everything is placed in the atonement of our Lord Jesus Christ.'"

The epithets "Rationalist," and "Unitarian,"—and by those who used them, these were intended to express a thoroughly reprobate state,—were, however, freely flung at him. In Edinburgh these names were sure to poison public opinion, wherever that opinion absorbed any of the spirit of the religious world. That world in Edinburgh is narrow-minded, imbued with a harsh sectarianism and a bitter essence of extreme Calvinism. Divided, as it is, into Established and dissenting coteries, it is, as a whole, characterized by this; and any supposed heretic is hunted down by the whole pack. In these coteries a formidable power is lodged in certain "devout and honourable women," who, along with much zealous well-doing and activity, wield an indefnable influence as the conservators or as the destroyers of clerical reputations. This influence was ever set against Dr. Lee. Men, but chiefly women, who had never heard him preach or lecture, or had never read a word that he had spoken or written, were not ashamed to rake up out of the gutters of vulgar slander every charge that stupidity or jealousy or ill-will could forge against him, and to put the garbage into new circulation, with an added flavour of their own. Slander is a vice seldom preached against, and slander of Dr. Lee was never preached against. Dr. Lee himself had always a strong suspicion that some of his brethren rather enjoyed the slander, and helped it quietly when they could.

Be this as it may, between them, for the most part, and him, there was no sympathy and little intercourse. Cut off from alliance with men of his own profession, it was inevitable that he should seek for friendship and society among others : and he readily found this among the most intellectual and cultivated laymen that Edinburgh possessed. His most intimate friends were Lord Murray and Mr. George Combe. He became, also, a frequent visitor at the "Scotsman" office, a friend of Mr. Russel, and a welcome contributor to his columns.

What has been said as to his relations to the clergy will throw light on an entry in his diary in March, 1854: "Had a call from Lord Murray. His benevolence and good sense appear to me equally conspicuous. He called to tell me plainly that my contempt of the clergy is too conspicuous in my preaching, and, in short, to hint to me what I have indeed often myself been conscious of—that there is too much asperity and bitterness in my preaching—too much personality. 'Dull wasps sting,' as Lord Murray very wisely reminded me. Let me pay particular attention to this. It is indeed a sin that doth too easily beset me. And may God give me grace to imitate the meekness and gentleness of Christ—ἀληθεύων ἐν ἀγάπῃ."

The following correspondence shows his own impression of the feeling with which he was regarded by the clergy, and indicates that Lord Murray's cautions were probably not uncalled for :—

“EDINBURGH, 6th December, 1853.

“To Dr. ——

 “My dear Sir,

  “I am sorry I missed you yesterday. I have never thought of publishing the sermons which I have preached the last two Sundays, as they contain only matters which are quite familiar to one class of the community, and which another class seem anxious to shut their eyes to. I cannot expect that these would attend to anything I could say. I am not aware that they contain anything inconsistent with the standards of the Church, or anything on account of which I could be annoyed by any Church court: so that I have no apprehension on that score, though undoubtedly some of my views are very offensive to many of my brethren. As I am writing on this subject I may mention a thing which I have wished to hint to you some time past. The circumstance that so many persons now attend our church who are known to have held opinions inconsistent with the doctrines of the Church of Scotland, cannot but attract attention ; and I doubt not some persons would be very glad if they could infer from this fact that my preaching commended itself to those persons, because it taught their own heresies. You, and all my hearers, know how absurd this is : yet it is a conclusion not too absurd for ignorance or malignity to draw. Now I think some of my hearers have sometimes given occasion to such speculation, by speaking of my preaching as if it might expose me to question by the Church courts, &c. And what I have to request of you is, that if you hear any of them talking in this strain, you will point out to them the impropriety of so speaking ; as such observations can only tend to produce the result which they apprehend—very unnecessarily, I believe. The Church courts are showing no inquisitorial activity at present, and I should be sorry that any of my own flock, who are also, I believe, all of them my sincere friends, should speak in such a way as may put it into their heads to give me trouble. At the same time I should preach before the General Assembly any of my sermons on the Laws of Nature and fear no ill consequence.—I am, &c.,

“R. Lee.”

REPLY.

" 6th December, 1853.

" MY DEAR SIR,

"I thank you for your letter, and will attend to what it contains. I hope that nothing will occur which is calculated to interrupt your career of usefulness. I do not doubt that you are within the rules of your Church in what you preach, and I think the better of the Church of Scotland, which is the Church of my youth, because of the excellent matter which flows from one at least of her pulpits. I am occasionally led into conversation by others on the subject of your sermons, and, on these occasions, have employed language similar to what you once said to me on this subject:—that it seemed to me, that, without disavowing the peculiarities of the Church of Scotland, you did not think it necessary to insist on these to the exclusion of a sort of matter which is more useful and practical, and far more to my taste.

"My expressions yesterday arose from a consciousness of what you mention in your note, that you are surrounded by certain persons to whom your liberality is the greatest of heresies, and who would torture your expressions into heresies if they could. The fate of Dr. Wright, of Borthwick,* for writing some excellent works, has often presented itself to my mind when I have heard you combating some popular error or delusion. But this was before the disruption, and I trust that common sense has a better footing now for encountering such miserable fanaticism and illiberality as that which you have been lately controverting; and that a day is coming when it will supplant within the National Church much of that cold formalism on the one hand, and that rampant intolerance on the other, to both of which your preaching is so decidedly and so honourably opposed. It seems to me that the condition of a man's thinking for himself upon religion, is that he must not expect to find his individual opinions closely represented in any church, though he may find in some churches much useful instruction. Of the first of these propositions I have had ample experience. Of the last, my experience, since I became your hearer, has been so completely satisfactory that no church I have ever attended has afforded equal satisfaction to me and to my family and friends; and I will add that had there been such a church

* Deposed by the General Assembly of 1841.

to be found among the Established Churches of Edinburgh when I wandered from them in search of something more to my mind, it would have saved me from much trouble and disappointment.

"Yours always sincerely,

"Rev. Dr. Lee."   "————."

The sermons, which excited at once the admiration and the apprehensions of his friends, were, more especially, those on the Laws of Nature, and those on Toleration. The former were preached in November and December, 1853, and appear to have been suggested to his mind by Lord Palmerston's letter to the Presbytery of Edinburgh. The cholera was in the country in the autumn of this year. The Presbytery, "thinking that from their position they were bound to take the lead,"* wrote a letter to Lord Palmerston, the Home Secretary, to ask if the government was going to appoint a Fast Day because of the cholera. Lord Palmerston, in reply, read the Presbytery a lesson upon the natural laws of health, which, if observed, would, he averred, protect the people against infection, and, if neglected, would revenge themselves, in spite of Fast Days. He advised them to see to the cleaning out of the dirty haunts of poverty and disease, and the removal of the sources of contagion, which, if suffered to remain, would "infallibly breed pestilence, and be fruitful in death, in spite of all the prayers and fastings of a united but inactive nation."

This answer took the Presbytery very much aback, and scandalized the religious world sadly. But people with a more intelligent faith in the Divine government,

* See Buckle's "History of Civilization," vol. ii., p. 590. Readers, acquainted with the mode of observance of "Fast Days" in Scotland, will be struck with the unnecessary vehemence of Mr. Buckle's indignation, which proceeds on a total misconception of the usages of the Scotch people.

approved of the sound common sense of Lord Palmerston's letter. Mr. Combe writes to Dr. Lee on 31st October :—" You appear not to have been at the meeting of Presbytery when Lord Palmerston's letter was read. It is making a great impression among *laymen* against the Presbytery. Mr. Robert Cox met Sir David Brewster in a railway carriage, and gave him the letter to read, when he said that Lord P. was quite right. He is the scientific oracle of the Free Church. I am told that a collection has been made of the newspapers that noticed the letter, and sent to Lord P. to show him how strongly he is supported by the press."

Dr. Lee tried to improve the opportunity which the occupation of the public mind with Lord Palmerston and the Presbytery offered, by his discourses on the Laws of Nature. "Divines," he says in beginning the first sermon, " commonly show great impatience, and even resentment, when any one insists on what are called *Laws of Nature.* I propose to inquire a little into this subject; but as I am speaking to many young people, and perhaps to some illiterate people, the philosophers among you will pardon me if I talk in a very familiar style, and insist on things which every one knows who has paid any attention to such matters." He then defines the laws or properties of nature, " on whose uniformity the sciences are built;" and, stating the ordinary objection, that if we admit universal and unchangeable *laws,* we dethrone *God* the first cause, and set up nature and second causes in His place, he repels it at some length, arguing that " if perfect order and regularity shut out the Deity, perfect disorder and confusion must bring Him in, and so Chaos be the proper throne of God," who, S. Paul teaches us, is the God "not of confusion, but of order." He shows that, in fact, the uniformity of the Laws of Nature (as is pointed out by Paley, &c.) is the great argument for the unity and perfectness of God. Then, with a direct reference to the Presbytery and their letter; and warming, towards the close, into the more eager and half-satiric tone which those who used to hear him will remember well, and which they knew betrayed no bitterness of feeling, but only his restrained impatience of bigotry and his zeal for truth, he says :—"Is it not surprising to find people now talking as if every new disease, every pestilential visitation, were, in its nature, miraculous, and therefore should be cured or prevented miraculously ? For if it come, like the plagues of Egypt, miraculously, it must also go like them miraculously. But if it come according to the common laws of nature, it may be expected to go according to the same. And if the crop fails, we find a whole host of men vociferating, as if such failure were a miraculous visitation—the punishment of some sin which has no visible connection with the calamity—and suggesting, if not insisting, that a miraculous remedy must be effected. We find the language of the Old Testament, and cases derived thence, quoted as applicable to the calamities which befall *us*, as if those who so quote did not know that they are not Jews, and therefore not under the law, that the Old Testament dispensation is abolished, and that the language which they so abuse was the language of a dispensation which claims everywhere to be miraculous, and that the language is totally inapplicable regarding a dispensation which we know, by experience, is not miraculous.　Such use of Scripture language I should call a daring impiety, were it not an incredible stupidity. . . . .　You may ask me whether I think God may not occasionally vary the laws of nature, and whether the doctrine I have held does not virtually thrust God aside, and make us trust to these laws of nature?　I reply, I believe God has as much power to alter the laws of nature as He had at first to establish them; and I believe that He would change them if they could be made better.　But knowing they cannot be improved, I conclude they will not be altered out of deference to the ignorant fancies or weak wishes of foolish men, who would soon ruin themselves and the world, if God were not so merciful as to save them from the effects of their own foolish desires."

Many people, he says in the second sermon, seem to think the world is the Devil's, rather than God's, and nature the enemy of revelation.　On the contrary, he explains, nature and revelation are in perfect harmony, parts of one great whole, each illustrating the other. The Bible teaches us that nature is a revelation of God. Science helps us to understand the Bible,—as, for example, in enabling us to interpret rightly the Scriptural language about the creation of the world, the Second Advent, the Body and Blood of Christ in the Sacrament,* and other points.　The laws of nature have been fixed, that men, understanding them, might *obey*

* The controversy as to Transubstantiation is just a "question whether the language of Scripture is to be understood according to the interpretation which science suggests, or literally.　The Bible says, 'The bread is my body.'　Science says, 'The bread is not flesh and blood, but simply and physically bread; for when analysed, the sacramental bread is found to have the same constituent parts and all the same properties as other bread.'"
—*Sermon.*

them. "And," says Dr. Lee, "what I wish to impress upon you is that you are under *obligation* to obey these laws, and that if you do not obey them, neither prayer nor any other means of grace will save you from the punishment of your neglect." He goes on to illustrate this with much force and directness:—"In one of the hospitals, of which we have so many, prayers are offered daily, as for other blessings, so for the *health* of the inmates. The children, some years ago, were lodged in a damp building; the rooms were too small, and ill ventilated, and the mortality during eight years was no less than one in $37\frac{1}{2}$. Various changes were introduced, however, in the diet of the inmates, and in improving the internal arrangements, particularly in the rooms where they slept, till from one dying in every $37\frac{1}{2}$, there died only one in 66, one in 120. Now, it does not appear that more prayers were offered in this hospital of late years than before; on the contrary, it is certain that there was as much prayer for health when one died in 37, as when only one died in 120." If these be facts, he urges, we must accept their teaching, and not call it "piety," to shut our eyes to them, for facts are God's lessons. And to expect that prayer will avert disease, the physical means of averting which we neglect, is to expect that God will work a miracle to remedy the evils of our ignorance and sloth. In common life, he says, men would laugh at such expectations. "If one ship in a fleet was attacked with scurvy, while all the rest escaped, should we seek for an explanation of this difference in the fact that in that ship prayers were not offered regularly and devoutly? Would the Admiralty receive that as a satisfactory solution of the difficulty ? A person who offered such an explanation, would be considered as fit for Bedlam ? And yet men do propound such theories, and are revered as shepherds of the people!* Pious men are as much concerned as philosophic and philanthropic men, to put a stop, if possible, to the fanatical notions which are sought to be maintained on this subject. Prayer is too important an ordinance connected with our spiritual affairs, too precious a means of grace, too powerful an instrument for purifying our souls of their evil passions, and rendering us fit for a better world, to be reduced to a scavenger, made a substitute for sweeping our streets, draining our towns, cleaning and ventilating houses, practising temperance and moderation, and, in short, doing those other common duties which involve some trouble, require some expense, and demand some self-denial. But prayer demands none of these. Because *it is cheap*, the Pharisee, who is a great economist, and would serve God at the smallest possible expense, is always for prayer. This he would virtually make a substitute for all duties and all sacrifices. . . . . ' Wash you, make you clean; put away the evil of your doings from before mine eyes; cease to do evil; learn to do well. . . . . If ye be willing and obedient, ye shall eat the good of the land : but if ye refuse and rebel, ye shall be devoured with the sword : for the mouth of the Lord hath spoken it.' This is the reply of God to that people, who, in the days

---

* It was common to represent the cholera as a plague sent because of the sins of the people. Similarly, at a later date, the rinderpest was occasionally described as a punishment for Sunday trains.

of Isaiah the prophet, refused to give him obedience, to wash them and make them clean, but were most liberal in incense, Sabbath meetings, prayers, and fasts. 'He that hath ears to hear, let him hear.'"

The third sermon is on the duty of prayer, in its relation to the laws of nature, and shows that "prayer itself is enforced by our Lord on this very consideration, that it is connected with certain blessed consequences with the fixity of a law—a law of the spiritual world." In the spiritual sphere we are to expect the answer to our prayers, not in a disturbance of the order of nature for our sakes. " So then, you will say, has prayer nothing to do with our outward condition ? Has it no part to act in the material improvement of the world ? Quite the contrary. Its effects are most powerful, its exercise most beneficial here also, as well as in that spiritual region which is its appropriate sphere. But how ? Not surely by suspending the laws of nature, but by leading us to observe and study them, and rendering us so docile that we may obey them." * But the age of miracles being over, he maintains that prayer can no longer be expected to produce healing, or the like effects, which S. James, and other apostles in that age, taught their disciples to look for. He enlarges at much length in the fourth and last sermon, on this distinction between the age of miracles and the miraculous dispensation, and the present age and dispensation, with the view of demonstrating that nothing affirmed as to the power of prayer in the former, can warrant our belief in

* Some very valuable thoughts in connexion with this subject will be found in the Preface to the second edition of Dr. M'Leod Campbell's work on the Atonement. M'Millan and Co., 1867.

its possessing a similar power in the latter. Passing on to a very earnest, and indeed solemn, exposition of the uses of afflictions, such as those which were over-shadowing the land at that time, he says :—" We should desire something much more earnestly than even to be delivered from them, and labour for something much more diligently than even to have them removed ; that they may be so sanctified to us, by the grace of God, as to work in us the peaceable fruits of righteousness, as to make us wisely number our days, and consider our work upon the earth; and so to prevent our living without faith, and dying without hope. . . . . Let us be washed in those waters of repentance and reforma-tion, which at once cleanse and save the soul, and not bring upon ourselves that penal fire, which will indeed cleanse the world, but only by consuming the im-penitent workers of iniquity. For God will have his world cleansed, either by water or fire, either by our being reformed, or destroyed."

These four sermons, and the series on Toleration, preached in March and April, 1854, produced a very strong impression.

The series on Toleration forms one closely connected treatise on that subject, and can hardly be called sermons in the usual acceptation of the term, although arranged in four separate discourses for the purpose of delivery. Dr. Lee intended to publish these, but did not live to carry out the intention.

Another noteworthy sermon of this period was that preached on the National Fast Day, 26th April, 1854, on account of the war with Russia.

The subject is the lawfulness of war; and he takes the

opportunity of replying to the arguments of the Peace Society, which had already done no small mischief by misleading public opinion on the Continent; and was still, as Dr. Lee says in his introduction to the reprint of the Sermon, in "The Family and its Duties," extremely turbulent and noisy; so that it might be said of its members, as Cowper said of the Whigs of his day, "They talk of peace till they disturb the State." Mr. Combe, who was a very constant and almost always eulogistic critic of Dr. Lee's sayings and doings in those days, writes to him about the sermon thus :—

"EDINBURGH, 13*th May*, 1854.

*   *   *   *   *   *   *

" Please accept of my best thanks for your very able and eloquent sermon on war. I belong to the Peace Society, but am not a non-resisting member. I lament that what I consider a good cause is rendered ridiculous by absurd fanaticism. Your defence of the present war is vigorous, and, as an answer to the fanatics, it is irresistible ; and I do not dissent from your conclusions. Still there is a view of the question which I have never seen stated, and which I have no time now to detail, but which some day we may discuss, that leaves a shade of doubt on my mind whether the war might not have been avoided by us. I can merely state a general outline of my difficulty. I have a thorough conviction that this world is actually under a real, practical divine government (although, for believing this, many persons think me a fanatic in my own way). No course of action can be sound, or in its ultimate results beneficial, that does not harmonise with the principles of this government. One of these seems to me to be that nations must proceed in improving their whole faculties as individuals, and their institutions and modes of action as nations ; otherwise undergo the natural consequences of neglecting to do so. One of these is conquest by a barbarous but more energetic neighbour; and out of these conquests ultimate good is evolved by God's laws, even although, in human eyes, the aggressors may have been morally unjustifiable. Both parties are in the *animal phase of national existence,* and the natural law is, that in the conflict of animals, the strongest prevails. But the conquering nation is itself under divine rule. Its barbarism renders it feebler, the more it extends itself; and hence Russia, with Turkey under her sway, would actually be less able to conquer civilised Europe than in her present state. Great intellect and great morality are necessary to keep a great heterogeneous empire permanently united; and greater still, to combine and direct its force aggressively against more enlightened nations. History shows that an ignorant and fanatical people cannot permanently be upheld by foreign friendly hands; and if there be any degree of soundness in these principles, the Russians might have been left to deal with the Turks in their own way, and Russia been weaker, and Turkey ultimately roused and improved either by Russian oppression, or Russian wisdom, most probably the former. England and France have undertaken the task of saving Turkey from the natural consequences of her own neglect of God's imperative laws; and although I feel all your indignation against the falsehood, hypocrisy, and grasping ambition of Russia, I do not see my way clear to the conviction that God has given to England and France the commission to arrest her in her iniquities, and to save defaulting Turkey from the consequences of her sins; but I have a secret suspicion that had the Turks and Russians been left to themselves, God's laws would have evolved out of their conflicts consequences more beneficial to both of themselves and to Europe, than are likely to be achieved by France and England taking the place of Providence.

"I state this, however, as a view that is perplexing me, and not as one that I have adopted as absolutely true and sound. Time will test it, although I shall never see the issue. If England and France are acting in conformity with the laws of the divine government, good will come out of it; if not, evil; and I leave the issue to God, without blaming our rulers, who are obviously acting under a high and noble sense of duty. If the Turks had been a people like the Swiss, I should have said 'they have not brought this invasion on themselves: it is pure wanton aggression on the part of Russia;' and I should then have held that God's law justified all moral nations in protecting a moral and intelligent people from the outpourings of animal aggression, and should have anticipated success and advantage to the *protégé* and the protectors also from such conduct. But heaven is weary looking on the aggressions exercised by the Turks on their Christian fellow-subjects, and their other iniquities."

Dr. Lee, about this time, was probably preaching at his best. He always wrote and spoke most vigorously when under the stimulus of opposition; and he had been led to sundry subjects of discourse, on which he felt compelled to speak his mind stoutly against current opinions and traditions. He also had the incitement afforded by the intelligent sympathy of a highly cultivated and steadily increasing congregation. Men, especially, of liberal ideas, and who loved practical Christianity better than dogmatic theology, rallied round him. He had, moreover, sufficient leisure for research and thought and composition, having to preach but once on the Sunday. All this helped to make his preaching peculiarly substantial, interesting, and telling. He regarded the pulpit as the chair of Christian instruction, and he used it conscientiously as such—week after week striving "with all diligence" to expound to his people all he himself had learned of that truth which should make them free. Heated declamation, tricks of rhetoric, theatrical attitudes, florid illustration, he heartily contemned. He went to the pulpit to impress on the minds and consciences of his hearers neglected or misunderstood truths and duties—not to tickle their fancy with mere oratory. His manner of delivery was sometimes cold and measured—professorial rather than clerical; and the academic "Gentlemen," which now and again would slip out, instead of the sermonic "Brethren," showed how habitually the idea of instructing those whom he was set to teach was present to his mind. He looked on his congregation much in the light of a vaster and more varied "class." He never went into the pulpit without having something to say, when he got there, which justified his going. And didactic, or even dry, as a lover of rousing declamations might consider him at all times, and as he certainly was at some times, he yet almost always, as he drew his argument or counsel to a close, warmed into a fervour of feeling, and rose to a clear, terse eloquence, which from him was far more memorable and impressive than any loud or excited flights could have been, or ever are. "As a preacher," said Principal Tulloch, in his funeral sermon at Greyfriars, on Sunday, 29th March, 1868—

"Dr. Lee had, especially during the last fifteen or twenty years, acquired great distinction, and yet it may be certainly said of him that he never courted popularity in the pulpit. He had none of the mere dazzle of rhetoric; he had but little of the customary fervour of the evangelist. He never aimed to impress by the mere declamatory force of what he said; with all his powers as a debater, and his frequent eloquence as a speaker, he had little or none of the abandonment of the oratorical temper. There was no hurry, nor glow, nor strong colour in his preaching. He valued, perhaps too slightly, the efficacy of such qualities in the pulpit; he could be sharply critical on any extravagant display of them. But withal he was a preacher of a high order. I do not mean merely that he showed in his sermons all the clearness, vigour, and life of his remarkable intellect; but that he had the highest of all qualifications of the preacher. He had always something to say. Sunday after Sunday he came here with his mind well informed and exercised by some Christian doctrine or duty, which he considered it important to declare to you. He was constantly going deeper into the great truths which it is the business of the Christian preacher to handle; and, therefore, like the householder in the Gospels, he was constantly bringing forth from his treasures things new and old. His idea of preaching was undoubtedly that of a continued education more than that of a mere outpouring or traditional commentary respecting any truths, however important. He freely handled all topics which he considered to have any bearing on the religious intelligence or the religious life, and in this manner gave a constant variety and interest to his sermons. Not merely the numbers, but especially the character, of the congregation which he here gathered round him testify, more than any words of mine can do, to the attractiveness, the instructiveness,—above all, to the spiritual force that was felt to lie in his teaching."

The congregation which he formed was certainly, in itself, a striking evidence of the power of his preaching. No doubt, many were attracted by his manner of conducting the devotions of his people, but by far the greater number came for the sake of the instruction which he imparted. A more intelligent and more critical congregation—one combining so many varied interests and different elements of mental culture, and composed so largely of men—could not be found in Scotland, and probably never had before met in any church in Edinburgh. To many of the men who had attended Dr. Lee's church, preaching like his was so new, they expected so little to hear it in one of the National Churches, that they were apt to express their admiration too freely. It was not perhaps altogether wholesome for a clergyman, who was a kind of Ishmaelite among his clerical brethren, to find himself hailed as the Christian oracle of a highly refined, intellectual, and benevolent set of men, who, he could not but feel, were in all mental gifts and graces,—in beauty of character and social attractiveness,—very different from the mass of those who called him, or encouraged others to call him, a heretic and a rationalist.   The natural tendency was to make Dr. Lee regard, with an increasing impatience and scorn, the opposition he met with in the Church Courts and the opinions of the majority of his clerical brethren.   The more sure he felt of the concurrence and sympathy of the educated laity around him, the less he attended to the scruples, tenets, and traditions of the clergy.   This was an inevitable consequence, but an unfortunate one, leading to wider estrangements and more hostile feelings.   Few men, probably, have been as little moved by popular approbation as Dr. Lee.   For mere applause indeed he cared nothing; but he could not fail to value the feeling for him manifested by thoughtful and influential men; which was allowed, it seems to me, too open an expression.   It was all very well for Lord Murray to warn his minister against showing too freely his "contempt for the clergy;" but his lordship did not add the best commentary on his advice, when he wrote such a note as this :—

"DEAR DR. LEE,—Lady Murray and I were much delighted with your sermon yesterday.   It was clear, concise, and well reasoned, and at the same time went over a great deal of ground, defining clearly every proposition you laid down, and making your conclusions almost self-evident.

"Lord Handyside compared it to a discourse of Principal Campbell's in 1780, which I think I once had."

Mr. Combe writes in a like strain frequently.   "Mrs. Combe* reported to me," he says on one occasion in 1853, "that your whole service on Sunday, in manner, style, and thought, was the highest she has heard in

---

* Mrs. Combe was a daughter of Mrs. Siddons.

Presbyterian Scotland; and she has heard some of the celebrities." Again: "Mrs. Combe and Mr. —— gave me a very interesting report of your concluding sermon yesterday. They say that it appeared to them to make a deep impression on the audience. It may form an epoch in preaching." In reference to the sermons on the Laws of Nature, a well-known gentleman writes :—"Your sermons have given the greatest possible satisfaction to those among my friends who have heard them, as well as to myself. When one considers the immense pulpit-power running to waste throughout Scotland, and how vast is the amount of good that might be done with it, if rational and well-informed men were to wield it, one is apt to grow melancholy over the spectacle. Your example will in due time produce excellent fruit." This was the kind of letters that came to him, assuring him of the support and regard of those whose opinion he, or any man, was justified in rating at a very high value. Over against these he had to range the demonstrations of Dr. Muir and the Rev. John Stewart, the minister of Liberton. We can scarcely wonder that his respect for his own order did not grow apace.

In his diary for 4th May, 1853, is this entry :—"Finished this day the most laborious labour I have ever undertaken, the Reference Bible. On the whole, it was, as far as time is concerned, a very improper work for me to have engaged in, occupied as I am with other duties, though, as an exercise connected with the Scriptures, most useful and profitable. Now it is finished, I do not regret having undertaken it; and I am truly thankful I am spared to complete it. My friend, Dr. Barclay, did part of the work—from Proverbs to

Malachi, both inclusive. I hardly know what character to impute to the work. I hope it will be found to be an improvement on the Reference Bible commonly in use."

It was published in 1854. This edition of the Bible has been found of great service to attentive readers of the Scriptures. It contains about sixty thousand carefully collated references. The "Witness" newspaper, which was then the champion of dissent, disgraced its columns by a clumsy and stupid attack on Dr. Lee, in a review of the work. The reviewer, who was understood to be a learned doctor of the "Free" Church, tried to fasten on him the charge of propagating heresy by means of his references, and especially of attempting to inculcate the doctrine of "Universal Redemption." There was no conceivable ground for the attack, which was met in a set of brilliant replies in the "Scotsman." The malicious assailant, whose blundering assault proved nothing but the general ill-will of which it was the indication, was convicted of almost every crime which a critic could commit,—gross ignorance, and grosser misrepresentation, contradictory statements, misuse of terms, and above all, a venomous intention. He skulked off the field amid the laughter of every man who possessed common scholarship or common honesty. It is in reference to this subject that Dr. Lee writes to Mr. Paisley:—

"MY DEAR PAISLEY,

"I am much obliged by your note. By professing that the References want 'sectarian bias' I mean to say that they are intended to make the Scriptures say what they really say, and not what any sect whatever wishes them to say, or may have made them say. I do not understand how you can infer that I include all sects except the Unitarians within the censure of 'Sectarianism,' unless it be made to appear that I had constructed the References to favour their views, which of course may easily be asserted, but cannot be proved. As to Socinianism being imputed to me, I shall only say this,—I am not aware of any one who has said anything in theology, beyond the flattest commonplace, to whom it has *not* been imputed. I am, however, very confident that I have never taught any such doctrine, for I do not believe it. That the Divinity of Christ is taught in John's writings, and also in Paul's, is to me certain and evident. This outcry is of old standing, and arises from various causes and quarters. Whether envy and spite are not its chief sources I do not know or care. It is very likely all this murmuring may take shape at last. I cannot help it. I do not intend to turn out of my way for any such reason. My enemies would, I dare say, have had me before the Church Courts long ago, unless they felt that they really wanted grounds, and feared a discussion of which the result cannot be very obscure. It is my resolution, by the grace of God, to go on teaching what I think true and feel to be useful, not doubting that all things will work together for good. I am disposed to think that this 'Witness' outbreak has done a great deal of good, and from the most orthodox ministers I see testimonies to that effect, as also assurances that they find the references 'wholesome and sound.' The enemy has been very unhappy in his choice of a field of battle. I agree with you that the religious mind in this country is in a most uneasy state. A spark might at present create a vast conflagration. The good men who are labouring to prevent religious progress do not know what they are doing. Indeed, I feel myself singular in giving them credit for sincerity. Many very observing men hold them quite hypocritical. This I do not believe. But, whatever their intentions, their conduct is infatuated so far as the interests of Christianity are concerned. I see so few ministers that I don't know much of their thoughts and feelings; most of them must be very idle, else they could not find time for so much evil speaking. With kind regards to you and Mrs. Paisley, in which Mrs. Lee unites, believe me, my dear Paisley,

"Yours most sincerely,

"ROBERT LEE."

Before quitting these busy and useful years, 1853-4, we must take some extracts from the diary.

"*March* 3, 1853.—This day reached my old parish, Campsie, and having dined at the Manse and felt the change of human things and myself a stranger in my former home, I went and lectured at Lennoxtown to the Mechanics' Institute, and having escaped suffocation, I slept in the room where our dear Jane was born and baptized. Alas! what a changing world, and how we change, and how should we shrink to go over our past journey again, and to be what we were. *Nulla vestigia retrorsum.*"

"*July* 1.—Not being able to keep one horse, I have bought two; one for myself, and another for George, though Miss Napier paid for the latter. The acquisition of a new horse is always a small event, as it always brings considerable comfort or vexation. *Note.*—One grew wild with ease, like Jeshurun, and, having been tamed by labour, relapsed again into insubordination, and was sent to Laing's (October 1) to be sold, but would not sell, and now stands lame (November 5); was sold at last for 20*l.*, having been bought for 31*l.* 10*s.* Have got no good of her. *Mem.*—More caution. Query, Any more? Respond, *Prudentia.*"

"*Oct.* 5.—The summer vacation, as I may call the month of August, has a considerable tendency to exasperate that propensity to dissipation of mind which I fear is among my faults, and, indeed, is almost sure to be engendered by a multiplicity of employments. I find myself now running from book to book, from subject to subject, from thought to thought.

"Man is a great congeries of faults. His very virtues become vices, his wisdom swerves into folly, his strength degenerates into weakness, unless he jealously guard himself not only as to the *character* of his actions and habits, but also their *degree.* Who is so stupid as not to feel this? Who so careless as not to sigh for a higher life, in which this painful struggle will either be superseded, or at least will always result in progress and triumph? How ineffable a delight to find one's self always advancing in those things which constitute our dignity and happiness; instead of reproaching one's self, after the lapse of years, with the same follies and sins which were inexcusable before we had suffered so much bitter experience. Light of the world, enlighten me, and in Thy light I shall see light."

"*Nov.* 2.—It is my wish or purpose this winter, if God be pleased to spare me, so to apportion my time as to visit my congregation, every family, and, if possible, every individual, at least once. To do myself justice I have done a good deal of late in the way of visiting, or at least, calling. And no doubt it has important uses, particularly as conciliating the good will of the people, and, if judiciously managed, their esteem.

"I calculate that two days every week, applied in this way, will suffice for this duty, though sometimes more may be required. The days most convenient may be *Tuesdays* and *Wednesdays* or *Thursdays*. But good days must be used, for *exercise*. God give me wisdom and resolution. He who has many employments needs much of these, but he who has none, needs much more."

"*Nov.* 6. To-day I have felt much what I am very frequently conscious of, the difficulty of speaking in one's natural voice, and the tendency to speak on a high key. This has many evil consequences. It is fatiguing, it spoils the voice, it makes it shrill and unpleasant to the hearer. Even in lecturing to thirty students in a small class-room I commit the same error continually."

"*April* 1, 1854.—I finished my seventh session last Thursday. I have to be thankful for good health on the whole. The Session has been neither an unpleasant nor an unuseful one, I think. I have again repeated the fault of allowing too much of the Session to pass before inviting the students to the house and becoming acquainted with them. May God grant to them and me His grace and blessing."

"*April* 6.—Wonderful are the ways of Providence. When a student at St. Andrews, I had a presentiment that I should be one day Principal of S. Mary's College—the highest dignity which then presented itself, though I almost trembled at my own presumption in venturing to harbour such a thought. To-day Mr. Craufurd, the Solicitor-General, called to offer me that appointment, which, of course, I respectfully declined. This is curious certainly.* To-day poor Wilson† is to be laid in his

---

* It was a less valuable office than the one he held in Edinburgh.

† Christopher North.

grave. So passes fame with all earthly things. But χρυσέα ἐλπις, blessed be God, still lingers among men."

"*April* 26.—The National Fast on account of the war with Russia. I preached the longest sermon I ever ventured on—an hour and a quarter—on the Principles of the Peace Society. A very tempting subject certainly."

"*May* 22.—I wonder whether others share that self-dissatisfaction with which I am generally oppressed. What is it? Is it self-reproach for living and acting below the standard which one apprehends to be the true one? Is it wounded vanity that others are superior to ourselves? Is it envy? What is it? This at least is certain, that the feeling is a very unhappy one, and should be resisted, because it neither makes one happy, nor helps one to be good. 'Render to all their dues; honour to whom honour.' 'Honour all men!'"

"*June* 3.—Mrs. Lee, Maggie, and myself, returned this afternoon from a visit to Stirlingshire, Bridge of Allan, and Arngomery. We were charmed as usual with our excellent friends at the latter place, full of goodness. May God bless them. It is charming to know and love such people. Better than all the literature, science, ambition, fame, and glory of the world is such quiet happiness, such geniality and kindness."

"*Sept.* 1.—Returned home from a charming rustication at Fintry for five weeks. The country grows dearer as life advances. I feel, indeed, that I grow more imaginative and romantic as the dark shadows draw nearer."

"*Sept.* 10.—Last winter I did more, I think, in the way of solid, original work than in any former winter. I preached two courses of sermons, &c., &c., &c., besides writing many reviews, and getting through a good deal of reading. I have also visited the whole, or nearly the whole, of my flock during the summer."

"*Sept.* 24, *Sunday.*—This has been to us a dark day, for this morning George's pony, Brunette, died; the pet and servant of the whole family. She strangled herself with her head-collar on Saturday morning, and lingered till this morning. She was the best pony I ever saw; handsome, strong, swift, and safe, gentle and full of spirit, without a fault. All of us have shed tears over her untimely end; for they who are useful to us, and contribute to our enjoyments, cannot leave us without drawing our sighs after them. She was a present from Miss Napier to George in July last year, and she cannot be replaced.

"'The creature also shall be delivered from the bondage of corruption.'"

"*Dec.* 31.—I have repeated my accustomed folly in buying horses. At present I have a useless one which I wish to sell. This, I hope, will be my last folly in that kind."

"*Jan.* 6, 1855.—My wife gave me a rebuke this morning which made me angry, as rebukes generally do, in proportion as it was just; namely, that I find too much fault with myself as well as others. I dine out, and I find fault with myself. If I think it right to dine out only once in the week, make a rule to that effect, and adhere to it, and say nothing about it farther. But I grumble against everything, and yet agree to everything. This is folly, to speak mildly. Be firm and mild, not cross and facile. Who can tell how oft he offendeth? I, at least, cannot."

"If the dissenting bodies be Churches as much as those which are established, the established Churches are sects as much as the dissenting bodies. For no one, I presume, will maintain that the accident of being supported or recognized by the State is that which constitutes the distinction between a Church and a sect."

"*Jan.* 22.—One of the greatest and most necessary instances of self-denial, particularly for a person like me, is to restrain one's self from speaking of people and speaking ill of them, as one will speak if one speak at all. 'Keep thy tongue from evil, and thy lips from speaking guile, if thou wouldst see good and enjoy peace.' May God enable me to be more and more careful in this respect."

"*Jan.* 24.—To-day a very long debate of a very full Senatus on affairs of Reid Fund. This reminded me much of the foregoing caution. 'Keep thy tongue from evil and guile.' For this purpose keep it from much speaking. O Lord, 'keep the door of my lips, that I sin not with my tongue.'"

"*Feb.* 24.—Thomas Ross died to-day. He was in my employment as groom and coachman about three years. A model of sobriety, truthfulness, honesty, good sense, and kindly dispositions. No man, perhaps, in his station ever united more valuable qualities, so that he became an object of lively affection and interest to all of us. I regarded him as a friend, and the death of few persons would have given me greater regret. He has left a wife and five young children."

"THE TEACHING OF THE SPIRIT.*

" When Christ was about to depart, he did not say 'I will give you a Bible, or certain books,' nor did he say, like Moses, 'A prophet like me shall the Lord your God give you.' But he promised to send his Spirit, the Spirit of truth, righteousness and peace and love : and this promise was not confined to the time needful for composing the New Testament Scriptures, or to the lives of the apostles, but it should abide with his disciples and his Church for ever. If so, it is difficult to deny that the Christian Church is always inspired. Did Christ withdraw his Spirit ? When ? Christ did not die, or cease to act or work when the apostles died. God is still the living God; still his Spirit teaches, breathes, stimulates, sanctifies. Why may we not expect new revelations ? What hinders ? Christianity is a new revelation in regard to Judaism. The Pharisee rejected it on this very ground. They thought that God died after the time of Moses, that his Spirit could speak no more. Why may we not look for new revelations in regard to Christianity ? In fact, have we not received them ? Moses thought the world had lasted a thousand years or two. The apostles thought it would end in a few years. If the apostles were wrong respecting the time when the world would end, why may not Moses have been regarding the time when it began ? Both were grossly mistaken. God has taught us what they were ignorant of, and thus made us wiser than our teachers. So of many things else in the New Testament. Human reason is the organ of God's Spirit, *it* is the standing inspiration. When men generally are educated and taught, the saying which is written will be fulfilled: ' It shall come to pass in the last days, I will pour out of my Spirit upon all flesh.' 'They shall not teach every man his neighbour, saying, Know the Lord, but all shall know him, from the least even to the greatest.' "

"THE MESSIAH.

"One who is to do all we think should be done,—to teach us

---

* From his note book.

all we desire to know. 'I know that Messiah cometh : when he is come he will teach us all things,' to surmount all our difficulties and to make us triumphant over all our enemies. Have not all nations had some dim faith of such a Redeemer, and some faint hope that he would at last appear? Does not faith in God seem to imply this hope? Yet, alas! the Messiah has been 2000 years in the world and yet the ignorance remains, the difficulties still press; enemies conquer and death triumphs.

"It must, therefore, be by the presence of the Spirit of the Messiah in the hearts of his disciples that they shall know and do,—fight and conquer. The Messiah is the Son of God. God grant us the Spirit of His Son, that we may learn our lesson and do our work."

CHAPTER VIII.

NATIONAL EDUCATION.—PHYSIOLOGY IN SCHOOLS.—TOUR.
ON THE CONTINENT.—PROPHECY.—DIARY.

> "Truth is fair, should we forego it?
>   Can we sigh right for a wrong?
> God Himself is the best poet,
>   And the real is His song.
> Sing His truth out fair and full,
>   And secure His beautiful."—E. BARRETT BROWNING.

DR. LEE was asked to deliver the closing address to the members of the Philosophical Institution of Edinburgh, after the lectures of 1865—6. He consented; and taking National Education as his theme, addressed the members on the 8th of April.

He embraced the opportunity of expounding his opinions pretty fully; and published the address afterwards, as he was eager to disseminate these opinions, while an Education Bill—one of many—was before Parliament. He had great faith in his principles, though but little hope of seeing them generally adopted.

As this address expresses the convictions upon Education, which he had been urging amidst many difficulties, wherever he had influence, and which had no small effect on public opinion, I shall make some extracts from it.

" Education must contemplate all that the man is, all that he has to do as a man—else you will make a tool, frame a machine, not educate a man.

"In the first place, we bring a body with us into the world. This is the animal we ride upon into that arena in which we must fight—an animal, however, which is part of ourselves. By it we must act; through it we must suffer. It is the medium of our communication with the external world; the organ of thought and emotion, of knowledge, of pleasure, of pain; the seat of appetite. Its condition is destined to affect, and that deeply, not only our enjoyment, but our virtue. As a body is not the attribute of any one rank or class of men, it would seem to follow that every individual of both sexes should be instructed in the value and nature of this great talent; shown how to use it, and keep it from harm as much as may be; as also, how it may be misapplied, abused, ruined; and the terrible penalties which must follow such abuse; and all this should be taught as matter of duty and of religious duty. When, however, we speak of teaching such things as these, we are met with the objection that this knowledge is much too refined and recondite for common people. Only, I would remind ladies and gentlemen that ploughmen, sailors, carpenters, servant-maids, and even scavengers and sweeps, have bodies—human bodies as well as they—that those bodies may be in health or sickness, may be preserved or destroyed—that pain is an evil to a poor man as well as to a rich one, and disease a much greater evil. I conclude, on the whole, that since every man in the community has a body, every one should be made so far acquainted with it as to comprehend the more simple and essential means of promoting its well being, and avoiding its hurt.

"Here it is necessary I should state more specifically what kind of instruction I refer to. I do not mean such general precepts as that we should avoid damp feet, cold draughts, eating and drinking too much, and the like. Such general rules make little impression, especially upon young people, and are of very little use to them, because they neither understand the facts, nor comprehend the principles, upon which the rules are founded. We must teach them the structure and functions of the different parts of the body, and the relations and reciprocal influence of its various organs, such as the heart, lungs, stomach, skin, brain, &c.; because it is on the preservation of a proportional action in each that health depends; and we cannot know the influence of our habits and of external objects, such as cold, damp, heat, food, &c., on these organs, individually and reciprocally, without knowing their structures, functions, and relations ; and this knowledge is obtained by studying anatomy and physiology, and their application to health.

" The possibility of rendering these subjects intelligible and even deeply interesting to young persons, as well as to the mass of the people, is no longer a question. It has been demonstrated by the Lectures which Dr. Hodgson has delivered to the Heriot Boys, the Pupil Teachers, and others, during this winter and the last.

" No community in which this kind of instruction is not generally diffused, can be justly considered as possessing even the elements of education. For this knowledge, besides its immediate connection with the preservation of health and the prolongation of life, has also most intimate relations with the moral and religious interests of men. It teaches them to regulate their conduct in many personal and domestic respects, so as to avoid or diminish certain formidable temptations, and to promote mental by increasing bodily health.

" Yet, strange to say, this first, this fundamental knowledge is taught in very few schools. With great difficulty it has been introduced in a few instances ; and in other cases the attempt has actually been made and failed—the wise men opining that it was more important a boy should know that the Latin nouns *collis* and *orbis* are masculine, and the Greek nouns ὁδός and νῆσος feminine, or how men wore their togas who have been rotten in the dust some 2000 years, or accented a syllable which nobody has spoken almost as long, than how their own living bodies are formed and sustained—how they digest, breathe, and perform their other marvellous functions—by what treatment they are injured, and the consequences—what connection temperance, sobriety, and self-denial have with health, happiness, and long life !

" Even in our colleges, the ingenuous youth are left without any attempt being made to initiate them in this science, or to induce them to practise its lessons. Nor is there in any university in the kingdom, so far as I know, provision made for the physical training and exercise of the students. They are left, in ignorance and thoughtlessness, to violate all the conditions of health to any extent they please; and hundreds of them pay the penalty in carrying their useless knowledge and their vain distinctions to a premature grave—literally "perishing for lack of knowledge"—while they have been consuming themselves in the pursuit of knowledge. It appears most amazing that we should tolerate and perpetuate this deplorable folly, or should suffer any system of public or national education to be organized which does not remember that the subjects of education have each a body whose welfare is to be consulted. Will the time never come when parents will see that no education which their children can require demands pale faces and anxious looks?—that bone and muscle require development as well as understanding and memory—and that the hand, the eye, and the limbs need education and daily exercise no less than the mental powers?

"Every human being has a body—therefore every human being should be taught those things which concern its welfare. *Somatology* is an essential part of every man's education.

" Man is placed in the midst of a physical universe, composed of matter in various forms, acted on by various influences, regulated by certain laws. The better he understands these, the better is he prepared to avail himself of them, and to avoid the mischiefs in which ignorance would involve him. In that great laboratory of nature in which every human being finds himself, he is both agent and subject, the matter and the workman, and also the tool, though he uses other things also as his tools and instruments. It will depend upon his knowledge chiefly whether he be lord of those powers or their slave—whether they drag him on, a helpless victim, or he yoke them to his chariot and triumphantly guide them whithersoever he will. Every man, whatever his condition, is destined to work amid the tremendous wheels of nature, which fly round for ever with resistless speed; and as this machinery cannot be screened off or boxed in, they who are not so instructed as to know the danger and guard against it, must be caught and crushed. How many poor creatures are continually sacrificed to such ignorance it is sad to think. 'The people perish for lack of knowledge.'

" I might, in the next place, remind you that, as every person is born into a family, so there are a certain instruction and training, connected with this relation, which are indispensable parts of his education. First, the fundamental virtue of obedience is here learned, if it be learned at all : reverence and affection are here cultivated, faith in his parents supplying the first rudiments of the great lesson—faith in God. This is the school of those virtues and those habits which form the substance of the worthy character, and the ornaments of the refined character. The elements of the social virtues are here imparted, wherever else they may be practised ; and religious impressions, wherever they may manifest themselves afterwards, are first sown in this holy ground. At the fireside, around the family board, the young acquire the feelings, tastes, habits, which after-life does little more than develop or confirm. Good manners, courtesy, are learned here, if they be learned at all. On this momentous subject much might be usefully said. I shall, however, only stop to make two remarks. One is, that many parents are so unreasonable as to expect that the schoolmaster should perform their work, and feel disappointed that he does not teach what they leave untaught ; or does not undo what they themselves have done. The other is—that every mode of bringing up the young which interferes with family life or supersedes it, is a sacrilegious violence done to a divine institution, and is a conspicuous example of human ignorance, folly, and conceit. Such schemes, instead of purifying and refining mankind, tend to demoralise them ; they weaken the holiest ties which bind human beings together, and they foster powerfully that selfishness from which they spring. ' By their fruits ye shall know them.'

" Man has wants and powers, and he must exert these powers to supply those wants. This he does by practising various trades, professions, callings, by means of which are produced food, clothing, shelter, and the multifarious things which minister to the sustenance, comfort, and adornment of human life. That skill he gains by a special professional education, and it constitutes his craft. But there may be many things needful for them to know who practise any particular craft, which the master of it does not teach, and which the apprentice will not learn from his fellow-craftsmen ; and yet this knowledge may so deeply concern him, that the want of it may be ruinous. A master mason does not teach his apprentice what will be the effects upon his lungs of the continued hewing of sandstone ; nor does a needle-grinder initiate his pupil into the danger of steel-dust, and the remedy. A youth who learns in a factory to spin cotton or to print calico, does not learn there the laws of demand and supply, the causes which determine wages, the effects of combinations, strikes, and the like ; yet his notions, and those of his fellows, on these momentous points, will determine them to act, and if they act amiss, they and their employers, and the business on which both depend, may all be ruined together, as has taken place many times."

He then speaks of the advantage of imparting *political* knowledge, and goes on to the vexed question of religious instruction.

"I may, I hope, without offence, make this remark, that notwithstanding all the machinery for imparting moral and religious instruction, we are forced to acknowledge, when we look upon society, and witness the exposures which are incessantly made—the adulterations, evasions, petty rogueries, the atrocious villanies, and the brutal violence, which are constantly brought to light—that there must be, after all, either a great deficiency in the quantity of moral and religious instruction, or, what is more probable, some glaring defect in its quality. If the right thing were taught rightly, we might expect that the records of our criminal and bankruptcy courts, and the whole social history of our people, would be very different from what unfortunately they now are. We have higher authority than probability for expecting that, 'if a child be trained up in the way he should go, when old he will not depart from it.' Admitting exceptions, this is the rule. But when we see crowds of persons who have received the best education which the public provides, or which parents can hear of, showing, in their dealings, no regard to the dictates of morality or the precepts of religion, we are tempted to suspect that something must be very wrong in the moral and religious instruction and training of such persons. 'By their fruits ye shall know them.' This is the infallible criterion for testing not only doctrines and men, but all systems.

" If we consider religion not as one of many powers which divide among them the territory of human life and action, but as an all-comprehending influence, from which nothing that man does, speaks, thinks, can lawfully be exempted—which has to do with everything, however small or secular it may in some respects be—we shall, perhaps, be brought to conclude that of all branches of education this is that to which least justice is done, even in those systems of education which are professedly founded upon it; and that reformations which are needed everywhere are needed here most of all.

" When we speak of national education, or of any system of education, we naturally think of those elements of knowledge which are proper to be communicated in schools ; because it is with these the public is more immediately concerned, and over these alone the public has any direct control. It would seem, therefore, that all those things which men need to know to fit them for the common duties of life, but which they are not taught in the course of acquiring their several callings, or within the domestic sphere, should be comprehended in the list of things proper and necessary to be taught in schools—for the family is also a school, so is the workshop ; but by the school we mean specifically that place of instruction where that is taught which every one needs to know, and which cannot be so conveniently or so effectually communicated in the family or the workshop. According to its very idea, therefore, it is merely supplemental or preparatory, and does not profess to do the whole work of education, but only a limited part of it, and this varying according to circumstances. These considerations, though obvious enough, have been too little attended to by those who have discussed systems of instruction for the people. The propriety of teaching girls domestic economy in school will be shown, if it can be proved that they are not generally taught it at home. And this, I take it, is the only argument or justification for introducing religion as a formal branch of instruction in schools,—that the people generally are disinclined, or negligent, or unqualified, to teach their children religion ; and that the instruction they receive in church (if they attend church) is not suited to the capacities of the young. For few, I think, would contend that if parents perform their part, and the clergy perform their part, there would be any necessity to employ the schoolmaster in the same work, or any advantage in doing so. If it be judged necessary to attempt this, it must be done at such times, and under such regulations, as shall compromise the rights of no one, and shall respect the conscientious opinions and scruples of all. We must recognize the right of the parent to determine absolutely in what form of religious doctrine his child shall be instructed, or whether he shall receive, in connection with the school, any religious instruction at all. The difficulties connected with this matter are, however, so great, that the practical result would probably be, that the teaching of religion would be left to the different Churches, whose proper business it is, and above all to parents. If the cessation of such teaching in schools should have the effect (which probably it would have) of stimulating parents and Churches to a more earnest performance of their duty, incalculable benefit would result to all parties.

"Having, in this imperfect way, spoken of the *matter* of education, or the things which should be taught, I should next have considered the question—To whom does it belong to communicate that part of education which it is proper to communicate in schools? There are *three* answers to this question—One is,—This business belongs to any one who chooses to undertake it. I shall say nothing to refute this theory, hoping it is sufficiently exposed when it is nakedly propounded. The second answer is, that the duty devolves upon the State ; the third, that it belongs to the Church. Besides the advocates of these two simple propositions, there is a third and a very powerful section of educationists who hold that the State should educate the people by and through the Church. This being interpreted, means that the Church should perform the work according to its own ideas (not to say for its own purposes), and that the State should furnish to the Church the necessary funds. This last conception has the merit of great simplicity. It is the doctrine of spiritual independence extended to matters educational. Some of our statesmen who have felt themselves called upon to take a lead on the subject of national education, are seen to steer their course dubiously and painfully among these different answers to the great question, being evidently rather drifted onward by the currents of opinion, and presumed expediency, than guided by any enlarged theory, or indeed any theory at all. I regret to say that the speeches, in Parliament and elsewhere, of those by whose views government has of late years been guided, and is likely still to be, do not inspire much hope of enlightened legislation regarding public or national education; because they do not seem to indicate that the question is understood. Whenever a person comprehends a subject, he rises to simplicity. Simplicity is the attribute of thorough comprehension; but the speeches in Parliament of those who are dealing with this matter, and their general proceedings, appear to me to demonstrate that they are destitute of any theory, and are adopting make-shifts, stop-gaps, and, in short, are under the trammels of a short-sighted expediency, which will spend much money, work much confusion, and at last (we may hope) will find grace to acknowledge it knew neither what was to be done, nor how.

" We must presume that Her Majesty's present government, and the governments which preceded it, since public action was taken by them in education, adhere to the notion that national education should be, or must be, carried on mainly through the Church or Churches—for their grants to the schools of all denominations mean this, if they mean anything. And they seem inclined to go on in the same course. I shall conclude with a remark or two on this way of proceeding.

"1. My first objection is one of principle. The Christian Church is an organization for teaching religion—the Christian religion. It has no qualification, call, or authority, to teach anything else—not arithmetic, geography, grammar, any more than masonry, carpentry, weaving, painting, or sculpture. And this applies to directing or superintending education, as much as to the immediate communication of it. However much these duties may belong to Christian men, they do not, in any way, belong to the Christian Church as such ; and, in so far as she undertakes them, she transgresses her proper function.

"2. Education by the Church means, in this connection, nothing but education by the clergy ; education controlled and directed by them according to their peculiar and professional views and feelings. Is the propriety of this self-evident ? Do the people desire this ? Are they prepared to submit to it ? In conducting the education of a people in religion, it is natural and proper that the clergy should have much to say; but happily they are not now the only persons who understand reading and writing, arithmetic and geography. The sciences of physiology, social economy, and others, whose introduction into schools is seen by all intelligent men to be indispensable, are much better understood by members of other profession than by ministers of the Gospel. Why, then, should the better qualified classes be excluded, that all authority may be engrossed by the worse qualified class? Is it to please the clergy, especially of the Church of England, that Governments act thus? We should 'please all men for their good to edification,' as S. Paul teaches. But we should not please any one to his hurt, or to the hurt of others. And we always hurt a man when we devolve upon him duties he is not qualified to perform, or bestow privileges which belong to others. The people are a more numerous body than the clergy; and it is of some consequence to please them also in a matter in which they have so deep an interest as the teaching of their children.

"3. It is pleaded that as religion extends to all the departments of education, therefore the Church should superintend all departments—*i.e.*, the clergy should. But I object that the clergyman is not religion, nor is religion the clergyman. He is not necessarily even the impersonation or expression of true Christianity. He may be rather the impersonation of narrow-mindedness, intolerance, bigotry, sectarianism. This is no bare possibility. The largest charity must admit that it has been often realized. And saying so, I do not libel the members of my own profession; I only acknowledge that we are men like our neighbours—certainly, no worse—and, as certainly, not so much better or wiser, that the State should treat us as if we were superior to the common infirmities.

"It is very true, and very important truth, that the whole work of teaching children and youth should be carried on in a religious spirit. But this is only saying that teaching should be done, as all other things should be done. We should do all that we do, even eat and drink, 'to the glory of God.' Shoemakers and tailors, smiths and carpenters, masons and plasterers, and craftsmen of every sort, should perform the operations of their several callings in a religious spirit. So should merchants traffic, physicians treat their patients, advocates plead, and judges weigh and determine. All should be done in a religious spirit, 'to the glory of God.' But we do not from these admitted premises draw the practical conclusion that, therefore, the bishop of the diocese should exercise a general superintendence of all farming, manufacturing, and other operations within the same; or that the Presbytery of the bounds should be empowered to visit all places where trades are carried on, or business is transacted, or should be armed with a commission to exercise an inspection over the civil courts, lest advocates should overstep the limits of forensic propriety, or judges transgress the bounds of law. I submit for the consideration of those wise men and statesmen, who habitually confound the two things, that the influence of religion and the superintendence of the clergy are not one and the same thing, but two things, so distinct and separate, that the presence of either is quite compatible with the absence of the other.

"4. I shall offer only another observation on this subject. The various Churches or sects (for in one respect they are all Churches, and in another they are all sects), are labouring to promote education, some with greater zeal, others with less. It would be uncharitable to doubt that all of them are desirous to promote education, according to their own ideas of it. But this cannot be overlooked that, with all of them, education is such instruction as shall dispose those who receive it to embrace or adhere to the Church or sect which supplies it. It does not even profess to be such education as shall either dispose or qualify the youth for judging which among all the sects is the best, or, if you like it better, which of all the Churches is the true Church, or the truest Church; but it regards education as one, and the most powerful means of proselytism. Under ecclesiastical management, the schoolmaster is just the minister with modifications; and the value of the school is its tendency to serve as a *seminarium ecclesiæ*—a feeder for the church or chapel. The interest which Churches or sects take in education is naturally, and even necessarily, a sectarian or Church interest. This is what they seldom say, but always mean. Nor can it be otherwise. In saying this, I express neither blame nor wonder. On the contrary, as I have said, acting thus, sects or Churches act according to their nature. If sects support or manage schools, they will always manage them with a view to their interests as sects. But what I wonder at and venture to blame is, that any Government should make itself a party to such action—should stimulate this process by grants of public money to all parties who profess to teach any sort of religion—should thus recognize in an indirect and irregular manner, religious opinions which are not recognized in any direct or legitimate manner—and should aggrieve the conscience of the subject by compelling him to support and propagate doctrines which he privately considers erroneous, and it may be pernicious, and which are unknown to the law and constitution of the realm."*

The reader will have noticed the reference to Dr. Hodgson's lectures on physiology. These lectures were the evidence of a great advance in public opinion touching education, and of the triumph of principles which Dr. Lee had zealously advocated. It was under the influence of Mr. George Combe, the great apostle of physiological education, that he had interested himself keenly in the efforts made to introduce instructions in physiology into some of the Edinburgh seminaries.

These efforts had begun, under Mr. Combe's direction, a few years before. They had encountered violent opposition. As one of the Commissioners of the Society of Writers to Her Majesty's Signet, Mr. Combe was a manager of John Watson's Hospital, and he tried to get his favourite subject added to the usual course of instruction for the children of the hospital; but he was baffled by the prejudices of his co-directors and their constituents, the Society of Writers to the Signet. Their immobility only made him the more eager to see the cause taken up by others, and he urged Dr. Lee to propose the teaching of physiology in Heriot's Hospital and

* This address is reprinted in "The Family and its Duties."

schools, which he did.   In reference to this, Mr. Combe writes to him in February, 1855 :—

"In your last note you remarked that only something very elementary could be taught to such young children as attend Heriot's schools.*   Will you allow me to mention that we selected the older boys and girls to receive physiological lessons in Williams' School, and that we found them capable, at ten years of age and upwards, of understanding the *structure* and its uses, and its relations to health.   Our directors† have the opinion that the children will *not be capable* of understanding the *structure*, and they propose to introduce *talk* on the functions and the laws of health, as something more elementary and more level to the young capacity ; but it is the old blunder continued, of supposing that *words* instruct better than *things*. It is by teaching the structure that all the rest becomes interesting and intelligible."

Again, a little later, after hearing of Dr. Lee's vigorous advocacy of his views, he writes enthusiastically, "You are doing glorious service to your country.   Oh, for a score of men of your calibre !" and, mentioning some facts connected with the lessons in physiology given to the Royal Family by Mr. W. Ellis, "going to show that *God* governs the world by laws of which princes and men's sons are only the administrators," he adds, "this will, I hope, give encouragement to your soul, as it has given consolation to mine."

Dr. Hodgson, whose admirably lucid expositions rendered physiological studies as attractive to his pupils as the exploration of a new and beautiful country is to the traveller, has kindly furnished me with his recollections of this movement, and I cannot do better than insert his letter here.

* Schools in Edinburgh established by the governors of the hospital.
† John Watson's.

"41, GROVE END ROAD, ST. JOHN'S WOOD, N.W.,
"10th November, 1868.

"MY DEAR MR. STORY,

"Your inquiry relates to a most interesting chapter in the history of education, and especially in the educational history of Edinburgh. The facts are briefly these. In the year 1855 (I think), Mr. G. Combe, then a director of John Watson's Hospital, asked me if I would undertake to give a course of lessons to the elder pupils of that institution on human anatomy and physiology, with reference to the conditions of health. I consented at once to do so, if requested by the governors. Mr. Combe made the proposal at the board that I should be invited, but he was met by an inquiry about my religious opinions. Mr. Combe replied that I was not about to teach theology, directly or indirectly, explicitly or by implication; that my services would be gratuitous; that I was not likely to submit to any inquisitorial searching into my opinions in theology; that, in my name, he would undertake that at every lesson any or all of the governors would be permitted to be present, as well as the head master, and that in event of any dissatisfaction arising, I would at once retire, if requested. An adjournment was decided on, in order to allow inquiry, not from me, but about me. At a subsequent meeting it was reported that no information could be obtained, and it was then resolved, chiefly at the instigation of Mr. Gibson, W.S., that no one should be engaged to teach at all in the institution without his signing the standards of the Church, or without his orthodoxy being ascertained. To this affair I owe my introduction to Dr. R. Lee. He speedily took the subject up, and succeeded in inducing the governors of Heriot's Hospital to invite me to introduce physiology into their out-door schools. Mr. Combe greatly rejoiced to find that the Town Council and clergy of Edinburgh were more liberal than the Writers to the Signet. About a dozen boys and as many girls were selected from each of the schools; they, their teachers, and assistant-teachers, met me twice a week in the Phrenological Museum lecture-room, and I think I gave about twenty-five lessons, always in presence of one of the governors, Dr. Lee himself being often present, and Mr. Combe once. I owed much to the kind support of the late treasurer, Mr. Dick, whom I shall ever remember with love and respect. I received from the governors a very handsome letter of thanks. A set of nine diagrams (then issued by the Government, and prepared by Mr. Marshall) was bought for each school, and a box provided in which to keep them safe. I was next invited, through Dr. Lee's influence, to give a similar course to the boys in the hospital itself. This I did, and through the sympathy and encouragement of Dr. Bedford, the house governor, a man equally zealous and enlightened, the course was very successful. It was concluded by an examination in presence of the governors. I next gave various courses in Edinburgh, one to the senior pupils of the High School, on the invitation of Dr. Schmitz; one to the pupils of the Training College of the Church of Scotland, Dr. Cook giving me very kind support and encouragement, and Mr. S. S. Laurie, too;* one course in Nicolson Street to ladies and gentlemen; two courses in successive winters to two hundred working men; one course to the young ladies in the institution in Park Place. A course was offered to the Training College of the Free Church, but declined. Of subsequent courses in London and in other places, I need not speak, as they were not at all connected with Dr. Lee, except in so far as it was by him, in conjunction with Mr. G. Combe, that I was induced to devote myself seriously to this subject. Of Dr. Lee's earnestness in this, as in so many other good works, it is vain to attempt to speak. His enthusiasm and energy, courage and hopefulness, were quite contagious, and he stands in my esteem, and affection, and gratitude, beside three of my chief benefactors, Professor Pillans, Mr. George Combe, and Mr. William Ellis. His death has been to me a very great affliction, and my own personal bereavement is aggravated by the thought (often recurring) of the loss which the world, and especially his own country, has sustained. I know not whether I more admired his activity of mind, his indomitable perseverance, his boldness in denouncing and resisting the bigotry that ever stood in the way of the good he aimed at, or loved him for his frank, genial, and cordial manners, which gave such a charm to his society. I rejoice that the memoir of him is in your hands.

"Yours ever,

"W. B. HODGSON."

* Dr. Cook, Minister of Haddington, and Principal Clerk of the General Assembly, the Convener, and Mr. Laurie, the Secretary, of the Church's Education Committee.

Dr. Lee's correspondence in 1855-6, as far as I have seen it, turns very much on questions of education; and his most constant correspondent is Mr. Combe. He corresponded, also, on the same subject with, among others, Sir James Clark and Lord Dunfermline. The latter writes on one occasion—in February, 1855—"Physiology, as you view it, is closely connected with morality; but what I wish is that the acknowledged laws of morality should occupy a more important place in popular education, and I anxiously hope that this point will be strongly pressed. So far from greater attention being directed to the teaching of the laws of morality being injurious to religion, I believe that it would be the means of removing danger from, and giving fresh strength to, real religion. There is nothing that has pressed so strongly on my mind, since I returned to my native land, as the conviction that the deficiencies of female education are a main source of the vices that prevail." This letter referred to speeches of Dr. Lee's at Heriot's Hospital, in February and March, 1855, in which he urged the introduction of physiological instruction. In the course of one of these he had said, " I should like to have distinct, detailed, and fully illustrated lessons on the common Christian virtues, such as truth, honesty, sobriety, industry, contentment, humility; and on such essential habits as punctuality, order, cleanliness, cheerfulness, and the like; for there is a strict relation between the knowledge of such duties and their performance."

The general question of national education, before the Church courts year after year, was debated in the Assembly of 1856, of which Dr. Lee was a member, and, just before the Assembly met, in the Presbytery of Edin-

burgh. In his diary, under April 30, 1856, he writes :—
" Meeting of Presbytery.—The Lord Advocate's Bill was
discussed, and I was well abused and insulted. May
God defend me from malice, which will hardly stop
here."

His speech in the Presbytery, like many of his other
speeches, shares the fate of all advocacies of opinions
which are much in advance of their age. At the date of
their utterance, regarded as extreme, they come, after the
lapse of a due season, to look like the mere demonstra-
tion of undeniable principles, hampered with a needless
weight of argument and illustration. After they have
served their time and done their work, they hardly
admit of much quotation. Dr. Muir and his friends had
raised the cry of " The Church in danger," because the
Bill proposed to remove the test, and relax the connection between the parish school and the parish church—
the old cry, said Dr. Lee, but with as little sense in it
as ever. They must consider, he pointed out, their duty,
not as members of the Established Church only, but as
citizens and members of the Church catholic ; and if the
interests of the State and of the Church, which were
primary and general, required it, the lesser interests of
the Establishment must yield. But he did not admit
that the two interests were opposed, for the schools, he
held, belonged to the State, and not to the Church. Dr.
Muir's argument, that our Lord's admonition to Peter,
" Feed my lambs," implied and authorised the inalienable
connection of the parish schoolmaster with the Established Church, did not appear to Dr. Lee altogether
conclusive.

It is painful, in reading over the reports of these

meetings, to mark the bitter spirit of personal hostility to Dr. Lee which shrills like an east wind through the speeches of some of his opponents. I do not wish to revive the wretched memory of this; but it is not just that it should be entirely lost sight of, as it has never been repented of and honestly confessed before men. If Dr. Lee was occassionally, as some people thought, too sharp in tongue, he had an almost intolerable provocation, and yet he never once spoke of an opponent in the tone of studied insult and of intense dislike, which was constantly used towards himself. With some of his co-presbyters — such as Dr. Grant, of S. Mary's, and Dr. Crawford, at this time one of the ministers of S. Andrew's Church—it was possible to contend without the risk of other assault than might be expected from courteous foemen; but with others—whom it is unnecessary to name,—this was not possible.

In the Assembly he spoke at great length in favour of the Lord Advocate's Bill, pointing out the good features in it, such as its providing increased salaries for the schoolmasters, securing effective inspection of schools, and virtually leaving the election of the schoolmaster as it had been, in the unfettered hands of the minister and heritors. All this, however, availed nothing if the *test* were abolished, and Dr. Lee argued for the bill in vain.

The same Assembly, with a curious inconsistency, resolved to accept, from the Indian Government, grants in aid of secular education in India. It was an inconsistency which Dr. Lee did not fail to expose. He rejoiced, he said, during the debate on Indian education, " in the improved atmosphere of the house, for when

Scotch education was in question, the secular system was heartily denounced, whereas, when India was concerned, it was all that was excellent."

He spoke also, again, in favour of private communion, but was left in a minority. On this occasion he had one of his first encounters with Dr. Pirie,* an ever zealous opponent, who, with odd logic, discovered an "Episcopalian movement" in the proposal to relax a rule, the strict retention of which only served to force those, who desired to receive the communion privately, to secure the services of an Episcopalian minister.

After the Assembly rose he says,—" It has been a very pleasant Assembly on the whole; and I have got through my part of it creditably, wonderfully so, considering how obnoxious some of my opinions are. I made speeches on the Education Bill (being left in a minority of 3 to 120), on the Jewish Committee,† the Procuratorship,‡ the Colonial Committee, Private Communion, besides many other topics. The habits of reading and reflecting a good deal give one a great advantage in a popular assembly. I imagined I had quite lost the power of extemporary speaking. Instead of that I find I possess it much less imperfectly than I ever did before. Experience in affairs also comes greatly to one's aid. May God be glorified."

In the summer of 1856 he treated himself to a brief tour on the continent. He was to have gone with Mr.

---

* The Rev. W. R. Pirie, D.D., Professor of Theology and Church History in the University of Aberdeen; and latterly the leader of a strong party in the General Assembly.

† Whose affairs had got into a sad mess.

‡ The office of legal adviser to the church, which had at this time to be filled up (by the appointment of Mr. A. S. Cook).

and Mrs. Combe, but was detained by a slight illness, and they had to proceed without him. "You must not delay an hour on my account," he writes to Mr. Combe from Edrington on the 27th June. "I had resolved to come to London on Friday, and give myself time to visit Sir James Clark, and present some letters of introduction, but I am afraid this may prove a slow affair. I *prophesied* a little before leaving home—that was all. But the people seemed to like the cheerful prophecies quite as well as the gloomy ones, and I am certain they are much more truthful. We happened to spend Saturday evening quietly at Lord Murray's; when talking of the subject, I undertook to prophesy, and predicted distinctly and solemnly that the north-east gale then blowing would cease before sunset next day. It did, and I sent my doubting auditor next morning the following lines to confirm her faith and that of all others in future :—

> "Dear Lady Murray, now you see
> I *have* the gift of prophecy.
> Long ere the sun had sunk to rest,
> Last night, the wind was in the west,
> And Boreas quite had ceased to rage,
> Exactly as I did engage.
> Now we won't care for Dr. Cumming,
> Newton or Elliott, Bush or Fleming—
> Or any such predicting elves—
> Since we can prophesy ourselves,
> Besides—and this will weigh with you—
> Their signs prove false, while ours come true.

"This place is charming, and such weather I hardly remember. I wish you and Mrs. Combe were here."

About a week later he was able to begin his journey, having arranged to join the Combes on the Lake of Geneva.

He went up to London, and thence across the Channel, and by Amiens to Paris. At Amiens he says :—

"It is affecting to see numbers of women come to Church of a morning to say their prayers (having first sprinkled themselves with holy water) with much appearance of sincerity.

"*Paris, July* 6.—Paris is just the place for a person who would live out of doors—out of his own house—out of his own family —out of his own thoughts—in short, out of himself. . . . Went with Mr. Cochrane and visited various churches, Madeleine, S. Etienne du Mont, &c. Very, very, very fine indeed.

"But these Catholics really believe their religion ; and their everlasting Virgin and Child disgusts us Protestants, who are (I fear) among half-believers."

From Paris to Lyons, thence to Geneva by diligence.

"We rumbled on at a capital pace till midnight, when we began to ascend the passes of the Jura, which we could not see —the more the pity ! but we saw six, and even seven horses, all dragging us up the cragged ascent.

"*Geneva, July* 12.—It rains most of to-day ; but Geneva appears to me splendid, and unites all the requisites of a residence. Till I saw Geneva, I thought Edinburgh the finest situation in the world, but there is no comparison."

From Geneva to Chamouni, by Salenches :—

"Delightful smell of Alpine forests. Montanvert, Mer de Glace, amazing, sublime beyond measure. Theory of colour of glacier torrents,—all greyish-white, from mixture of pulverized granite."

"16*th*.—Great day. Started with guide for Tête Noir. Met a severe thunderstorm on the way, but arrived safe. Warmed myself at the wood fire and drank brandy-and-water.

"N.B.—One should never take more than the smallest quantity of this.

"Went to Martigny, having walked from Chamouni without fatigue. It is twenty-four miles from Chamouni to Martigny."

Next day he takes the diligence down the Rhone Valley.

"The Rhone very muddy, but water of lake very blue, even at top. Thought of the purifying effect of contemplation and gentle influences upon the furious passions of men."

He hereupon expands into verse, which, however, we shall not reproduce.

"To Vevay: perfection of beauty.

"18*th*.—Sailed from the inn, Trois Couronnes, the best in Switzerland, by steamer to Geneva, and saw the lake favourably. The upper end is by far the finest.

"19*th*, *Thursday*. — This day I hope my dear George has made his mother and sisters happy by joining them at Edrington. This will cheer them the fortnight or three weeks which may elapse till my return. Heard the worship to-day in the church at Geneva: began with the organ and read prayers. Very good. Small congregation, almost all women.

"This evening went with the Combes to hear Concert on Rousseau's island. Very good music, excellently played. The scene, lamps, trees, water, people, very pretty.

"21*st*, to Friburg. The evening has been splendid, and looking on Friburg from the heights beyond the river under this splendid summer evening's gleam, it looked like something one had dreamed of, or read of in romances, rather than a substantial reality. The grasshoppers were chirruping as loud as linnets, which made me understand the allusions in the Greek Poets to their *singing*.

"22*nd*.—High Mass in the Cathedral. Heard the organ, played — by far the most wonderful musical representation I ever listened to. Indeed, it so far surpassed anything I had heard, that I felt as if I had never heard music before. Sunday seems to be very little regarded on the whole either in the Protestant cantons or the Catholic—though perhaps less in the former. From Friburg, to Berne, Thun, and Interlachen; climbed the Wengern Alp,—found quite a fair. The Jungfrau stands up before you in glorious majesty; never saw aught so sublime, had there been but quiet. Descended to Grindelwald.

"*25th.*—Climbed the Scheideck, rested at Rosenlaui, where we had a shock of an earthquake. Walked rest of the way in torrents of rain. Did not care; in capital spirits. Reached Meyringen, went to bed and got all right.

" Next day walked over the Brunig with knapsack."

And so, on to the Lake of Lucerne, where, at Weggis, at the foot of the Righi, his notes abruptly stop.

He writes, however, on the 28th July, from Lucerne, to Mr. Combe,—

"I ascended the Righi, but the sun would not shine. I got to this beautiful place yesterday morning. We set out this morning for Zurich. I have picked up two very nice English youths, who will probably go with me as far as Baden."

And on the 29th from Zurich,—

"I have not seen much of this, having been seized in the same way as at Lyons. I have been most affectionately nursed by two young English gentlemen whom I have met on my journey. Professor Schweizer has been most kind and attentive, but as he can speak neither French nor English, we were forced to betake ourselves to Latin, which the Germans pronounce so differently from us that it is sometimes not easy to understand them. We propose setting out to-morrow for Basle and Baden."

He reached Edrington House, near Berwick, where his family awaited him, on the 7th August.

A young friend and former pupil, too thoughtful to find the signing of the Confession an easy form, and too conscientious to accept it save on terms satisfactory to his own conscience, had written to Dr. Lee to ask his advice in a difficulty into which he had got with his

Presbytery, — which reverend court, with keen nose, scenting heresy in some of his trial discourses, had evinced a disposition to worry and obstruct him in passing his examinations for "licence." Dr. Lee promptly replies,—

"I received this morning, on my return from the Continent, your most interesting note, which surprised and grieved me exceedingly. I could not have believed such proceeding was possible as you describe. By this time you probably see your way a little better, and have come to some conclusion as to your future proceedings. All I shall therefore venture to say is that I hope you will do nothing rashly, but will take full time to consider the whole subject, which even those violent people you have had to do with cannot refuse you. Perhaps you are aware that I don't feel much sympathy with Mr. Maurice's theological views, though I respect and admire the man; and I am not well up to your present state of mind and feeling; but I know you too well not to feel confident you do not hold any opinions which should disqualify you from signing the Confession, liberally interpreted. They are zealous in pulling down the Church of Scotland with their own hands, and not knowing what they do. Your excellent mother's zeal for the Church, as now existing, proceeds probably from not knowing what it really is, and what temper animates it. This will probably tend to enlighten her. I shall be glad to hear from you, and if I can do anything I shall be too glad. But don't despond. We are always safest in doing right—'all things shall work together for good, &c.' If you be a true minister of God, He will put you in a position to speak His truth—in spite of small men in a little authority."

This letter is but one illustration of the spirit of frank sympathy and kindness with which he was ever ready to enter into the troubles of any friend, and to do what he could for him. And this not for friends only, but for old pupils—for struggling writers or preachers—for any one who appealed to him. Among his papers I have found, again and again, touching expressions of thankfulness for the help and encouragement which had been found in him. "Now that the fruit of my labours is laid before the world," writes a poor author whom he had befriended, "I will truly and gratefully say that if it have any success, you are the kind friend to whom I shall ascribe that success; and if it be spurned and neglected, I will never cease to dwell with pleasure on those generous efforts which you made to bring it into favourable notice. May God bless and reward you for your disinterested kindness."

After his return to Edinburgh this autumn he was much occupied with the subject of Prophecy. The Rev. Dr. Cumming had published "The End," and a variety of worthless pamphlets and volumes, such as "The Coming Struggle," had recently been imposing upon the foolish, and vexing the spirits of the wise. Dr. Cumming's "End" was reviewed in the *Scotsman* with much wit and pungency, the reviewer, who can be identified, maintaining that on Dr. Cumming's own principles of interpretation, the author of the "End" could be none other than the prophet Elijah "which was for to come."

"We do not conceal from ourselves that between Elijah and John the Baptist on one side, and our contemporary antitype of those ancient seers, there are, with this admitted identity, also certain points of difference. But it is an established maxim that as 'every parable limps on some foot,' so every parallel, the closest, fails in some particular. We, therefore, hold very cheap such objections as that 'Elijah and the Baptist were not fashionable preachers—did not make fortunes by prophesying —did not brag of their intimacy with Ahab, Herod, or Pilate, their courtiers and ministers—had not their town house and country house—and that they did not lay hands on other people's prophesyings and do them up for the market.' To all

such quibbles we have two short answers—first, that these dis-
similarities, even admitting their reality, are unimportant, and
of very small significance ; and, secondly, that in so far as they
do exist, our Modern Prophet has plainly the advantage over his
predecessors.   Nor can we seriously think there is much weight
in another reproach that we have heard uttered—as if a person
who knew that the world was to surcease in ten years should
throw it away and contemn it; whereas true wisdom rather
suggests that those good things should be diligently used and
eagerly enjoyed which are so soon to be taken from us. Neither
Elijah nor the first John had enjoyed the benefit of a classical
education, or had been initiated in such sound philosophical
principles as these—

> Dum loquimur fugerit invida
> Aetas : carpe diem, quam minimum credula postero.
> Φάγωμεν καὶ πίωμεν, αὔριον γὰρ ἀποθνήσκομεν."

His attention turning strongly to the subject, he, as
usual with him in such cases, preached on it.

On February 24, 1856, he writes : " Finished to-day a
series of twelve Lectures on Prophecy, including some
of the general topics, and an exposition of the Book of
Revelation, to the end of the 11th chapter. I daresay,
if published, they might do something to check the mad-
ness of prophesying which has seized so many preachers.
It is a popular topic, and secures crowds of hearers for
sermons and purchasers for books." These lectures have
not come into my hands; and I cannot speak as to the
exposition of the portion of the Apocalypse. His principle of interpretation agreed with that of Eichhorn and
De Wette. He treated the Revelation as already fulfilled, and criticized severely the presumption with
which dabblers in prophetic exposition are wont to apply
prophecy to past, and current, or future events, as their
fancies or prejudices may suggest.

The following rough outline from one of his note-books will help to illustrate his view of the general question :—

"A large number of people, generally idle and imaginative, and often women, occupy their time in what is called a study of Prophecy ; *i.e.*, in reading the speculations of others who add to the same tendencies, semi-literary or other ability.

"To such, Prophecy becomes not only their Religion, but a chief subject of their thoughts; and they are apt to judge that they who neglect this study neglect the greatest part, or a great part, of Religion.

"Several objections to this proceeding and temper :—1. Prophecy is confessed to be obscure; not accidentally, but purposely. If our study remove that obscurity, it removes what was intended to remain. Thus we *pry*.

"2. We are informed that the day and hour of Christ's second coming (the grand subject of New Testament prophecy) is hidden from the angels and the Son of God himself. And the reason is, that we should be *always* watchful. If from the Prophecies we may know that Christ will come between 1854 and 1858—as it seems we may—all the foregone Christians might and should have known the same. And, therefore, they had no motive to expect Christ's coming in their days ; and so watchfulness and expectation could not be duties to them.

"3. Whatever we should believe is *revealed*. Prophecy is not revealed, till the event unfolds the meaning. (Such is a popular theory at least.) So that any meaning we attach to it is merely our *conjecture*. Our faith, therefore, is in a conjecture of our own. And the variety of such conjectures shows how many of these must have been false.

"4. The Prophecies of the Old Testament which have been fulfilled in the events of the New, have not supplied any *principle* of Interpretation which we may apply to the unfulfilled predictions. Each appears to be dealt with in a manner of its own. No ingenuity could have taught a person, who lived before our Saviour, that the predictions respecting Him should be accomplished as they actually were. And no ingenuity can enable us to guess how the unfulfilled predictions will be accomplished. Even if we fall upon the right conjecture, we cannot know it is the correct one.

"5. It does not appear what advantage we can reap from this presumed Study of Prophecy. For we can find no new rule of duty, and no motives to it, other than those more clearly supplied by the preceptive parts of Scripture, which are plain and clear.

"6. These multifarious speculations and interpretations tend to excite doubt and foster scepticism, because they suggest the suspicion that vaticinations which can be so easily twisted to such a variety of senses—which can be made to mean so many things—can really mean nothing, and that those predictions which can prove *anything* can prove *nothing*.

"7. As God permits other creatures to exist as long as is needful to accomplish the purposes of their existence, and to attain the perfection of their being, so may we not presume that he will not cut off the aggregate creature, man, till he has accomplished his purpose and unfolded all that is in him? No wise man will admit that he has yet approached the goal. The art of printing is not yet 400 years old;—the mariner's compass not much older. America has been known only three centuries and a half (1492). It is only yesterday that we knew the use of steam, railways, and the electric telegraph. The effects of these inventions we cannot yet appreciate. We are only learning to till the ground, to construct our habitations, to educate our children. In short, a hundred facts show that the world is only in its infancy. Look at the state of government, law, prison discipline. Look at the state of Christianity, and the notions which prevail regarding it—the superstition, the Judaism!—at the state of morals, and the corruption of morals! Curious how the idea of the end of the world and the dissolution of it has deadened in modern times. This is caused by scriptural discovery and the experienced perpetuity of κοσμος."

DIARY.

"*March* 27, 1856.—To-day finished my ninth session, not having lost an hour by bad health or any other cause. The class was much inferior in quality generally to previous classes. I fear the *status* of our students is deteriorating. I hope I have been not slothful in my duties, though I fear a good deal of the seed sown has been lost; yet who can tell which shall grow, whether this or that? May God, ὁ αὐξάνων, make the seed which is good grow abundantly to the honour of His name. Amen. Now for other work.

"*June* 21, 1856.—Our twentieth wedding-day. Goodness and mercy follow us all the days of our life. We are all alive and in health, and all in peace and love. How great mercies are these ! Bless the Lord, O my soul.

"Our children are rising ; some of them have arisen up like olive plants around our table. God keep them from all evil, and prosper them in all good things.

"This day of midsummer is cold and bleak. Summer is not yet begun. Easterly winds have prevailed since January, with a few days' exception, and I am sitting by a good fire in my thick dressing-gown.

"*June* 30.—Jack —— appeared here this evening, and told me he was living at the Royal Hotel. I found he had come here three days ago, and having no money, like a prudent man, he set himself down in the most expensive hotel he could find. I paid his bill for the poor fool, and sent him on to ——. He had *smoked* twice as much money as would have kept a person who had any sense. ' Bray a fool in a mortar,' &c.

" *July* 20.—Preached this day on Justice. Have never been absent but one Sunday since the beginning of last September. Thanks unto God.

" *July* 21.—Went with Maggie to Greenock ; and (22d) with Lord and Lady Murray to Ardlussa in Jura, where I enjoyed three weeks of kind hospitality, and plenty of exercise and fresh air.

"*Aug.* 12.—Returned to Rosneath ;* and 15th, strained myself, and was confined to bed and house ten days."

From Rosneath, he writes to Mr. Combe on 27th August :—" I passed three weeks very pleasantly, and so far as health is concerned, very profitably, in Jura, where we had also some very pleasant society. . . . I propose returning to Edinburgh on the 3rd or 4th prox., leaving Mrs. Lee and the young people here till the end of September. I am of opinion that the banks

---

* Where he had a house this Autumn.

of the Clyde are, on the whole, little inferior, if at all, to anything to be met with on the Continent. The view from this cottage is so beautiful that I sometimes ask myself whether even Vevay surpasses it."

"*Sept.* 29.—Returned from a very pleasant visit to Minto, to dine and spend the evening with my dear and excellent 'Mamma,' Miss Napier, who this day completes her eightieth year. Though frail and weak, she is cheerful and patient, and so good that it is a sermon to see her. God bless her, the dear old lady!

"*Oct.* 2.—To-day rode with Mr. Ramsay to visit Mr. Learmonth, who appears dying. I hope I may have spoken to him what may be useful; but God only knows, who also can work effectually in us θέλειν τε καὶ ποιειν.

"*Oct.* 2.—To-morrow I expect the return of my family. I have spent a month quite alone here; and it has been so happy, so undisturbed by any unpleasant feeling of any kind, that one is tempted to question whether, after all, the single state is not the better?

"I am satisfied, on reflection, it is not. A family tries, tempts, exercises us in various ways; but it is a perpetual call to patience, forbearance, self-denial—to a relinquishing of our own inclinations, to controlling our feelings. It is, in short, such a discipline of self-control as cannot otherwise be found; and all this takes place in an atmosphere which makes the exercise possible and wholesome—the atmosphere of *love*.

"The family, however, may be rendered a hell upon earth, where bad temper is indulged, where differences of opinion are urged by either party, where there is a radical want of sympathy, or the like. Many worthy people, I am inclined to think, grievously afflict each other during their whole lives by not exercising a little wisdom and forbearance with each other in such matters.

"The treatment of their children often forms a constant field of battle to such persons. The mother defends her son against the reproofs and complaints of the father, 'who is too severe and exacting,' &c., &c., and so this youth is defended till he is spoiled.

"It is bad for children to know the disagreements of their parents; it makes them (in heart at least) partizans of either, and sows the seeds of disunion among themselves. May God give to me, and to my dear wife, grace to avoid all such evils, that we may live together in peace and love all the days of our life."

"*Dec.* 13.—On this Saturday evening I feel disposed, on looking back, as one naturally does at the end of a week (or of a year), to reflect that I lose a good deal of time by dissipation, —*i.e.*, running too much from one book and one study to another. This fault I have always felt inclined to. I weary with much of one thing. The thoughts of the same author after a while begin to fatigue me. I feel as if I knew beforehand all he would say; as if one had got all his associations, and even all his trains of thought, and even all his ideas. Thus, after having attended Dr. Chalmers's classes at St. Andrews, I felt always after unable to hear him with interest, or even to read his books. It was like reading my own writings, or listening to myself. Is this an ingenious apology for desultoriness? I think not. It seems to me the truth.

"Knowledge, like food, needs relish, else it is not digested, nor does it prove nutritious."

His life at this time was at its calmest and happiest. His family was undivided—all beside him in peace and safety. There had no evil befallen him, neither had any plague come nigh his dwelling. Separation and trouble were soon to come; but as yet they had cast no shadow before them. One could not see a brighter group than gathered round his table in 24, George Square. How many merry evenings one recalls in that house, with their music and dances, and charades; Dr. Lee always among his children and their guests, himself the gayest of the gay. How often do the words come back, which the memory of the golden past wrung from the sad heart of Lockhart as he wrote

of Scott and Abbotsford—"Gay voices for ever silent,
bright eyes now closed in dust, seem to haunt me as
I write."

> " Alas ! that all we loved of them should be,
> But for our grief, as if it had not been,
> And grief itself be mortal ! Woe is me !
> Whence are we, and why are we ? Of what scene
> The actors or spectators ? "

CHAPTER IX.

DR. SLOWMAN.

"Of Truth, of Grandeur, Beauty, Love, and Hope,
And melancholy Fear subdued by Faith;
Of blessed consolations in distress;
Of moral strength and intellectual power;
Of joy in widest commonalty spread;
Of th' Individual Mind, that keeps her own
Inviolate retirement, subject there
To Conscience only, and the Law Supreme
Of that Intelligence, which governs all."
WORDSWORTH, *Preface to the Excursion.*

AT this point in Dr. Lee's history, we may pause to look at a sketch, to which he gave the name prefixed to this chapter, and to which he kept adding line after line for several years, between 1850 and 1860. "Dr. Slowman" is not a real character. He is, I should rather say, the ideal of a real character, which has a certain affinity to the character of Dr. Lee himself. Whether Dr. Lee meant to construct an imaginary biography, and to publish it, or whether he merely sought in this form an outlet for his thoughts and speculations, does not appear from what he has written about Dr. Slowman. Probably, with the idea of ultimate publication in his mind, he occupied and amused his leisure by recording, under the guise of Dr. Slowman's biographer, his own convictions, speculations, or feelings, on many of the questions which interested him. I do not know that anything else among his MSS. admits us to a more intimate knowledge of his mind than this compilation, which fills the greater part of a tolerably thick octavo note-book. Having gone carefully through it, I shall make such extracts as seem most characteristic.

The title is " Some Account of the Life and Opinions of the late Rev. Samuel Slowman, D.D., by one of his Parishioners."

EXTRACTS.

After a somewhat Carlylese condemnation of modern biography-mongers, and of the publicity into which every life is now-a-days dragged, he proceeds :—

" Would to God one were forty days and forty nights in the wilderness ! The fasting, the wild beasts, even the devil, would be worth encountering, to hold communion with ourselves and with the Divinity without us and within us.

" I may here, once for all, introduce a remark which this last passage suggests, and which will be exemplified in many other cases in the course of this biography, that, Dr. Slowman, being a person of warm temperament, was apt, when he got into his rhapsodies, to go a little too far, at least it appeared so to us, but perhaps that was our mistake. I am not forward to pro-nounce judgment upon a man who was so much wiser and better than I can ever hope to be. I therefore entreat the gentle reader—flattering myself that gentle readers are not yet extinct —to receive my sentiments, when I venture to express them, *provisionally*; as matters of question submitted to him for consideration, not dogmas already defined, sanctioned, and to be received under pain of heresy and damnation. It would ill become the biographer of Dr. Slowman so to dogmatize or denounce ; for he, loving soul, could bring himself to hate only three kinds of creatures—devils, tyrants, and inquisitors."

" But is it not interesting, and useful also, to see the minutiæ of men's characters, and to know somewhat in detail the thoughts and lives of eminent men ?

" ' Yes, sir,' he would reply, ' if they really thought thoughts or lived lives of their own, I should like to know a good deal about them, if the truth could be reached. But I tell you, that either living or thinking on a man's own account, is as rare nearly as are angels' visits. Are you not sick hearing the same things over, and over, and over, from pulpits, platforms, parliament, and all other elevated places, each fellow conceiting himself clever if he can but alter a little the order, or vary the phrase? I have heard sermons for the last sixty years; and I speak in sober earnest when I affirm that, in that time, I have not heard six men who had anything of their own to tell me—traditions all, hearsay, repetition. Some few, indeed, have succeeded in startling the world with a strange phraseology; and for a little the world, poor fool! stood amazed, and cried, "Here at length is a new thing under the sun." But before he had listened a few minutes, he found that it was just the old song bawled out in a new manner. "Is there anything whereof it may be said, see, this is new? It hath been already of old time which was before us." No people that live so little in retirement as we do, can ever be original. If we habitually live with the vulgar, that is, with the crowd of our fellows, we shall not only speak with the vulgar, but think with them.'

"Now Dr. Slowman was a great admirer of retirement. This was one of his crotchets, as he used to think and say; and we shall meet this notion again more than once before we take leave of him.

"But would it not be delightful to know more of many persons who have lived and done mighty acts, and said wise sayings?

"'Perhaps so,' he would answer musingly. 'I should like to know what Moses thought when he stood upon the summit of Nebo, or Elijah when he felt himself borne up in the fiery chariot, also what Paul thought when he heard Stephen pray for his murderers; though, perhaps, we should be disappointed if we knew. As for the heathen sages, most of them have told us more of their notions than we care to listen to. Plato and Cicero are both of them too loquacious. We grow weary at last of their infinite talk, and only render thanks that Providence permitted Ali to burn the Bibliotheca at Alexandria, and zealous monks to scrape out whole acres of unedifying heathen lore. It was a merciful dispensation, whatever classical professors and editors may exclaim or groan.'

"And then he would lower his voice and add, 'There is but one person of whose acts and words I should earnestly desire to have a more minute record. And yet the evangelists, not without a higher than human wisdom, have judged their concise and scanty narratives sufficient for our information, even regarding the history of Jesus Christ.'"

"My late revered friend was settled, at the age of twenty-nine, as minister of a parish, in this highly-favoured and ancient kingdom of Scotland, which had enjoyed the light of a Gospel ministry in an eminent degree. Three successive pastors had laboured in it during long lives with conspicuous zeal, if not with eminent success. They were all three undoubtedly, and even emphatically, evangelical ; so that, as was acknowledged in all the country round, great were the privileges enjoyed by the people of Cailsie. Notwithstanding the administration so long of word and ordinances in singular purity and power, it was a sad and puzzling fact, that the inhabitants of this favoured parish were not decidedly better than their neighbours. Nay, it was maintained, with but too much appearance of truth, that the people of Knockbrae, and Drunkie, and Strathdune, who had been cursed with a succession of dry moderate and legal ministers, were better than the folk of Cailsie, a parish which had been a hundred years and more 'as a watered garden,' &c. Without moving further this ticklish question, I am bound to confess, that at the time when Dr., then Mr. Slowman, became minister, though there was much piety in the parish, and a great zeal for religion of a certain kind, there was so little morality that, as he said, the parishioners seemed so absorbed with the first Table of the Law that they had never got so far as to find out there was a second.

"It being suspected that Mr. Slowman was tinged with what is called *moderation*, or, as English folk would say, was of the high and dry school, and would feed the flock with the dry husks of morality, good works, and such garbage, instead of regaling their hungry souls with the sappy and soul-satisfying doctrines and promises of the Gospel, a formidable opposition was raised against his settlement by a few men who had much to say with the population, being reputed sound in the faith, and able judges of doctrine. These persons did not relish the prospect of Mr. Slowman coming to be minister of Cailsie ; not only because of his suspected moderation, but also because he had the character of a clear-headed man with a mighty strong will, so that they feared if he got himself fairly installed, their influence would be weakened or destroyed."

"While the parish was in a tumult of agitation, and the more evangelical portion of the people had organized a formidable opposition to Mr. Slowman's induction, he settled the matter in a way which made an impression on the parishioners that never wore off as long as he lived. It showed *he was an honest and a bold man :* and in no profession are these qualities more esteemed or more necessary, than in that of a clergyman.

"While the tumult was at the height, Mr. Slowman caused it to be intimated that he was to officiate in the parish church the following Sabbath. The people flocked to hear 'the dry stick' they had heard described. But the first few sentences of his morning prayer began to dispel the delusion, which was completely dissipated long before the sermon was finished. And the revolution of feeling was completed by the way in which he concluded the sermon.

"'Friends,' said he, 'I am informed there exists among you a great opposition to my settlement in this parish. As you do not know me, and never heard me preach, I thought it only justice, both to you and to myself, to come and introduce myself to you in this way, and let you hear what kind of things I have got to say to you. And now I have to inform you that if you don't wish me to come I will not come. If twenty persons out of this congregation will come into the Session House and tell me seriously that, in their opinion, the doctrine I preach is not likely to do them any good, I will to-morrow return the presentation to Lord ——, the patron. Don't think I wish to come here simply to draw the stipend. I have another end in view. I believe that you are a set of hypocritical, canting, lying, cheating, tippling, psalm singing, and praying scoundrels, and I should like to try my hand at pulling off the mask from your faces. And I give you fair warning that, if I come here, by the grace of God, I will not spare you. You know now what to expect. And now I shall wait my twenty honest friends in the Session House.'

" I was a boy at that time, but I was in church, and heard that strange appeal. I shall never forget it, or the excitement it produced. The display of fearless honesty and manly truth, overcame universally the indignation which so fierce an assault on the religious character of the parishioners of Cailsie tended to excite. The general truth of the satire, also, was far too evident to be denied; and so it was that, captivated by his eloquence, impressed by his earnestness, and actually electrified by his manliness and honesty, the whole congregation, as soon as the service was finished, rushed as one man into the Session House, shook him by the hand, told him they had been quite deceived, begged he would come and be their minister, promised to be attentive to his instructions, and, in short, from that moment Mr. Slowman took the place in their hearts which he held during his own life and theirs, without interruption or abatement."

" It was the custom in that part of the country, and, indeed, is still, to assemble crowds of people at funerals. And it was considered by those who were bidden a point of almost religious duty to attend. The people, coming from considerable distances, and regardless of punctuality, as country folks generally are, here seldom assembled till an hour, or even two hours, after the time at which they were bidden. This had become a grievous nuisance, which was long and loudly complained of, but still it continued.

" The week after Mr. Slowman's ordination, he preached from this text, 'Thou shalt not steal.' In the course of his sermon he made his audience prick up their ears by the following statement.

" ' I told you the first time I preached here what a bad report I had heard of you ; and I am sorry to confess, now I know you a little, that you are even worse than I expected. I find that you are guilty of stealing also, which I had never heard laid to your charge. I have lived among you only ten days, and two valuable pieces of property have already been feloniously abstracted from me by men living in this parish. I know who the guilty parties are ; I see several of them in church at this moment. You look amazed. Well you may. The two pieces of property which I have lost are two *Hours*—which were stolen from me at a funeral last Thursday. Perhaps you don't reckon time property, but I do. I value it as much as money, or rather, far more. I was bidden to a funeral at twelve o'clock, and you assemble at two, and I lose two hours:—120 minutes or 7,200 seconds waiting you. For shame! it is almost worse than theft; it is a kind of sacrilege.

"'What account shall I give at the Day of Judgment of those two hours? What can I do but accuse you of theft? "They were stolen from me," I must say, "by my dishonest parishioners, the people of Cailsie." There it is. Look to yourselves. You must be arraigned for theft, transgression of the law "Thou shalt not steal.'

"Some persons may, perhaps, feel disposed to censure this style of preaching as inconsistent with '*the dignity of the pulpit.*' Many years after the period I am now writing of, I mentioned this to my venerated friend. 'Dignity of the pulpit!' said he. 'What is the dignity of the pulpit? The dignity of dulness! the dignity of fine sentences, holiday phrases, and good-for-nothing generalities! There is no dignity, sir, in being of no use. True dignity is the doing effectually what you propose and profess to do, whatever that may be. The most dignified jockey is he that rides his horse best; the most dignified ploughman is he that makes the best furrow; the most dignified king is he who rules his subjects most wisely; and the most dignified minister of the Gospel is he who preaches in the way most suitable and most impressive to the people he preaches to, who employs the language they best understand, the illustrations and arguments they are most likely to feel. True dignity is nothing but real worth. God forbid that we should seek any dignity except that of labouring to render the people wiser and better. Believe me, sir,' he added, 'the only dignity a clergyman should aspire to is that of simple, honest earnestness, without all cant, hypocrisy, finery, and affectation. It won't do for a man whose business it is to teach rough peasants to affect the fine gentleman or the *petit maître.*'"

"Mr. Slowman often spoke of the necessity of suiting the address to the apprehension and habits of the audience. 'When you wish to chastise an animal,' he would say, 'you consider whether the instrument you have taken up is such that *he will feel it.* You would never think of applying a light driving whip to the hide of a donkey. You must make people see and *feel.*' Acting on this principle, Mr. Slowman sometimes produced the most wonderful impressions on the rude people with whom he had to deal. He one day overtook on the road a carter, named Jamie Brown, a coarse blackguard, notorious for his cruelty to his animals, and his wife and children. He had just been thrashing his horse when the minister overtook him.

"'I think your name is Jamie Brown?' said Mr. Slowman, stopping his horse and addressing the carter.

"'Yes, sir,' said Jamie, who, like many such characters, had a sort of superstitious reverence for the minister.

"'Ah, indeed,' he continued, musingly, and looking at Jamie, 'so you are Jamie Brown! Poor fellow! ah, indeed, so you are the man!'

"'Ods mercy!' cried the man in amazement; 'what are you saying?'

"'And do you really not know,' interrupted the minister, 'what is going to happen to you?'

"'Me?' exclaimed he; 'what is it? Mercy on us, what is it?' his face now filled with an alarm which he could not disguise.

"'Oh,' replied Slowman, in the deepest tones of his solemn voice, and looking intently in Brown's face, 'something very awful, Jamie, is to happen—the devil is coming very soon to carry you off to the bottomless pit, and there the ghosts of all the horses you have tortured and killed will be appointed to kick, bite, and trample on your miserable carcase to all eternity. Now, Jamie, you had better consider what is to be done; and when you have thought over the matter, come to me, and I will give you my best advice. Don't linger, my good fellow, for I tell you—*the Devil is upon your track.* Good-day. Mind my words.'"

"I visited Dr. Slowman once when two clergymen also were his guests, Mr. Alpha and Mr. Omicron. Mr. Alpha was a learned man, and deeply read in the critical and biblical lore of modern Germany; and if not infected deeply with the sceptical temper of that people, he evidently had ceased to be either horrified or startled at their bold innovations. Mr. Omicron, on the other hand, was *orthodox*, according to a most rigid standard. He believed all that the Church taught, and he refused to look into any book or to listen to any person who threatened to disturb his convictions. As he said himself, he had 'found rest to his soul,' and he treated every one as an enemy who attempted to disturb it.

"After Alpha and Omicron were gone, Dr. Slowman and myself had much discourse respecting those two men, and the states of mind which they respectively represented.

"I argued that Mr. Omicron was at least the more consistent and honest man of the two. True, he knew very little beyond his own creed and catechism, and what went to establish and explain these ; but then, this narrowness, or bigotry as it might be termed, was sincere. He loved truth; and having been taught that this was truth, he was afraid to trust himself with those who, he feared, might seduce him into the fatal paths of error. His refusal to read the books which Mr. Alpha recommended, was therefore really a determination not to enter into temptation. For, admitting that he might obtain from such books much instruction and great enlargement of mind on some points, yet, his apprehensions that, on other points, and these more vital, he might be perverted, seemed to justify him in confining his reading to those authors who fortified him in his own views, and strengthened his orthodoxy.

"Dr. Slowman thought that Mr. Omicron did not deserve this commendation at the expense of Mr. Alpha. For he held if Mr. Omicron had not some suspicion that some of his opinions were ill-founded, or at least questionable, he would not fear to listen to those who impugned them. We don't much applaud a judge who insists on deciding a question after hearing only one party. This is what Mr. Omicron does. He has heard the Presbyterian and the Calvinist, and he has affirmed their arguments. But the Arminian, the Episcopalian, the Independent, the Quaker, the Papist, the Unitarian, the Rationalist, all put in their claims to be heard, and promise that they can refute the reasonings of the Presbyterian and Calvinist; and what does the judge, Mr. Omicron, say? Because Calvin and the Westminster Assembly have first got my ear, I have attentively listened to them and seriously weighed their arguments : and I therefore proceed to give judgment that they are right and all that differ with them wrong. In vain do their adversaries protest against giving sentence against them in absence. Mr. Omicron replies that his two advocates have told him all about the opposing parties that he cares or needs to know, and so he turns them out of court. 'I cannot,' said Dr. Slowman, 'consider this any high type of honesty. Men seek truth, certainly, by such proceeding, on no subject but religion. In fact, however he may disguise it, Omicron makes Calvin and the Westminster divines Christ and the Apostles. To *them* he imputes *Inspiration* and *Infallibility*. He is a slave to that human authority which he is always denouncing; and when I hear him talk of the authority of Scripture, &c., I always think of that proverb of Solomon, "He that answereth a cause before he heareth it, it is folly and shame unto him." Besides,' added Dr. Slowman, 'our friend Omicron is a teacher of Christianity. By assuming this position does he not claim to understand a subject? But how can any one make such claim (consistently) who refuses to learn what a host of the most able, learned, and acute men have advanced on the subject? A friend of mine, a banker, had a country house in Omicron's parish, and used regularly to attend the parish church. Being a man of much intelligence and serious reading, he had become acquainted with certain opinions respecting the Scriptures. Observing the way in which Omicron treated such objections both in conversation and in preaching, Mr. B. once took occasion to mention his doubts and difficulties to him, telling him at the same time that he should feel very thankful for any assistance or light. But he was astonished to find that Omicron knew nothing of the subjects on which he had dogmatized, that he simply repeated what he had heard from others not much better informed than himself. Mr. B. frankly told Omicron that though he had never admired, he had always respected him; but now, as he could do neither, he must attend some other church to save himself from becoming an infidel. Poor Omicron was sadly disconcerted at this, for he was rather flattered by the regular and serious attention of so intelligent a man as Mr. B., and his withdrawal, he knew, would create much speculation and remark.'

"'You will allow, at least,' said he, ' that I am honest in holding my own opinions.' 'That, sir,' replied B. 'is for yourself to decide. You are placed here, and maintained to teach the Christian religion, and you know almost nothing of the subject, you are therefore unable to afford any assistance to one of your flock who seriously wishes help. You refuse to look into books which many of your parishioners read, and think it their duty to read. If you had a higher honesty, you would follow their example, and then you would be either qualified to refute what they advance, or to cease denouncing opinions which you do not understand, and which, for aught you can tell, may be correct.'

"Mr. B. is now a hearer of Alpha, who, he says, has given him much light and done him great good. A remark he lately made to me on this subject illustrates well the different effects which such men as our two friends produce. 'Under Omicron's preaching,' said he, 'I began to doubt whether anything was true; all the dogmas, however doubtful, were urged with the same confidence; whereas the effect of Alpha's instructions is to deepen my conviction that *religion is true*, that it is a genuine part of man's nature, and one of his primary necessities; that to deny this is to deny himself. The doctrines involved in this idea, and plainly arising out of it, appear to me as certain as any other necessary truths, so that faith rises into knowledge, and having become convinced that Christianity is speculatively true, I feel it also practically efficacious in urging me to live a higher, purer, and more self-denying life, than any I ever thought of attempting before. In this state of mind,' he added, solemnly, 'I hope, Dr. Slowman, I am neither an infidel nor a heretic, though I feel Mr. Omicron feels some difficulty in determining to which class I belong, or perhaps whether I do not belong to some other community worse than either.'

"Dr. S. ended our conversation with this remark, 'As men know less they believe more; as they know more they believe less, that is, fewer things. The ages of faith have always hitherto been ages of ignorance, perhaps they always will and must be; which is only saying, that when we don't know ourselves, we are the more ready to listen to those who say *they know*. Germany now believes less than England, England less than Ireland, Spain, Italy; everywhere the creed contracts as the popular understanding expands. The priest and the schoolmaster are natural antagonists: no wonder, the priest is jealous of his rival, and would keep him in his pay and under his authority. But the struggle can only end in one way. Learning is called in to defend the faith, but always ends in turning round to attack its patron.

'A friend who went with me to church to-day, and who had heard Dr. S. preach before, remarked, ' that he did not seem to insist much upon the *mysteries of religion.*' On my asking what doctrines he alluded to, my friend mentioned the doctrines of the Trinity, the Divinity of Christ, the Personality of the Holy Ghost, the Fall, the Atonement, Election, Reprobation, and the like.

"On the first opportunity I mentioned this to Dr. S. His reply was to this effect, ' When younger I used often to discourse on these topics, because, being persuaded they were truths revealed, I supposed it was my duty to insist upon them. I have ceased for many years past to do so, for this reason;—I find I cannot explain any of those doctrines in any degree, neither can I turn them to any practical account. Any hypothesis I may propound depends entirely upon my own ingenuity, or that of some other man, and may be correct; but more likely is merely imagined. To discuss these subjects is apt also (as experience has taught me) to raise up doubts and questions which are not easily satisfied; besides, is it not absurd to confess that these are mysteries, and then to discourse of them as if they were matters within the scope of our understandings ? *i. e.,* first to acknowledge that we cannot explain or comprehend them, and then to proceed as if we could do both. Besides, these doctrines, if handled at all, should be handled in a philosophical way. S. François de Sales was both a great preacher and a great saint, and a very wise man to boot, as his wonderful success in reconverting the Protestants shows. In his treatise, "De la Prédication," he offers the same advice. "Si dignè de mysterio Trinitatis dicere nequiverimus, eo argumento abstineamus. Si idonei non simus exponere istud Joannis *In principio,* supersedere licet. Sunt alia majoris utilitatis argumenta, nec omnia omnes facere necesse est."

"'Some doctors, you see, are wise as well as orthodox, and yet both our Lord and Paul have taught us this, "I have yet many things to say, but, &c." "I have fed you with milk .... to bear it." '

"Among many other strange opinions which he advocated, this was one, that sermons should not be *declamations* but *teachings*. When people said they had heard a fine sermon, he was accustomed to ask 'What has it taught you?' If they said, 'Nothing in particular,' or 'they could not tell,' or something quite trite and common-place, he told them they did not understand what was the use and intent of preaching. 'It is wonderful,' he would remark, 'that men and women should hear sermons all their lives, and yet should know almost nothing of their religion, nothing in short but the catechism. In what subject are men willing to be pupils and scholars all their lives without making any progress?'

" He gave very curious advice to a young preacher who consulted him whether he should read or recite his sermons. 'If you can speak sense,' he said, 'by all means *recite;* reading is an unnatural, and, therefore, an ineffectual mode of address ; and is preferable only to talking nonsense. But however you prepare your *sermons*, always prepare your *prayers*, and that with anxious care : simplicity, dignity, comprehensiveness, are not to be attained without careful study. A Church which uses a Liturgy will always gain upon a Church which employs extempore prayers, among an educated population. *Its want of a Liturgy will prove the overthrow of the Church of Scotland :* and at no distant period. I have talked to many pious and intelligent people who had seceded to the Episcopal Church, and I found that 'the superiority of the Episcopal prayers' was the reason alleged, and I doubt not truly, in almost every case. Write your prayers very carefully and deliberately, and revise them again and again, till they become fit expressions of the Christian heart, and if you cannot commit them to memory, *read them.* The laws of our Church allow the reading of prayers as much as the reading of sermons, and even more : for Knox's Liturgy is still the Liturgy of the Church of Scotland, which was intended to be read, and was read : and the people (I presume), would much rather their ministers should read prayers than sermons. Besides, whatever reasons may be alleged for the one practice, stronger may be for the other. If it be necessary that our speeches to our fellow men should be well ordered, it is yet more needful that our addresses to our Maker should be so.'

"Some discussion arose one evening, whether Dr. Chalmers was a great man? One of the company denied this, and endeavoured to prove his point by arguing that all his grand positions in philosophy, political economy, Church politics, &c., were false. Dr. Slowman thought the fact that Dr. Chalmers had persuaded so many people that he *was* a great man, was itself a proof of a certain amount of greatness; 'for,' said he, 'there is always some divinity in human idols, they are universally superior to the herd in some quality fitted to excite admiration; if not in wisdom, knowledge, &c., yet in strength of will, energy, perseverance, and the like. And in these latter, the greatness of the person in question chiefly consisted. He was, also, a great rhetorician, though not profound or accurate as a thinker, and very shallow in his knowledge of most subjects.'

"'Our Church,' Dr. Slowman once said, 'teaches the doctrine of eternal torments to the wicked. I feel it a duty to believe that I am one of the elect, and also all my kindred, and all I love and care for; because it being my duty to love God, I feel I should have too strong a reason to hate Him, if I thought either myself, or any one else, whom I care for, created by the Almighty to glorify Him (who needs no glory), by unceasing and endless torment.'

"' Is this hope of Immortality,' he would exclaim, 'the inspiration of God, or of our own selfishness? Is it our covetousness grasping for more life, after we have had enough; refusing to retire from the banquet though we have eaten and drunk enough? Is it the glory or the shame, the strength or the infirmity of human nature? or has our experience in this world only awakened the consciousness of a capacity which has had no satisfaction, and could have had none in the present state?'

"A young minister, a person of some talents and acquirements, who had lately been settled in a neighbouring parish, officiated one day for Dr. Slowman. He dealt very hardly with the literary and scientific men of the time, the periodical press, and, in short, with those who lead public opinion: representing them as deeply infected with a spirit of ungodliness or infidelity. As we were walking in the manse garden, before dinner, this young divine turned the conversation to the sermon, pardonably anxious to know Dr. Slowman's opinion of his performance. After receiving one or two hints to this effect, he at last confounded the preacher, and all of us, by remarking very gravely, that he very much admired the composition of the sermon, and thought several passages very effective ; but he confessed he did not like sermons which attacked the Christian religion, and he felt uncomfortable when a minister of the Gospel set himself to pull down what he should labour to build up. Being both a sincere and a zealous man, Mr. Steven exhibited that degree of astonishment, and even horror, which may be imagined. With great agitation, he asked Dr. Slowman to explain what he meant ; for he had found out that he always meant something when he spoke. 'Be not surprised, my young friend,' said the much reflecting man, 'at what I have said: on a moment's consideration, you will perceive how you were, by that strain of discourse, dishonouring and weakening that faith which you designed to uphold and honour. Your argument amounted to this, that the learned, the inquiring, the reflecting portion of the community doubt or disbelieve the Christian religion ; while they who believe it are the illiterate, the uninquiring, the credulous, they who take everything for granted and believe, or profess, anything they are taught. Analyse your expressions, and you will see that with you, the " wise and prudent " are just the men of intelligence and thought, the *babes* are just the boors and simpletons. Now, sir, if this representation were just, what inference could any man of common sense draw but this—that the religion which the latter party believed, and the former rejected, can be nothing but delusion ? Don't be hasty, my good sir, to call any one an infidel because he denies many things which you hold ; or a heretic because he believes very differently from you. He may have more *faith* than you, though he has less *creed :* and the most enlightened Christians have generally been *heretics* to contemporary Theologians and Dogmatists, and the multitude, who are always led by them. Our Confession of Faith makes Milton and Jeremy Taylor, not to say François de Sales, Fénélon, Chrysostom, and Basil, and all the Fathers, Saints, and Martyrs of the ancient Church, both Greek and Latin, heretics ; yet I hope to meet them in heaven, if I am counted worthy to find entrance there. And, besides, I console myself with the thought that I may see in the same place great numbers, whom the Polemics had consigned to everlasting flames. "For many shall come from the east and the west, &c.,' *i. e.*, many of the heterodox shall be in heaven, and crowds of the orthodox shall be in another place.' . . . .

. . . "Let me set down in this place what the Doctor said to me respecting the sin against the Holy Ghost. 'It is very remarkable,' he said, 'that when our Lord says so much about the divine mercy, and preaches so much forgiveness of sins, he should make an express exception in respect of this one sin. This particular wickedness, as you will observe by looking at the passages in which it is mentioned, was the imputing *Christ's* miracles to *Demons;* in short, ascribing God's works to devils ; a proceeding, doubtless, which displayed a peculiar malignity against Christ, and detestable disregard of moral distinctions. Now,' added he, 'to impute evil works or malevolent dispositions to God, appears to me the same sin in a more hideous form. To hold that God wishes, intends, or necessitates that any of His creatures should be miserable, much more that they should be eternally so, is such an outrage upon the character of God, that to teach it may well be deemed the sin against the Holy Ghost, and that in an aggravated form. Fortunately, however, good men mean no evil by the doctrines they embrace. When they feel their contradiction or impiety, they call them *mysteries.* And we should charitably accept the apology which is implied in the use of such terms.' . . .

"Among the peculiarities of Dr. Slowman was this, that before going out to dinner, and before going to dinner in his own house, especially if any one was to dine with him, he went to his prayers. 'We are never in greater danger,' he would say, 'or as Martin Luther would express it, the devil is never closer to our elbow, than when we dine in company :—in danger both as to what goes into our mouths and what comes out of them. It is then we are most apt to trangress in the way of intemperance, being stimulated with variety of delicacies, wines, &c., and by sympathy and example to commit excess ; and, also, we are tempted to exceed truth in various ways, in order to render ourselves agreeable, to indulge in gossip and other foolish talking, and in 'jesting which is not convenient.' So that, on the whole, he is a perfect man who, in such circumstances, can eat and drink to the glory of God.   Therefore, sensible of my danger, I say my prayers.'

"I am afraid such superstitious notions and practices may lower my friend in the estimation of my enlightened readers.

"Dr. Slowman said: 'A great evil in itself, and a fearful temptation to weak and unscrupulous men, is this, that whatever a preacher says, he need fear no contradiction.   I, myself, have heard numerous downright falsehoods uttered in the pulpit as the Gospel of our Lord Jesus Christ.   This very summer, being in London, I heard a popular preacher there assert with the greatest coolness, not in any confidence, as glaring an untruth as ever was spoken by human lips, and that in presence of a well-dressed and even fashionable-looking congregation ; among whom, however, it seemed to produce no sensation, or even to excite any surprise, or, as far as I could observe, any particular attention.   This apology, no doubt, may be made for him, that he did not know it was false. But, on the other hand, neither could he know it was true.   So that at the very least, and giving him all the benefit of absolute ignorance, he still lied ; for he asserted what he did not know, and could not have ascertained, to be the fact.

"'If custom had permitted any of the hearers to stand up, and modestly to ask the proof of such assertion, it never would have been made ; and, by such a check, if it were practicable, (and I do not see it is not, for it prevailed in the Apostolic Church,) a salutary revolution would be produced in preaching. Nonsense and fallacy, wild assertions and absurd statements, would not flourish as they do now.'

"A person observed, that some of the provincial newspapers appeared to derive their whole matter, even the substance of their leading articles, from the 'Times.' Dr. Slowman said that every thing that grew to be monstrous became a prey and plunder to others. It is a law of nature ; one is fat, the others are hungry. It has happened to this Leviathan of News as it did to another Leviathan, of whom it is written, 'Thou gavest him to be meat to the people inhabiting the wilderness.' (*Ps.* lxxiv.)

[At the Zoological gardens at Edinburgh I found that the elephant could not protect himself against a rat that ate his foot.]

"An acquaintance had lost a daughter, a beautiful and very

interesting young lady, of whom he was very fond, and had expressed an inclination to pray for her. The person who related this circumstance was inclined to censure pretty severely this superstition, as he considered it.

"Dr. Slowman said he saw no reason for pronouncing any grave censure upon this dictate of parental affection, for our feelings, said he, are often wiser than our understandings. Besides, he added, 'it can do no harm to the father, and certainly not to his departed child, and not being anywhere forbidden, I cannot see why our friend may not do what affords comfort to his wounded spirit.' This strain of reasoning much scandalized our companion, who objected that all Protestants considered prayers for the dead as superstitious, if not impious; and it appeared preposterous to pray that persons might be saved whose doom was irreversibly fixed, their probation being ended, and their day of grace past.

"Dr. Slowman admitted that the Protestants were generally unanimous against this practice, but he said that the ancient Christians were nearly as unanimous in favour of it ; and as to the other argument, he did not think it had much force in the mouth of a Calvinist, who prayed for the salvation of all men, though at the same time he held that God had, by an absolute decree, doomed to everlasting damnation the great mass of them, and that before they were born, or had either done or thought good or evil.

"'If you pray that all men may be brought to the knowledge and obedience of the truth, why,' asked Dr. Slowman, 'may not Mr. —— implore God to look in mercy upon his dead daughter, to keep her in his holy keeping, to make her partaker of the joys of Paradise, to shorten any correction she may need, and to hasten her perfect felicity ? God (I trust) will forgive, if he does not answer, such prayers.*

"'Many different opinions,' said Dr. Slowman, 'have been held concerning the happiness of heaven. Indeed, probably no two persons agree in their conception of the nature and elements of that happiness. Richard Hooker, harassed with controversies, and agitated with the factions of his time, imagined heaven to be a blessed order and submission to authority.

"'My idea of heaven,' he added, 'is freedom from *doubt*, a state

* Dated " The night after Janie's burial."

in which we can inquire without suspicion, remain ignorant without apprehension, and reason without danger of making shipwreck of our faith. In this world inquiry is the parent of doubt or unreason, and both pay dreadful penalties, and expose us to frightful dangers.'

"A London barrister met Dr. Slowman at our house, and had much conversation with him on a great variety of subjects.

"He said he had never met a better informed man, or a more instructive or pleasant companion. He also expressed surprise to find a man so perfect a gentleman who lived in so obscure a corner, so out of the world. He was a union, he said, of two almost incompatible characters, the recluse student, and the practical, easy, refined, man of the world. He must have conversed a great deal with other men, added the barrister, and yet more with himself. We should not do him justice if we said he was free of all vanity, pride, ambition, for he is evidently *above* these passions.

"One Sunday we had a stranger, who preached a long explanatory and doctrinal sermon, of which we were extremely tired.

"I asked Dr. Slowman what was the reason why ministers continued to afflict people with such discourses, seeing the whole matter was contained in the Catechism, which everyone should be presumed to be acquainted with. He said the reason was because they considered the Christian religion, and called it, a scheme of salvation, and so very intricate and puzzling a scheme, that they could never take too much pains to explain all its intricacies and complications.

"'But,' I asked, 'was not the Gospel in turn such a scheme?'

"Dr. Slowman said, smiling, 'If it was, S. Paul would probably have known the fact. It was a scheme of salvation, as a father's or mother's love was a scheme for the good of their child. It no doubt tended to good and sought it, but the very thought that it was in any sense a scheme or plan was felt to to be shocking and even absurd. These schemers should not think God altogether such an one as themselves.'

"Much preaching, he said, does far more harm than good. This mania for sermons we owe to the Puritans, who left us a very mixed legacy, combining much good and perhaps even more evil.

"'I have heard a good character of Mr. Davidson,' said Dr. Slowman, 'and yet I cannot think well of him, for he is not a just man. Now without justice no one should be considered good. Coming with him from Glasgow this afternoon, I observed he put his feet upon the cushions of the railway carriage.' I remarked in reply that this was a very small matter, and I did not see how it involved the character of justice. 'Its being a small matter,' answered Dr. Slowman, 'is the very thing that renders it a test and indication of a man's principles. It is in little things that the acute and educated conscience shows itself. I do not suppose Mr. Davidson would steal a thousand pounds, or injure his neighbour in any matter which was so big that every one must see it to be wrong who has any conscience at all. As to that practice, however, being unjust, a moment's reflection will prove it. It is contrary to a regulation of the company, who warn all passengers that it is forbidden. By using their railway, you are constructively a party to their laws and regulations. It destroys and wears out their property prematurely, and by unfair usage. A gentlewoman comes into the carriage and sits down upon the cushion which Mr. Davidson has filthified with his feet, and spoils her dress, and he thus wrongs *her*. No, sir, no man is worthy to be considered just who does not perceive that such proceeding, besides being socially rude and offensive is morally wrong, a violation of the rights of our neighbour. It would be well for the people, and for themselves, too, if the clergy, instead of speculating regarding the constitution of the divine nature, and the secret policy of the court of heaven, would instruct their hearers more in such common-place matters as these, that by reason of use their moral senses might be exercised to discern both good and evil.'"

The reader will see from these extracts, which give a fair sample, what the range and character of these " Collectanea " are. They are the same throughout, a *mélange* of thoughts, some original, some borrowed, and with the thin thread of biographical identity running through it, reminding one now of " Sartor Resartus," and now, of " Friends in Council," in a subdued way.

In sundry note-books and scraps of MS., there are jottings evidently designed to be wrought into the tissue of this web, but too fragmentary or disjointed to be quoted here. Dr. Slowman comes to no end ; and probably much would have been added to his sayings and doings, but for the "*ineluctabile fatum.*" In Dr. Lee's diary, of July, 1861, among other projected works, he specifies "Life of Dr. Slowman, and a System of Theology, by Same." Some of these projects he fulfilled, but this remains incomplete.

CHAPTER X.

RESTORATION OF OLD GREYFRIARS' CHURCH—ANNUITY
TAX—SERMON AT CRATHIE—UNIVERSITY REFORM—
CORRESPONDENCE—DIARY—TROUBLE AND SORROW.

> " Who knew the seasons when to take
> Occasion by the hand, and make
> The bounds of freedom wider yet."
> TENNYSON, *To the Queen*, 1851.

AFTER much municipal delay, the Church of the Old
Greyfriars' was restored. A large sum was added by
the congregation to the legal funds, in order that the
restoration might be effected in a style worthy of the
historical renown of the Church. The outside could not
be altered in any way; but the interior was repaired
and fitted up, gracefully though simply, and all the
windows were filled with painted glass—then a novelty
in Scotch churches. The great east window was the
gift of the congregation. Among the others, which were
presented as memorials, were, one in memory of Principal
Robertson—to which his nephew, Lord Brougham, contributed; one in memory of Dr. Inglis—the founder of
the Scottish " India Mission "—given by his son, the
present Lord President of the Court of Session; and one
in memory of Dr. Erskine (Robertson's colleague), the
joint gift of Dr. Lee's distinguished friend, Mr. Erskine,
of Linlathen, and other members of the Erskine family.

"It was very sad," says Dr. Lee, "to leave the Assembly Hall, where we had been since Feb. 1845. Dear S——,* may God bless him abundantly. I have preached more than half of my ministry in this church, and I suppose far the most useful and important part of it.

The restored church was opened on June 14, 1857; Dr. Lee conducting the service in the forenoon, Dr. Barclay in the afternoon. At the close of his sermon, which was from the text, Hebrews vi. 1-3, Dr. Lee said: —"I have endeavoured, though in much ignorance and weakness, to set forth the Gospel in its more practical applications, to the persons who have hitherto attended my ministry, rather than to entangle them in metaphysical speculations, or to stun them with theological dogmatism; and instead of being frightened or disheartened by the opprobrium which this way of proceeding never fails to draw down, I desire, and by the grace of God I intend still, to pursue the same course, with, I hope, greater wisdom and energy and decidedness, and, may God grant, with increased success. Though I acknowledge, with thankfulness and humility, that I have not been left without the satisfaction of seeing some good fruit already; and I hope more may have been produced than I wot of now,—but the day will declare it. Still, it is my purpose to look upon 'the colours of good and evil;' to study the *religion* of Christ in the spirit and character of Christ; so to consider His life that we may live with Him; His death, that we may die with Him; His resurrection, that we may rise with Him; His ascension and reign in heaven, that we may ascend to a loftier moral elevation, and

* Rev. Dr. Smith, minister of the Tolbooth parish, whose congregation met in the Hall.

reign in spiritual life, disenthralled from the bondage of the flesh and the world, both in earth and heaven ; may so believe that we may work ; and so work that we may receive the reward in that day when God shall bring every work into judgment, and we shall know how small a matter is the praise or blame, the admiration or the contempt, of our fellow-creatures."

Immediately afterwards he went up to London to oppose a bill concerning the " Annuity Tax," then before the House of Commons. He says in his diary, in reference to this, " *Mem.* : to keep out of turmoils and discussions as much as possible, for the future. The life of a salamander is not agreeable. ' As much as lieth in you live peaceably with all men,'—even with dishonest knaves like the members of the T. C."

This tax, which has long had an unhappy prominence in the civic and ecclesiastical annals of Edinburgh, was, at that time, a charge of six per cent. on the rental of shops and houses in the city, for the stipends of the clergy. The tax was first imposed in 1634, and the area of its incidence was extended as the city increased, —the last extension having taken place in 1809. The College of Justice, comprising all the members of the legal profession, was exempted from payment; an ancient privilege, designed as a bribe to induce the Courts of Law to settle themselves permanently in Edinburgh. The tax was levied from occupiers, not from owners ; and this, as well as the exemption of the lawyers, fostered the popular dislike to it. As dissent grew, dislike ripened into hate, and hate into resistance. Although the clergy were most lenient in their collection of the impost, and voluntarily sanctioned many exemptions from it, the fact of their claiming it at all was eagerly used by local agitators (as an oppressive sample of clerical rapacity) to inflame the uninstructed public mind against Church Establishments in general, and the Establishment at Edinburgh in particular. Sundry efforts were made at different times, in Parliament, to adjust the "Annuity Tax" on a basis which should conciliate the opposition to it, without entirely forfeiting the rights of the clergy. None had succeeded. Indeed, the local demagogues found the tax too serviceable a stalking horse for their own ambitions and jobberies, to allow it to be quietly driven into the background. They would either have total and immediate abolition—which they knew they could not get—or nothing. So year after year passed, and the agitation continued ; the clergy were exposed—as the local demagogues desired—to the odium of collecting the tax from recusant payers ; and persons of tender and delicate conscience were, on every needful occasion, to be found, who, rather than pay peaceably their legal share of it, suffered the spoiling of their goods by the sheriff's officer, and enjoyed the brief glory of a dubious martyrdom. In 1857 another Annuity Tax bill, introduced by Mr. Adam Black, then member for Edinburgh, was before the House of Commons ; and its provisions were so entirely subversive of the position of the Church as an Established Church, that the Presbytery did all they could to secure its defeat. It was on this errand Dr. Lee went to London. He took a keen interest in the question ; being anxious at once to secure adequate stipends for the clergy, and to remove every reasonable cause of grievance on the part of the taxpayer. But he had no tolerance for the tactics of the local demagogues,* and no belief in the conscientious scruples which obliged people to break the law rather than pay their taxes.

He made a long speech in the Presbytery, shortly after his return from London, on the subject of the Bill. He maintained that the principle to be kept in view in any adjustment of the tax, was, that the stipends of the ministers should be so secured as to bear a proportion to the progress of society, the expenses of living, &c. ; and that therefore it was necessary to perpetuate their relation to the rental of the city, and not to fix them (as had been proposed) at a definite sum, which, as the value of money lessened, would become proportionally insufficient. He pointed out, what the local demagogues shut their eyes to,—that the incomes of all other professional men were rising steadily, while those of the clergy were relatively falling, and this, in a great measure, because of their own gentleness in exacting the Annuity Tax.† At that time there were fully 16,000*l.* of arrears due to them.

---

* In a squib which I find among his papers, Dr. Lee enshrines the names of some of these obscure worthies. Here is a verse of it :—

> " Those venerable saws
>   That Magistrates the laws
> Should both enforce, and eke themselves obey,
> Are now exploded quite,
> For Stot, and Neil, and Wright
> Have shown the lieges all a better way.

Chorus.

> Wright, Neil, and Stot,
>   Shall never be forgot—
> With Tully's and with Chatham's name,
> In company their deathless fame
> Right on to Immortality shall trot."

† For instance, in 1807 the salary of a judge of the Court of Session was 1280*l.*, and that of a minister of Edinburgh 330*l.* In 1857 the salary of a judge was 3000*l.*, while that of a minister was barely 600*l.*

We find him, again and again, speaking in the Presbytery on the question, and trying to guide the deliberations of his brethren to the only satisfactory end—a practicable compromise. In a long speech in March, 1859,* he argues against a fresh bill of Mr. Black's, then before the House of Commons; and urges, as the basis of an adjustment which the ministers could accept, the transfer of the patronage of the churches from the Town Council to the several congregations; the extension of the tax to the members of the College of Justice; and the concession of the seat rents, at present paid to the Town Council, to the Church on behoof of the clergy.

These terms were not obtained; but in 1860 a different settlement of the vexed question was secured by the bill of Mr. Moncrieff, then Lord Advocate. This bill effected a compromise, to which the clergy, somewhat unwillingly, assented. It reduced to a minimum the amount of the tax; it levied it from the College of Justice,—to which that body readily agreed—but it reduced the number of ministers from eighteen to thirteen, and it fixed the stipends at the inadequate pittance of 550*l.* a year. It further vested the management of the city churches, and of the fund raised by the tax, in the hands of a board of Ecclesiastical Commissioners; of whom Dr. Lee was appointed one.

As a final solution of a prolonged dispute, this arrangement was accepted by the city on the one hand, and the clergy on the other. All the concession was, obviously, on the part of the latter. They agreed to the reduction of their number from eighteen to thirteen, and also to a serious loss of revenue; for the tax on the in-

<hr>

* *Scotsman,* 31st March, 1859.

creasing rental of the city was rapidly growing in annual value. But these sacrifices they resolved to make for the sake of peace.

Dr. Lee writes to Lord Campbell in reference to the Bill on July 14, 1860 :—

"DEAR LORD CHANCELLOR,

"Though I feel very reluctant to intrude, even for a moment, upon your valuable time ; yet, knowing the lively interest you take in the welfare of the Church of Scotland, I venture to draw your attention to a Bill which has just been read a first time in the House of Lords, I mean the Edinburgh Annuity Tax Bill. Though not giving us all that we consider ourselves fairly entitled to, we—I mean the ministers of Edinburgh and the Presbytery—regard the passing of that measure as of great consequence, as well to the peace of the community as to the prosperity of the Church and the comfort of ourselves and our successors. We hope it will meet with no opposition in the Lords, at least with no serious opposition. But if such should occur, I venture to solicit your lordship's good offices in getting over any difficulty that may be raised. The Bill settles an old and vexatious question in a manner highly favourable to the community, and we hope not very detrimental to the Church. Hoping you will kindly excuse this trouble,
"I remain, dear Lord Chancellor,
"Your lordship's faithful servant,
"R. LEE."

The local demagogues, however, were not to be deprived of their pet grievance ; and no sooner was the compromise effected to which they and their representatives had been parties, than they began to clamour for the repeal of Mr. Moncrieff's Bill, and for the absolute withdrawal of the stipends of the clergy. During the whole of Dr. Lee's incumbency this unprincipled clamour continued, and it continues still. Mr. Moncrieff, who had carried the Bill with the concurrence of the clamourers, and who had a proper regard for the terms of the arrangement which it had effected, found he must either prepare to violate these or cease to represent Edinburgh; and he honourably chose the latter alternative. This sorry chapter in the annals of the metropolis has, in the meantime, closed, in the triumphant elevation of a pair of the local demagogues to the seats once occupied by Jeffrey and Macaulay.

To return;—this letter to Mr. Combe tells us something of his life, this summer of 1857.

"EDINBURGH, 1st August, 1857.

"MY DEAR SIR,

"I am quite ashamed to have been so long in writing to you; the more so that though I have twenty reasons, such as they are, I doubt if I have one good reason. Certainly I have been pretty busy, and about not pleasant matters. To-day has been the 'capping of the doctors;' when ninety-four young lads have been sent forth, duly authorized to poison and slay Her Majesty's subjects, without risk of criminal proceedings against them for so doing. Mrs. Lee also and our children all left me this morning for Callender; so that unless John Findlay had remained on the other side of the square, I should realize the feelings of Alexander Selkirk or Robinson Crusoe. I am perusing with very great interest letters from the slave States of America, by James Stirling, just published. I know the author a little. He is a shrewd Scotchman, pretty well informed, and observing and reflective also. . . . . I have had a most extraordinary summer, quite a miracle for an adhesive and unmigratory animal like me; twice in London, once in Forfarshire, also in Berwickshire, and all this before the proper season for travel has begun.

"The church, which I have preached in regularly till last Sunday, is improving as a speaking trumpet; but the Town Council show their spite by resisting all applications to ventilate it, putting forth the most ridiculous excuses.* My opposition

---

* The Town Council are the patrons, and were then the conservators of the city churches.

to their Annuity Tax Bill has inflamed their rage to the utmost ;
and they appear to think it a good opportunity to suffocate me
and all the heretics who hear me. . . . . Edinburgh is gone out
of town ; to-day the solitude is quite striking. This empty
echoing house is a specimen of the city.

"*August* 2.—To-day I have been nearly suffocated. I shall
not be found preaching again in that church till their high
mightinesses see proper to admit fresh air. Literally, I hardly
knew what I was saying. . . . I hope we shall see you home
about the time you anticipated, and that you and madame will
both feel much recruited. My affectionate remembrances to
her, and accept the same for yourself.

"Believe me, my dear sir,

"Yours always most sincerely,

"ROBERT LEE.

"P.S. Being all alone this evening I have read again the introduction to your new book. I think it equal to anything you
ever wrote, in clearness, vigour, and animation. It is also
pervaded by a *most religious* spirit ; and it will be felt to be
deeply interesting and important even by many who are not
prepared to sympathize with its views."

Mr. Combe's book here referred to was "The Relation
between Science and Religion," and is frequently mentioned in their letters. Dr. Lee revised the proof-sheets.
"If at any time you can suggest a modification of expression which will render the text less offensive, I shall
be grateful for it," says Mr. Combe, in reply to some
criticism. "I write," he continues, "under strong activity of *conscientiousness, benevolence, and veneration* ;
and my head becomes hot in the region of these organs
after an hour or two's application, and I then throw
all aside till next day ! "

DR. LEE TO MR. COMBE.

" 15th March, 1857.

" MY DEAR SIR,

" I have looked over the appendices, &c., and do not find anything particularly requiring remark. I admire your good temper in dealing with adversaries. It is certainly a great triumph over the irascible passions to suppress the contempt which it is impossible not to feel. During the whole of last week I have been so much afflicted with toothache, arising, I think, from rheumatism, or tic, or some such cause, that I have done very little but groan and meditate upon the mystery of pain. To-day I have been thinking of a series of lectures or sermons on natural religion. Your present remarkable book suggests a great deal, and supplies a vast amount of thoughts and facts on the subject ; though, of course, my point of view is different from yours. . . . . With our united very kind regards to both of you,

" I am, my dear sir,
" Most truly yours,
" R. LEE."

MR. COMBE TO DR. LEE.

" EDINBURGH, 17th March, 1857.

" MY DEAR SIR,

" I beg to thank you very sincerely for all the trouble you have taken in regard to my proof sheets, which are now very near an end. . . . . I regret to hear that you are suffering from toothache. May it not arise from excitement of the brain, caused by too much work ? I know that this is a fertile cause of it in men whose brains are vigorous and active. My late brother* cured me of an *awful* toothache (it was so overpowering that I could only lie in bed), by sending me in cold April weather to Dumfriesshire *in an open carriage.* The cold air during the drive to the 'Crook Inn,' a long day, so allayed the nervous excitement, that I was relieved and slept soundly, and after a week's excursion came home well. I was in ecstasies writing the 'Constitution;' and he said that had not the tooth-

---

* Andrew Combe, M.D., died 1847. " Life and Correspondence," published by George Combe in 1850. His character is sketched by Sir James Clark in the introduction to the 9th edition of A. Combe's " Management of Infancy."

ache arrested me, I should have brought on cerebral disease. I was then young, ignorant, ardent, and self-willed ; but ever since I have read in pain a serious warning that *something* is wrong ; but we are all still so ignorant that we are often sadly puzzled to find out what it is that is wrong, but my *faith* never falters on the point why pain was instituted.

"It appears to me that with half the violence that has been done to the Scriptures in framing the Westminster Confession, a new creed could be constructed from them, every point of which would harmonize with a sound natural religion, adding, from them, doctrines beyond the reach of, but not contradicting, reason ; and I have a strong impression that within the next fifty years this must be done, or Christianity, as now taught, will perish.

"We shall be greatly disappointed should you fail us on Wednesday evening. I expect Mr. John Young, who, in July, 1839, was introduced to me in Quebec. He was then one of my disciples, although personally unknown. He is *now* the member for Montreal in the Canadian Parliament, and a moral reformer, in whom you will be interested. He has heard you preach, and was astonished to hear such sound practical sense from a Scotch pulpit !

. "With our united kind regards to you and Mrs. Lee,

"I remain, my dear sir,
"Very truly yours,
"Geo. Combe."

MR. COMBE TO DR. LEE.

"St. Roque, 28th May, 1857.

"My dear sir,

"The visit of yourself and Mrs. Lee last evening did us much good, and gave us much pleasing matter for reflection.

"I have explained to Mr. Robert Cox the project I threw out yesterday of having a voluntary board or boards in Scotland, for the examination of middle-class schoolmasters, and he approves of it. If you, Professor Kelland, Professor Allman, Mr. Macadam, Chemistry ; Dr. Goodsir or Struthers, or Mr. Gardner, for Physiology, and Hodgson as paid Secretary—could be formed into a Board, with the function of the Committee of Council, and if Boards in Glasgow, Aberdeen, and St. Andrews were subsequently formed, Hodgson being secretary to them all, I should anticipate good results to the education of the country.

"I have been thinking with deep interest on your now influential position, which throws great responsibility on you.[*] You know 'there is nothing like leather,' so excuse me for saying that I wish you were a practical phrenologist, to aid you in your recommendations of ministers. Sheriff ——'s head, for example, is such a palpable index of his true character, that no phrenologist, accustomed to observe, could mistake it; yet you would have erred from your impressions of his qualities. If you should ever recommend a man, however admirable in intellect, and however liberal in speech and profession, but in whom the moral organs, especially conscientiousness, were deficient, he would turn out to be the man the brain indicated, and disappoint you, and there is constant risk of this. If you can find time and inclination this autumn to read the system of phrenology, and are disposed, when I return, to receive a practical lesson in the museum, I should be happy to give it, if I recruit sufficiently during the summer. This may appear really 'like leather,' but I am in earnest.

"With our united kindest regards to you and Mrs. Lee,

"I remain, my dear sir,

"Very truly yours,

"GEO. COMBE.

"The Rev. DR. R. LEE."

DR. LEE TO MR. COMBE.

"MY DEAR SIR,

"I think most of the gentlemen you mention would be willing to act on such a Board as you name, or others would who are equally well qualified. For myself, I should be willing to act, for a little at least, till matters were set a-going. I should rejoice to see Hodgson so employed. It is a duty he would discharge better than anybody, and it would afford him a recognition and give him a position to which he is well entitled. You mistake if you suppose I imagined Sheriff —— to be a man of any moral probity or conscientiousness . . . . I thought him to possess that low kind of amiability which may consist with a

---

[*] In recommending ministers for Crown livings.

self-indulgent temper; a constitutional kindliness with no self-denial, and a low *moral.* Don't imagine, however, I could ever recommend such a person as worthy of confidence or proper to be put into a situation of trust. I thank you for your advice about phrenology. And though I despair now, at my age, and with my occupations, of doing much in a new study, I am not only willing but wishful to learn what you can so well teach me on the functions of the brain. I shall accordingly endeavour to read the system of phrenology, which indeed has stood among my *legenda* a year past; assured by much experience of your writings that I shall find great instruction, whether I may be fully convinced or not. Of the truth of phrenology in a general way I have long had no doubt. Your friendly offer, I hope, I may be able to embrace; for which, and for all other instances of your kindness, I thank you very much."

The following extract from another letter to Mr. Combe expresses his warm regard for the latter as a friend, and illustrates the frank and candid spirit in which each regarded the other's opinions.

" You will never lose my affection and esteem so long as I can appreciate moral principle, love of truth, courage, and benevolence ; that is so long as you continue what you are, and I retain the same capacity of admiring what is good which I now have.

"I am not yet in circumstances to give any opinion of your work as a whole ; but I am satisfied it contains not only what is highly important, but highly needful.

"I do not disguise from myself, what you, I believe, are quite aware of, that you and I have some very deep differences of opinion. Your philosophy teaches that this world is a complete system. Mine, if I may presume to call my poor thoughts by that name, regards it as a great vestibule only to a mansion far greater than itself. I am thankful, however, to you for the great light you have thrown upon this vestibule: the vast mass of new and important truths which you have discovered, systematized, expounded, and made practicable and useful : and the vast mass of sophisms and errors you have refuted. Also your religiousness of spirit, and constant habit of associating nature with God, as his creature, and depending upon him, and expressing his character and his will, attract my sympathy strongly towards you. I am thus delighted to agree and sympathize with you so far; and in the matter respecting which we hold different views, it is useless for us to speak, for it is not likely either of us will ever relinquish his present opinion. For myself and all my friends I pray constantly, that the Father of Lights may teach us all that is needful, and preserve us from all errors that are hurtful and dangerous; and sensible of my own ignorance, I am not disposed to call those that differ with me by hard names, or even to think of them harshly. On the contrary, I desire to love what is good, and esteem what is excellent in all men. After this explanation we may feel at perfect ease. Considering how little we know, and how imperfectly and dimly even that little is comprehended, we may well practise forbearance towards each other in these matters in which we may differ, while we entertain a cordial sympathy in these respecting which we agree."

Of the many letters which passed between Combe and Dr. Lee, the four interesting ones which follow originated with an article on Dugald Stewart, which Dr. Lee had written for the *Scotsman*; and which had pleased Mr. Combe, who writes:

"EDINBURGH, 17th March, 1858.

"MY DEAR SIR,

"I have now read your notice of Dugald Stewart's Philosophy, and was really refreshed by seeing so much sound sense, accompanied by so much kindly feeling and critical acumen, applied to that huge, gilt, painted, and inflated India-Rubber Ball. The law which enforces attendance on the Professors of the 'Scotch Philosophy,' is retarding our social progress, and I most earnestly wish that you may succeed in getting it altered. By the way, you are probably aware I had the audacity to offer myself as a candidate for the Logic Chair in opposition to Sir William Hamilton, and obtained three votes out of the thirty-three electors. But did you ever see the testimonials which I produced ? If not, I beg you will allow me to send you a copy, as a curiosity. I have several, and they are of no use ; and their interest to you lies in the fact that they caused a storm in the Senate of the University, in which some of the Professors were stamping with rage, through fear that that ignorant squad, the Town Council, might be blinded and seduced by their number and speciousness. One of the Professors, Jameson, I believe, told this to Dr. Neill, who told me. Good men ! They had no notion how safe they were !

"I was struck with your remark about Confucius and God ; for I very lately had two analogous cases stated to myself, in addition to six or eight previously known to me. The statement is in these terms, varied slightly in individual instances, and the persons are all well-educated, moral, and well to do ; in short, above par in moral, intellectual, and practical qualities : viz., referring to science and religion, each says, 'I see the powers inherent in matter ; I see their adaptations, and the results which these evolve : I see that the tendency is benevolent on the whole ; and I see great beauty, and skill, and power in the adaptations and combinations ; but, nevertheless, no feeling, sentiment, intuition, or conviction—call it what you will—of a God arises in my mind from all these perceptions.

"The case is so entirely different with me, that I feel, on hearing such statements, precisely as I do when a person tells me that he hears the sounds of the sweetest musical instruments, but recognises in them nothing corresponding to what people in general call melody and harmony. They indicate a cerebral defect, and I am anxious to find out its precise nature and locality. One feature is found in all their brains, so far as I have observed, viz., they are deficient in Wonder and Ideality. Some of them have a fair share of Causality and Veneration ; but all of them are deficient in the power of going out of themselves and embracing a wide sphere of thought. I have found them looking perfectly blank, when an abstract argument was being carried on to its logical but distant conclusions, so distant that an exercise of imagination was necessary to give those form.

"Such confidential communications are at once interesting and instructive ; and should teach us all forbearance and humility. I often think how a being who possessed an organ that enabled him to discern the *nature of things* would look on us. We should appear to *him* pretty much as the inferior animals appear to us.

"With our united kind regards to you and Mrs. Lee, and hoping that the milder weather is benefiting your daughter, I remain,

"My dear sir,

"Very truly yours,

"GEO. COMBE."

[REPLY.]

"EDINBURGH, 18th March, 1858.

"MY DEAR SIR,

"I had no notion that your 'certificates' would prove one of the most interesting volumes I ever opened. I have done nothing but read it this evening, though I have plenty other work before me.

"It is quite *dramatic* and most striking. I am quite annoyed that your modesty has prevented you mentioning to me this curious chapter of your history sooner. I did not imagine, in writing the remarks on the works of Dugald Stewart,* that you had been so deeply implicated in the same question. Many thanks for this very amusing and instructive volume. I wish I had written anything worthy of being sent you in return for your many kind contributions to my library —all of which, without exception, are full of interest and instruction.

"Believe me, my dear sir,

"Most sincerely yours,

"ROBERT LEE."

MR. COMBE TO DR. LEE.

"EDINBURGH, 19th March, 1858.

"MY DEAR SIR,

"I return the 'Record' with many thanks. It affords an excellent text for your projected work on Preaching. It ignores your remarks on pages 24 and 25 of your sermon You should hold the opponents close down to answer *that*

---

* Collected works. Edited by Sir W. Hamilton.—Constable & Co.

question.* Again, does grace operate in *harmony with*, or in *opposition to*, the laws of nature ? They must answer this also. It cannot act on the human faculties, so far as I can conceive, *independently* of the laws of nature ; for *without brain* we have no evidence of mind, and the *brain* certainly acts under laws.

"I had forgotten my 'Testimonials,' and all that they contain, for many years, until your observations recalled them to my recollection. I never had any hope of being elected. My sole object was to promote the study of phrenology, and in this respect I was as unsuccessful as in obtaining the Chair. I distributed the volume to all the authorities, scientific, medical, and legal, in Edinburgh, and it only provoked greater dislike and hostility. The testimonials were a condemnation of themselves, and affronted them ; and they scowled on me for my presumption. 'Academicus' is Dr. W. P. Alison, and he and the other Professors redoubled their 'refutations' to their classes, and phrenology in Edinburgh went back.

"It is quite true that my rejection was to me a great benefit. It threw me on the world ; and my ideas have been greatly increased by my travels in America, on the continent, and by the position which the testimonials acquired for me in London. In 1836, I was still breathing only an Edinburgh and provincial atmosphere. The rejection made me a citizen of the world ; and I now see the littleness of many persons and things here, who and which then appeared to me great.

"I remain, my dear sir,

"Very sincerely yours,

"Geo. Combe.

"The Rev. Dr. Lee."

DR. LEE TO MR. COMBE.

"9th April, 1853.

"My dear sir,

"I returned this afternoon from Kippendavie, near Dunblane, whither I went on Tuesday. As soon as I am at leisure I shall endeavour to look into your paper on D. Stewart's philosophy. I have no doubt you have pointed out its fatal

---

* "Is it part of Christianity that we should obey these sanitary commandments, under pain of the anger of God, under pain of guilt ? "

defects. Some good remarks on the subject appeared in the *Times* a few days ago. I fear students are less likely to read objections to Stewart's philosophy than some things which they need less; though till this new edition appeared, D. Stewart was about as dead as Albertus Magnus or Abelardus. Nor will even this grand issue preserve his vitality. Whatever truths he has to tell are familiarly known, and we are now too busy to read ponderous tomes for the sake of fine sentences. . . . . I was very sorry to leave you so soon, the more so as I was doomed to suffer semi-suffocation to hear what was more than semi-nonsensical. It is enough to tempt one to despise the human understanding, when it can accept such talk for philosophy and wisdom.* I fear we are a *silly* generation.

"Believe me most sincerely,

"R. Lee."

He preached on Wednesday, 7th October, a sermon which attracted a good deal of attention. This day was the fast-day appointed by government on account of the Indian rebellion. Dr. Lee declined, he said, to regard this terrible disaster as a punishment of our national sins. He wanted to know what special sins it was sent specially to punish. " Punishment can afford no instruction, and be no instrument of moral government, unless a connection can be traced between the thing punished and that which punishes it." He did not hesitate to condemn the idea that we should use our power in India to promote Christianity. He held the Government had no right to employ Indian taxes to spread British religion ; and he believed that the mutiny of the troops had arisen chiefly from the Hindoo dread of this, and of other changes, wrought upon by Mussulman fanaticism. " Perhaps," said Dr. Lee, towards the close, " the sin

---

* At the Philosophical Institution, apparently.

that will be least thought of to-day is our being rulers of India at all."

A good deal of dispute was going on about India at this time in religious circles. It was maintained by many persons that the Government should directly use its influence and authority for the propagation of Christianity. This view was zealously opposed by others, who contended that it was unjust to employ secular power to spread religion of any kind. Opinion was also considerably divided, in the Church, upon the question of the evangelization of India; one party holding that "the preaching of the Word" must be the great instrument, another that the native mind must be first prepared by education for the reception of the Gospel. Dr. Lee was steadfast to this latter principle.

In the Presbytery of Edinburgh, in March, 1858, Dr. Macfarlane, backed by Dr. Hunter and others, urged that the Church should press on the Government the duty of authoritatively recognising and teaching the Christian religion in India, and that an "overture" should be adopted to this effect. Dr. Lee moved a negative to this proposal, and in the course of his speech he said :—

"The overture, as he understood it, called on the Government to take every means for the Christianizing of India. He could agree to no overture that called on the Government to do any such thing. Dr. Hunter had quoted this most solemn passage —'When thy judgments are on the earth, the inhabitants will learn wisdom.' He (Dr. Lee) read it 'will learn righteousness;' and he hoped the lesson which they would derive from the recent judgments in India would be the righteousness which was inculcated by our blessed Saviour, when he said, 'All things whatsoever ye would that men should do unto you, do ye even thus to them.' They had heard reverend gentlemen telling them that they were advocates of the principle of toleration, and (what was more astounding to him) that all the members of this Presbytery were advocates of the same principle. He supposed they were, but the toleration of which they were the advocates seemed to differ exceedingly from that which was usually understood to be toleration, and from that of which he was a humble advocate. The toleration which they supported was not a toleration which told them to do to others that which they would that others should do to them, but to do that which if done to them they would rebel against. They propose to call on the Government to do something. What was the Government? It was the body that wielded the civil power, which held the purse, and disposed of the money and lives of the people; the body that carried the sword, and was the minister of wrath—they called on that Government to do whatsoever it could to promote Christianity. And they proposed that the Government should carry on its operations by establishing schools in order, he supposed, to teach Christianity directly. But what did they mean by that? Did they wish Government to erect a civil establishment for the promotion of Christianity in India? Did they wish Government to set up an Established Church in India? The arguments of reverend gentlemen would go to this, that they should take the money of the Hindoos, and that, contrary to their opinions, however erroneous, and their convictions, however absurd, they should pay a priesthood for teaching them the Christian religion? Was that what it was desired that Government should do? If the doing of that by a Government was consistent with *their* ideas of toleration, it was not consistent with *his*. The thing proposed to be done was that Government should erect schools in which Christianity was to be taught. That was just erecting a Church Establishment in another form, though calling it a school; and he held that, if Government did so, it would violate every idea and definition of toleration that ever he heard. Some might say, why was it done in this country? It was done for this reason, that this country was reputedly a Christian country, and that it professed to be a Christian country, and because Christianity was understood to be part and parcel of the law of the land. It was on the idea that the people were Christian, and acquiesced in that application of their money, that the Established Churches in Great Britain could alone be defended. If the course proposed could be defended on abstract grounds, every man in his senses, every man who had the faculties of observation and reflection, must see that it would be most inexpedient, and for this plain reason that it would only tend to strengthen those objections to the Gospel, and to fortify those prejudices which were already too strong ; and hence, instead of hastening the coming of the kingdom of God in that benighted land would only tend to postpone it indefinitely. There could be no doubt that the progress of European enlightenment, and of Christianity itself, had had a great deal to do with this very rebellion. It was proved, beyond the shadow of a doubt, that the constant increase of European influences among the population of India had laid the foundation of that rebellion, the effects of which had been so disastrous. But what would be the effect if this course were adopted ? How much stronger would be the suspicion that would agitate the minds of the Hindoos ! And the result would probably be another rebellion, new murders, new devastation, new wars. They had heard a great deal about idolatry in India, and about the contributions levied for the support of Juggernaut ; but had not these things been answered again and again in the House of Commons ? Had not Mr. Mangles, Colonel Sykes, and every man acquainted with the facts, given a direct negative to all this ? Had they not told us that the money so applied was not our money ? If it were taken out of our pockets to support the worship of Juggernaut, Siva, and Vishnu, and the other Hindoo deities, he could very well understand the objection ; but the money was not ours, it was that of the people who worshipped these gods ; and many territories had been ceded to the British Government under the express stipulation that the moneys contributed, not by us, but by them, should be so devoted. Did they want these treaties to be broken, and the feelings and consciences, such as they were, of these people violated ? Certainly that would be a curious way of illustrating the Christian principles of which we boasted so much. But how, after all, did Government show its neutrality in this matter ? It supported three or four bishops, as many deans and archdeacons, and a great number of chaplains, belonging to the Church of England, and several Church of Scotland chaplains, all teaching Christianity out of these funds—not our money, but the money of the natives of India.

He submitted, therefore, that the people of India had in these facts a sufficient indication of what were the inclinations of the British Government, and as to whether the British Government thought its own religion true and beneficial, or not. He maintained that in this matter they had gone as far as either principle or expediency would permit them to do . . . . . It would be said, 'Well, but ours is the true religion, and theirs is a false religion.' That did not matter in this respect, for *they* thought theirs true, and ours false. That should make us all the more careful to use argument alone, in order to convince them. Dr. Hunter had stated that it would be better for the Hindoos to have no education at all than an education without Christianity. With every respect for the reverend doctor, he must say that he held an entirely different opinion. He spoke in the sense of every one who knew anything of Brahminism, Buddhism, or any of those great Oriental superstitions, the professors of which were the great majority of the human race, when he said that the communication of the common knowledge which inculcates in a European school the elements of science, would effectually refute and explode the superstitions which now held the Hindoos in thraldom, and the power of which was such as to forbid their votaries even to think. If a Hindoo were to be convinced of the folly of supposing that there are thirty millions of gods, and were to be convinced that there is but one true God, that was a conviction which he would derive from the common instruction everywhere communicated by Europeans. In like manner, could any man deny that the communication of secular knowledge was of immense benefit? Could our prejudices be so gross as to make us doubt that it was of importance that that knowledge should be imparted, and that a man in possession of that knowledge was not in a better position to receive the truths of the Gospel than a Buddhist? Buddhism was a system of Atheism ; the teaching of our science therefore would teach the Buddhist that there was but one God, and was that nothing? He could hardly believe his ears when he heard reverend gentlemen propounding such a doctrine as this, that Buddhists were better let alone in their degrading superstition. Were they not, after such teaching as he had alluded to, incomparably better fitted for the reception of that which was the power and the wisdom of God unto salvation ? Now.what must be done ? In his opinion, Government should be petitioned to take every obstruction out of the way of the diffusion of truth, whether physical, moral, or religious; that everywhere the missionaries should be protected; that every man should have liberty of speech; and that truth and error should have a fair field; and then, as always, the truth would prevail. They must not forget that in India we were conquerors and foreigners, nay, that we were oppressors. These people had tried to throw off our yoke, and God forbid that we should attempt to palliate the atrocities which they had committed in the attempt to do so ! But they were only doing what we called patriotism among ourselves, and what we extolled as patriotism in other nations. Their resistance to our rule, therefore, was not of itself what we ought strongly to condemn, though the means by which they had sought to accomplish their end could not be too strongly reprobated; and since we were called upon to remember what our faults were, he thought that our faults had not been that we had not persecuted them, but that we had allowed the lust of dominion, and covetousness, and other such lusts, to be the prompting causes in our government of that great empire. He thought that, if we could not govern them without persecuting them directly or indirectly, we ought to cease to govern them at all; for we had no business there if we could not rule over that people without applying principles which he contended to be in opposition to the principles of Christianity. We ought to use no physical constraints whatever in the propagation of the Christian religion. It was wrong in itself to do so ; and it was doubly wrong because they were ineffectual for the purposes for which they were intended."

Dr. Lee, on moving that the overture should not be transmitted, carried his point by the narrow majority of one.

"A noble sermon," said an English newspaper in a notice of his discourse on the Fast-day;—"its author, we are glad to see, is commanded to preach before the Queen." This command, which came in the autumn of

1857, had been anticipated for some time. In June 1854, Mr. Combe, who was then in London, had written to Dr. Lee, "I had the honour of an hour and a half's conversation, *tête-à-tête*, with Prince Albert, in the Palace to-day, and I found an opening for telling him about you; your talents, attainments, position as Professor, and the good you are doing in reconciling Christianity with the thinking of progressive minds. I mentioned, also, the consequences, in seducing the young students to the side of antiquated doctrines, flowing from the use made of patronage to support particular opinions.* Your sermon on war was read by the Queen, who spoke to Sir James Clark of it with approval."

And again in June 1856. " On 28th May, Sir James Clark wrote me a note expressive of his admiration of your speech on the Education question,† in which he adds, ' Dr. Lee might preach a good sermon on Religion in the common affairs of life, taking up the subject where Mr. Caird left it off.' I delayed writing to you till I had seen Sir James, and asked where he wished you to preach such a sermon; and he answered, ' on Dee side.' I concur with Sir James, that a sermon such as he suggests, published by the Queen's authority, would greatly aid the progress of the country, and by strengthening your influence, render you a more efficient instrument, high as you already stand, in doing good." " As to going to Crathie," Dr. Lee replied, " I can say nothing at present. If any intimation comes, I must consider it. *I am, however,*

---

* Referring, apparently, to the Church patronage of the Crown in Scotland, with the mode of exercising which Dr. Lee had been much dissatisfied.

† In the Assembly of 1856.

altogether indisposed to go. If I go, I shall preach something *very practical.* But it is rather embarrassing to preach to order. Besides, I seldom make much of a *single* sermon. It is in a series of discourses, where one has room to fully unfold a subject, that I ever succeed to any tolerable degree." Mr. Combe's and Sir James' benevolent desires were however at length fulfilled, and Dr. Lee preached in Crathie Church on the 11th October. "To-day," he writes at that date, "I preached in the Parish Church of Crathie, a sermon on 'Glorify God in your body.' I had afterwards the honour of meeting the Queen, the Prince Consort, and the Princess Royal, and of dining at the Castle, and remaining there all night. The Prince Consort came to my room before dinner, and talked somewhat more than an hour, in a very intelligent manner. The Queen was very gracious; commanded me to sit at her right hand, and chatted like any other well-bred, sensible lady."

This sermon,—urging the Christian duty of caring for the body, and that "the Platonizing Christianity which would induce men to care for their souls by teaching them to contemn the fleshly tabernacle, is not less pernicious in its practical influence than theoretically vicious and false,"—was published at Her Majesty's request.

"*Dec.* 5.—This day the sermon was published, after many delays. What the result may be I cannot tell; but probably Adam Black's opinion may prove correct, that it would not be very popular. Blackwood expressed the same opinion, though for an opposite reason; the first saying it was too good, the other that it was too bad to be popular.

"*Dec.* 12.—A great variety of newspaper articles, mostly very laudatory; but some few Scotch and Free Church papers spitting out their venom plentifully, very much chagrined evidently because they cannot find some heresy or other deadly sin to comfort themselves with. How often do we break God's laws through zeal. Such zeal, however, is zeal for ourselves, our notions, or our party, not for Him."

The Queen did well to command the publication of the Sermon. It is an earnest Christian protest against the unwholesome divorce of the body from the spirit, and the exaltation of pietistic sentiments above practical duties, which the popular religious teaching of the day not only sanctioned but helped to produce. The influence of Combe's philosophy is sufficiently discernible. The sermon will be found in "The Family and its Duties," page 101 ; but we may take one or two extracts from it :—

"No one is so absurd as to deny that we can do *something* to promote the health and prolong the life of the body. But we should understand both that we may do a great deal, and that to do what we can, both for our own welfare and that of others, in this regard, is a matter of *strictly religious obligation*, being part of that duty which we owe *to God, to our neighbour*, and *to ourselves.* For we must glorify Him with *our body*.

"The power of man to destroy himself is exemplified every day; but for one that is guilty of this wickedness *directly*, thousands are destroyed by intemperance, bad or insufficient food, want of ventilation, noxious gases, excessive mental excitements, idleness, overworking, and the like. These paths, indeed, are often so circuitous, that people will hardly be persuaded that their 'end is destruction.' But that they lead down to the chambers of death as certainly as the shortest road, who does not know that ever took pains to trace them ? Who does not know, in his own experience, that ever walked in them ?

"It is reckoned that a *hundred thousand persons die annually in England of preventable diseases.* In the same proportion, more than *a million and a quarter* must die annually over Europe; and, probably, if we consider certain customs prevailing in China and India, the great centres of population in the East, not fewer than five or six times that number must perish over the whole world.

"We shudder to look upon the sanguinary track of war, as well we may; but the numbers that perish in war are a mere fraction compared with the countless throng of human beings that ignorance and vice are constantly tumbling into their graves. Can we think of this without horror and pity? Our religion, the religion of mercy and charity, should prompt us to study this dreadful spectacle—*sin thus reigning unto death.*

"Probably not fewer than four hundred thousand men were killed during the late Russian war. But during the same period, ten times as many died in Europe alone from preventable diseases. The slaughter of four millions of persons, during three years, in war against the laws of health! so appalling a fact is surely deserving the earnest attention not only of governors, politicians, and philanthropists, but of all men who profess Christianity, and especially of those who are appointed to teach it. Because (1.) the laws of health, through disobedience to which such multitudes perish, are God's laws; for He not only ordained them, but He executes them impartially and universally, before our eyes and upon ourselves; and (2.) because the gospel which we are appointed to teach, is the religion of Him who came into the world 'not to destroy men's lives but to save them,'—to save them in a temporal as well as a spiritual sense. . . . . .

"No martyrdom is acceptable to God, or a duty in us, except that which cannot be escaped without sin. 'Godliness has the promise of the life that now is, as well as of that which is to come.' It is written, 'The wolf shall dwell with the lamb, and they shall not hurt or destroy in all God's holy mountain,' *because* 'the earth shall be full of the knowledge of the Lord.'

"Let us not, then, invent crosses, that we may carry them; or be weighed down with any that we may lawfully put aside. Suffering is the most evil thing in the world—sin only excepted, and therefore tolerable only so far as it is the medicine and cure of that root of all evil.

"This world is indeed a valley of the shadow of death, where weeping and groans re-echo from every side. But disobedience and ignorance have made it what it is. As these diminish, sorrow and sighing, in the same proportion, will flee away; and even the King of Terrors, whose dire tribute we cannot evade in this world, will exact his due at a later day. Still debarred from the garden, in the midst of which grows the tree of life, we are encouraged to subdue the thorns and briars of the wilderness, to turn the desert into a fruitful field, and in the sweat of our face to eat bread; so fighting our way back to the lost Paradise—not without good hope that the flaming sword shall at length have abated its consuming fire, and that the guardian spirits, who drove us forth, not without pity, shall have received commission to welcome back the repentant exiles; that they may eat again of the tree of life—may hear the voice of God without terror—may see His face and not die.

"In short, unless men shall be taught to take a conscientious interest in their bodily welfare, they will hardly be persuaded to feel that concern which they ought, in the health and salvation of their souls. He cannot be expected to aspire after eternal life who has not learned to appreciate the blessing of temporal life. 'He that is unfaithful in that which is least, is unfaithful also in much.' Nor will he study to acquire ten talents, who sets no store by that one talent which the Lord and giver of life has already bestowed. In the order of his dispensations, God has suggested both the natural progress of ideas, and the manner in which these duties are evolved. He gave us first, in the Law, the rudiments of the doctrine of salvation—prescribing multifarious regulations for bodily purity and health; and afterwards, in the Gospel, the mystery and perfection of the doctrine; that we might be holy both in body and soul—redeemed, sanctified, saved in both. 'Howbeit that was not first which is spiritual, but that which is natural; and afterwards that which is spiritual.' The elements of that which is heavenly, are still contained and suggested by that which is earthly : a consideration well deserving the attentive regard of those who not only acknowledge, but deplore, the slow advancement which 'pure religion and undefiled' makes even in those countries in which it has been longest known, and is most generally professed."

"I gave the Queen your prayers and sermon," writes Sir James Clark, "which she received very graciously. I found she had sent for a copy of the prayers before." The following letter to Sir James' replies to some criticisms (which he had transmitted to Dr. Lee) of the view given in the sermon, of Plato's theory of the body.

"EDINBURGH, 22 Feb. 1858.

"DEAR SIR JAMES,

"I am much obliged to you for enclosing Mr. F——'s letters. The printed letter to the *Times* is very interesting— more to a clergyman even than to anyone else. It certainly is one of the greatest triumphs of conscience and self-denial to keep the waters sweet and wholesome in the stagnant pool of a small country parish. It would give me unfeigned pleasure to enjoy the personal acquaintance of one who has succeeded so well in so hard a task. Regarding the other note, I feel of course much interested, not only because it regards my own poor little production, but because it expresses almost exactly the views which another able clergyman of the Church of England urged in a note to me some time ago. Both, I think, have somewhat misapprehended what is said in the introduction to the sermon. I am myself partly chargeable with this, for what is printed is merely an outline (and a very short one) of what I wrote upon the subject when the sermon was originally composed. If I can lay my hands upon this MS. I will send it to Mr. ——, and he will find (as it appears to me) ample authorities in support of my statements.

"What I really state is not that the Greeks paid no attention, or little, to the body. No person who knows anything, can forget that they were excessively addicted to the *mos decoræ palæstræ*, and in fact worshippers of the human form, which suggested and dictated their ideas of the divine, so that Lucian truly says, 'their men were only mortal gods, and their gods only immortal men.' What I speak of is not *practices* or *customs* which prevailed among the Greeks, but the *philo-*

sophical speculation, the δόγματα on the subject from which the former almost never spring, and with which they have almost no connection in many instances.

"Neither did I call the notions in question 'Greek philosophy,' or the 'philosophy of the Greeks,' knowing how discordant the opinions of different Greeks (even of Plato and his pupil, Aristotle) were on almost all these subjects. But I call it 'heathen philosophy,' and 'the philosophy of *the Gentile* sages.' I demur to the inference that 'heathen of course means Greeks.' With our present knowledge of ancient Oriental speculation, 'heathen' means (I submit) something very different, pointing to those whose pupils and copyists the best of the Greeks (and Plato specifically) were. That the philosophy of Plato, and specifically his notions regarding the body, were derived from Oriental sources (directly and also indirectly through the Pythagoreans) can hardly be doubted. Apuleius states expressly that he derived his mental philosophy from the Pythagoreans, (*De Doct. Plat.* i., 4). It is popularly known that Plato had communication with not only the Egyptian priests in their own country, but with the magi in Phœnicia, as is stated by Olympiodorus in his life of Plato.

"I do not question that in the works of Plato may be found expressions, perhaps whole passages, which may appear inconsistent with that view of his doctrine regarding the body which I have given. Not having read all his works, I cannot speak positively on the point. But if Mr. —— will look over the *Phaedo* again, *in which dialogue he expressly and formally treats of this subject, and from which therefore his δόγματα on the matter should be learnt*, he will see that I have not misrepresented the great teacher. Beside the general scope of the Dialogue, I refer him particularly to §§ 24, 26, 28, 29, 32, 100, 148, *Ed. Bekk.* With these passages before me, I can have no doubt that Plato's doctrine is what I have stated, nor do I feel any doubt that, as it is distinctly *Oriental* in its character, so it was drawn from the East. That the *followers* of Plato held the views I have imputed to the master is, I suppose, not to be doubted,—an argument that they understood him as I have done: not, however, that they were indebted to him alone for them; for evidently there mingles a larger element of Orientalism in the Neoplatonism of Plotinus, &c., than in the teaching or mind of Plato himself. The same holds of Philo in a greater degree. The doctrines of *Mani* themselves appear to me only an exaggeration of the spirit of Oriental speculation on the subjects of mind and matter. I do not hold that the monasticism of the Christian Church was derived from Plato directly, though favoured in the east of Europe by the authority of his writings, which the Christian Fathers felt had a great affinity with Christianity, or what they imagined was Christianity; but that monasticism was a later and a Christian development of that philosophy which appears in a mild form in the Phaedo, and which displayed itself in India in the form of Buddhism; on the banks of the Dead Sea as Essenism; in Libya and Egypt as Therapeutism. The *language* of Paul appears to me to be deeply tinged with this philosophy, though I have endeavoured to show that we should interpret that language as importing something different from the sense which it would have on the lips of a Gentile sage. Indeed, I confess that I am not quite able to reconcile Paul's language on this subject with itself, differing as it obviously does from the other New Testament writers. I do not think that Mr. —— differs from me on this point.

"So many objections have come from various quarters to the doctrines contained in this sermon, that I have had serious thoughts of writing a defence of it. As to the Greeks particularly, and their cousins in Latium, no doubt, as your correspondent truly says, they had a high appreciation of the human body, and were much, even excessively, addicted to its exercise and development. But that was only a strong *animalism* not resulting from such doctrine regarding 'the flesh' as science unfolds and Christianity (as I hold) does not contradict. I am very glad, that regarding the more practical and important matter in the sermon, Mr. —— thinks with me. The approbation of so enlightened a judge is very comforting. Many objections that have been urged imply that the pulpit is a place whence nothing but useless platitudes and mystical jargon should be heard. Accordingly when anything is spoken there which tends to 'utility or adornment of man's life,' it is instantly denounced as 'not the Gospel,' which would prove that 'the Gospel' is of small use, and hardly worth preaching or being zealous about. This barrier must be broken down. We must preach what is proved to be true, and experienced to be useful, and felt to be necessary, and leave those who feel called upon to settle for themselves whether or not they will call it Gospel, or by whatever other name they will distinguish it. Submission to the dictation of a miserable and hypocritical cant is rendering preaching useless, and the clergy contemptible."

In 1857 and 1858, University Reform was the great topic in Scotland. The repeal of the tests had paved the way for further changes. After much public discussion, the Act was passed in 1858, by which the University Commission was appointed and empowered, and the numerous reforms were initiated, which have resulted in the present constitution of the Universities, with their courts, councils, chancellors, rectors, parliamentary representatives, and other apparatus. Dr. Lee entered zealously into the discussion of this subject, and wrote a series of letters on it, which appeared simultaneously in the *Scotsman* in Edinburgh, and the *Daily News*, in London, for some months in 1857 and 1858. In these letters he reviews almost every point in the whole range of University Reform : the number, emoluments, and status of the professors ; the mode of their election ; the system of teaching ; the division of the academic year ; the constitution of the governing body ; the theory of examinations and graduation, &c., &c. The letters had, no doubt, a salutary effect in helping to guide public opinion through the difficulties of a somewhat complicated question. Lord Minto, and others of his correspondents in and out of Parliament, refer to them again and again in their letters ; and he was urged to republish the series in a pamphlet, but did not do so.

One point on which he was keenly set, was the rescue

of the patronage of the chairs in Edinburgh from the hands of the Town Council. It was gained in part only; the patronage being vested by the Bill in a board of seven Curators, four of whom were to be appointed by the Corporation. " I entirely agree with you," wrote Lord Minto,* "in condemning the preponderance given to the Town Council in the body of Curators in Edinburgh; on whom it is proposed to confer the rights of patronage, which would have been better placed in the hands of the University court. I should also have been glad to see the post of Principal still reserved for a clergyman of the Established Church."

"We have only been partially successful," writes another correspondent—the liberal representative of a great Scotch constituency—"in eliminating the municipal element from the University courts; and Edinburgh has the unenviable distinction of retaining the corporation as the dispensers of literary patronage. . . . The voluntaries made a shabby, and, as I think, an unconstitutional attempt to prevent any part of the funds being applied to theological chairs; thus anticipating the future decision of Parliament, and, with admirable inconsistency, forgetting that not a month ago they had voted sums in supplement of the salaries of Divinity chairs in almost every University of Scotland. Mr. Gladstone's clauses as to a University for Scotland, are most valuable. It will be for you, and those who can get the ear of the commissioners, to work them out."

Dr. Lee was one of a deputation which went to London

---

* The late Lord Minto, second Earl, who died in 1859.

to represent the interests of the University while the Bill was before Parliament. "Dr. Bennett and myself have seen a good many people," he writes to Mr. Combe; "and most of them seem to favour our ideas of University reform. Of all the new men I have seen, Gladstone struck me most. . . . I fell into conversation with a very talking gentleman, at the Wellington last night, regarding Mr. Buckle. I had read a great deal of the book at Sir James Clark's last autumn ; and certainly was not impressed with anything but the amazing reading—a very equivocal merit. But there must be some merit in it, as so many people say it is a great book and Mr. Buckle a great man. As, however, I insist on walking by the light of my own candle, I shall refuse my faith till I see reason to yield it. . . . I told my talking friend that almost everything of value on the subject in Buckle's book was in yours. But he overwhelmed me with a vast ocean of words, which drowned me quite ; and said something of intellectual laws ruling the world, which appeared to me a very stale discovery. . . . I saw Mr. Ellis at Miss Johnston's ; a remarkable man, unquestionably."

He writes again, a little later: "The University Reform Bill has, as you will see, passed the second reading without a division. What gratifies me and my fellow-deputy much more is, that of five amendments which I proposed, four are to be adopted ; *and no other amendment is announced as to be adopted.* After this it is not wonderful that I feel a *quasi*-paternal interest in the measure. Mr. Black and the Town Council will now find out how little influence they have in Parliament ; and how easy it might have been to denude them entirely—as in my opinion they should have been—of all management and power in University affairs."

Although lamenting this blot, and one or two other defects in the Bill, which was carried by Lord Derby's Government in 1858, Dr. Lee hailed it as on the whole highly satisfactory; and regarded it as the beginning of a new and fruitful era in the honourable history of the Scottish Universities.

During the winter of 1857-8 his diary has few entries. He records his friend Dr. Barclay's appointment to the Principalship of Glasgow University in December;[*] and his only son George's departure to Croydon, preparatory to going to India in January. "Into thy hands, O God of my fathers," he writes, "I commit my dearly beloved son. Keep him by Thy mighty power, and save him for Thy mercy's sake, through Jesus Christ our Lord."

"*March* 16.—"Went like a fool last night to the Royal Society, where very dry food was provided. Lost my time and caught some cold.

"*March* 27.—"To-day a painful meeting at the Senatus. Several members whose votes I expected,[†] forgot their promises. 'All men are liars,' as David said in his haste, and I say at leisure. An awful row also between B. and S. What a world this is!"

---

[*] In reference to Dr. Barclay's appointment, he writes to Mr. Combe on 8th December—"Whatever I can do I have done, or am doing, to obtain the appointment of Dr. Barclay. . . . . Our friend Sir James Clark is taking an active interest in the matter, and it has occurred to me that you might encourage him by mentioning in the first letter you write him the kind of person Dr. Barclay is. As to his liberality, honesty, fearlessness, consistency, and all that, you need no information; as to his scholarship and fitness for the Professorship of Biblical Criticism, proposed to be combined with the Principal's office, I can give you the most solemn assurance. In these respects he is immeasurably superior to any one whom I have heard named as a candidate. Having deserved as he has, and being thus qualified, I cannot comprehend how any government which desires to promote the intellectual, and social, and religious interests of the people, can ever think of setting Dr. Barclay aside."

[†] The University returns a member to the General Assembly.

And now begin such sombre records as had hitherto never cast their gloom upon his pages ; records of which henceforth there were to be but too many, often filling the annals of his life, like the prophet's roll, with lamentation, mourning, and woe.

" *Sunday*, 18*th April*, 1858.—My dear friend, Miss Napier, died this morning. I saw her last night, when, though spent and weak, she was in full possession of her mental faculties, and showed the same wonderful love to me, which she has shown ever since I knew her. She was fully sensible of her condition ; and well prepared to leave this world, if genuine, and ardent, and unwearied, goodness can prepare any one for that solemn event. Of all the friends I have had in this world, outside of my own family, she has been the most ardent, constant, and endeared. We quickly discovered a strong affinity, which has bound us together with ties that ever strengthened : till at the end of fourteen years we could not have loved each other more, had she been actually my mother, as she was accustomed to call herself.

"I feel it is a high privilege to have known such a character, and a singular honour and felicity to have enjoyed so much of her affection; for a friendlier, a purer, nobler, more unselfish, or more generous character, no one has seen. A heart so large that she sympathised with every one : no one, within the range of her knowledge, had a joy or a sorrow, but it was hers also : and her hand was as open as her heart was tender. Without a tinge of vanity, malignity, or selfishness, she exhibited the best traits of the Christian character, with an abhorrence of cant and pharisaism. Such a spirit was indeed fit for the kingdom of God : and going over the beatitudes, one by one, I believe she enjoyed the blessing of them all. What a blank does her departure make, that old woman of eighty-two years of age ! How many, when they hear of her death, will feel that a friend is gone whose place can never be supplied in this world ! May she have a joyful Resurrection, with all the Saints who sleep in Jesus !

"Another friend, of whom I have seen a good deal, of late years, died yesterday, Lord Dunfermline :* a man of strong

---

* First Baron Dunfermline, formerly Speaker of the House of Commons.

faculties, an acute, vigorous, and comprehensive understanding; and withal, honest, consistent, and ardent in his love of liberty.

"He said to me some time ago, and it appeared to be more than a passing thought with him. ' We are still living among the dregs of oligarchy.' In Lord Dunfermline I have lost a sincere and steady friend."

"23rd.—To day laid in the grave the mortal remains of my ever dear friend. She lies beside her father, her mother, and her brother, in the West Kirk grave-yard."

"July 26th.—Our beloved son, George, left us this evening on his way to India. Another sad trial; but we must bear it with what patience and resolution we may! May God Almighty and most merciful protect and save him."

"August 3rd, 12 P.M.—Our darling Janie, now more dear than ever, and more lovely and attractive, is sinking rapidly; and our hearts are torn with grief and pity. My heart by turns is submissive and rebellious; sometimes I believe, sometimes doubt, all things.

"O my God! I will hope in Thee for my child and myself; yea, and for all Thy children, for we have all one Father."

"August 17th.—Yesterday arrived the intelligence that my steady and ardent friend, Mr. George Combe, died on Sunday, 15th, at Moor Park.

"It would seem as if all my friends would die together. Mr. Buchanan, Miss Napier, Lord Dunfermline, Mr. Combe, all in one summer; to be followed by my dear, dear Janie! What a crash! But they had all reached the natural goal of human life. My Janie alone is a flower untimely blasted!

"Dear Combe! I knew him as an affectionate and persevering friend, as well as a philanthropist and man of science,—in which character all the world knew him. Probably, he was the most famous man in Scotland at the period of his death; more famous, indeed, abroad than even at home. One of the blessings of death, according to Bacon, is that it diminisheth envy, and openeth the gate to good fame. This will be exemplified in Mr. Combe. He will now, by all the world, be recognised as a great man.

"It is too soon to appreciate his exact position as a thinker, or measure the effect which he produced upon his age, and the character of that effect. His was a mind which did not so much originate new trains of thought, as appropriate ideas which others had originated, yet with such completeness that they became truly his own, and with such force that they acquired from him both an original form, and an intensity and power they wanted before,—so that he was as truly identified with them as if he had been their parent. He loved and cherished his foster children."

" *August* 19*th*, 1858.—This evening, at 9.30, our dear Janie ceased from her sorrows, and was delivered from all her pains. I feel as if I had never before known grief. The same morning she took leave of us with words and looks that can never be forgotten by those who witnessed them. Her hope was that God would permit her to be a ministering spirit to comfort her parents, and to console her brother in his distant pilgrimage. Her beautiful countenance grew more and more beautiful as her strength decayed; and to the last her words bore the stamp of that original, witty, powerful, and beautiful mind which distinguished her even from a child. She lived in an atmosphere of beauty; she found it in everything, or put it there. She neither did nor said anything in a common-place way; all was fresh, original, picturesque, and joyous. A brighter spirit never lived upon the earth, or left it, than Jane Ann Lee. May I be her companion in that world where God is the Common Parent, and all happy spirits are alike his children; and having this hope, let me purify myself as Christ is pure. Her hope was that we might be soon a family in heaven! I console myself with the thought that she is now with my dear Miss Napier, who loved her with a peculiar affection, and to whom heaven itself will be made more happy by her presence.

" In thy good time, O Lord, grant that we may all of us inhabit those mansions which Christ, thy Son, has prepared for them that follow Him."

" *Tuesday, August* 24*th*.—To-day I laid the head of my beloved child in the dust; and now only I feel that the separation is complete. But perhaps it is not so. May she not be, as she wished, a ministering spirit, sent forth to console and aid us poor mortals, still encumbered with the flesh, and sighing for the adoption, even the redemption, of our bodies. It was a sweet thought, as all her thoughts were sweet and beautiful like herself."

This letter to Mr. Paisley refers to the same sad theme :—

"BENRHYDDING, 10*th September*, 1858.

"MY DEAR PAISLEY,

"I should have written you, as I intended, long ago. We have lost, as you know, our Janie, an affliction which no one can appreciate but those who have experienced the like. . . . This is a charming country, and Benrhydding is a charming place. I had no expectation of finding anything so delightful and beautiful in the centre of Yorkshire. It appears to me the more delightful after my long confinement to Edinburgh, where I have been all summer. This Death is an awful fact which we can never feel in its terribleness till it tears from us some one who is like our own souls. Nor is it easy, at least for me, to appropriate those consolations which are provided for us in the Gospel; nor do I think that state of mind is uncommon. On the contrary, I know it is very general. May God bless you and yours !

" Yours affectionately,
" R. LEE."

And this to Mrs. Combe was written on hearing of her husband's death :—

"I do not know what to say to you,—alas ! none of us can as yet know, not even yourself, the extent of the loss you have sustained. And yet how many consolations you have even in this irreparable bereavement !

"The news will strike many to the heart as it has done me, among whom admiration of your late husband's genius is almost lost sight of in the thought of his affectionate heart, high principle, steady and warm attachment to his friends, and noble aims and motives.

"Our sad family has been made much sadder by the news of your affliction. May you and I, dear Mrs. Combe, find in our sorrows that consolation which they only can have who trust in God and love Him. Your husband was too noble a creature to perish in the dust.   May we be all reunited, superior to sin and death !   Our Janie creeps gradually into the dust, tearing our hearts as she goes."

" *October* 26*th*, 1858.—This day my dear wife, with dear Bella and dear Napier, set out for Italy.   May God bless and restore them to me in health and happiness.

"I am alone, but, thank God, I am not desolate; as no one can be who loves many persons and is loved by some."

" *November* 11*th*, 1858.—This is my fifty-fourth birthday, on which I have reopened my class, which I feel is my true sphere. I get accustomed to my solitude.   Good news from my absent ones also cheers me.   God grant to them and me that while we live we may live unto the Lord, and that afterwards we may be united in τη βασιλεια τοῦ Θεοῦ."

"*December* 25*th*, 1858.—Our Christmas party, which dear Lord Murray had made for us, was sadly darkened by the death of poor Mr. Bringloe, who was called away rather suddenly this morning.   Another warning ! "

"*January* 2*nd*, 1859.—What an eventful year in my personal and family history has the last been !   During its progress, or a few days before it commenced, died Mr. James Buchanan, our kind friend; and our connection Mrs. Young.   Besides many other friends, such as Lord Dunfermline, died my dearest Miss Napier, my dear friend Mr. George Combe, and my never-to-be forgotten Janie, my lovely and endeared child.

"Our dear boy, our George, left us for India ; Bella returned home from school alarmingly ill; and our Maggie was married.* Finally, my wife, with our two remaining daughters, is gone to Italy; and here I sit, this first Sunday of the year, alone, solitary, desolate.   It is to myself a wonder how the human heart is able to bear such a load of sorrows ; and yet I am wonderfully cheerful, and even happy.   In spite of ourselves the wounds heal.   We resolve that we shall not and cannot be happy again; but the active duties of life mercifully draw a skin over our most painful sores.   And yet this is not happiness; grief and happiness cannot dwell together, the eye strains too painfully after those that are gone before.

"In a former notice at the end of the year, I expressed my

* In October, to Mr. Lockhart Thomson.

apprehension, or rather knowledge, that the dark and cloudy day would come; and come it has, darker and cloudier than I could have anticipated. Shall we receive good at the hand of the Lord, and not evil also? O God, sanctify whatever Thou sendest, through Jesus Christ our Lord. Amen."

This year, which opened amidst so many mournful memories, saw another dear friend withdrawn, Lord Murray, "the wise counsellor, the considerate and sympathizing friend." He died in February, after a brief illness.

"In him, I and my family," says Dr. Lee, "have lost a most kind and valuable friend, of whom we should ever think with gratitude and affection. Almost all the people of consequence I know, I know through his means; and his kindness in that and in many other ways was uniform and great. . . . I was induced, Feb. 13, to depart from my usual custom, and preach what may be considered a funeral sermon for our venerable and excellent friend."

In the sermon, which was printed, he says :—

"I have been deterred from the practice of preaching what are called funeral sermons, from having had occasion to observe the great abuses into which it is apt to degenerate, and the inconveniency and embarrassment which it is almost certain to occasion. Nor should I have been tempted to depart from my former practice on the present occasion, even by the virtues of the eminent individual who has just been taken from the midst of us, unless his public position, his intimate connection with almost all the great men and great events of the last half century, his long residence among us, his abounding munificence, and the *goodness* which distinguished him in public and in private, had made his reputation a public property, and caused the whole community to feel that in his death they had indeed lost a friend." .

For the sake of unity I have grouped together these

extracts and passages from Dr. Lee's diary; but before the date to which they have led us, events had occurred, to whose origin and character we must now attend.   The cry of "innovation" had been raised, and Dr. Lee had begun his long contest with the Church courts, in which this war-whoop first swelled into noisy chorus.

CHAPTER XI.

INNOVATIONS, 1859.

"When I look at the blessed liberty and godly order which Christ's Church had amongst us at the Reformation, and compare it with the bondage of forms, and the obstruction of times and circumstances which now prevails, I am grieved at my heart, and cry out in the bitterness of my soul for some deliverance."—EDWARD IRVING, *Preface to the earlier Confessions of Faith and Books of Discipline.*

LONG before his church was reopened in 1857, Dr. Lee had been much dissatisfied with the mode in which worship was commonly practised throughout Scotland. Watching, with keen eye, the condition of the Church, he had come to see that, among the evils afflicting her, an unimpressive and ill-ordered worship was practically the worst. A wrongly exercised patronage might, here and there, alienate the mass of a rural congregation; and the illiberal exigency of a minute formula might exclude, in occasional instances, thoughtful and earnest men from office in the Church; but an ill-ordered, slovenly, uncertain service was a fault and grievance which, wherever it obtruded itself, either blunted all reverential feeling, or drove devotion and culture from the sanctuary which it profaned. The service was but too often ill-ordered, slovenly, and uncertain. It followed no definite rule. The manner of its performance was fixed to no positive standard. It might not only differ essentially in one church from what it was in another; but it might vary, in substance and detail, from Sunday to Sunday, in the same church. The ordinary Scottish idea of a public worship, of a divine service, was in fact rudely chaotic. If it had any distinct features at all, these were a long sermon, with variable and nebulous adjuncts of long extemporary prayers and untrained psalmody. Regular and consecutive reading of the Scriptures; carefully chosen and well-executed music; united prayers in humble attitude, and in which the topics should succeed each other in one recognized sequence, and the worshipper should be able to join in the supplications, and not merely listen to them; audible response on the part of the congregation; reverent reception of the closing benediction, as though it were truly "the blessing from the Lord," and not a mere licence to quit the place of worship—the thought of these never troubled the placidly unconscious irreverence of the ordinary Presbyterian worshipper. But the absence of them, nay, the denial of any worth or advantage in them, estranged the hearts of many who were capable of some visions of the beauty of holiness. People utterly indifferent to religious forms or religious impressions might care for none of these things, and find their presence or absence alike a matter of little concern; or persons into whose natures habit or old persuasion had ingrained a rough love of the usual mode of worship, might cling to it tenaciously, overlooking its rudeness for the sake of its alleged simplicity and apparent venerableness of usage; but educated and enlightened men and women could not but feel repelled by the frequent defects of a service which, undoubtedly impressive when reverently performed by a clergyman of piety and eloquence, was apt to be positively irksome when performed by one of mediocre gifts.

"The fault that I have to bring against our Scottish service," says a complainant not very long ago, "is that it is too bare and lifeless, too purely intellectual in its nature and aspect. Look at any country congregation, and deny this if you can. The congregation assembles, coming into church with hardly any show of reverence for the sacred place, sitting down without any sign of prayer or blessing asked. The minister enters the too often ugly and ungainly pulpit, or preaching-box, as one might call it. A few verses of a psalm are sung, the singing led by some discordant or bull-throated precentor. A long, often doctrinal and historical, and un-devotional, prayer is uttered by the minister, the people standing listlessly the while, most of them staring at the minister or at their neighbours. Then, as he nears the end of his supplication (in the course of which a number of women have generally sat down), there is a universal rustle, and before he is fairly done with the ' Amen,' in which the people never join, they are in their seats. A chapter is read, more psalm singing, then probably an exposition; then again 'praise and prayer' as it is called; then a longish sermon, then more singing; a concluding prayer, which is regarded as merely a matter of course, and to which the inattention of the now wearied congregation is more obvious than ever; and a benediction, during which the men get their hats ready, and the women gather up their bibles, and draw their shawls and cloaks into the most becoming drape; and as soon as the last word is uttered, they are all charging out of the kirk as if for their dear lives. This picture is no exaggeration; you and I have seen it a hundred times. Now a service of such a nature as this is very remote from the ideal of true Christian worship."

Dr. Lee marked how extremely remote it was from that ideal. He saw that, year after year, the faulty service was sending people—especially among the aristocracy and the educated classes—away from the Church to the Episcopal chapels; where they could at least calculate on finding a reverent and orderly service, which did not vary from day to day, according to the mood, or fancy, or health of the minister. He saw that this secession was specially active among the young; and that thus the Church was losing a large number of those who in a few years would be in positions of influence and responsibility. He desired to stop, if he could, this process of depletion ; not only for the sake of the national Church, but for the sake of those who were abandoning her. "We might conclude," he says, "that it is unfortunate and even dangerous for the aristocracy of a country to profess one religion, and the body of the people another, even had we not, at our own doors, a terrible proof of it in the turbulence, bloodshed, and miserable disorganization which are the chronic distempers of society in a neighbouring island. God grant that the Scotch aristocracy may not find out the grievous mistake they have committed when it is too late!"* The question was, how was this exodus to be arrested ? This question resolved itself into another, How was the Scottish Church-service to be restored to a just model ? This was the more vital query. Whether reform of the Church's worship would stop the secession or not, it was due to the Church, and

---

* Reform of the Church, chap. vi.

for the glory of God, that the reform should be effected. Dr. Lee prepared to essay this task. He saw that reform was needed, that it was a reasonable need, and therefore he began the work. He was urged by this conviction, and not by any silly hankering after Episcopal forms, or any sentimental love of high ritual; not even by any special or innate sympathy with the "fair humanities of old religion," the antique sacredness of venerable words and rites. Some of Dr. Lee's own tastes and views, as shewn by the boldness with which he ventured to alter the Te Deum, and to defend his alterations, and even by some of the prayers in his Order of Worship, prove that he was defective in this higher liturgical feeling, and lacked something of that tender reverence for Catholic usage, that subtle sense of rhythmic harmony and fitness, which guide the hand and breathe from the lips of all true Liturgists. But he saw and felt the urgent necessity for an altered worship, and resolved the alteration should be made. His practical sagacity indicated the only feasible way of effecting it. It has been common to find fault with him for not bringing a scheme of the reforms he sought before the General Assembly, in order to get its sanction ere he should introduce any of them. He knew how completely useless any such proceeding would be. He would have been told that, if he did not like the Church's service, he might leave the Church. This was what he was told, when afterwards he was brought to the General Assembly against his will. In the Assembly and out of it, the great argument against "innovations" was, " so long as ministers are bound by their ordination vows, they cannot attempt the introduction of any change without perjury."* He held that he did not need to ask leave to do that which no law forbade his doing. There was no law against any of those changes which he resolved to introduce. There was no law against kneeling at prayer, against standing to sing, against the minister's reading the prayers, and the congregation's responding " Amen."

While his congregation assembled along with Dr. Smith's, it would have been impossible to begin the course of improvement. As soon, however, as he regained his own church, he had the desired opportunity for which he had been preparing himself, and educating the minds of his people. They were ready to adopt the changes which he suggested, and to support him heartily in carrying them out. Accordingly, on the restoration of the church, Dr. Lee requested them to kneel at prayer, and to stand up to sing. He read the prayers ; and altering the first act of the service, which usually is the singing of a psalm, he conformed to the recommendation of the Directory (to which the common practice is opposed), " The congregation being assembled, the minister, after solemn calling on them to the worshipping of the great name of God, is to begin with prayer."†

All this was contrary to general custom ; but Dr. Lee knew that custom, even if universal, could not have the force of law. And the custom was not universal. There was no complete uniformity throughout the Church. Even the practice of beginning the service with singing, which was the most general of all the customs, was not without exception. As to the number of prayers, lessons from Scripture, and psalms sung, there was nothing more

---

* See a pamphlet, "Innovations in Public Worship," &c., 1863, p. 8.

† Directory : "Of the Assembling of the Congregation." The Westminster Directory was approved by the General Assembly of 1645.

than a general—by no means a universal—agreement.
Even had the substance of the service been always unexceptionable, this looseness of method would have de-
tracted seriously from its propriety and effect. Dr. Lee
therefore directed his efforts both to improving the substance of the service and rectifying its order. In the
latter, he adopted that which he thought at once the
most logical and the most agreeable to the Directory.
The former he attempted to effect through the preparation of an elaborate series of Church services. These he
read from a printed book.*

"The author of these prayers," he says in his preface, "has
studied that they should assert, or rather imply, Christian
doctrines in a catholic spirit; avoiding all sectarian vehemence
and controversial exaggeration. It has also appeared to him
becoming that the prayers of the Church should express
Christian doctrines, especially those doctrines which are termed
mysteries, as much as possible in the language of Scripture :
and that they should perpetually suggest the connexion of the
duties and graces of the Christian character with the great
gospel verities ; aiming at the production neither of a dead
morality on one hand, nor of an equally dead and far more
useless orthodoxy on the other ; but seeking to combine
Christian life with Christian motive and feeling—*faith working
by love.*
"The only deviation from the order generally practised in the
Church of Scotland, which will be here remarked, is in beginning the service with calling upon the people to unite in the
worship of God, instead of commencing with singing. This is
done not only out of compliance with evident propriety, and
with the practice of the Presbyterian Liturgies, but in obedience
to the express Rule of the Directory for the Public Worship of
God ; a document which contains the present law of the Church
on this subject, and indeed on the whole subject of public
worship ; and to which a recent General Assembly has 'earnestly

* Prayers for Public Worship : 1st edit., 1857.

called the attention of all presbyteries and ministers of this Church, trusting that its regulations will be duly observed."*

Much attention and keen discussion were naturally excited by these new things.

It was freely alleged, by the foes of change, that Dr. Lee was subverting the Established Church,—" playing at Episcopacy,"—and introducing novelties never before known in the Church of Scotland.

This talk came of mere ignorance and ill-will. Dr. Lee, and many with him, honestly believed that his reforms would tend to build up and not to overthrow the Church. He knew, as every person acquainted with the real differences between Presbytery and Episcopacy must have known, that certain postures in worship and the reading of prayers had nothing to do with these. The historical and legal warrant for his proceedings was a point a little less obvious,—but, in regard to this also, he knew he had the right on his side.

The reading of prayers was not an unknown novelty in the Scottish Church. Immediately after the Reformation, the Prayer Book of King Edward VI. was ordained to be read in the parish Churches.† In a few years the Book of Geneva, as modified by Knox, and commonly called Knox's Liturgy, or the Book of Common Order, supplanted King Edward's Book, and was commanded to be used, by the Assembly of 1564.‡ This command was never repealed by any lawful assembly; and at the time, in 1637,

<hr>

* Recommendation and Declaratory Act of Assembly, 1856.
† Knox's Hist., Book i. He states, in the Second Book, that Queen Mary on coming to Holyrood, "discharged the Common Prayers, and forbad to give any portion to the principal young men who *read* them."
‡ Calderwood; Wodrow Society's Edit., vol. ii., p. 284.

that Laud's Liturgy was arrested by the cutty stool of Jenny Geddes, the prayers of the Book of Common Order were regularly read in S. Giles'.[*]

When, in 1645, the Westminster Directory was approved by the Assembly, no act was passed to supersede Knox's Book; and the reading of the old prayers continued, probably, for a few years longer, and then gradually was laid aside.[†] It was proposed to abrogate the use of them by Act of Assembly; but Calderwood, among others, opposed this, and it never was done. Thus, while under the stress of the Directory, *usage* drifted away from the old prayers and the reading of them in public worship—no obstacle to the reading of prayers was ever created by *law*. A similar remark applies to the " Amen," or other response of the congregation. It fell out of use; but it never was forbidden.

The kneeling at prayer introduced by Dr. Lee, was the ancient custom of the Reformed Church in Scotland; and, judging from the way in which the tunes are printed in some of the old psalm books, we are led to conclude that standing was the attitude during praise.[‡] Dr. Lee thus felt no scruple in undertaking to restore the service in his own congregation, and to set the example to other congregations, of a restoration, to the more decent and catholic usages of former times, before the harsh infusion

---

[*] Row's Hist.; Wodrow Society's Edit., p. 408.

[†] Wodrow Correspondence, vol. iii., p. 494.

[‡] The tunes are printed so as to be read by persons standing opposite each other, and holding the book between them. Many authorities for the statements in the text might be quoted here; but it is better to refer the reader to Mr. Sprott's " Introduction to the Book of Common Order " (Blackwood, 1868), in which almost every source of information as to the laws and usages affecting the worship of the Church is quoted; and results, which can only be reached after long and patient investigation, are lucidly presented in the compass of a few exhaustive pages. No recent treatise is so valuable a guide to the historical studies of the Scottish Churchman.

of English Puritanism had soured and hardened the spirit of the Northern Church. He aimed at nothing which the laws of the National Establishment forbade, or which was foreign to the original constitution of the Church, or at variance with the ideas of her great reformers.

The Act of William and Mary (1693), ordaining "that uniformity of worship and of the administration of public ordinances within this Church, be observed by all ministers and preachers, as the same are at present performed and allowed therein," which was quoted as forbidding any such alterations of the service as Dr. Lee's, appeared to him to be intended only to secure the Presbyterian worship, to the exclusion of the Episcopalian. The order of this worship, as sketched in the Directory, was the only order, or "uniformity," of which the law could take cognizance; and therefore the Act of William and Mary must, he held, be interpreted in the light of the Directory. The Directory nowhere forbids the reading of prayers, or prescribes or forbids any special posture in worship. The often quoted Act of Assembly of 1707,* against "innovations," could, in Dr. Lee's opinion, hardly be cited with justice as prohibiting any of his reforms; inasmuch as it—(a Presbyterian Act adopted in dread of a toleration of Episcopacy)—proceeded on the preamble that the Church, "ever since her reformation from Popery," had "enjoyed and maintained" "the purity of religion, and particularly of divine worship, and uniformity therein." This "uniformity," which had been maintained and enjoyed "ever since the Reformation," could not mean any order of worship from which read

---

* Acts of Assembly, 1707. Act xv.

prayers were excluded, since from the Reformation until after the acceptance of the Westminster Directory, such prayers had formed part of the ordinary public service.

Upon the whole, and taking a general view of his position, Dr. Lee believed that his reforms were not only salutary, but entirely legal.

For a time all went well. The church was crowded—the congregation was unanimous. The service, with all its adjuncts, was felt to be invested with a solemnity and beauty rarely to be witnessed, in a like measure, within a Presbyterian temple.

But opposition and trouble, before a year was over, began to darken the horizon. In the Assembly of 1858, of which Dr. Lee was not a member, "overtures" were presented from the Synod of Dumfries and the Presbytery of Aberdeen, praying the venerable House to prevent innovations in public worship. Neither the Synod nor the Presbytery could point to any innovator within their own borders; and the supporters of the overtures, among whom Dr. Pirie figured prominently, could only refer vaguely to "certain quarters," in which novelties were believed to have sprung up. Sir John Heron Maxwell ruffled the temper of the House by frankly expressing the opinion that it would have been more "fair and open" to name Dr. Lee, and move that he should be summoned to the bar. And Sheriff Tait,* whose close relation to an Anglican bishop might be held to account for, if not to excuse, the irreverent allegation, confessed his belief that "in country congregations, churches, instead of being the 'House of Prayer,' had become little better than preaching stations;" and that his impression was

---

* Brother of the present Archbishop of Canterbury.

that " in the country churches the great body of the congregations, during prayer, just stood and stared about the church."* A motion was adopted, after a lively debate, to the effect,—" The General Assembly earnestly and solemnly warn all members of the Church against the rash adoption of changes in the order and form of public worship as recommended in the-Directory, confirmed by Acts of Assembly, and hitherto practised by this Church ; and in conformity with the laws of the Church and the enactments of Acts of Parliament, do expressly enjoin all Presbyteries, where such innovations are represented to them as having taken place, to inquire into the reasons assigned for them, and to take with due prudence and discretion, such a course as seems to be most advisable for restoring uniformity and preventing division in the Church." This deliverance, which implied that the order and form of worship established in the Directory, and the order and form practised in the Church, were identical—which they are not—left the subject, as a member of Assembly† shrewdly pointed out, as vague as it found it. Some future Assembly would have to settle the question as to what the "uniformity" to be "restored" was.

" I intend to reply to the talk in the General Assembly," Dr. Lee says in a letter to Mr. Combe, on 11th June, " with a new and greatly enlarged edition of ' My Prayers for Public Worship.' " He says in the same letter, " I do not know whether your consciousness is mine ; but from a child I have always felt disposed to be proud when depreciated or undervalued ; and on the contrary, to humble oneself, perhaps excessively, when commended. I presume this is a not unnatural reaction

---

* *Scotsman*, June 1, 1858. † The late Sheriff Arkley.

and adjustment in minds not ill constituted." His second edition was out by the end of 1858. It was considerably larger than the first; containing four Sundays' forenoon and afternoon services; forms for the administration of the Sacraments, for Marriage, and for Burial; and "Meditations, Songs of Praise, and Prayers for Christian Worship, extracted from the Psalter and other parts of Scripture." This publication and the use of the book in Greyfriars' did not tend to lessen the public interest and disputation, which had been increasing ever since the sittings of the General Assembly closed, in June.

At length the Presbytery of Edinburgh, although no member of the congregation of Greyfriars' had made any complaint, or requested the Presbytery's interference, made up its mind to take Dr. Lee to task. After some preliminaries, his case was fairly grappled on the 23rd of February, 1859. "To-day," says Dr. Lee, in his diary under that date, "I was called to make my defence before the Presbytery. I spoke two hours; and I think the speech has produced a considerable impression, and has opened the eyes of many people who had no notion that I had anything to say for myself. May God guide me in this and in all things."

The form which the proceedings assumed was, that the Rev. Dr. Balfour, minister of Colinton, whose sole distinction was his advanced age, put this question to Dr. Lee, "Have you not introduced into public worship, as conducted in old Greyfriars', an order of divine service, together with the use of a Liturgy, or formula of public devotion, and certain forms or postures in devotional exercises, unknown to this Church, and inconsistent with the rules and practice thereof?" After some fencing

with Dr. Balfour, about what he meant by the order of
service known to the Church, and agreeable to its rules
and practice, and by a Liturgy, Dr. Lee proceeded to his
speech.   He said :—

"The first question here is whether an order of divine
service unknown to the Church of Scotland, and inconsistent
with its rules and practice, has been introduced in the Greyfriars'
Church.   I say, no—nothing of the kind.   The order now
practised in the Greyfriars' Church, is minutely the order of the
Directory for the Public Worship of God.   It is the order of
worship which was solemnly sanctioned by the General Assembly
in the year 1645, and three days after confirmed with no less
solemnity by the Estates of Parliament, which the General
Assembly ordains and commands every minister within its
bounds uniformly to observe, and unless, therefore, such oracles
as charge me with violating my ordination vow can tell us when,
where, and by what competent authority this Directory has
been abrogated, I beg to say that, whatever others may do, I
myself, my kirk-session, and the members of my congregation,
observe the only rule for determining the order of worship
known to this Church, or consistent with its laws.   Allow me to
read you the words in which this Directory has been established.
I think it will meet such observations as have reached me from
the other side of the house.   The General Assembly, on the 3rd
of February, 1645, 'doth unanimously and without a contrary
voice agree to and approve the following Directory in all the
heads thereof, together with the preface set before it, and doth
order, decern, and ordain that, according to the plain tenor and
meaning thereof, and the intent of the preface, it be carefully
and uniformly observed and practised by all the ministers and
others within this kingdom whom it doth concern '—and, among
others, the Rev. Dr. Balfour, of Colinton.   And three days
afterwards, the Estates—that is, the Scottish Parliament—'do
ratify and approve all the heads and articles thereof, and do
interpone and add the authority of Parliament to the said Act
of the General Assembly, and do order the same to have the
strength and force of a law and Act of Parliament, and execution to pass thereupon, for observing the said Directory according to the said Act of the General Assembly in all points.'   Now,

sir, I ask again, when this solemn Act of legislation was repealed? It is commonly said that the Directory for the Public Worship of God was not ratified at the Revolution in 1690, and that it does not enter into the Treaty of Union, and is not mentioned in the Act of Security. Is there any minister or elder in the Church so ignorant as not to know the reason why it was not so ratified? Was it not ratified at the instance of the Church, or was the mind of the Church that it was not then obligatory? It so happens that we know that very distinctly. At the very time when the Estates of Parliament were discussing the Revolution Settlement in 1689, there appeared an address of the Presbyterian ministers and Professors of the Church of Scotland to the Estates of Parliament. This address shows what they understood to be the law of the Church. They state that their advice to the Estates is, that they sanction the Confession, the Larger and Shorter Catechisms, the Directory for the Public Worship of God, and the form of Presbyterial Church government and discipline —that is to say, the whole five documents compiled by the Westminster Assembly—all of which they knew that the Church had solemnly committed themselves to; and the only reason why the Estates did not sanction the whole was that their patience was exhausted by the hearing of the Confession of Faith, and they would hear no more. But instead of the Church applauding them for their indolence, we are told by one of the pamphlets of the time that the indignation of the Churchmen was so excited by this that the influence of the Commissioner had to be interposed in order to quiet and soothe them. They did not understand that any practice that might have crept in was the law of the Church. They knew full well that the Directory was the only law.

Now let us come a little farther down. We find that in 1709 a work of great authority was published in Scotland. Walter Steuart of Pardovan, a man of known proficiency in Church and in civil law, published a book which you all know familiarly—his 'Collections and Observations on Church Government and Discipline.' This work he divides into four books, and the second book relates to public worship. Now, let us see what the understanding was when Pardovan published this Collection of his, which has always been regarded as of such authority that Peterkin, the last editor of it, states that this work has been the chief source

whence our leading Churchmen during the last century have
derived their information on these subjects ; and, indeed, he says
it has as much authority in regard to our laws as the work of any
constitutional writer in respect to the civil law.   The authority,
therefore, of Pardovan, as a collector and expositor of Church
law, is beyond all question, and Peterkin wrote this when he
published his ' Collection of the Laws of the Church ' at a very
recent period—so lately as 1830.   What, then, does Pardovan
say ?   In the second book, instead of treating the Directory as
a document of no force, instead of supposing that the customs
which happened to prevail had become the law, he actually
goes to work and he details the laws relating to public worship
in the very *ipsissima verba* of the Directory.   He does not
mention even that any suspicion had arisen that the document
was not still legal and valid.   He quotes the Directory throughout
as the supreme and only authority for the public worship of
God known or acknowledged in the Church of Scotland.   Now,
the insinuations which have been directed to me in this
house at present, and which were also very plentifully made in
the discussion which took place in the last General Assembly,—
where certain Doctors were extremely eloquent on the same
principle that Falstaff was very brave when he had Hotspur's
dead body to hack and hew, who always speak eloquently and
strongly when there is nobody to answer them,—have without
much scruple charged me—I suppose perjury was the meaning,
though the word was not used—in having followed the Directory
(for that is what I have done and what my congregation have
done)—have charged me with perjury and with a breach of
my ordination vows.   The words which a Rev. Doctor * now
present is reported in the newspapers to have used are these—
for there was no doubt who was the person attacked, though
the Assembly did not choose to let my name be mentioned,
and reproved an hon. Baronet who, in a manly way, like an
honest sailor, wanted me called to the bar, thinking that if a man
were accused he should be enabled to speak for himself ;—the
words used by the Rev. Doctor on that occasion were these—' His
ordination vow was he should not follow divisive courses from the
doctrine, discipline, and worship of the Church. He was not speaking of the propriety of one form more than another, but what he

* Dr. Muir.

affirmed was this, that having found certain forms in the Church when he entered it he was not at liberty to make any deviations from these forms without the authority of the Church itself.'

" Now, the Act to which reference is made is the Act which regulates the obligations and vows imposed on licentiates when they are licensed, and on ministers when they are ordained. When was that Act passed? It was passed in the year 1711, exactly two years after Pardovan had published his Collection, containing an exposition of the authoritative mode of divine worship prevailing in the Church of Scotland, and, therefore, I tell my accusers that, instead of being bound to any practices which prevail to-day, they and I have both committed ourselves most solemnly to those practices which prevailed in 1711; for can any man maintain that the practices which were then held to be authoritative are not those to which we swear when we say that we will adhere to the order of worship, &c., presently in use—in use, that is to say, when the Act was passed? I say the Directory of Public Worship was the authority for the order of worship at that time, and it is to that, and to that alone, that any of us have committed ourselves. We have nothing to do in regard to obligation with other practices that have crept in, and which may be good, which may be bad, or which may be indifferent. We may comply with them or not; but' as to our ordination vows, our ordination vows relate to the Act passed in 1711, and to the practices which were then held to be of authority. In 1694 a formula was passed which agrees in effect with the other Act. That formula requires ministers and others signing the Confession of Faith to declare as follows—' As likewise, that I own and acknowledge Presbyterian Church government of this Church now settled by law, by Kirk-Sessions, Presbyteries, provincial Synods, and General Assemblies, to be the only government of the Church, and I will submit thereto, concur therewith, and never endeavour, directly or indirectly, the prejudice or subversion thereof; and that I shall observe uniformity of worship, and of the administration of all public ordinances within this Church, as the same are at present performed and allowed.' How were they allowed? What other Act is there to be named that had allowed anything else than the Directory, which had been established by civil and ecclesiastical authority only a few years before?

"Now, it certainly might seem superfluous to prove here that the Directory for public worship is now in force, and that its order of worship is the only legal one. The Rev. Doctor has drawn attention to the year 1856, when the General Assembly passed an Act on this subject. I might quote many other Acts of Assembly showing that the Directory never was out of view. But I shall quote to you the Act of 1856:—'The General Assembly had laid before them an overture on public worship, the tenor whereof follows:—Whereas it has always been the desire of the Church of Scotland that in every part of its bounds the people should, as far as is practicable, enjoy in an equal degree the benefits of public instruction and the administration of divine ordinances, it is overtured to this General Assembly that a recommendation or declaratory Act shall be issued for the purpose of reminding all who labour in word and doctrine that every congregation at each diet of public worship should have access to the advantage of hearing a portion of the Old or New Testament read, and that there should always be included in the service of every Lord's Day not only a sermon but a lecture on a passage of the Holy Scriptures. The General Assembly approve of the overture, and enjoin all the ministers of this Church to observe the recommendation conveyed in it respecting the reading of the Holy Scriptures of the Old and New Testament at each diet of public worship ; and, further, on the subject of the overture, the Assembly earnestly call the attention of all the presbyteries and ministers of this Church to the regulation on this and other particulars connected with public worship and spiritual instruction contained in the Directory for the Public Worship of God, trusting that the principles maintained in that Directory will be duly observed.' Let me ask the rev. brothers of this presbytery if they have duly observed that Act of the General Assembly? Have they modified the public worship as the Act enjoins them to do ? Have they looked back to the Directory to see whether they were complying with its instructions or not ? Or, on the contrary, have not the great majority—almost the whole of you—gone on transgressing that Directory from Sunday to Sunday, which the General Assembly commanded you to look to and to observe ? I have endeavoured to comply with the Directory. I have endeavoured to obey not only the statute law of the Church in the

Directory, but the admonition of the Assembly that it should be obeyed; and because of this compliance I stand here with my kirk-session and congregation—for I say we are all involved in the same accusation, and stand here accused before you this day. I say I have done, or I have endeavoured to do, what the General Assembly admonished all ministers to do, but what very few of you have done or pretended to do. That, I think, will settle the question respecting the Directory.

"Now, I hear people say that the *custom* is the law. I put the question to the rev. father of the Presbytery, on whom I don't wish to bear hard, considering his venerable age, his respectable character, and many other good things I could say of him,—and I expected just the answer—had he been a younger man I should have said the foolish answer—which he has given. But I don't apply that epithet to him, because of his venerable age and his respectable character. He says that the custom has put aside the law, and because a certain custom of conducting public worship has prevailed so long, therefore the law of the Directory is no longer in force, and a minister or a congregation who complies with it is to be found fault with. Did ever any lawyer —did ever any man accustomed to consider legal questions— did ever any man of common sense hear such a doctrine gravely propounded as this doctrine contained in the answer of our rev. father? The way of conducting public worship now in use is the authoritative way, and none other is lawful or to be tolerated! It is very true that, in some cases of private right, custom is allowed a great force by most laws; and we all know that in England there is a law of custom called the common law, and that the civil or Roman law also gives a certain validity to custom,—but mark the conditions. Before anything can be admitted in England to be a part of the common law, or the law of custom, three conditions must meet. In the first place, there must be no statute law in that case made and provided. Here we have a statute law made and provided—and in force—alive. In the second place, it must, in order to be valid, be a custom time out of mind. Your present customs are not customs time out of mind. The introduction of them is within the ken of history—some of them within the ken of human memory. And, in the third place, before any custom can be admitted a part of the common law, the evidence of its being a custom must be found in the decisions of the courts. It won't do for a man to come into the court of common law in England, and say—This is the custom. He has to produce decisions of the courts of law in order to prove that it is the custom. Have you any decisions of your General Assembly telling you that the customs that prevail are to be accepted as of authority in opposition to the Directory? Is such a thing to be heard of? Now, the civil or Roman law does not admit custom so far as that, but it does admit it, but in no case unless there be wanting a statute law. In point of fact, the case is this. We have a law, and we have certain customs; that is to say, if we call them by their right name, we have a certain tradition. Now, as the Pharisees made void the law of God by their traditions, so we have made void the law of our Church by our traditions and our customs in many particulars. I am not blaming any individual on this account. I am not blaming any one who has gone with the stream of custom. Very far from it. I am not censuring Dr. Balfour because he conducts public worship according to the custom; but I venture to find fault with him, and I venture to find fault with as many as have gone with him or sympathised with him, because doing that themselves they find fault with those who I think are doing better and are setting aside the tradition in order that they may comply with the law. We have a Confession of Faith, which regulates the doctrine we should preach, or should regulate it. I would ask any minister here if it had become the custom for half a century, or for a whole century, for all the ministers, or a great many of them, to preach Popish, Arian, Socinian, Bourignian, or other tenets, doctrines which they ought to abjure—if it became the custom to preach instead of abjuring these doctrines—I would just ask whether any man could have stood up here to accuse any brother who chose to return to the doctrines which we all had vowed to maintain and preach, and whether you would have thought such a custom as that a valid reason for charging a minister with an impropriety? Would not the reply have been—These doctrines are the law, and if any one departs from the law, the worse for him.

" During the last century it was a custom almost universal to omit the reading of the Sacred Scriptures in church. Over nearly the whole of Scotland, I believe, that was the custom, and it is so at the present day in some districts; but the Directory commands that we shall read the Scriptures twice in every diet of public worship. Now, I will ask you this—for it is a parallel case—whether a minister was to be censured who chose to depart from that custom—that venerable custom, as it was, if age will give any authority—and to read the Scriptures as he was commanded by the laws of the Church to do—I ask whether any man of sense would have had the face to accuse a minister because he chose to comply with what was the undoubted law, although it had fallen into total, or almost total, disuse in practice? I am sure no man here or anywhere else will contend that any such thing would be right. Why, then, does any man think himself warranted to call me up here, and to charge me with an impropriety because we have put aside customs which have no more authority, and followed the order of worship which is laid down in the authoritative books? Now, as to this custom, I should like very much to know what it is. If it be our law, it would be very edifying and very instructive to know what the custom is that we are bound to observe. The uniformity of worship, I ask what is it? For my part, I have never heard of it. It is the general custom to begin with singing. But there are some churches in which they begin with reading a chapter. I know at least one church in which that is uniformly practised. I know another church in which the minister begins with an exposition of the psalm that is to be sung—that is, with a lecture. Some ministers sing two psalms during the worship—some sing three—others sing four. Which is the custom? Which is the law? In some churches two chapters of the Bible are read at each meeting—in others one—in others none. Which of these is the custom? In some churches they have choirs, in some they sing doxologies, in some they sing doxologies in the afternoon and not in the forenoon—which of all these is the custom? In point of fact, every man does what is right in his own eyes. He sings as many psalms as he pleases, reads as many chapters as he pleases, brings in this reading and singing wherever he pleases, and nobody finds fault with him so long as he does not depart from the tradition that happens to circulate around him. It is only when he begins to obey the law that he becomes a transgressor, and is found fault with. Those who are following practices which differ so much from the practices which prevailed in 1711 and 1694, when the formula was passed and the Act regulating the vows we should take, should be very slow in charging their brethren with a breach or violation of their ordination vows. Now, sir, that is my answer to the first question, whether an order of service contrary to the law and unknown to the Church, and inconsistent with its rules and practices, has been introduced by myself in the Greyfriars' Church. I say the order is that of the Directory as minutely as it can be made, as I understand it; and I know no other order which is known to the Church publicly and authoritatively, or has any sanction of a public kind whatsoever. This is my first answer, and I hope it will proves atisfactory to the Rev. Doctor.

"Now, the second question which he puts is, whether a liturgy has been introduced into the public worship of God in the Greyfriars' Church? I have looked a good deal into liturgical literature, both ancient and modern, but such an idea of a liturgy as the one that has now been propounded is quite original — quite new, so far as I have ever heard or read. Writers on liturgical matters tell us that a liturgy is a form of public worship, a service ordained by public authority in the Church, and binding on those who minister in the Church. It is having *public* authority that is the very essence of a liturgy, without which it is no liturgy at all, whatever else it may be; and they divide liturgies into three classes—the first are those which may be called strict or absolute liturgies, where the prayers and succession of the services, the ceremonies and attitudes, not only of the officiating minister but of the people, are all strictly laid down, and where no discretion whatever is allowed to the minister in any respect. Such are the Greek liturgies—the three great Greek liturgies—such is the Roman liturgy in its various forms, such is the Lutheran, and such is the Anglican liturgy. Then there is a second liturgy, where the prayers to be used in public worship are furnished by public authority, and are obligatory on the ministers officiating in the particular Church, but where a certain discretion is allowed to add, to omit, and to alter to a certain extent. Such was the liturgy employed in the Church of Scotland from its foundation to 1644, John Knox's Book of Common Order; such were all

the Calvinistic or Presbyterian liturgies founded on Calvin's
liturgy, and adopted by all the Presbyterian Churches whatsoever.*   And there is a third kind of liturgy, which Mr. Baird
has very judiciously described as containing rubrical directions
without examples, suggesting the matter and the order, but
not the language ; and such is the Directory for the Public
Worship of God, which succeeded Knox's liturgy.   Now, this
Directory for the Public Worship of God, though not a liturgy
in form or strictly, is yet a liturgy, I maintain, in its essential
character — and it is very remarkable that our Dissenting
brethren, as they were called, in the Westminster Assembly,
objected to the Directory on that very ground — that though
not a liturgy in form, it was really a liturgy.   And it is also
very remarkable that John Milton, in his reply to the Eikon
Basilike, attacks the Directory on that very ground, that it
was in fact a liturgy.   He says Service Books and Directo-
ries are all the same in effect if they be imposed, though the
Service Book is worse than the Directory, because it is superstitious in itself, and in fact nothing but the mass in England ;
yet the one is to be resisted, that is, the Directory is to be
resisted as much as the Service Book, because the two in fact
are liturgies in essence.   Now, not only so, but by implication,
the authors of the Directory itself call it a liturgy.   They say
they have been moved by certain considerations to put aside
the former liturgy.   What do they allude to ?   What was the
latter liturgy ?   It was this very Directory.   And there is not
in the preface to the Directory one syllable against liturgies.
There is a great deal against the Book of Common Prayer,
against that particular liturgy, but not a syllable against liturgies in general ; and how could there be ?   They say they had
two reasons for putting aside the Book of Common Prayer—
because it had offended the consciences of many sincere believers
at home, and in order to content the foreign Protestants—that
is, the foreign Reformed or Calvinistic Protestants.   How content them by denouncing a liturgy when all of them had liturgies themselves ?   Many of them had composed and used
liturgies ; and Baxter, the great leader of the Presbyterians,
whom it was the intention of the Assembly to content, made a
liturgy himself, and was the author of a book called ' Baxter's

* " Baird on Liturgies."   London : Knight & Son, 1856.

Reformation of the Liturgy,' the influence of which is felt in the Presbyterian Churches to the present day. I cannot sufficiently express my astonishment at the Ministers of the Church of Scotland pretending that a liturgy is unknown to the Church of Scotland, and inconsistent with the laws and practice thereof, when you have a liturgy subsisting for a hundred years, and since that time you have had what was a liturgy in its essential particulars, if not in its outward form. But whatever may be in this, how can I be charged with introducing a liturgy? I have chosen to compose and print and publish certain prayers. These are my own prayers. I have not stolen them from anybody, except a few of them from those ancient Fathers with whom the brethren around me are so well acquainted, which I have not indicated, knowing very well that they would know where to go to look for them. I say these prayers are my own composition, except so far as otherwise indicated. How then can I be charged with introducing a liturgy because the prayers happen to have been printed? This is a perfectly new charge. I have lying on my table about half-a-dozen volumes of prayers for public worship printed and published in like manner by ministers of the Church of Scotland. Well, why am I to be a criminal for doing what so many other people have done? I should like to know what specialty there is in my case that that which is innocent and commendable in everybody else must, forsooth, be blameworthy or criminal in me? A printed form of prayer is a liturgy! If it be so, there is a considerable number of ministers in the Church chargeable with the offence, and I do wish there were a great many more."

Dr. BALFOUR—"There is a printed form of prayer; but the prayer is read by the minister instead of in the usual way in Scotland."

Dr. LEE—"That is the liturgy, is it?"

Dr. BALFOUR—"Yes."

Dr. LEE—"Well, that is another most original idea. How does the Rev. Doctor ascertain that I read these prayers?"

Dr. MACFARLANE—"Dr. Balfour only asked the question."

Dr. LEE—"Then I intend to answer the question in this way: As there is no law of the Church respecting the reading of prayers any more than the reading of sermons, I take the same liberty in respect to the reading of prayers which everybody else does in respect to the reading of sermons. If the one be right, both are right; if one be wrong, both are wrong; if the one be allowable, both are allowable. I don't say that I read prayers, or to what extent I read prayers. But I say I have as much right to read my prayers as you have to read your sermons, and that that is a question you have no more right to ask me than you have to ask whether in the pulpit I read without spectacles or with them. It is very remarkable to hear gentlemen raising an outcry against a liturgy when they themselves have appointed a committee to compose a liturgy, which liturgy is now in course of publication, called ' Aids to Devotion.' If a printed form makes a liturgy, I am afraid the Rev. Doctor is now completely in the net—if a printed form makes a liturgy, then the Church of Scotland is guilty of a liturgy, because it has appointed a committee to compose forms of prayer, and upon those forms of prayer those very Doctors have been working for years past, with what effect I shall not say. And ' Aids to Devotion ' are all the more a liturgy because the book has a public authority or a *quasi*-public authority. I know that we are told very industriously that these ' Aids to Devotion '—this liturgy is only for the laity, and not for the ministers. But if a liturgy be a bad thing, why should it be supplied to the laity ? If it contradicts the spirit of prayer, as the Rev. Doctor told the last General Assembly, and if no man who understands the spirit of true worship or Presbyterianism can do anything but resist the introduction of anything like a liturgy, how does it happen that himself and so many others have concurred passively and actively in the production of these ' Aids to Devotion ? ' Because they are for the laity ! But I say, why for the laity ? If a liturgy be inconsistent with the spirit of devotion as used by a minister, why not also by the laity ? It is said because the laity are not supposed to be able to pray extempore. But I beg to say that many of the laity can pray extempore as well as we can, and perhaps some of them better. But if they are to have a liturgy because they need it, I fear many of us too will want this kind of assistance. If a layman must have forms of prayer supplied to him, because he cannot pray in an edifying manner without such assistance, do not many of the clergy want the same ? I think many of us do always, and some of us do—all of us do at certain times. I do not know what other men feel, but I feel it to be an impropriety to address extempore effusions in my own name, and in the name of my fellow-worshippers, to Almighty God, to the Majesty of Heaven and Earth. Does any man presume to make an extempore oration to the Queen? No; that would be resented as an impropriety; and when I consider how few men have the power of speaking extempore with perfect accuracy and propriety, how difficult it is to avoid repetition, to avoid misquoting Scripture, to avoid confusion, and how difficult to attain to order, simplicity, propriety, and dignity in an extempore speech—when I consider these things, I say I have wondered at myself, and I have wondered at my brethren, that they have ventured to conduct public worship in this most unedifying manner—for it is most unedifying, at least to their more cultivated hearers. And particularly when by composing and reading their sermons, at least by carefully writing them, they show that they have no confidence in their power of speaking in this manner. If they know that they can speak extempore with such propriety, why do they write so carefully and even read their sermons? My prayers, whatever may be their merits or demerits, can in no sense or way be a liturgy according to any idea of a liturgy which I have ever heard propounded. I deny therefore that I have introduced a liturgy.

"Now, sir, the third question—the third accusation I should call it, for it is an accusation—regards certain forms or postures introduced in public worship in the Greyfriars' Church. I suppose the forms or postures alluded to are standing to sing and kneeling to pray; and we are told by implication by the question that these postures are unknown to the Church of Scotland and inconsistent with its rules and practice. This third insinuation fills me with as much surprise as any of the former. It is a wonderful insinuation. Standing to sing is unknown to the Church of Scotland, and inconsistent with its rules and practice! I dare say many of you have seen copies of the old Psalm and Prayer-Book used before the middle of the 17th century, and you may have observed that these Psalm Books have the music printed in such a way as to allow two persons standing in different pews to use the same book. And, accordingly, in the distant parts of the country, where the old customs

of the Church hold their place—such as the Orkney Islands—
the people stand, and apparently have always stood to sing
since the very period of the Reformation. I suppose Dr.
Balfour never heard of that, but he should have taken better
advice before he said that this attitude was unknown to the
Church of Scotland. The Rev. Doctor has, during half-a-
century, been a member of the General Assembly, and at the
conclusion of the Assembly it is the custom to sing a psalm.
The members of Assembly always stand to sing this psalm,
and, I believe, have always stood to sing this psalm. And now
we are to call on the General Assembly to come down on the
unfortunate members of the Greyfriars' Church, and to tell
them they are doing something unknown to the Church of
Scotland and inconsistent with its rules and practices, when the
Venerable Assembly itself stands, and has always stood to sing.
I think the Assembly would do a very wise as well as a very
consistent thing if they should issue any such order or regulation ! The late Principal Macfarlan was a man almost as well
acquainted with the laws and practice of the Church, if I may
speak it with reverence, as our Rev. Father; he was Moderator
of the General Assembly in 1843, commonly called the year of the
Disruption. That year it was thought edifying to hold certain
prayer meetings in S. Andrew's Church ; and, as I am informed, when the psalm was given out, the Venerable Principal
called upon the people to rise to sing, and they did so. I think,
sir, Principal Macfarlan had a pretty good idea of what practice
was known and legitimate in the Church ; and if he had known
that standing to sing was forbidden in any way, he would hardly
have advised the General Assembly to adopt that practice.
Now, sir, the congregation of the Greyfriars' choose to stand to
sing. They do that because they think they can sing better
standing. I don't see what interest you have in preventing
them taking the attitude which they feel most comfortable.
They are not disturbing you nor anybody else in doing so. In
the second place, they stand because they believe it is an
attitude of reverence, and that sitting is not an attitude of
reverence, or proper to be taken in worship. You sit at a
concert, but when ' God Save the Queen' is sung you stand.
Why ? To show your respect to the earthly Majesty. But you
sit at your ease while the praises are sung of the Majesty of

Heaven and Earth. We think that an impropriety—we don't censure you, however. We don't bring questions before the Presbytery regarding your doing this, but we choose to do it ourselves for these reasons; and we most humbly request that you will either leave us alone in following what seems to us propriety, or give us good reasons at least for doing otherwise. Now, as to the kneeling to pray, we are told that this is unknown to the Church of Scotland, and inconsistent with its rules and practices. On that point I shall only say this, that if it be unknown it is a great pity, and it is time that it were known. If it has been unknown hitherto, it is a great pity, and it is full time it was known, both speculatively and practically. I hope the Scriptures of the Old and New Testament are not unknown to the Church of Scotland. We find that Daniel kneeled down upon his knees and prayed. We find that Peter, when he was sent for, knelt down by Dorcas and prayed. We find that Paul, when he sent for the elders of the Ephesian Church, after he had admonished them, knelt down and prayed with them ; and that, when he landed at Troas, in the open air on the seashore, where there was no convenience, he there also, with the saints, knelt down and prayed. We have been taught that nothing is contained in the Holy Scriptures without a meaning and a use. Is it recorded in vain that that attitude was assumed in all these cases? I think not; and I think it would be somewhat harsh and a little presumptuous if the Presbytery of Edinburgh or the General Assembly were to take it upon them to censure me and my congregation for doing what was done by Daniel, by Peter, by Paul, and, so far as we know, by the Christian Church universally, or almost universally. Not only is this the case, but the attitude of kneeling is so associated with the act of prayer, both in the Old and the New Testament, that it is actually put as a metonymy for prayer. 'To me shall every knee bow' —that is, every man shall worship me, but the attitude of kneeling being so associated with prayer, the attitude is put instead of the act. And, again, Paul says to the Ephesians, 'For this cause I bow my knee'—he does not say I pray, but takes it for granted that that was the universal attitude, and says—'For this cause I bow my knee to the Father of our Lord and Saviour Jesus Christ.' It is very true the Pharisee stood, and so did his more respectable neighbour the publican ; but we don't wish to follow, even in this, the example either of Pharisees or of publicans.　We think it is possible to be pious without being Pharisees.　We think it possible to be rational without being Sadducees ; and therefore we think it respectful and better to follow the exhortation of the Psalmist, 'Let us worship and fall down, and kneel before the Lord our Maker,' and to follow those venerable examples given us by the apostles of our Lord. I say, therefore, that if kneeling has been unknown to the Church of Scotland hitherto, it is full time that it were known, for it is well known to the Scriptures, and to the men by whom they were written.

"Now I shall say a very few words more, but these on a point which cannot be passed over.　It has been said by many people to myself — These alterations may be very well, they may be very proper, but there ought to have been a law to sanction them ; you ought to have gone to the General Assembly and got a law to sanction these alterations, however proper they may be in themselves.　Now, I should like, if I could satisfy the brethren of this Presbytery—perhaps they are already satisfied—that I am not to be charged with any crime in not having taken this course.　A law on this subject must either be compulsory or it must be only permissive.　Now I say we don't want a permissive law.　The Directory does not forbid any of these things.　Neither do any of our Acts of Assembly forbid these things.　And therefore we don't want to go to the General Assembly to get a permission.　What is not forbidden is permitted.　Where there is no law there is no transgression. Brethren, are we living under a constitution, or are we living under a despotism ?　The difference between a constitution and a despotism is this, that under a constitution, if the law do not forbid something, the subject is at liberty to do it ; but under a despotism, where there is no law but the will or caprice of the tyrant, he may interfere and put down anything which he has never intimated his wish should be put down.　If we be living under a constitution, we need no permission to do what we have done.　If we be living under a despotism, that is another matter.　Now I say the law must either be permissive or it must be compulsory—that is to say, it must either allow all congregations who like to do as we have done, or it must

require all the congregations in the Church to stand at singing
and kneel at prayer. Now, I for one would never advocate any
such law. I don't want to enforce my ideas on other people,
neither do those who think with me. We want all ministers
and congregations to be left in these matters to their own discretion. That may be very prudent—very edifying—in the
case of one congregation which it would be very wrong indeed
to attempt in the case of other congregations. The feeling of
the people is to be consulted—unity and peace are to be promoted—the prosperity of the Church is to be regarded ; and if
it were found that these were impinged upon, I would advise
any minister who happened to have the same opinions as I
have, by no means to attempt any such thing. If I had been
in a different congregation, or in a different part of the country,
I should never have attempted to do what I have attempted ;
and, therefore, to ask for a compulsory law to require ministers
and people to do in these indifferent matters what is not agreeable to their feelings, would be a most improper thing. Therefore I say, a law was not wanted—either a compulsory law,
which it would be wrong to enforce in many cases, or a permissive law, which we have already. But it is said, again, that I
and my elders should have gone to the General Assembly, or to
the Presbytery, and got their sanction before making these
changes. Now, I have to say, in the first place, that the General
Assembly is a body that moves very slowly, and it is not easy
to get matters through the General Assembly. A committee
was appointed about Paraphrases and Hymns, I don't know how
many years ago, and it is still hanging in the same condition,
and, for aught I know, before that committee gives in its report,
our grandchildren may be carried to the place appointed for all
living, where our controversies are all forgotten. There was no
chance, therefore, of getting this permission during the life of
myself or anybody now alive. But I have one thing more to
say. I would ask my brethren whether they have got the
permission of the General Assembly to do all the things which
they do, even to transgress the notorious laws of the Church,
which most of us, I fear, do transgress ? Moderator, it is
according to the law of this Church, which I suppose you all
know, that baptism shall be in public in the congregation. I
ask have all the members of this Presbytery obeyed this law ?

Have none of them baptised in private? and have they sought to obtain the sanction of the General Assembly before they presumed to break a notorious statute? Again, according to the law of the Church, marriage ought to be performed in church, in the face of the congregation. Which of you, most rev. brethren, have not broken that law without permission? In like manner, the rebuking of offenders is to be conducted in public before the congregation always, except on some special occasions. Well, which of you does that? Which of you brings the penitent before the congregation, and rebukes him or her according to that practice which prevailed at the time when the Acts were passed, to which you have committed yourselves? Not one of you. Not only so, but I am afraid some of us have broken the Confession of Faith as well as the Directory and other statutes, and without any permission. The Confession of Faith tells us, and the Larger Catechism tells us the same thing, that fasting is an act of religious worship. The Directory tells us, and other documents tell us, what that fasting is, which is an act of religious worship you are bound to perform. It is that you shall abstain from all food during the whole time of that fast, and the only exception to be allowed is in the case of persons who are sick or infirm. Now here is both the Confession of Faith telling you that fasting is a religious duty, which, therefore, you are bound to perform, and you have the regulation made as to what fasting is; and yet, is it not shrewdly suspected that some of you have both eaten and drunk on fast days as well as on other days? It might be possible, Moderator, to quote other instances in which the venerable members, fathers and brethren, have, without coming to the Presbytery and getting permission, or going to the Assembly to get permission, done that which was right in their own eyes; and, therefore, seeing they are all in the transgression, and most of them to a far greater degree than I am, I hope they will bear with a weak brother who, in good faith, with good intentions towards the Church of Scotland, and with a sincere desire for the edification and peace of his own congregation, has ventured to do what the Assembly of 1856 commanded and required us all to do, and who has done nothing, so far as I know, that is forbidden by the Church. I hope you, sir, and others who have broken the laws of the Church unquestionably without any sanction or permission, will not be too severe in condemning or punishing myself and my respectable kirk-session, and, perhaps, I may venture to say, my respectable congregation, for doing what we have done.   Perhaps I may be permitted to add, that the elders of the Greyfriars' have desired me to state that they sympathise entirely in the views which I hold on this matter, that they approve the innovations, if such they may be called, which have been made, which are conducive in their opinion to solemnity, and propriety, and edification ; and that, so far as they know or have learned, every individual in the congregation is of the same mind with them : so far as we know, there is not one person, young or old, male or female, who is not perfectly satisfied. There is no division, no controversy has been excited. The Church has not been weakened—no scandal whatever has been created.

"Now, I have carefully gone over the various Acts of Assembly on the subject of innovations in public worship, for I was most particular not to do anything which was forbidden by the law ; and instead of these Acts condemning anything we have done, it appears to me that they either have no reference whatever to the matter, or rather favour what has been done. I shall just mention one or two of them. The first Act of the General Assembly, in regard to unity of religion and innovation, was passed in the year 1639. That was the year after the great Assembly at Glasgow. The purpose of that Act is to prevent the General Assembly making a revolution in the Church. Then there was the Act of 1642, which is in fact a repetition of that of 1639, both of them being the precursors of the Barrier Act : —viz., that the General Assembly shall not without the consent of Presbyteries introduce innovations into the Church. The next Act was passed in 1641, between the Glasgow Assembly and the sittings of the Westminster Assembly, and it is intended to prevent any form of Church government being established in the Church until the Directory had been framed and adopted. It cannot be pretended therefore that these Acts have any relation whatever to anything now in question. Then in 1695 the Acts of former Assemblies made anent innovations in doctrine, worship, or government are revived. In 1707 an Act was passed in reference to the innovations within the Church; this Act was made against the Episcopalian and Jacobite party in the north and the Covenanters or hillmen in the south ; and anybody who reads these Acts will see that the drift of the whole of this is against what we now call dissent—against men who, though in the Church, were making factions and drawing away the people from the Church, laying the foundation, in fact, of dissension ; and it is notorious that at that time, to the north of the Tay, some of the Presbyteries had a majority of them Episcopal ministers."

Dr. MUIR.—"May I be permitted to request that, instead of these Acts being spoken of generally, we shall have them read ; and particularly I would call the attention of the Rev. Professor to Act 15 of 1707, and the Act of 1641."

Dr. LEE.—"The Act of 1707 says :—'The General Assembly of this Church, taking to their serious consideration that the purity of religion, and particularly of divine worship and uniformity therein, is a signal blessing to the Church of God, and that it hath been the great happiness of this Church, ever since her reformation from Popery, to have enjoyed and maintained the same in a great measure, and that any attempts made for the introduction of innovations in the worship of God therein have been of fatal and dangerous consequence. Like as, by the 5th Act of the Parliament anno 1690, and 23rd Act of Parliament 1693 years, and the Act lately past for security of the present Church establishment, the foresaid purity and uniformity of worship are expressly provided for '—that is, the uniformity established by the Directory—'And being well informed by representations sent from several Presbyteries of this Church, that innovations, particularly in the public worship of God, are of late set up in some places in public assemblies within their respective bounds, and that endeavours are used to promote the same '—I think the Rev. Doctor will rather repent that he drew attention to this."

Dr. MUIR.—"I want the fact stated."

Dr. LEE.—"Very well, sir. I shall read the fact, 'and that endeavours are used to promote the same by persons of known disaffection to the present Establishment, both of the Church and State.' Is that not what I have just been saying, that this Act was directed against the Jacobites in the north, who were resisting the ecclesiastical establishment and the civil establishment altogether, laying the foundation of dissent, and drawing the people out of the Church ?——"

Dr. MACFARLANE.—"Go on."

Dr. LEE.—"I will go on when it pleases myself to go on. I shall just go as fast or as slow as is consistent with propriety in my opinion. I say that justifies to the letter what I said respecting the design of this Act of 1707; and to show you still further what the practices aimed at are, the Act says that these practices are introduced by 'persons of known disaffection to the present Establishment both of Church and State, the introduction whereof was not so much as once attempted, even during the late Prelacy; and considering, also, that such innovations are dangerous to this Church, and manifestly contrary to our known principle (which is that nothing is to be admitted in the worship of God but what is prescribed in the Holy Scriptures)—to the constant practice of this Church '—that could be no practice but the Directory, to which the men who wrote this were solemnly pledged—' and against the good and laudable laws, made since the late happy Revolution, for establishing and securing the same men in her doctrine, worship, discipline, and government, and that they tend to the fomenting of schism and division, to the disturbance of the peace and quiet both of Church and State.' Is there any schism here—is there any breach of quiet here? There was nothing of the kind till this matter was introduced by the Rev. Doctor and his questions. 'Therefore, the General Assembly being moved with zeal for the glory of God, and the purity and uniformity of His worship, doth hereby discharge the practice of all such innovations in divine worship within this Church, and does require and obtest all the ministers of this Church, especially those in whose bounds any such innovations are or may happen to be, to represent to their people the evil thereof, and seriously to exhort them to beware of them, and to deal with all such as do practise the same, in order to their recovery and reformation, and do instruct and enjoin the Commission of this Assembly to use all proper means, by applying to the Government or otherwise, for suppressing and removing all such innovations, and preventing the evils and dangers that may ensue thereupon to this Church."

Dr. MUIR then asked the Rev. Doctor to read the Act of 1641.

Dr. LEE read it as follows :—"' That according to the aforesaid Act of Assembly at Edinburgh, and that at Aberdeen, 1640, no innovation in doctrine, worship, or government, be brought in or practised in this Kirk, unless it first be propounded, examined, and allowed in the General Assembly and that the transgressors in this kind be censured by Presbyteries and Synods.'   Now, when was that Act passed ?   It was passed three years after the Assembly of Glasgow, which, in opposition to the authority of the civil power, made a revolution in the Church, put aside Episcopacy, and introduced Presbyterianism ; it was made four years before the Directory was sanctioned, and what is the purport of it ?   It is this—that neither the ministers of the Church, nor any others, should set up a Church government till the Directory should be completed, to which they were all looking, and according to which it was their intention and wish that the Church government should be established.   Can any man, looking at the Act, and remembering the circumstances in which it was passed, doubt for one moment that that was the intention of it.   Then there are three Acts in 1713, 1714, and 1715, against innovations.   If you read these Acts you will find that certain disturbances had arisen regarding the oath of abjuration, and that certain ministers who refused to take that oath would not assist their brethren at the sacrament. These Acts have reference to that matter alone, and have nothing to do with the present case.   Now, I shall take the liberty of quoting to you the Act of 1735 :—' It is recommended to ministers and others, that they do what they can to prevent and suppress the growth of deism, infidelity, Popery, and other gross errors ; and in order thereto, it is recommended to all ministers to maintain, as far as in them lies, brotherly love, peace, and unity amongst themselves and amongst the people under their charge, and in all their more public appearances to· avoid uncharitable reflections and all just grounds of irritation tending to engender strife more than to promote edification.'

"Now, I shall conclude with stating that, though I did not take an appeal against the mode of proceeding, at the last Presbytery, I expressed my disapprobation of it, because the General Assembly had given to this Presbytery—for this Presbytery was undoubtedly in view—an instruction how they ought to proceed in the case. They were to proceed if a representation was made to them.   No representation has been made ; yet the

Presbytery has proceeded. It is said, indeed, that they proceeded according to the general law of the Church, and not under that special Act. I don't know what authority the Presbytery have to proceed in any way but that which the General Assembly have recommended; but if they be proceeding according to the general law of the Church, this is not the way in which the general law of the Church appoints that a minister shall be proceeded against. It was said indeed that there was a *fama clamosa*. I say, sir, in reply that there is not any *fama clamosa*. A *fama clamosa* is the imputation of a crime. I understand that is the meaning of the phrase in Scotch law. It is not a talk; when a popular preacher or actor comes here there is a great deal of talk. But is that a *fama clamosa?* By no means. There has been a great deal of talk about what is done in Greyfriars' Church, but we have not heard that anybody disapproved what was done who was present, neither have we heard that any one charged these innovations to myself and the people as an offence or a crime. I say there is no *fama clamosa*. There has never been any *fama clamosa*, and if there were a *fama clamosa*, there ought to have been a criminal charge brought forward in the usual way, and not in this way. Now I have only this to say, and perhaps it will astonish some of the persons present when I tell them that not one member of this Presbytery has ever spoken to me privately in the way of remonstrance, or even of inquiry, as to the grounds I might have for what I had done; not one individual in this Presbytery has ever waited upon me or spoken to me one word as to what I was doing, or what the ground might be of what I had done. The intimation of that question was the first intimation I had that anything in my conduct was considered by the Presbytery to be amiss. I say is that according to the rules of the Church? Is it according to the rules that honourable and manly men follow in dealing with each other? Is it according to the rule which our great Lord and Master has given us? Why, sir, this conduct is the more astonishing when I tell you that we have had in the Presbytery a great many private meetings. At one of these private meetings last summer, I took occasion to draw the attention of the Presbytery to what appeared to me an impropriety in the conduct of two of the brethren in a particular matter in which, as I thought, they had acted improperly, and broken the law of the Church. I need not disguise what it was. It was the lending of their churches to ministers not of the Church of Scotland. Here was an excellent opportunity for the reverend brethren turning round and saying to me—'What! do you find fault with my breaking the law?' Is it not alleged that you do it? We are here all alone—the public is excluded; those dragons the reporters are not here, is it not the fact that you have broken the law? No, sir; not a man had the courage to stand up and say—'You have done the same yourself.' I was allowed to make remonstrances, and nobody said to me—'You have done amiss.' There are some of the members of this Presbytery whom I should not expect to speak to me on that or any other subject; but there are many others of them from whom I certainly might have expected that, if they were dissatisfied with anything I was doing, they should have had the candour to say—'What is it you are doing? and why are you doing it?' But not one word to that effect has ever been addressed to me, until the question was laid on the table to which I have now endeavoured to give a reply." *

The Rev. Dr. Bryce † moved that the Presbytery, having heard Dr. Lee, find it unnecessary to proceed further. But this was far from meeting the wishes of the majority; and after considerable debate, in which it was very apparent that the Presbytery knew less of Church history and law than Dr. Lee, and in which none of his positions were attempted to be impugned, the following motion was carried by a majority of 21 to 14, "That having heard Dr. Lee in answer to the question put to him, and not being satisfied with the explanation which accompanied his answer, the Presbytery appoint a committee of their number to inquire more fully into the

---

* *Scotsman*, Feb. 26, 1869.

† Formerly one of the chaplains on the Indian Establishment; author of a ponderous history of the " Ten Years' Conflict ;" in his Church politics a strong Moderate, but a man of much good sense and liberality.

facts of the case in connection with the question put to Dr. Lee; instructing them to confer with Dr. Lee and his Kirk Session, and to report on the book laid on their table, in so far as Dr. Lee admits it to be an exponent of the mode in which public worship is conducted in his church." Dr. Grant and Dr. Crawford voted with the majority.

The committee, having done its best to carry out the instructions of the Presbytery, reported, in about six weeks, the results of its labours. The report was, in effect, little else than a special pleading in reply to Dr. Lee's speech. It added nothing to the facts already ascertained; and the only new light it cast on the theory of public worship had to be extracted from the vague declaration that the requirements of the Directory were properly met by a service in the course of which three prayers, agreeing substantially with the Directory, and including the Lord's Prayer, should be offered, the Scriptures read, a sermon preached, and "convenient" psalms sung.* This barren document was by a majority of 15 to 9 received and ordered to be printed; and on the 26th of April the Presbytery met to consider it. Dr. Bryce again, in vain, advocated no further procedure. Dr. Simpson made a long motion to the effect that the Presbytery should find that standing to sing and kneeling to pray, as practised in Greyfriars' Church, were inconsistent with immemorial usage; that the prayers in that congregation were read, and that the order of worship differed from the order recognized by the Church, inasmuch as it began with the recitation of sentences from Scripture,†

---

* *Scotsman,* April 9, 1859.

† In accordance with the injunction of the Directory, that the minister should, first of all, call the people to the solemn worship of God.

and included certain verses or "comfortable words,"
analogous to the Absolution in the Anglican service, and
that the congregation said "Amen" after the prayers.
All which Dr. Simpson moved should be found to be
"innovations," unknown and unauthorized in the Church,
and therefore to be "discontinued" by Dr. Lee and his
congregation.   Twenty-three voted for Dr. Simpson,
against twenty for Dr. Bryce.

The case, first appealed to the Synod of Lothian and
Tweeddale, which on the 3rd of May affirmed the sentence of the Court below,* was taken up by the Assembly
on the 24th of May.   Never since the days preceding
the secession of 1843, had so much public interest centred
in any case before the venerable House.   "The excitement was so great," says Dr. Lee, "that I could with
great difficulty find my way into the Assembly.   I stated
my case in a speech of about two hours.   The Assembly
decided for me, substantially, by a majority of 140 to
110.   It is a wonderful result; and has surprised many
people, and delighted far more."   The result, unexpected
as it undoubtedly was, must be ascribed in a great
measure to the masterly defence which Dr. Lee made at
the bar.†   Going over much the same ground as he had
traversed in the Presbytery, he spoke with even greater
cogency, animation, and eloquence.   "His speech," says
one critic, "was one of the finest addresses, logically,
rhetorically, and historically considered, that ever won
the sympathy or led captive the judgment of an ecclesiastical tribunal."   "It was one of the finest pieces of

* In the Scotch Church Courts, an appeal lies from the Presbytery to the
Synod, and from the Synod to the General Assembly.
† See Report in *Scotsman* of May 25, 1859.

historical and argumentative eloquence," says another, " ever heard at the bar of the Assembly."

In the debate which followed, as in the pleadings at the bar, the weight of reason and of sound historical argument was overpoweringly on the appellant's side. His opponents, although arguing with all their skill, could not shake the accuracy of his statement of historical facts, or the soundness of his deductions; nor could they establish for the vague uniformity, whose existence they asserted, and whose enforcement they claimed, any such legal warrant as he had vindicated for his " innovations."

A motion condemnatory of Dr. Lee's proceedings, and forbidding alike read prayers, and any change of posture or of order in public worship from the postures and the order commonly used, was proposed by Professor McPherson, of Aberdeen, a good and able man, whose word was supposed to have weight with the northern ministers. But the motion in Dr. Lee's favour was brought forward by another and still more able and influential northern divine, the Rev. Dr. Bisset.* He was supported by Dr. Norman McLeod, and Principal Tulloch; and after a long and exciting contest, he won the day.† The cheers which greeted the announcement

---

* Minister of Bourtie; Moderator of the General Assembly of 1862; a prominent member of the Moderate party in the " Non-Intrusion " times; and a " Moderate " of the best type; in the general policy of the Church conservative, but in thought and sympathy liberal and catholic; a powerful debater, and a ripe scholar, overflowing with a wealth of classic lore, rather wasted, sometimes, on the learned Thebans of the Assembly.

† As much, in the later history of the Innovation controversy, hinged on the scope and meaning of Dr. Bisset's motion, the exact words of it are subjoined:—

" It was moved and seconded—That the General Assembly sustain the appeal, and recall the judgment of the Synod in so far as the same affirms, *simpliciter*, the judgment of the Presbytery of Edinburgh, pronounced on the 26th of April, 1859; but find it established by the Report of the Committee of the Presbytery of Edinburgh, referred to in this judgment, and by the admis-

of the majority in the House, were caught up by the crowd which thronged the stairs and lobbies outside. This decision of the Assembly, " rara avis in terris," was really a popular triumph.

It was as favourable as the most sanguine could have expected. It virtually sanctioned all that Dr. Lee had introduced, except the reading of prayers from his present book. This it condemned as " contrary to the laws and usage " of the Church; repeating the common but erroneous assumption that the laws and the usage agreed together. The judgment of the Assembly was announced to the parties at the bar; upon which Dr. Lee stated that he acquiesced therein, and would endeavour to comply with the injunction as he understood it.

The man of greatest mark who, in this debate, opposed Dr. Lee, was his colleague, Professor Robertson. He however gave but a very qualified opposition; conceding at once a congregation's right to adopt whatever becoming postures in worship they thought fit, and admitting honestly that it would be no transgression of the Directory if a clergyman were "week after week to write out and read his prayers, adapting them to the circumstances of his people, and endeavouring in that way to promote their edification." "I am perfectly aware," added Dr. Robertson, "that our freedom of prayer has, in times of excitement, led perhaps to the utterance of what we

sions of Dr. Lee and certain members of his Kirk Session, that the prayers in the services of Greyfriars' Church are read by Dr. Lee from a book in manuscript or printed, entitled 'Prayers for Public Worship,' a copy of which was laid on the table of the Committee, and is now laid before the House: Find that this practice is an innovation upon and contrary to the laws and usage of the Church in the celebration of public worship; and the Assembly enjoin Dr. Lee to discontinue the use of the book in question in the services of his church, and to conform in offering up prayer to the present ordinary practice of the Church."

should have been glad never to have uttered; yet, taking the good along with the evil, I am free to confess that I would rather adhere to our own practice." But Dr. Robertson fell into the common Scottish error of regarding prayer, as well as every other part of public worship, as mainly intended to promote the "edification" of the worshippers; and also of conceiving that the circumstances of any ordinary congregation could be so changeful as to require the adaptation to them of new forms of prayer every week. Besides, he virtually yielded the chief question at issue, which was, the legality of reading prayers, when he admitted that a minister might lawfully do so, provided only he wrote them out once a week.* When the most logical debater in the Assembly could take up no stronger position in antagonism to Dr. Lee than this, we need scarcely wonder at the decision.

The decision was hailed throughout the country, and by the press, with hearty and loudly expressed gratification. It was felt that a new era of useful progress had begun. Many earnest clergymen who had hitherto sighed in secret over the baldness of the services of the Church, and the bareness of the once "holy and beautiful house" of their fathers' worship, thanked God and took courage when they saw that the Assembly recognized the right of a minister and his congregation to order their sacrifice of praise and prayer after the seemly model which had been too long forgotten. Every restoration, or change, which Dr. Lee had introduced had received the Assembly's sanction, except the reading of certain prayers in a certain church, from a certain book. This sanction was

* Charteris' "Life of Robertson," chap. xiii.

a long and emphatic stride towards liberty of worship ; and as such was thankfully welcomed by all who understood by that liberty something higher than a minister's right to utter extemporary prayers. With their joy mingled a strong sentiment of gratitude to the champion who had, so boldly and sagaciously, vindicated the rights of the clergy and the people. All the credit of the triumph over prejudice, ignorance, and dull conservatism, which had done honour to the majority of the Assembly, was justly ascribed to Dr. Lee.

This was the first "fytte" of the Innovation Controversy. Dr. Lee had not sought the strife ; it had been forced on him against his will, and by his own co-presbyters, in the absence of any complaint from his congregation, or the faintest outcry against his proceedings from any section of the laity whatsoever. The anti-innovation crusade was a purely clerical crusade ; there was no popular response of " DEUS VULT " when the angry Presbyters fulminated against the innovator. There was, on the contrary, much jubilation when, the combat over, he remained master of the field.

END OF VOL. I.

LONDON:
BRADBURY, EVANS, AND CO., PRINTERS, WHITEFRIARS.

9 783744 661294